EMILY HILDA W9-AOE-793

(1880-1949) was born in Northumberland, the daughter of a ship-broker. She was educated at Gateshead High School and Penrhos College, Colwyn Bay, Wales. In 1902, after her marriage to a solicitor, J. A. H. Daniell, she went to live in Bristol, which was to become the setting of most of her novels. Her first, *A Corn of Wheat*, was published in 1910, followed by *Yonder* (1912), and *Moor Fires* (1916).

During the First World War Emily Young worked in a munitions factory, and as a groom in a local stables. However, after her husband's death at Ypres in 1917 she left Bristol for London, going to live with a married man, Ralph Henderson, Head Master of Alleyn's school in Dulwich. She continued to write. *The Misses Mallett*, published originally as *The Bridge Dividing*, appeared in 1922, preceding her most successful novel, *William* (1925). Then came *The Vicar's Daughter* (1928), *Miss Mole* (1930) – winning the James Tait Black Memorial Prize, *Jenny Wren* (1932), *The Curate's Wife* (1934) and *Celia* (1937). She lived with the Hendersons in South London until Ralph Henderson's retirement at the time of the Second World War when he and E. H. Young went, alone, to live in Bradford-on-Avon, Wiltshire. Here Emily Young wrote two children's books, *Caravan Island* (1940) and *River Holiday* (1942), and one further novel, *Chatterton Square*, published in 1947, two years before her death from lung cancer at the age of sixty-nine.

Virago publish *The Misses Mallett, Miss Mole, Jenny Wren* and *The Curate's Wife. Chatterton Square* will be published in 1986.

VIRAGO
MODERN
CLASSIC

NUMBER
177

Jenny Wren

E. H. YOUNG

With a New Introduction by Sally Beauman

Published by VIRAGO PRESS Limited 1985
41 William IV Street, London WC2N 4DB

First published in Great Britain by Jonathan Cape 1932

Virago edition offset from Cape first edition

British Library Cataloguing in Publication Data
Young, E. H.
    Jenny Wren.—(Virago modern classics)
    I. Title
    823'.912[F]   PR6047.046/

    ISBN 0-86068-436-9

Printed in Finland by Werner Söderström Oy,
a member of Finnprint

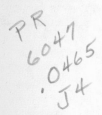

INTRODUCTION

JENNY WREN is the first of a close-knit pair of novels, about two sisters, Jenny and Dahlia Rendall, and—although it can stand on its own—it is best read together with its powerful sequel, *The Curate's Wife*, completed by their author E. H. Young some two years later.

Although both novels deal with the lives and sentimental education of both sisters, using them in counterpoint, rather as Jane Austen used Elinor and Marianne in *Sense and Sensibility*, one sister is the prime focus for each—Jenny for *Jenny Wren*, Dahlia for *The Curate's Wife*.

In each case, the title E. H. Young has chosen is revealing: the Rendall sisters, though very different as women, are both seeking the same thing: an identity of their own, one that is neither inherited from their parents, nor acquired by means of a husband. Both are, initially at least, to be thwarted: Jenny takes refuge in the false name and false identity that gives this novel its title; Dahlia discovers that to be herself and to be a wife is neither as easy nor as admirable a proposition as she had hoped, and that the two identities, far from merging, are all too often in conflict with one another.

The two novels, then, move into territory which, interestingly, is uncharted by E. H. Young in her earlier novels *The Misses Mallett* and *Miss Mole*. Unlike them, they do not end in the traditional manner, with a romantic proposal and an assumption that now all, for hero and heroine at least, will be well. *Jenny Wren* is left deliberately open-ended; its sequel moves on to the stuff of marriage itself, to life *after* the ring has been slipped onto the third finger.

But that is to run ahead. Here, in this novel, we are apparently on more familiar female novelist territory, although, being by E. H. Young and therefore as idiosyncratic as all her other novels, the reader should be forewarned that the familiar terrain may prove a great deal odder than was expected.

We have the two sisters, whose experiences will be the lynch-pin of the novel. And both are very young. They have energy and spirit; neither their vitality nor their optimism has yet been drained. When the novel begins they have not long left school. They are about to embark upon life; their surroundings are limited and confined; both girls are exhibiting distinct signs of impatience. Life, they both feel, seems to be taking an unconscionable time to get started . . .

Jenny Wren was published in 1932; it was E. H. Young's eighth novel, following immediately after her most acclaimed and celebrated book, *Miss Mole*, which had been awarded the James Tait Black Memorial prize. Emily Young was fifty-two when it came out, and she was to write only three further novels, *The Curate's Wife* (so close-knit as to be virtually the second volume of *Jenny Wren*), *Celia* (1937), and *Chatterton Square* (1947).

Almost all Emily Young's postwar novels were set, as is this one, in Bristol, which she christened Radstowe for fictional purposes, and at first sight this is only the most obvious of the similarities between this and her earlier work. Like *The Misses Mallett* and *Miss Mole*, its main location is the desirable Clifton area of Bristol. Beulah Mount, where the Rendall sisters have moved with their mother Louisa, to manage a boarding house, is an area of beautiful eighteenth-century squares and crescents still remarkably unchanged to this day. The Rendalls, like the Malletts of the earlier novel, live close to the cliffs of the Avon Gorge; indeed, from their lodging house they can see both the celebrated suspension bridge that spans the gorge, and the verdant and alluring countryside of Somerset on the further shore. It is a view, and an expressive divide, to which Young returns again and again in her novels; here, as before, her female characters, situated in Clifton, yearn for the other side. It represents to them different things at different times. Occasionally the bridge seems to lead to a magical and threatening place, associated with sexual experience, the woods of fairy tales. At other times, more simply, it is a place apart from the petty hypocrisies and compromises associated with the city, a place where truthfulness—and love—become a possibility. At other times, and for the Rendall sisters particularly, it is associated with social stigma and with shame. Nevertheless, whatever aspect it takes on, they yearn for it, as Chekov's three sisters yearn for Moscow; it is there, they sense, that their lives will begin.

Socially the Rendalls are poised midway between the Mallett family and Miss Mole—but poised is perhaps not the right word, for almost every aspect of their lives in their cliff-edge house is a precarious one. Their father, Sidney Rendall, who has died shortly before the point at which the novel begins, was a gentleman of good family, cut off from his relations by his impulsive marriage to Louisa, a working-class countrywoman who has, on widowhood, borrowed the money to exchange her farm for the boarding house. Both Jenny and Dahlia have received a private education; both are ladylike in an era when such concepts still mattered; both are beautiful; both have manners and accents that, unlike their mother's, are socially flawless.

But their parentage has made them stateless persons, belonging neither to their father's class nor their mother's. They inhabit a peculiarly English twilit area, one which causes Jenny embarrassment and shame, and which

vii

infuriates their acquaintances, most of whom, being English, want to pigeonhole them, and are enraged when they cannot.

Besides belonging to no particular class, they belong to no particular place. They have been educated away from the farm where they spent their childhood; they do not fit very easily into the rigidly structured provincial society of Bristol either. That they should be living in a lodging house when we first encounter them is an example of E. H. Young's craft, of her ability to make imaginative points by simple factual means. It is not a very successful lodging house, and it is a place of many comings-and-goings. People turn up there, stay a while, and depart. They do not put down roots; they are even constantly obliged to change rooms, their sitting room of today being appropriated for a new lodger on the morrow. Everything about this lodging house, in short, is suggestive of the transitory. It is the perfect location for Jenny and Dahlia, girls who are themselves going through the process of transition, and who move, in the course of this novel and its sequel, from being girls to being women.

There is also one other major respect in which *Jenny Wren* closely resembles E. H. Young's other fiction. Like her earlier novels it focuses on the question of class, on a social structure so rigid, so confining and ultimately so absurd, that it distorts and twists people's lives, spawning hypocrisy, inhumanity and unhappiness. Like them, and tellingly, it also focuses on the question of carnal desire, on the one force which (other than love) arcs across all social divides and disrupts alike the lives of the rich and the poor, the estate owners across the bridge and the *petit bourgeois* of Beulah Mount. Desire, in all E. H. Young's novels, is a double-edged sword that cuts through the social fabric. She treats it with an honesty quite remarkable for her period, with gravity and with humour.

Hedged in and distorted by the romanticism of both her male and female characters, desire is seen calmly as a force for good and a force for evil: it can bring, with even-handed justice, both revelation and delusion. Here the attraction of Sidney Rendall for the low-born Louisa has not endured; it has led to a miserably unhappy marriage, and—in her case—to an equally unfulfilling adulterous affair with the farmer, Thomas Grimshaw. Neither episode seems to have brought anything other than harm to any of the participants, and, to Louisa's distress, the stigma of her adultery is quickly attached to her daughters by jealous neighbours only too delighted to sully their name.

Yet—and it is this duality which gives the novel its strength—E. H. Young simultaneously presents sexual desire from the very opposite viewpoint. Writing in the thirties, at a time when—particularly for the middle classes—sexual propriety and social acceptability meshed, and sexual decorum was still regarded as a prime female virtue, Young relentlessly and courageously, in novel after novel, questions and mocks such moral assumptions. Physical love is seen, it is true, as capricious, unpredictable and dangerous: it is also seen as a liberating force. A morality beyond propriety is constantly explored. Miss Mole's pre-marital affair, for instance, or, here, Louisa Rendall's incautious marriage and adultery are both, ultimately condoned. They are seen as the actions of a free heart; they speak with a vibrant rebel voice; and to ignore that voice, to dismiss the promptings of the heart, to toe the line of conventional morality is seen, in instance after instance, as a denial of life itself. Those who do so may be pillars of the church or the community, but they suffer the consequences of their choice every bit as much as Louisa Rendall does. In *Jenny Wren* there are two such women, the spinsters Miss Morrison and Miss Jewel. One, gently drawn, drifts sadly through life on an ocean of unfulfilled gentility; the other, more overtly and savagely portrayed, becomes a monster of thwarted longings, living a virginal and 'blameless' life, eaten alive by malice and jealousy.

Besides these two semi-dead women, Louisa Rendall, the social and sexual outcast, is seen as vividly and unrepentently alive—a mother who could teach her daughters much, if only she could overcome her guilt, and they their shame.

At heart then, this novel is deeply subversive to the values of the society of its time. It is with the unconventional that the sympathies of this apparently conventional author lie. That fact is a little obscured, perhaps, by the quiet tone of the writing, by the absence of all stridency from its arguments. Certainly it must have caused E. H. Young some dry amusement to see contemporary critics miss altogether this subversiveness in her writing, and praise her novels for their wit, for their assured portraits of provincial life, for their quiet 'good taste'. They dubbed her a novelist in the Austen tradition, which to some extent, of course, she was. Yet they failed singularly to notice that Young took her fiction into territory that was, quite simply, out of bounds to earlier women novelists.

That this concern with sexual transgression and redemption should have been so central to Young's work is less surprising when one considers that it was also central to her own life. Born the daughter of a prosperous Northumbrian ship-broker, Emily Young married, at the age of twenty-two, a solicitor, J. A. H. Daniell. It was her marriage to Daniell which first took her to Bristol, where she lived for sixteen years. Daniell was killed at Ypres in 1917, and her husband's death marked a turning point in her life.

In 1918 she moved to London, and went to live with her lover, Ralph Henderson, who had been at school with her husband, and his close friend. Henderson was—in name only—still married. He and his wife never divorced, and for twenty years, under extraordinary circumstances, they and Emily Young lived in a virtual *ménage à trois*. Henderson was then Head Master of the public school, Alleyn's. Perhaps because any gossip of his adultery would have certainly ended his academic career, perhaps for other reasons also, the Hendersons and Emily Young (or Mrs Daniell as she was always known in private life) maintained this façade assiduously and with total success. Mrs Henderson accepted the situation; all three lived tranquilly together in Sydenham Hill. In the mornings Emily Young walked to the house of her close friends the Gotchs (Mr Gotch was a colleague of Henderson's at Alleyn's), and there she spent the mornings writing, taking a coffee break with Mrs Gotch, with whom, however, she never discussed her work or commented in any way on its progress.

Thus, in her own life, deviation from the prescribed code of sexual behaviour seems to have brought E. H. Young few of the tribulations it brings her characters. In a very English way a potentially explosive situation was defused. In 1940 Henderson went into semi-retirement, and after the war, this time without Mrs Henderson, he and Emily Young moved to a house in Bradford-on-Avon in Wiltshire, where they lived together, still unmarried, but very happily, until her death from lung cancer in 1949. Thus E. H. Young herself lived a double life for nearly thirty years, and returned, obsessively, in her novels to the clash between social propriety and individual morality, making the confrontation between those two different ethical codes a troublous and perplexing one, capable of resolution only through a frankness that—in her case—eluded her all her life.

Jenny Wren begins in a slow, dreamy, ruminative way—but then it is a novel about a girl who is a dreamer. Young unfolds a series of images: the boarding house on Beulah Mount; the gorge; the bridge; the country beyond. Audible from the house are the sounds of ships and steamers whistling as they disembark for the sea. A girl—Jenny—lies in bed; the same girl leans out of the window and watches the passers-by; or dusts, in a desultory fashion. Constantly she looks out of the house, towards the far cliffs, and towards the future. Her idea of the future is forceful but vague: it will be a time of 'gilded happiness'; the agency of that happiness, it becomes increasingly clear will be a man. At least Jenny conceives of it like that.

Jenny resembles her father. She is tiny, graceful, refined, with such delicate sensibilities that even people's ugliness dismays her. She is also proud, and a snob, bitterly ashamed of her mother, embarrassed by her accent and appearance. She loathes Thomas Grimshaw, who is still pursuing her mother, whom she sees only as a coarse and uneducated man who somehow, through her mother's lack of discrimination managed to supplant her own gentlemanly father. She detests her mother's sister, her Aunt Sarah, not so much because she is a singularly unkind and deceitful woman, but because she is common, in service, and ugly to boot; E. H. Young, who made something of a speciality of unsympathetic heroines, treats her with severity, and yet also with understanding. For in some respects, Jenny, egotist though she is, resembles her sister. She is spirited, and desperately vulnerable; the journey she goes on, in the course of the novel is not at all the magical gilded expedition that she had imagined for herself, and her courage and resolution, once she realises that, does much to rescue her from the two-dimensional.

She, then, to pursue the *Sense and Sensibility* parallel, is the Marianne. Dahlia is the Elinor, but Elinor transformed and made a great deal more sensual and warm-blooded. If Jenny resembles their father, Dahlia resembles their

xii

mother. She has the same flamboyant beauty, the same generosity, the same robust common sense. But she shares one characteristic with her sister. Like Jenny she does not admit it, but like Jenny she wants to get married. Marriage, for two very different young girls amounts to the same thing. Love—of course. Romance, excitement and an interruption to the humdrum tedium of their days. But, above all, freedom. For both Jenny and for Dahlia marriage is, quite simply, the only ticket out.

It should be said that E. H. Young makes the available male candidates a pretty unpromising lot. The circle of the Rendalls' acquaintances is a narrow one, made up for the most part of their lodgers, most of whom come to them through the agency of the local church. There is Edwin Cummings, who works in a bookshop, and aspires to his own antique shop in the country, and who has 'never wanted anything that wasn't for sale'. There is the curate, Cecil Sproat, who wears rusty ecclesiastical black, and is in constant need of a haircut. There is the slightly vulgar Mr Allsop, fiancé of Mary Dakin next door, but appreciative, nonetheless, of other women's charms. Beyond these apparently lacklustre specimens there is a dull and depressing circle of other misfits from Clifton society, most of whom, lacking all common ground, are brought together by the Church and its Mission, and that terrible, suffocating, if well-intentioned ideal, 'good works'.

The Rendalls' social life, such as it is, is one of grinding monotony, emphasised by the fact that, apart from the curate and Louisa, virtually nobody does any work. Jenny and Dahlia, young, energetic and intelligent, have nothing to occupy their time, and even less to feed their imaginations. It is a major event to make little dolls for a church bazaar; only one social event of any magnitude takes place in the novel, and that is an open-air performance of *Twelfth Night* in, of all places, the Clifton Zoological Gardens. The Rendall daughters' response to this confinement is very similar to that of Miss Mole in Young's previous novel: Jenny takes refuge in fantasies and subterfuge; Dahlia takes an obsessive interest in the characters and affairs of the few odd fish that swim into their net.

Both Edwin Cummings and Cecil Sproat, it is true, prove to be far more considerable than either Jenny or Dahlia first imagined: Cummings is gentle and kind; Sproat reveals both a surprising independence of judgement and a capacity for humour which is quite unexpected. Still, the sisters are cramped, by the circumstances of their own background, and by the assumptions of their period as to what it is fitting for a young woman to do. But it is fairly clear what will happen when Jenny finally meets the one glamorous male figure in the novel: the young, the handsome, the dashing, the rich Mr Merriman, heir to Merriman House across the bridge, on the other side of the river.

Jenny first encounters Merriman when he is on horseback, and she is out for a walk with Edwin Cummings, trying not to mind the fact that his suit is cheap, ill-cut, and poor-fitting. She encounters him again, under more romantic circumstances, some while later, and instantly, predictably and inevitably falls in love with him.

E. H. Young treats her infatuation gently, but it is firmly placed: 'Music and books and pictures did not exist for him, though she was sure he enjoyed a good tune on the gramophone and read the sporting papers . . . and, with shameful disloyalty to her old beliefs, she decided that this was how a man should be.' It is, in any case, not really the man, but his class and material circumstances that entice Jenny: 'A world like Cyril Merriman's was one in which she could be at happy peace. He had the old house, the lawns, the trees of her desire. He had work, but he had ease and leisure, beauty surrounded him as naturally as air, and was as little consciously regarded . . .'

So, with a slow even tempo that echoes the uneventfulness of their lives, the novel moves towards its close. Its climax is the performance of *Twelfth Night*, where an audience caged in by their own beliefs sits surrounded by cages of wild animals, and watch a play about love while, in the course of the evening, all their own ideas on the subject will be upended and overturned. It is a scene of gentle irony, in a novel filled with ironies, the greatest of which, centring on Jenny, is her search for romantic love while at the same time being utterly incapable of understanding the mute, awkward and immensely generous love of the mother who embarrasses her.

The novel ends, conventionally, with a proposal—but it is a very unconventional one, and E. H. Young makes it clear that this is by no means the satisfactory resolution of her story. To find that, one must move on to the second novel in this sequence, *The Curate's Wife*, a more flowing and better organised book than this one, in which E. H. Young moves into the new territory of marriage, and—responding to the challenge—is writing at the height of her powers.

Sally Beauman, London, 1984

CHAPTER I

In the sloping, one-sided street called Beulah Mount, no two houses are alike. Some of them are flat-fronted, a few are bow-windowed and some have flimsy, roofed balconies outside the first-floor windows, and these, even when they are in need of painting, give an effect of diminished but persistent gaiety to a terrace built in an age of leisure and of privilege. Differing in breadth, in height, in the shape of chimney-pots and the colour of roofs, in the size and number of the front steps, which rise directly from the pavement, the houses, standing shoulder to shoulder, like a row of eager but well-behaved spectators, are united in an air of personal dignity, unmoved by changes of fortune, and in the proud possession of the finest view in Upper Radstowe. On the other side of the road the ground drops for a steep two hundred feet to the river, and beyond that stream, which varies in colour according to the sky and in size according to the tide, the opposite cliff rises still more steeply, carrying with it trees of every shade of green. On the right the suspension bridge spans the gulf: away on the left, masked by the houses built on the more gradual slope, are the docks, the low swing bridges, the factories close to the water's edge, the ships loading or unloading, and at night, when the day-time noises have ceased, mysterious sounds rise from that quarter of the city and are pierced, at high tide, by the mournful, challenging cry of steamers making for the sea.

5

The houses in Beulah Mount were built when ships had not found a voice and when there was no easy passage across the gorge, yet, when Jenny Rendall looked from the bow windows of No. 15 she did not resent the presence of the bridge, though she had an inherited liking for what she imagined of the past: and when she lay in bed and heard the steamers hooting, she knew she was richer, by that sound, than the ladies in hooped skirts and the gentlemen in brocaded waistcoats who had taken the waters at the wells, down by the docks, and made Beulah Mount gay with their wit and elegance. She could not resist this conclusion: unwillingly she had to accept the law of compensation when she heard the steamers, just as she forgot some of her discontent when she opened the window on a bright spring morning and leaned out to feel the breeze on her head and to fancy she could smell the primroses which grew on the banks in the country beyond the river, where she was born. And each day there was some change to be noted; on the cliff a larch tree had flung out a new sleeve of green tassels, the trunk of a silver birch, hardly noticed before, had become lustrous by some accident of lighting, the packed colour of last year's leaves was brighter or duller than it had been yesterday: the tide was low and the mud-banks were iridescent, or it was full and ships were going up and down: gulls swooped, like fragments of white cloud which were shaped and sharpened as they fell. Country carts trundled across the bridge, cars slackened their speed for the passage, the man at the little toll-house popped in and out, taking or giving tickets. In wet weather, when all this colour and all this movement was dimmed and lessened, the beauty was only veiled by the soft, west-country rain: behind the thin, shifting screen there was promise of more brilliance when the sun shone, and the characteristic drizzle did not daunt the spirits: it produced a feeling of muffled peace, a sense of waiting for ultimate happiness.

There was very little rain, however, in that first April of the Rendalls' removal to Upper Radstowe, and every morning, at nine o'clock, Jenny could have been seen at the open bow window of what was called Mr. Cummings' sitting-room. It was her duty to dust this room, but each time she flapped out her duster she paused to look at the view and to see what could be seen of her neighbours. When she returned to her distasteful but thoroughly executed task, she looked in vain for any signs of Mr. Cummings. After the removal of his breakfast tray and his departure, the room retained no impress of his personality. No newspaper, no open book, no pipe or cigarette ends betrayed the late presence of a male lodger. The cleanliness of his habits was a satisfaction to her own daintiness, the external barrenness in which he seemed to live, matched a personal reserve which was too simple to be affected and baffled the curiosity she would not show. Yet she was less curious about Mr. Cummings than surprised that he was not curious about her, and inconsistently she resented in him the indifference she wished she could notice in others. Mr. Cummings apparently found nothing remarkable in the fact that Jenny and Dahlia, with their pretty precision of speech, should have Louisa Rendall, who spoke with the local accent, for their mother, and nothing to make him feel abashed when they waited on him: yet the Dakins, next door, on the lower side of the terrace, had thought it necessary to subdue their natural impulses towards friendship, and Miss Jewel, on the other side, with her two permanent, respectable lodgers, had shown symptoms of the distrust which is roused in elderly virginal bosoms at the sight of beauty unprotected by a husband. Louisa Rendall, as Jenny uncomfortably realised, had the

7

appearance of a woman who has enjoyed the experiences of matrimony without its obligations, and she and her daughters made a trio which might attract the kind of lodger Jenny did not want, but a trio from which curates and professors and maiden ladies would certainly turn away. They had been fortunate in Mr. Cummings, though he did not belong to the professional classes. He worked in a large bookshop on The Slope: he was silent and seemed unappreciative of his privileges, but he was well-mannered: he was also sturdy in build and firm of jaw and might, Jenny thought, be trusted to frustrate burglars and to do what was necessary to gas leaks and burst boilers: he had shown no desire, dreaded by Jenny, to keep Dahlia in the sitting-room when she carried in his tray, but Mr. Cummings could occupy only one bedroom and there were two more, and an attic, awaiting tenants.

Jenny heaved a sigh and leaned out of the window to take her daily look at Miss Jewel's professor as he left the house. He never banged the door, but, standing on the step, he fumbled for his latchkey, put it in the lock and drew the door towards him without a sound: then, on his rubber soles he went, like a wraith, down the street, peering over his untidy, jutting moustache at the pavement as though there were no cliffs and gulls on his right hand, no Jenny Rendall looking at the top of his dusty hat, and no Dakin girls willing to smile to him from their windows. He was middle-aged, his clothes were crumpled, the bright April morning was clouded for him by doubtful passages in classical authors or the erratic behaviour of substances caught in test-tubes, but he was a professor at the University of Radstowe, he was respectable. He was wasted on Miss Jewel who, experienced and impregnable, could deal adequately with people who did not pay their bills and with vulgar young men or coarse older ones who would dally with Dahlia or crack jokes

8

with Louisa, if they were admitted to the Rendall household. Jenny lived in dread of the arrival of such lodgers. She saw her mother and her sister in moral, if not in physical, peril from people who were as yet unknown but who walked the world, charged with potential evil, and though she believed herself to be comparatively immune, she feared that life, which should be exquisite, was bound to be smirched with sordid details, as already it was troubled by the contrast between what was her rightful inheritance from her father and the conditions imposed on her by her mother. The fierce pride of her eighteen years rebelled against the social stigma of keeping lodgings: her loyalty, rooted in irrational affection, defied the criticism from which she shrank. She wanted to proclaim her quality, yet she withdrew disdainfully, telling herself that it must be apparent, and under the disguise of her slim, compact body and her sleek dark head, she was perpetually conscious of division in herself. There was the Jenny Rendall who had been educated as befitted her father's daughter, and there was the other who dusted Mr. Cummings' sitting-room and suffered because the Dakin girls narrowed their normally broad smiles when they met her in the street. This state, however, would not endure for ever. With a misleading pallor of complexion, with wide grey eyes which often made her expression tragic, Jenny had the good health that produces optimism, and she had the faith of her years in the future she wanted. It would come, with that sense of security, that single-mindedness, that gilded happiness which it was impossible she should lack for long and, in the meantime, there were hours when she forgot to be discontented, when she was satisfied with the small, important occupations of planning her clothes, watching the neighbours and looking in the shop windows—though she did this with less than Dahlia's ardour—when she was more than

9

satisfied with the view from Beulah Mount and the sound of the steamers, bleating farewells or shrieking greetings through the night.

Spring was the season Jenny loved, and spring, on the very edge of Upper Radstowe, had its wind and rain, scented by the country beyond the river. Her memories of that country were not happy, but already the life there was taking on the charm of what is past, and no one born there, to the smell of rich soil, damp moss, wood smoke and apples, to the sight of little orchards with white-washed tree-trunks and a sense of the persistent fertility of the earth, could get a waft of its presence and fail in response. Jenny responded more eagerly than she had done when she lived in the midst of it. There was a strange excitement in knowing that a county, singularly unchanged amid changes, was lying just beyond the rampart of the cliffs across the water, while behind Beulah Mount there was the rest of Upper Radstowe, behind that again were all the newer suburbs, and below were the docks and the big city spreading away out of sight. There was something determined and a little stealthy in the way the country lay and waited. It seemed to have a half-smiling scorn for the new noises made by machinery, noises that changed their note and volume, while country noises remained the same, and for the growth of brick and mortar of which the ultimate decay had no fruition. Jenny was familiar with every lane and field and wood-land, but the short distance now set between them and her gave them a different aspect. They were still a pleasure to the eye and a solace to the spirit, and she believed they had attained wisdom. They knew the true value of what men disdained or prized, and they had some special knowledge about Jenny Rendall and for her.

Conscious of all this, forgetting the professor as soon as he had passed out of sight, she knelt down in front of the window. She had her eyes now on the bridge, now on the cliffs or the river, while her ears were stretched for sounds from either of the flanking houses. In the affairs of their occupants, she took the exaggerated interest of an exile watching the activities of her proper world, and of an imaginative person who, awaiting romance in her own life, must make it out of the lives of other people. The material she had to work on was not very promising, but she did her best with it. The four Dakin girls, ranging in age from about thirty-five to twenty-six, seemed rather old and weather-beaten to her, but she envied their cheerfulness, their pleasant relations with their parents and the hosts of friends who were constantly knocking at the door or shouting up at the windows. She could forgive, because she understood, their awkward retreat when they discovered that Louisa Rendall was not the cook, as they had at first believed, but the unlikely mother of these two girls. Jenny was no leveller, she respected differences, and the eyes which appreciated her mother's beauty were not blind to the unfortunate effect of the widow's cheap and hastily-bought mourning. She had looked forward to the moment when Louisa would appear on the area steps, in her bright overall, with the sleeves turned up to show the rounded forearms and the sunshine on her crisp, dark-red hair, but the moment had come and shocked her into the realisation that what was lovely and fitting in the little orchard of the White Farm across the river was startling and doubtful in Beulah Mount. A man like Miss Jewel's professor might absent-mindedly stray into Louisa Rendall's care, but curates would be too cautious, refined spinsters would be too suspicious to accept her as a landlady, and Jenny, for whom a body that was not comely was a tragedy, supposed that Providence gave Miss Jewel these lodgers in apology for making her plain and sallow.

11

'She's like a thin tin box,' Jenny thought, 'and she hides the key. And of course that curate would never notice her face. I'm sure he thinks of nothing except souls.'

He was less regular in his habits than the professor and much more varied in his manner, and Jenny had her private explanations of the changes. When he walked slowly down the street with his hands in his pockets and his head thrust forward, so that she could see the hair which grew too far down his neck, she decided that no parishioner was ill or dying, no girl had gone astray and everybody was behaving as they should. When he left the house in a rush and strode down the street, holding his head high and looking happy, she was sure that someone was in danger.

There was no sign of him this morning. It was Saturday and he might be writing a sermon. It was the day of the week that Jenny most disliked.

CHAPTER II

On Saturday afternoon Thomas Grimshaw usually drove across the bridge to call at Beulah Mount and sit for an hour or two with Louisa Rendall in the kitchen. Dahlia and Jenny took care to be out when he came, for he was an unwelcome memory of their childhood when they lived in the little White Farm on the other side of the river. He was mixed in their minds with that mysterious vagueness called the war, when heavily-laden lorries thundered down the road and shook the old white house, when the men they were used to seeing about the farms were changed into soldiers overnight and their father went away and returned at intervals in uniform. He was dressed like a soldier but, the children were given to understand, there was a difference between him and the others. He was not strong enough to go across the sea and fight and, though they were comforted, they heard, in their mother's statement, a faint disparagement. Thomas Grimshaw was a real soldier and returned wounded to his father's farm, but Dahlia and Jenny might have forgotten how often he came to their home, how often their mother threw on the old red shawl with the yellow border and went into the little orchard at twilight; they would have forgotten the whisperings when they lay in bed and the sound of doors opened and shut if the neighbours had not asked them apparently innocent questions, laughed and nodded at each other over the children's heads and created a feeling that, in their house, there was something that should not be. Then the war ended, their father returned and doffed his uniform and Thomas Grimshaw came no more and they were glad, for they did not like his jovial attempts to caress them: his big, coarse hands, his handsome dark eyes and his slow country speech roused their antipathy and they connected him with the nods and laughter, but, if they gained by his absence, they also lost. Their mother's radiant beauty, her high spirits and affection suffered a change. She was dimmed by a shadow in the house, she was silenced by the chilly reserve of Sidney Rendall, and in this shadow the children lived until they were sent away to school, but when they returned for the holidays it was always waiting, and as they grew older they understood that it must remain as long as their ill-assorted parents lived together. Their mother was an ignorant country woman, their father was a man of good breeding and education, and the passionate madness of his determination to marry her was guessed by his daughters but never told. They were isolated from his relatives and hers, they returned from a normal life at school to this strange one in which their father tried to be a companion and their mother withdrew into herself. When he died it was just as though a thin veil fell from their mother's face, as though her shackled limbs were freed, and they did not blame her, for with their regret they felt a relief from strain themselves. He had tried to seem loyal to his wife, but not even his self-control could always repress the little frown at her lapses in grammar and her local accent, and the girls had been torn between two allegiances, between appreciation of him and what he represented and the instinctive, dumb sympathy they felt for her. She had been repressed by his superiority, half cowed by his possession of the weapon she had given him and he disdained to use, because he would not take advantage of a technical fault when he knew that he was faithless to her in every other way. He had burnt his boats when he married her and he was too proud to admit his mistake, and they continued to live together in complete estrangement. He turned to writing for a refuge, and how she passed her time he hardly knew. When he was gone, she came to life again. She could see the children, young women now, as hers, and she could allow herself to love them, though she did not know how to get past the barriers she had helped to put up herself, her suspicion of criticism in their quiet voices, in the difference between their standards and her own.

And then Thomas Grimshaw came back. There were no whisperings in the orchard, no stealthy exits and entrances: he sat in the kitchen like a family friend and helped Louisa with the business she did not understand: he was treated by the girls with a distant courtesy, in which their mother saw disdain and feared suspicion of the past.

For Dahlia and Jenny, the removal to Upper Radstowe held a promise of escape from him, but they were disappointed. They had not reckoned with his pertinacity or realised that a man of his age could be in love, and they were only now beginning to suspect that, apparently against his own interests, he had helped their mother to buy the house in Beulah Mount. He was as shrewd as all successful farmers must be, and he would risk his money, and even lose it, in order to teach Louisa the folly of her venture and show her that there was only one way in which she could pay her debt to him.

She saw their brief affair as a youthful episode produced by the reckless atmosphere of war and her impulse to mate with a man like herself, one who was not restrained by delicacies that sickened her and made a simple instinct seem unnatural. She hardly remembered it when she was with him unless she saw it in his eyes and then

15

she saw, too, and resisted, his desire to merge the past into the future.

He came on Saturdays in his dog-cart on which his name and address were printed in black lettering for the Dakins and Miss Jewel to read, and Jenny and Dahlia were unfortunate if they did not find something to do outside the house. They fancied his visits were not warmly welcomed by their mother and, on this Saturday morning, Jenny was making plans for a family excursion when Dahlia came into the sitting-room.

'Why shouldn't we all go for a walk this afternoon?' she said.

'What fun!' Dahlia exclaimed. She was like a finer edition of her mother. She had Louisa's height without her breadth, the same reddish, wavy hair and cream-coloured skin: she was warm and glowing, while Jenny, like her father, was dark and cold; she had a gay beauty that made young men turn and look at her in the street. 'Besides,' she said, 'mother won't leave the house in case someone calls about lodgings.'

'Then I'll stay at home and you and she can go out.'

'I'm beginning to get rather anxious about the lodgings,' Dahlia said. 'We can't live on Mr. Cummings.'

'Have you been to the stationer's shop again?' It was in a glass case, outside a little stationer's shop down the street, that they had seen Mr. Cummings' advertisement stating his desire for lodgings in Upper Radstowe.

'Yes, I've been this morning. Nothing but peram-bulators and gramophones for sale—and charwomen. We shall have to put a notice in the fanlight.'

'I won't have my lovely fanlight spoilt. And the wrong people would come. Thieves would come.'

'Well, there's nothing to steal,' Dahlia said. 'I'll tell you what I'm going to do, Jen. I'm going to church.

16

That's the way to get what they call a connection. The vicar will call.'

'He won't like us.'

'He'll like you. You look so prim. I'm going to the church on The Green.'

'I've peeped inside. It's very cold and dull. There must be a nicer one somewhere.'

'I'm going there because Miss Jewel's curate belongs to it. His name's Sproat! We must make him interested in us. And it's his duty. He's a neighbour. I'm sure he'd like to do his duty.'

'Well then,' said Jenny significantly, yet carelessly, 'take mother out this afternoon.'

'I can't. As a matter of fact,' Dahlia said slowly, 'I've promised to go out with Milly.'

'And who,' Jenny asked in her grandest voice, 'is Milly?'

'You know perfectly well who she is. And I don't care, Jen. I don't care what you say. I hate her boots, and her calves bulge over the tops, but she has a nice face and she'll be somebody to talk to. We've been here nearly two months and it's springtime, and I haven't spoken to a soul except the people in the shops.'

'And Mr. Cummings.'

'Nobody can talk to Mr. Cummings. He isn't interested in anything.'

'Isn't he? Can't you? I haven't tried.'

'No, you wouldn't: but I have. And this is keeping lodgings! I don't see where the fun comes in.'

They were to get rid of the White Farm and go into Upper Radstowe and keep lodgings and have a bit of fun, Louisa said, when her husband died. She would not stay there any longer, cooped up like a broody hen. She wanted to see some life, after twenty years in the country, yet since their arrival here she had hardly stirred out of the basement.

17

'Take mother to the pictures,' Jenny said.

'I've promised Milly,' Dahlia said stubbornly.

'You can't go out with the Dakins' servant.'

'I'd go out with their chimney sweep if I liked him.'

'Yes, I believe you would,' Jenny said sadly.

'Don't be an idiot, Jen, pretending to be grand when we're nothing but servants ourselves—to Mr. Cummings!'

'But we're Rendalls,' Jenny began.

'We're Lorimers, too. We've got to live like Lorimers. And don't forget that Aunt Sarah's a servant.'

'She's a housekeeper.'

'She didn't begin as one. She began as a kitchen-maid, poor little wretch.'

'Don't talk about her,' Jenny said.

They had only lately heard of her existence and of an Uncle Albert who worked the farm where their mother was born, and Jenny thought of another aunt, her father's sister. Out of the night, she had appeared on the very day of his funeral, too late to see him. Wrapped in furs, with pearls round her neck, smelling of violets, she stood in the lamp-lit kitchen, indignant at being kept in ignorance of her brother's illness, plainly scornful of her sister-in-law whom she saw for the first time, and, while Jenny thought this anger unreasonable in one who had made no attempt to see him since his marriage, while she resented this treatment of her mother, all her desires turned to this representative of her father's world from which his daughters were shut out. And Aunt Isabel kissed her before she disappeared in her swift car. She gave Jenny her address, murmuring, 'You're so much like him. If I can ever help you—' and then she was carried away across the country. For days, for weeks, Jenny had expected a letter. Perhaps, she thought, Aunt Isabel would adopt her, or ask her to Herefordshire on a visit or, at least, send a few words which would preserve the

18

slender link between them, but Aunt Isabel was silent. She had come like a dream and like a dream she had gone. If Aunt Sarah ever came, Jenny was certain she would remain: she would put her umbrella in the stand and tell the cabman to bring in her luggage.

'Don't talk about her,' she repeated. 'If you think about nasty things you make them happen. And I don't know what father would think if he saw you with Milly.'

'He would know it was all his fault. If he sees me with Milly he won't be surprised. I know it's not true and I know it's silly, but I shall always feel that the sky's the floor of Heaven and the dead people can see through it when they stoop down.'

'It would make them unhappy.'

'Yes, that's why it isn't sense,' Dahlia said simply. 'And he won't see me.'

'No,' Jenny agreed, and she thought, with pity, of the utter helplessness of the dead and how their wishes could be disregarded, until she remembered her father as she had last seen him, white and peaked and wearing an expression of magnificent disdain for the mortality he had quitted, and she realised that, if he had any consciousness now, he was glad he need make no protests or decisions.

She looked again at the lovely day, blue and green and white, and felt in her heart all the impulses stirred, by springtime, in Dahlia's. Jenny, too, wanted pleasure, pretty clothes, laughter, admiration and love, but she would not stoop to get them. She would wait, holding herself erect, until these gifts came to her unsought.

'There's plenty to see in Radstowe,' she said aloud, consoling herself. 'I think on Saturdays I'll go and look at the things he showed us, the churches and the houses where famous people lived and the funny bits and corners. I didn't enjoy those days properly, when he took us out. I didn't make the most of them or the best of him. He knew a lot, but there was always the feeling that I could get it when I wanted it, so I didn't bother, but I wish I had.'

'Oh, you're the kind of person who always thinks that what you haven't got is what you want. I thought those days were deadly, except having meals in restaurants. I liked that, but he hurried us past the shops, which were all I cared about, and then made us stand for hours staring at Gothic and Perpendicular and Norman! I don't know which is which now, and what does it matter? I mean—there they are and we can't help it. My legs ached and my eyes ached and my jaw was stiff with trying not to yawn, and after all that he'd drag us up a hill to look at a view! I felt proud of being with him, and I liked the way he talked to waiters and treated us as if we were important, but I wouldn't care if all his old churches were blown up this minute. But, to-morrow, I'm going to the one on The Green. After all, I can always look at the hats. And don't you think I might trim my own up a little? He would have hated us to wear black.'

'He would have hated everything.'

'Oh, Jen, don't be so gloomy. Let's make the best of it. At any moment we might get a really interesting lodger.'

'I hope we won't,' Jenny said severely. 'Not the kind you would think interesting.'

'Prig!' Dahlia said, but Jenny was not ruffled. She saw herself as the guardian of this pretty sister.

CHAPTER III

THEY heard their mother calling from below. 'Dahlyer-r! Jennifer-r!' she cried, and Jenny gave her father's quick little frown. She hoped the neighbours would not hear their names pronounced in an unmistakable Radstowe accent, but already that accent must have been heard when her mother talked to the tradesmen on the area steps, scolded the greengrocer for his jaded vegetables and shouted after him for something she had forgotten. Jenny was always conscious of the neighbours; Louisa never thought of them; Dahlia, humorous and independent, watched them with interest, but was not troubled by their possible opinions. She met her circumstances frankly, she had none of Jenny's anxiety for acceptance as a daughter of Sidney Rendall, and while Jenny frowned and stiffened, she ran downstairs to the basement, ready to help the mother who was almost a stranger, who alternated between the determination to assert her authority, her only defence against the criticism she suspected, and a pathetic endeavour to pretend there was nothing difficult in her relationship with her daughters.

Jenny stayed in the sitting-room. She was wondering why, among so many disadvantages, they had to endure the daily annoyance of hearing their names mispronounced, when there were so many which could have been uttered without offence. This thought had often occurred to her father, and he had to blame himself. Louisa chose the first child's name, when he was still sufficiently in love to forget how she would misuse it but, when Jenny was born, he insisted that her name must not end, like Dahlia's, with a vowel, and characteristically overlooked the dangerous consonant. Jenny was registered, she was not christened, as Jennifer, and Louisa stubbornly refused to accept the abbreviations he and Dahlia used.

In other ways he had protected them at the cost of hurting her. It was he who saw them off to school and met them at the station on their return, for he would not expose them to the surprise of their friends at the sight and sound of her. He gave them the best education he could afford and died before he had planned their future. He might have done better for them if he had sent them to the village school and allowed them to revert to their mother's ways and thoughts, but he could not foresee his early death, and he left them friendless and dependent on Louisa, for he never revised the will he made on marriage. Perhaps not altogether reluctantly he had infected Jenny with his pride of family. He rarely spoke of his youth, but he answered her questions and she knew he had lived in a house rather like the one he took her to see in the village, a long, low house with the colour of the wistaria fainting against the red brick of the old walls.

'Merriman House,' he said, and the dryness in his tone was explained by his next remark. 'Renamed when this man's father bought it.'

With such occasional comments he betrayed the value he set on his own heritage and Jenny pictured him as a boy, with ponies to ride and all the other conventionally lovely things of childhood. She gave him a romantically beautiful mother with a rose tucked in the knot of her dark hair, a mother who sang in the drawing-room when her little boy was in bed, whose skirts swished softly on the stairs, and she gave him a father who could be approached, on whose knee a little girl could sit, who did not create, because he had no cause, a strange, cold shadowy feeling in the house.

Her own mother was beautiful, Dahlia was beautiful; Thomas Grimshaw came to see her mother; Dahlia liked to attract the glances of people in the streets, and Jenny, loving beauty though she did, wished that theirs had been less conspicuous. She believed her own appearance and her nature were safeguards against the dangers she saw for them. She would not condescend to walk out with Milly: no young man, idling away a Saturday afternoon, would want to talk to her, and what chance was there of acquaintance with such young men and girls as she would like to know? It seemed to her that she must grow old and sour in isolation or gradually learn to appreciate the Millys of Beulah Mount.

She heard Dahlia running up the uncarpeted kitchen stairs and turned to see her flushed, merry face.

'I've had a row, Jen,' she said.

'Oh dear!' Jenny clasped her hands. 'How horrid!'

Dahlia made a long face in mockery of Jenny's. 'I couldn't help it. She says I mustn't go out with Milly.'

'She's quite right.'

'But you can't break a promise to a girl like Milly. She'd think it was the boots. And so it is! I don't really want to go a bit, but,' she said, wickedly mimicking Louisa's accent, 'I couldn't disappoint the poor gur-rl.'

'Don't!' Jenny said.

'Well, I don't, often, but there it is and we've got to face it. Who are we to give ourselves airs? She tells us, one day, that she won't have them, and we've a servant for an aunt—'

'A housekeeper.'

'That sounds better, I know. And to-day she says we can't expect to get lodgers if I lower myself and the

23

house!' Dahlia paused and looked at Jenny a little nervously. 'So I said—'

'I don't think I want to know.'

Dahlia, however, was seeking relief for herself in speech. 'So I said, "What about Thomas Grimshaw, every Saturday?"'

Jenny caught her breath, Dahlia looked studiously at the view.

'I don't know how you dared,' Jenny whispered, for their mother was formidable when she was angry.

'I didn't give myself time to think, and the worst of it is, Jen, she wasn't cross. She looked as if she wanted to cry. She looked rather like a baby.'

'Yes,' said Jenny on a little moan, 'she does sometimes.'

'And she said she didn't want him, but she couldn't stop him. And then she did get angry and told me to mind my own business, and I said that was what I was doing and—things like that. And so I'm in disgrace. But, Jen—'

'Don't let's talk about it.'

'I'm sure it's the money,' Dahlia said. 'We've spent a lot. I don't know where it all came from. Father hadn't much, and think how he pinched to send us away to school.'

'We can't owe that man money.'

'No, that's how I feel about it, so we'll have to be hearty about the lodgers. I'm going to church to-morrow, night and morning, and I think you'd better come too.'

'I should like to be sure about the money before I begin doing that,' Jenny said. 'I'll go to the Free Library this afternoon and look at the advertisements in the Radstowe papers. I wonder if Mr. Cummings could help us.'

'If he's wise he won't try. He knows we only let him have the sitting-room because there's no one else to use it. He isn't paying for it, and he'll have to give it up when we get more lodgers.'

'Yes,' Jenny said, 'but I don't think he's like that.'

'I don't know what he's like! He never looks up from his book when I take in his tray.'

'What is he reading all the time?'

'Oh, books and papers about old furniture. Chairs and tables and china.'

'Oh,' Jenny said thoughtfully. Her desire for intellectual occupation was not great, but she had a genuine liking for the company of those who had their minds on what her head-mistress called the higher things. Her father's knowledge and taste, Miss Headley's enthusiasm for poetry and Italian painting, had given her a pleasant sensation of basking in the rays of culture and getting the benefit of the warmth and brilliance without any effort on her part. She missed these suns which had vanished from her world.

'I'd like to look at his books,' she said. 'They're never lying about when I dust the room.'

'I expect he brings them from the shop and takes them back again. He tried to make me look at the pictures, but I soon stopped that. He wanted me to say which chair was better than another, and what period it belonged to, and I know he hoped I'd guess wrong—he's that kind of young man—so I wouldn't guess at all.'

'I'd like to. I'll look after him to-night.'

'You can have him for keeps,' Dahlia said. 'Oh, bother Milly! I wish I wasn't going. But you never know. Some good may come out of it.'

'No, Dahlia!'

'I don't mean what you mean. Milly's boots will stop all that, but if there's a chance of saving a child from

25

getting run over, or any little thing like that, I'll take it. That's how people get fortunes left to them.'

'But not for a long time.'

'No, I'm afraid my face is my fortune. I shall have to take great care of it.'

'You think far too much about your face.'

'I like it,' Dahlia said.

'And it's rather hard on Milly's. Where are you going to meet her?'

'Outside the house, of course.'

Jenny frowned. While she admired her sister's frankness, her heart sank when she thought of Miss Jewel peering through her lace curtains, the Dakins at their windows and, perhaps, the curate seeing Dahlia for the first time, in Milly's company. Dahlia was a strange mixture, Jenny thought. She was frivolous, but she was capable of gravity. She had broken all the Rendall traditions of behaviour in outfacing her mother, and she had done it in the cause of the very traditions she had broken. She was not ashamed of such actions as she chose to take: she had, in fact, a carelessness of opinion, an aristocratic indifference to criticism which somewhat disconcerted Jenny, who generally assumed that all the Rendall virtues were her own.

'She's better than I am,' she thought, as Dahlia banged the front door, but she could not discipline herself into watching the two girls walk up the street. Ready to start on her own errand, she waited in the hall until they must be out of sight, and while she stood there someone rapped loudly with the knocker.

It was early for Thomas Grimshaw's arrival. She had not thought of him as she opened the door, but there he was, smiling at her with his soft, dark eyes. His dog-cart was in the road and, on the left, a few feet away, was a group of Dakins just setting off for an afternoon's golf.

26

Jenny did not look at them. Out of the corner of her eye she saw the figures in tweed skirts and leather jackets, and hoped they would soon pass out of earshot, but there was delay among the Dakins, and Jenny, fearing Grimshaw would address her familiarly by name, did not suspect that one of them had conveniently forgotten a handkerchief and would take some time in fetching it, sacrificing herself for the general good and knowing that the others would give her a full account of everything they saw and heard.

'Mother in?' Grimshaw asked.

'I don't know. I think she's gone down to the shops for a few minutes.' Should she ask him in, by the front door, like a friend? Should she let him stand there, smiling at her in his teasing way, as though he knew what she was thinking? She held herself very straight, noticing the darkness of his shaven chin and the surprisingly fair down on his cheek-bones, and, with the Dakins still on their step, it seemed an age before he spoke.

'I'll drive down and have a look for her. But wait a minute. I've got something for you in the cart. A nice boiling fowl and a dozen of eggs.'

Jenny took the basket and clearly, urged by the nearness of the Dakins who were now slowly going by, forgetting in her embarrassment that this was the question that had been knocking at her mind all day, she said, 'Thank you. How much do we owe you?' Then, seeing the dark flush on his face, and the Dakins beyond Miss Jewel's house, she retreated, stammering, 'I mean, was it an order?'

He stared at her for a long minute. 'You know very well it wasn't an order, Jenny Rendall,' he said at last. 'And I shan't forget it. And if you want to know how much you owe me, well, you can ask your mother. And you can ask her when she's going to pay me. She's got a big house and a little lodger, but she'll need a lot of

27

lodgers, and I'll not wait for ever. You ask her!' He looked at Jenny quizzingly, from top to toe. 'You're a fine lot to keep lodgers, but I daresay it'll all come right in the end—for some of us.' Then he smiled at her, and it was not an ill-natured smile, it was a little propitiatory. She tried to see him as a villain, to hate him for his part in her life, but she could only see him as a man whose feelings had been hurt.

'You'd no need to ask me that, Jennifer,' he said quietly. 'And you might want a good turn from me one of these days.'

She shook her head. She wanted to apologise, to express her real contrition, but her mother owed him money and she shook her head, offering him a hard, blank gaze.

'Just as you like, but at any rate, I'll have the basket back,' he said, and before he was fairly in his trap she had shut the door.

She liked the dimness of the hall where no one could see her, for she was ashamed. She was more worried by her behaviour than by the certainty of debt to Thomas Grimshaw. She had been rude simply because the Dakins were standing on the step, because she could not help responding to their natural view of him. She had plenty of reason for disliking him: she had none, except her weakness, her vanity, for caring what those people thought. Then, as she heard her mother coming up the stairs, her shame turned to anger against the woman who had imposed this burden of obligation on the family, but when she saw Louisa looking a little timid, a little mischievous and, somehow, innocent, her heart was softened.

'Who was that I heard at the door?' Louisa asked.

'Mr. Grimshaw.'

'He's in a hurry to-day, is he?'

'I don't know. I told him I thought you were at the shops. And I did think you might be.'

28

'Well, yes, or why would you say it?' Louisa replied mildly. 'And what's all this on the floor?'

'Presents,' Jenny said crisply.

'Bother the man! Who wants his presents? All the same, you needn't have left the fowl where the cat could get it. It'll help us nicely over the week-end. Oh well,' she added, in protest against Jenny's critical silence, 'we've got to use some sense. We can't afford to be pernickety with that Cummings' appetite what it is. Now, you go out and have a nice walk and enjoy yourself.'

'Enjoy myself!' Jenny cried. 'I'm going to look for lodgers. I'm going to the Free Library to see the papers.' The reproach she felt was in her voice. She waited for a moment with her hand on the latch, but Louisa did not speak and Jenny went out into the sunshine.

CHAPTER IV

Sʜᴇ wished she could dislike her mother. There would have been something heroic in hatred and life would have been simpler, but in spite of those remembered whisperings in the orchard and the perpetual awkwardness of the present—more trying to Jenny than her suspicions of the past—she had feelings of affection and loyalty for Louisa. In the first place, she was beautiful, and Jenny would not have been her father's daughter if beauty had not touched her, and then her mother had a simplicity that made it seem necessary to protect her. No sensitive person could remember her at the White Farm, bewildered by her husband's efforts to interest his children in intellectual and artistic matters, conscious of being ignored, without feeling sorry for her. Her occasional sullenness and anger, as Jenny well knew, were the remains of that unnatural life: she was still watching for opposition and criticism and suspecting signs of superiority, and this was almost inevitable, for while such tendencies were weak in Dahlia, they were strongly developed in Jenny. The strength of her desire to love and to be loved created constant comparisons between her picture of the mother she wanted and the one her father had given her. There was no guidance to be had from this one, and Jenny wanted guidance as well as love. She and Dahlia were worse than orphans, she thought. They had to take care of themselves and, at the same time, to see that their mother, in her ignorance, did not harm them: yet Jenny had a young animal's instinct to put her head on that broad shoulder and feel the warm strength of Louisa's arms. She was restrained by her mental reservations and by lack of practice. Since they were tiny children, a kiss at the beginning of the holidays and a kiss at the end were the only physical demonstrations between mother and daughters, and there was no other kind of communion. Dahlia, with her gaiety, could bridge the gaps: when Jenny looked at them they seemed to widen.

But, at eighteen, there is always hope of happy solutions to difficulties, and as Jenny walked up Beulah Mount she was persuaded of the goodness of the world, for the sun was shining, there was new green on the trees, the clouds were like fluffy lambs, chasing each other in a blue field, there was exhilaration in the sound of footsteps and voices and the fussy progress of a tug in the river.

Through the streets of Upper Radstowe, so beautiful in spring with their flowering trees, Jenny made her way to the library in Nunnery Road and conscientiously read the advertisements until, looking up to rest her eyes from the small print, she saw Mr. Cummings standing at the reading-desk next to hers, not following a column with a finger as she was doing, but standing well back from the newspaper, his hands in his overcoat pockets, as though he detached himself as much as possible from what he read.

It was not long since she had given him his midday meal, for on Saturdays he took it in Beulah Mount, and, muttering a perfunctory word of thanks, he had kept his eyes on his book, apparently unaware that it was she, and not Dahlia, who waited on him. He was still unaware of her, a worthy sign in a young man, perhaps, but irritating to Jenny, and she had to speak before he saw her.

He had a good smile, showing teeth not too small nor too big nor too white, his hazel eyes had a bright light in them, and his nose, though bluntly cut, was a definite feature.

'I come here,' he announced, rather unnecessarily, 'to read the papers. I never buy one if I can help it. Waste of money. There's nothing in them.'

'They're not very expensive,' she said, expecting him to ask why, then, she was in the library too, but he was telling her that a penny a day was sixpence a week: he multiplied that by four and explained how at the end of a month, by doing without what he did not want, he could get something worth having.

'One of your magazines,' she murmured, nodding her head.

He looked more animated. 'But they're not magazines —not stories.'

'I know,' Jenny said.

'Would you like to see them?'

She nodded again. She was learning her first lesson in one of the ways to a man's heart. Mr. Cummings was not interested in her, and that was less uncomplimentary than it seemed, since he was not interested in Dahlia either, but if she showed herself interested in what interested him she would have a value for him. She had no practical knowledge of young men, she had rarely spoken to one. Miss Headley's parties for the big boys of the neighbouring school and her own older girls had a carefully planned naturalness that made everybody self-conscious, and the men in the region of the White Farm were either not presentable from her father's point of view, or unwilling to be presented, and Jenny had not cared, yet with her first definite opportunity of making an impression she was rather shocked to find that she wanted Edwin Cummings to see her as a girl, with a slim body and pretty feet, rather than as a person who could appreciate works of art. She shut her eyes to this discovery and to the real nature of the impulse which encouraged him to talk about himself, and they were both content as they walked home together. They went slowly, by devious ways, to see what flowers and trees were blossoming in the gardens, and there was no tree that Mr. Cummings had not seen in greater perfection near his home in a little Somersetshire town, and no flower his sisters had not grown in the garden behind their house.

'An old-fashioned garden,' Mr. Cummings said, 'with cobbled paths between the beds, and the flowers and vegetables all mixed up. But they don't hurt each other, and our lavender's a sight. Fanny picks it and puts it into muslin bags, but our Kitty's all for leaving it on the bushes. That,' he said, with satisfaction, 'is what Kitty's like.'

Fanny and Kitty! Jenny saw them plainly, Fanny making and filling the little bags and putting them among the sheets, and Kitty looking sadly at the garden which had been despoiled. She was eager to hear anything Mr. Cummings would say about them, but at this moment, when they had crossed The Green and reached the point where the road from the bridge curved into Beulah Mount, another woman distracted her attention from Mr. Cummings' sisters.

Mary Dakin, walking rather languidly in the first real warmth of spring, seeming to find her bag of golf clubs heavy, was within a few paces of Jenny and her companion. It would have been an embarrassing moment, even if it had not been complicated by Mr. Cummings. The Dakins and Jenny had avoided meeting each other's eyes since the day when she had arrived, alone, at Beulah Mount to measure the floors and windows. They had waylaid her, in the neighbourly desire to offer her a cup of tea, and while they all talked together in their deep voices they revealed to the shrinking Jenny their belief that her mother was the cook. She did not enlighten them. She did not know how she could bear their embarrassment and her own, and as they were talkative and continually interrupted each other, it was not difficult to pretend she had not heard: but now they knew the truth, no doubt they remembered what they had said and she had left unspoken, and to-day, somewhere in Radstowe, Dahlia was wandering with Milly.

Prepared for mortification, but not willing to await it, Jenny smiled, and Mary, smiling back, came nearer, then stopped and rather breathlessly asked if Jenny did not think the day was fine.

'Lovely,' Jenny sighed. She was happy because, in spite of her mother and Thomas Grimshaw, Mary seemed to want to talk to her. Mr. Cummings had disappeared and she was alone with the youngest and prettiest of the Dakins. 'You've come back early, haven't you?' she asked.

'Yes, I'm early. The others think I must be ill. The Dakins practically live for golf, you see, but I felt sick of it and I thought I'd have a look at the trees and things.'

This was Mary's way of expressing the unrest Jenny had roused in her sensible bosom. She saw beauty and romance in Jenny and wished she could be like her. She had seen them first when the almond tree blossomed in the Rendalls' garden and, from her bedroom window, she watched Jenny touch one of the flowers lightly with a finger. She was half embarrassed by the sight. It was like watching a caress between lovers who were certain of each other and need not protest, but it was then she saw her own life dull and herself clumsy, and envied Jenny her grace, her supreme femininity and even the mystery of her contact with the queer woman who should have been the cook. There was nothing mysterious about the Dakins, and no Dakin would have known how to touch a growing flower. Mary smiled grimly as she tried to imagine one of them pausing in her stride and shifting

34

her bag of golf clubs to pay such homage, but what would be absurd in the Dakins was wonderful in Jenny, and Mary would not join her sisters in gossip and speculations about the Rendalls. She had stalked ahead of them, this afternoon, while they discussed the man with the dog-cart and the basket. What did it all matter? Could they not see that Jenny was different? She was romance walking in Beulah Mount.

The thought of Mary Dakin, who might become a friend, made a little excitement for Jenny, and it gave her confidence when she set out for church with Dahlia the next morning.

'But I'm afraid,' Dahlia said, watching the worshippers entering the porch, 'it won't be a good church for hats. Only old ladies in bonnets and good, dull girls who haven't looked in the glass. Never mind. This isn't pleasure. It's business.'

They took their seats at the back of the church to command the scene, and they sat close together, like schoolgirls, so that their messages could pass with decorum. Dahlia's arm pressed against Jenny's at the sight of Mr. Sproat in his surplice. Jenny returned the pressure in a friendly spirit and added another, of a sharper character, as a warning. She knew how a fit of laughter could seize Dahlia at unsuitable moments, and she could feel the desire to say funny things about Mr. Sproat coming like a tiny electric current from Dahlia's body to her own.

The church did not evoke a sense of awe, but Jenny was soon reassured about Dahlia's behaviour. Her levity could not live in the large, bare building which had austerity without grandeur. The glass of the east window was faintly tinted and cast no glow on the pale figures in the stalls: the other windows were not coloured and they gazed down with hard, dull eyes. The church looked cold, the hoods of the clergymen, far away, could

35

not brighten it, and Dahlia was right about the hats. It was a sombrely-clad congregation and not a large one. The old ladies and the good girls stood and knelt at the droning signals in the distance, and Jenny, a sceptic in religion but a respecter of ceremonies, wondered what comfort or exaltation these people were experiencing.

Sometimes she and her father had gone to the village church. He, too, was a respecter of ceremonies when they were hallowed by age and custom, and Jenny liked the feeling of friendship there. The mooing of cows and bleating of sheep came through the open door. At evening service, in the winter, the oil lamps made warm points of light in the cosy darkness and gave out a smell that reminded many of the people of their homes. The vicar knew all the members of his congregation and they all knew each other, and if there was no spiritual fervour there was a sense of unity. The long evenings had to be passed somehow: it was pleasant to sing a hymn to a good tune and, now and then, as the lamps flickered and there was a silence, there seemed to be a presence in the church. Here each person looked isolated from his neighbour, from the ministrants and the God they worshipped.

'Isn't this dreary?' Dahlia whispered, settling herself for the duration of the sermon.

Jenny shut her eyes when she saw that Mr. Sproat was not to preach. She would have listened to him in an attempt to learn something about the man who was her neighbour but, as the vicar tiptoed up the pulpit steps with the lightness of a stout man, she leaned towards Dahlia, as Dahlia had already done towards her, and enjoyed her own thoughts in the little circle of noise made by the preacher's voice.

She was in a hurry to be gone when the service was over. She hoped Mary Dakin would be on the hill or in the avenue that led from it, where the people of Upper

36

Radstowe walked and talked on Sunday mornings and the inhabitants of less favoured suburbs came, pushing perambulators, to look at the famous view of the gorge and the double row of elm trees.

'No. Wait,' Dahlia said. 'I want Mr. Sproat to see us.'

'He never sees anything.'

'He'll see me,' Dahlia said. 'If he doesn't it will waste the whole morning. What a pity there aren't any graves to look at. I don't like a church without graves round it. It seems wrong, somehow. We'll just have to pretend to be talking about something interesting, and then we'll smile and say good morning.'

'I won't smile at a person I don't know just because he's a parson.'

'But they like it. They're disappointed if you don't. And remember, Jen, we're not doing it to please ourselves. Think of the lodgers!'

'Then don't smile too much,' Jenny advised.

The vicar did not need encouragement, and the rotund little man had a quick good morning and a rosy smile for each of them before he trotted after his tall, thin wife.

'Afraid we'd be jealous if he didn't say it twice,' was Dahlia's comment on this generosity. 'Nice little man! I'm sure he'll help us. But where's Mr. Sproat?'

Mr. Sproat, when at last he appeared, walking slowly and unwillingly towards food and leisure, did not lift his eyes from the gravel path, but the two black-clad figures, lingering there after the rest of the flock had gone, must have made some impression on his consciousness, for he turned back and said, 'Er—can I help you?' His face became graver as he asked the question, and Jenny feared Dahlia had smiled too much.

'We were wondering,' Dahlia said, 'if we had to pay for our seats if we came regularly.'

This was badly put: it sounded like an attempt at bar-

37

gaining and Mr. Sproat frowned as he replied, 'All seats are free. There is a notice to that effect in the porch. And in the Parish Magazine.'

Dahlia shook her head. 'We haven't had one.'

'Perhaps you don't live in the parish.'

'Ah, but we do. In Beulah Mount. Number 15.'

'Do you, indeed? Yes, yes, of course. You ought to have had one.' His face brightened at the discovery of an omission in duty. 'I'll see you do, and I'll tell the vicar,' he said, hurrying off.

'And he's afraid we might want to walk home with him,' Dahlia said. 'I suppose some of them do. That's why he waits such a long time before he comes out. Well, that's a beginning, Jen. He'll take more interest in us now he knows we've been neglected. I'm afraid we'll have to come again to-night. He'll be on the look-out for us.'

Jenny said nothing. She was weighing integrity of conduct against the responsibility and unpleasantness of debt to Thomas Grimshaw.

CHAPTER V

This operation engaged Jenny while she and Dahlia crossed The Green where children and dogs were playing on the grass and their guardians sat on seats under the budding trees, and she thought that none of these people, enjoying the sunshine and Sunday leisure, could have difficulties like hers. Most of the faces she saw were placid and many of them were contented, and she noticed that the shabbiest people, the ones with children who would not come when they were called and babies persistently dropping things out of their perambulators or adding peevish clamour to the barking of dogs and parental admonitions, were the ones who looked the happiest. They were free from the burden of possessions, they wisely lived without looking much further than to-morrow and, with the gratitude of those who receive more than they expect, they took the spring day and the sunshine. Even tottering old men and women who ought to have been miserable because they could not move freely, whose limbs would hardly obey the injunctions of the brain, seemed to have cause for satisfaction, but they, Jenny supposed, had lived beyond everything except physical comfort or discomfort, and now they were like cats beside a fire.

And soon Jenny herself yielded to the general feeling that this moment would be permanent, though the secret consciousness of its impermanence was the chief ingredient in its delight. And in spite of all this evidence Jenny felt sorry for the old and the mature, for every one, indeed, who had passed the twenties. Life for them, she thought, must be an affair of making the best of little things. Their time was over for strong emotions and those adventures of the spirit that awaited her, and love, if they gave or took it, might be a consolation, but could hardly be a glamour and an enchantment, like daffodils and primroses and violets and the shining buds of chestnut trees expressed in human happiness. That was Jenny's thought of love: it was something that made every moment and action exquisite, as did, in an infinitely lesser degree, this April morning, and always she imagined herself as the recipient, not the giver, for Jenny Rendall was known to her in the flesh and she had not yet tried to picture the lover to whom she would wish to give. He was living now, perhaps in another country, perhaps close at hand, but never a glance did she throw at the young men walking round the hill, or leaning against the railings to look at the gorge and the river. It would have been strange if she had not sometimes thought of love, but it had not preoccupied her: she knew that, for her, it was not to be sought: it would be a gift from Heaven, recognised at once and accepted without doubt, and looking at chance young men with a calculating, though innocent, eye, offended her sense of niceness.

She was looking now for Mary Dakin, who did not appear, and she was hardly disappointed for she felt an unwonted gaiety, matching the gay world. The hawthorn bushes were crisp with green and the bunches of leaves looked like tiny lettuces, ready to be eaten: the flower buds would soon be breaking, for this was a forward season, and the Downs, above and beyond the avenue which lay between them and the place where Jenny stood, would have their big bushes laden with blossom, snow-white in the distance, but faintly pink in each small cup. Far away, on the right, Jenny could see the hills on the other side of the Channel. In their unearthly pallor they might have been the wraiths of hills, and it was difficult to believe that farmsteads and little cottages, redolent of Sunday dinner, clung to the sides, that sheep and lambs were nibbling the new grass there, and when Jenny turned her gaze from those lovely ghosts to the opposite cliff it looked very dark, in spite of larches and silver birches, and very solid. It was the wall of a citadel which lay further back, concealed by trees: behind it was country familiar and dear to her. Her past was there and to-day she had a feeling that her future might be there, too, yet the cliff still seemed like a wall, inviting in its beauty, forbidding in its strength, and the bridge, offering so airy a passage, might easily be guarded at the further end. One man could guard it, and suddenly she remembered Thomas Grimshaw, who was an inhabitant of that country.

'I don't want to stay here any longer,' she told Dahlia. 'Let's go home.'

Dahlia turned obediently. She wanted to stay in the sunshine and look at the people, but she always gave way to Jenny. Quietly, as by right, Jenny made her little demands and they were fulfilled. Her feelings showed in her face: when she was troubled it became wan and she had a gift for making people believe—as she believed herself—that she suffered more intensely than others and must be treated with a special tenderness.

'I suddenly thought about that man,' she said.

'I've thought of nothing else since you told me what he said. And just look at all these hundreds of people! Some of them must want lodgings. But Mr. Sproat will help us.'

'Not with young men,' said Jenny. 'I don't think he'd approve of that and I don't see why we shouldn't have women. Not old ones—they might get ill—but betwixt and betweens.'

'They'd be a nuisance. They'd be fussy about their food, but I suppose we shall have to take what we can get.'

'Oh, it's hateful!' Jenny cried. 'It's not fair!'

All about her on the hill, below her in the streets and on the bridge was the life from which she was exiled, and yet she asked so little. She wanted a home where things went smoothly, where there was not this constant discord between herself and her surroundings. She wanted to be out of this false position in which she was supposed to be her mother's daughter while all her instincts were her father's, and she thought of him with more love than she had felt for him when he was living, but she was angry with him, too. He had left them defenceless and, in this moment, she wished the dead were really permitted to look down and see the results of their deeds and their inaction.

'Well, Jen, suppose you had six children and no money and a drunken husband?'

'That's silly. Why should I have them?'

'Some of those women with the perambulators have,' Dahlia said. 'And you may have them yet,' she chuckled. 'You may look back at to-day and think how happy you were. After all, we've got a roof over our heads and enough to eat and lovely things to look at.'

'You don't understand,' Jenny said, and her chin quivered.

Dahlia understood very well. Jenny's pride, her fear of what people thought, her desire to be acknowledged by her peers, were her troubles. Dahlia thought them foolish, but they were part of Jenny and had to be accepted. Her own pride was in her independence, and owing money robbed her of it. She took this more seriously to heart than Jenny did, she felt less forgiving towards her mother, though hitherto she had been consistently kinder to her, and to-day, when Louisa met them in the hall, looking pleased at their return, she could not smile in answer.

'Cummings has gone off for a walk,' Louisa said, 'with some bread and cheese in his pocket, so there's no cooking till to-night. I was just thinking of having a bit of a walk myself.'

Neither of the girls spoke. Jenny always left the unpleasant tasks to Dahlia, and Dahlia happened to be cross.

'Well, perhaps it's not worth while,' Louisa murmured, saving them the necessity of making excuses or doing what they did not like. 'But I do think,' she said, going towards the kitchen stairs, 'it's time you got out of your black. Brush it as you may, it's bound to show the dust.'

'We can't afford new clothes,' Dahlia said sharply. 'I shan't have any until I can get a situation and pay for them myself.'

'Get a what?' Louisa asked.

'Situation,' Dahlia said.

Jenny ran up the stairs. They were going to quarrel and she could not bear it, but before she was out of earshot she heard her mother saying angrily, 'I suppose it's that girl next door that's put the idea in your head.'

The attic bedroom was a precious refuge. It was a long way from the basement and no one would climb the stairs without a definite purpose. Here was the furniture from the bedroom at the White Farm, less shining and ornate than Louisa's purchases for the lodgers' rooms, but serviceable and familiar. Here were their books and the little treasures girls always collect, photographs of school groups, Miss Headley, framed, on the narrow mantelshelf, and Dahlia's rough caricatures of mistresses and girls, fastened with drawing-pins to the wall.

If Sidney Rendall had seen those drawings, he might

43

have encouraged her talent and planned a future in which she could use her nimble fingers and quick eyes, but she had not thought of showing them to him, she was hardly aware of her own gift, and she was far from considering that a certain facility in this direction was an indication of the path she must follow. It was Jenny who had the artistic impulse, without the power to express it except, unconsciously, in all she did, and though she admired Dahlia's skill, the very ease of it and Dahlia's own indifference persuaded her that it was of no importance. Neither of them had considered the possibility of turning it to financial advantage, even now, while Dahlia was talking about a situation, making her mother angry and threatening to desert the sister who needed her.

Jenny was resentful for a minute. It was a shame to spoil a lovely day. To-morrow it might rain and that would be the time for argument and quarrel. She had her father's tendency to procrastinate, broken disastrously in his affair with Louisa, and she had a strong desire to preserve the present good even though it might lead to trouble, and the present good was the sunshine and all the signs of spring, and peace in which to enjoy them. She could see no more than the sky through the high-placed window, but she fetched a chair and stood on it. Though her head was almost level with the top of the opposite cliff, the coping-stone hid her view of street and river, but looking sideways she could see the bridge from end to end. The men in the little toll-houses had not much to do at this hour, for, however fine the day, the Sunday rite of roast beef or mutton had to be observed and a ceremonial hush had fallen on Upper Radstowe.

Jenny thought of Mr. Cummings, tramping across the country with bread and cheese in his pocket, and she wished she were tramping too, not with him, but with someone who combined youth and strength with other

44

graces. She wondered, again, where that person could be and, lacking him, she looked forward to Mr. Cummings' return. He was outside this tiny circle in which she and Dahlia and her mother lived: she wanted to hear more about his sisters and to make herself apparent to him. The whole of Radstowe lay below the slim feet on the chair, her father's books were in Mr. Cummings' sitting-room, his few published works were treasured in her chest of drawers, she knew she ought to improve her mind, to find absorbing occupation: she had time on her hands and she could not use it. Behind her little cameo of a face, Jenny was restless. The family anxieties were a good enough explanation, but not the true one. Life was beginning to dance in Jenny, keeping time with the beat of the season, the swaying boughs and driven clouds. Spring was the conductor of the orchestra and everything living had to follow the motions of his staff, but dancing alone is a poor pastime for youth, so poor and unnatural that it was impossible not to believe in the speedy arrival of someone who would partner her.

She turned on the chair and stood with her shoulders against the window-sill, when Dahlia entered. 'You can't go away and leave me,' she said. 'And you might have told me what you meant to do before you made me go to church.'

'I might, but I hadn't thought of it until I spoke. But I think it's a good idea. I could be a parlour-maid and marry the son of the house, or a waitress in a restaurant, with a big bow at the back of my head and dozens of young men to take me out.'

'And to take tips from,' Jenny said, with deep disgust. 'And your feet would spread.' She glanced at her own toes and, conscious of infamy but making a solemn declaration in the cause of beauty, she said, 'I'd rather be in debt for ever than have my feet spoilt.'

45

In Dahlia's place, Jenny would have protested. Dahlia said nothing for a minute. She had a natural tolerance, and Jenny's feet were very pretty. 'It all depends on who you owe the money to,' she said. 'And we ought to have taken her for a walk, Jen. It was horrid of us.'

'Did you quarrel much?' Jenny asked. 'But don't tell me, don't tell me!'

'I couldn't quarrel, because I'd been unkind. It was a shame not to ask her to come out. I meant to say something about the money, but we'd hurt her already, you know. And to think that he used to try to kiss me!' She brushed her fingers across her lips. 'It isn't that I mind about her. I mean, it doesn't seem to matter, does it? It hasn't made her any different. But I mind terribly about him. I don't like it, I don't like it,' she said quickly, 'but it's no use worrying. Mr. Sproat is sure to put the parish magazine through the letter-box and we'll go to the Bible classes for young women.'

'You won't go with me! And what about the situation?'

'I don't think I can leave you, Jen.'

'I should think not!' Jenny said.

'Or her,' Dahlia said.

'No,' Jenny agreed.

They felt responsible for their mother and they thought of her down in the basement, alone, rather bewildered and perhaps sad.

'There isn't really a single bit of unkindness in her,' Dahlia said.

'No, but I can't always remember that,' Jenny said.

She did her best that afternoon. She took a book and a chair into the little garden at the back where the almond tree had flowered and, as she passed through the kitchen, she asked her mother if she would not come, too, and sit in the garden.

'Not in that bit of a place. I don't like the walls. I'd as

46

soon be in a well, and I was never one for sitting outside the house. When I'm out, I like to be doing something, feeding the fowls or gathering sticks or digging up a few potatoes. That's what the outside's for. And don't you get cold, sitting there. The sun's all at the front of the house.'

It was certainly rather chilly behind the barricade of Beulah Mount, but Jenny was soon repaid for her slight discomfort. She could hear Milly in the basement imperilling the Dakins' china in her haste to finish work and put on her stout boots and get into the sunshine. Somebody was playing snatchily on the piano, someone whistled, someone laughed. It was a noisy but, no doubt, a happy household, and Jenny wished she had been born into a family given to laughter. Then she heard a whistle of another kind, rather stealthy, a call to attention, and there, marvellously fulfilling her hopes, was Mary Dakin, with her head and shoulders outside the back bedroom window.

Jenny approached the wall dividing the gardens, Mary gave her a little information about the weather and Jenny nodded. Mary said she was going away for a few days to stay with an aunt who lived in Wellsborough, and Jenny said she had an aunt who lived in Herefordshire. It was pleasant to mention Aunt Isabel, however vaguely, and when she returned to the kitchen with cold feet and a warm heart, happy in this budding friendship, it was a shock to be greeted with the name of her Aunt Sarah.

'I was just writing to Sarah,' Louisa said. 'She doesn't know we've settled here.'

'And need she?' Jenny asked coolly.

This was a mistake for which she was to suffer. Louisa was good-natured, there was a dogged patience in her blood, transmitted by people whose livelihood largely depended on circumstances they could not control, but she had her loyalty to these people and she had a temper, and they were both roused by Jenny's question. She had been in two minds about sending the letter. She wrote it because her loneliness cried out for her own flesh and blood, but her knowledge of Sarah warned her to avoid this sample of it. Jenny's lordly indifference settled the matter. Louisa fastened up the flimsy envelope.

'Go and drop that in the letter-box,' she said.

Jenny held the envelope between her two forefingers. The address was quite as grand as Aunt Isabel's, but one aunt sat in the housekeeper's room and the other in the drawing-room and dimly she felt that her own life lay between these two extremes and was balanced precariously like the envelope in her hands.

'Not,' said Louisa musingly, recovering from her little spurt of anger, 'that I ever cared much for Sarah, but she's the only sister I've got. She's a lot older than me and she was off to work before I'd started school. Albert comes between. I'll tell you what I've been thinking, Jennifer. I'd like to go and have a look at the old farm one of these days. It'd give Albert the surprise of his life to see us all.'

'Doesn't he know you've got us?' Jenny asked.

'Oh, yes. He knows. Sarah'll have told him. I've seen Sarah, every so often, when she's come through Radstowe on her holiday. She'll have told him. But then, she hasn't seen you herself. I'd like for them both to see you. All the same,' Louisa went on, 'I'd sooner go and have a look when Albert isn't there. On a Sunday morning when he's at chapel. We were brought up church, but he goes to chapel. Heaps of flowers there used to be, in the garden, and we'd put flower-pots on the top of the dahlias to catch the earwigs. That's how your sister got her name. Our dahlias were as good as the squire's any day, and I called her for them.'

48

'Well,' said Jenny slowly, 'let's go when the dahlias are out.'

'I don't know,' Louisa said. 'I don't know. I daresay Albert's planted cabbages instead. Perhaps it's better just to think about it.'

'I'll go and post the letter,' Jenny said. She was not anxious to cut short her mother's reminiscences: this was her way of saying that Aunt Sarah, with her part in those memories, could not be altogether excluded from her own life. It was a concession granted, because, like Mr. Cummings, her mother had given her a picture of a garden, a peep into the past of which she seldom spoke, and with it, as it were, a halting line of poetry.

'Of course, you'll go and post it,' Louisa said, spoiling the moment and destroying Jenny's faint sympathy with Aunt Sarah. She had always disliked the thought of her and, as she went to the pillar-box, she saw her again, as she had first imagined her, neatly dressed in black, carrying an umbrella and threatening to appear above the horizon.

CHAPTER VI

Dᴀʜʟɪᴀ went to church again in the evening.

'What's come over you?' Louisa said. 'I'd have thought Jennifer would be the one for church, not you.'

'Appearances are very deceptive,' Dahlia said. 'I'm really much more serious than she is.'

'Well, don't get serious about church. Wait till you've nothing else to think of. Not but what I liked going myself when I was young, of a Sunday evening, but that was more to look at the boys.'

'There aren't any in this church, and Jenny's staying at home to look after our gay young spark.'

'Cummings? H'm,' said Louisa. When, from the other side of the river, she pictured her new life in Beulah Mount, she saw the house full of jolly, lively people who would be friendly with their landlady and amuse her with their little jokes. Edwin Cummings was silent and respectful, and slowly, almost imperceptibly to herself, Louisa's views were changing. Men like Thomas Grimshaw, in a slightly more urban guise, were not compatible with Dahlia and Jenny, and what suited Dahlia and Jenny was gradually, though unwillingly, becoming the right thing for Louisa. 'That Cummings,' she said, 'never has a remark to pass.'

'He's harmless,' Dahlia said.

'And clean,' said Jenny.

She appreciated his cleanly habits. As her father had done, like Dahlia and herself, he bathed each morning, but the Rendalls, at the White Farm, had carried water to their tubs, and Mr. Cummings had the use of an enamelled bath with taps.

'And the first time in his life, I'll be bound,' Louisa said. 'Putting on airs, I call it. I don't mind the cold water, but when it comes to the hot—! I'd like to know how much of it he thinks he's paid for! And a fowl for his supper! I've given him the two legs and he may as well have a wing too. After all, I didn't buy it. And now there's no room for the vegetables. Hand me a dish, Jennifer, and let him help himself off that. He'll never have the face to ask for pudding.'

Mr. Cummings, however, managed the pudding. He had gone without tea, he explained. Tea at an inn would have cost him at least a shilling. He thought it wrong to encourage such high prices, and he had enjoyed his supper all the better.

'You're very careful about your money, aren't you?' Jenny said gravely. She was glad he had eaten the greater part of Thomas Grimshaw's fowl, but it would have been an economy for the family if he had spared the pudding.

'Have to be,' Mr. Cummings said cheerfully.

'Careful about everything,' Jenny went on, looking round a room left untouched by his comings and goings. To-night he was not even reading one of his precious papers, and all there was of him was his own body, a little more relaxed than usual, after his hours of exercise.

'Yes,' he said, with some self-approbation, 'I was brought up among things that needed careful handling.'

'Books?' Jenny asked.

'Well, our books came in bundles at so much a foot, or just as part of a lot of other stuff. We don't really reckon to sell books.'

'But I thought you were in a bookshop.'

'Here, yes, but down at home it's furniture. Second-

51

hand, antiques when we can get them, and repairs. We've got a workshop in the garden.'

'Among the lavender?'

'Pretty well. You can walk out of our shop into the back parlour and that leads into the garden, and the barn's at the end of the path. It's handy, but it would be draughty in the winter if we had as many customers, in and out, as we'd like. Summer's better, with people driving through, and Kitty clears out the windows and just puts a good piece of furniture in each of them. That's the way to catch the eye.'

'And what does Fanny do?'

'She looks after the house. She knows a good thing when she sees it, but Kitty's quicker. My father goes to the sales, but he can't get about the way he used to. Yes, you have to be careful. You can never be sure what you've got in our business. It's exciting, you know. I wouldn't be in any other, unless I could go back to the old days and make the stuff myself.'

'Then why,' said Jenny, 'are you in a bookshop?'

Edwin Cummings' eyes, which had been contentedly sleepy while he talked, now showed their bright light, and his combative nose widened slightly at the nostrils. 'I suppose,' he said, 'you think I'm spending my time handing novels across the counter? I'm in the Old Books! I've been here for weeks, and you didn't know I was in the Old Books!'

'I've been looking after you for a few hours and I know already!'

'Yes, you take an interest. I could never get your sister to be interested in anything.'

'Were you interested in her?'

'No. How could I be? She wouldn't listen.'

Jenny smiled in a provocative manner, unfortunately ignored by Mr. Cummings, and she leaned against the table and contemplated this young man who knew she was not Dahlia, but probably did not realise that her hair was dark and Dahlia's red, that her eyes were grey and Dahlia's a warm brown.

'What's Kitty like?' she asked suddenly. This was the sort of question that persuades men of women's lack of concentration. It was closely connected with her thoughts, but from the Old Books and Dahlia's lack of interest to inquiries about his sister was a long way for him to go. He managed it with an effort.

'She's very keen on walnut, and it's not often she makes a mistake. She's got a sort of intuition about things. It's in her fingers as well as her eyes. You can tell by the way she touches things.'

'I meant,' Jenny said patiently, 'to look at.'

'Oh, to look at! I've never thought about it, but of course I'd know her if I saw her.'

Jenny's laughter, clear and cool and thin as the sound of a tiny waterfall, caused Edwin Cummings to look at her properly for the first time. There was an elfin note in the laughter, and he half perceived that this girl who had carried in his tray, and would have carried it out again but for his detaining conversation, had a quality for which he was trained to look and would have discerned at once in anything but flesh and blood, and if he had not been puzzled by her laughter he might have decided that, in form and essence, she belonged to the best period in mahogany, but he was not used to evoking amusement, as far as he was aware, and he was trying to discover what had caused it.

'Yes,' he owned, 'it was a rather silly thing to say. I think her eyes are brown and she's very quick on her feet.'

'And Fanny?'

'Fanny does the cooking.'

'Oh dear!' Jenny sighed. She gave it up and, glancing

past his head at the rows of her father's books, she nodded towards them. 'Have you looked at those?'

'Yes, first thing I did. There's nothing there.'

'Nothing! Only the best books that ever were written,' Jenny said, with a quaver in her voice, and going towards them as though every word in them were dear to her and must be shielded from this young man's insults, she put her back and her outstretched arms against them. Yet, for her, they were not much more than symbols, and she was really protecting her father's memory from the usurping affairs of every day in which the dead are so easily forgotten.

Mr. Cummings would have had to turn his head to look at her, and he missed the taut beauty of her pose. She did not know it was beautiful, but she felt that it was right and, therefore, she sustained it longer than her feelings warranted.

'When we gave you this room,' she said coldly, 'and I knew you were in a bookshop, I thought you'd like the books, I thought you'd read them.'

'I wouldn't have taken the liberty of touching them!' he exclaimed. 'I'm getting much more here than I had any right to expect, and when I said there was nothing there, I meant in my own line of business. Rare editions.'

'I see!' The advantage was with Mr. Cummings. 'Well,' she said, 'I suppose my father cared more about the insides of them. He was a writer himself.'

A piece of information that should have excited him and led to interesting conjectures about herself, did not deflect his thoughts from their path. 'It was the bundles of second-hands that started me off,' he explained. 'I used to sort them out and put them on a bench outside the window, and I was soon on the track of the good ones. And I began reading about them and all that, till I thought I knew enough to learn some more, so I went

54

into a shop in Birmingham and then came here. I've been here for three years.'

'In the same lodgings all the time till now?'

'Yes. I oughtn't to have left them.'

'If you were more comfortable than you are here—' Jenny began, and she put her hands on the tray.

'I wasn't, but it was cheaper. I ought to have stayed, because I'm trying to save. I left because of the street. All the houses the same and bad at that. Boxes—grey boxes. I had a sort of feeling that they'd spoil my eye. You can easily get your eye used to ugliness. There was nothing else to see out of the window and I thought I'd better make a move. Of course, I knew these houses by sight, but I never thought I'd get inside one, and I stood for a long time, looking at this one, before I knocked, that night I called. It's a good house. I made sure it would be too expensive. It's a good knocker, too. The ring's new, but the rest of it was put up with the door. So I've been very lucky with the loan of this room, too, and the bathroom, but I'm not getting much nearer to my own shop.'

'For books?'

'A few. Anything that's really fine. I want a little shop with one small window and a brocade curtain for a background to a piece of furniture or a bit of china or a set of books. There won't be any trays in my window saying, "All these articles ten shillings each!"'

'Then I should think you'll have to save for a long time.'

'I saved a shilling this afternoon.'

'A shilling! You'll never do it. You'd better go back to your father's shop.'

'I generally get what I want in the end. If you want a thing badly enough you can get it.'

'Yes, if it's furniture or a shop, but suppose it isn't? Suppose it's something you can't buy?'

55

'I've never wanted anything that hadn't got a price,' he said simply.

'That must be very bad for you. And I can show you something, this minute, in this house that you'd like very much, I believe, but you can't have it. A piece of furniture.'

Edwin smiled kindly. 'It often worries me to think that if I'd known you a bit sooner I could have put you in the way of getting some decent stuff instead of what you've got. You might have had good, solid Victorian. I've got a chest in my room at home with drawers that run like silk. The ones in my bedroom here will neither open nor shut unless you shake them like a dog worrying a rat.'

'Yes, I've heard you,' Jenny said. She had been on the point of reproaching him for his rudeness, and then seeing his simplicity, understanding something of his pure passion for beauty and good workmanship, her little flicker of anger went out like a spark. 'The drawers are all right in the thing I'm going to show you. It's in the other sitting-room.'

Edwin Cummings might have discovered that walnut bureau for himself if he had been more curious and less courteous. He had not looked into any of the rooms except the ones assigned to him: he had no suspicion that a piece of furniture worthy of Kitty's window, though perhaps not of his own, was waiting there across the passage.

'It was my father's,' Jenny said, laying her hand on the lid. 'He used to write at it.'

'It's a beauty,' Edwin breathed. 'Mind you, it's not a museum piece, but it's a beauty.' His hands ran over it with the deftness of a conjurer's: he opened all the drawers and touched the little ivory knobs of the inner ones. 'Never been touched,' he said.

'Of course it hasn't. It belonged to the family.'

'It wants cleaning. Kitty'd love it. We'd give you a fair price for it.'

Jenny shook her head. 'It was the only lovely thing he had.'

'We'd give you more than a fair price for it.'

'It's not for sale. You can't have everything you want,' she said on a rising note of triumph. 'You can't have this.'

He walked away as though he gave it up, but he came back. 'I'd like to have it,' he said quietly. 'Whose is it? Yours?'

Jenny hesitated. 'He would have wanted me to have it,' was all she could bring herself to say.

He looked at her while she hung her head, afraid to see the remorselessness of the collector in his eyes, and in this little silence they heard Louisa Rendall's step on the stairs and her voice crying to Jenny to bring down the tray. Then Jenny did look up and she saw that his lips were set.

'Whatever are you doing in here?' said Louisa, with a note of surprise, from the doorway.

Jenny did not speak. She left the fate of the bureau to Mr. Cummings. 'I've never been in this room before,' he said pleasantly. 'You must get a little more view of the hill from this window. You've got the best view in Upper Radstowe.'

'Yes, it's a good view when you can see it,' she said, looking at the curtains drawn for the night, and downstairs, when she and Jenny were washing up the dishes she wanted to know whether Mr. Cummings thought he could pick and choose his sitting-rooms.

'It wasn't that,' Jenny said, 'but he's interested in houses and things and he knows a lot about them.'

'Then I hope he knows where he's well off,' Louisa said.

57

Jenny lay on her right side to see the sky. The sun cannot be faced, the moon floats by, indifferent and aloof, but the stars have messages for mortals, and the brightest star she saw, through the small square of window, seemed to blink at her, now and then, in disapproval. It liked her, it was friendly, and when it blinked, it was remembering, with pain, that she was not honest. The price of that bureau, whatever it might be, was owed to Thomas Grimshaw, and Jenny did not mean to let him have it. When she looked at the star, boldly defying its regrets, she had to look beyond Dahlia's bed, and Dahlia, too, would say the bureau belonged, morally, to Grimshaw. Then, thought Jenny, I must be careful not to let her know its value, and she saw another little complication added to her life. A new lodger, the vicar or Mr. Sproat, entering that room, would be a danger, and as she lay there she felt angry with the world and all the people in it, except herself and Mr. Cummings. He had done what she wanted, but everybody else seemed to have been born to worry her. No, she would not be honest in this matter. Beauty and the happiness it gave were of more importance, and Thomas Grimshaw should not become possessed, though indirectly, of the one luxury her father had allowed himself. She forgot that only this morning she had weighed integrity of conduct, when it was Dahlia's, against the debts: now she deliberately chose a crooked course and repudiated the debts at the same time. It was not fair that she should be made self-denyingly responsible for her mother's actions. If everybody behaved as they should, no one else would be forced into dubious ways. The fault was not hers, it went much further back, and why should she suffer for what she had not done? What was the use of trying to do her best unless others would do theirs, unless, indeed, all past errors could be erased from time? One little speck of good would only be wasted in this world where human beings seemed to have been created so that they might spoil it.

She glanced at Dahlia, who lay on her back with her hands clasped behind her head, an attitude for thought and not for sleep, and she was tempted to present her with these problems, but she feared Dahlia's less subtle views: she wanted to preserve, not only the bureau, but all future rights to take and keep the things she wanted. It would be better to make ethical inquiries of Mr. Cummings, who would not be able to trace their origin and whose replies, if inconvenient, could easily be disregarded. He had been very kind, and her heart warmed towards him as she remembered how his hands had fondled the bureau and how generously he refused his opportunity, and suddenly she wondered if he would have been as generous with Dahlia. She had hung her head and waited, not quite trusting him, but giving him the chance to be trusted and he had taken it. Was it, Jenny asked, stiffening her toes, because he liked the look of her? Wanting to laugh, she contented herself with smiling against the pillow, and then, frowning, she put him from her thoughts, but as she turned on her other side to sleep she remembered that he was not just an ordinary young man in a bookshop: he was in the Old Books, he was an expert, and he and Kitty, and even Fanny who did the cooking, were aristocrats in the world of taste.

59

She woke with the belief that something nice was going to happen, but this was only the result of falling asleep in a happy mood. The events of the day did not prove her a good prophet, for she saw Mary Dakin carrying a suit-case down the road and knew her friend had left her for a time, and the discovery of the parish magazine on the mat did not console her. She handed the paper to Dahlia, who read it carefully, letting out derisive little chuckles as she read, and warning her mother that the vicar would probably be calling soon.

'That means my black dress every afternoon till he's been and gone,' Louisa sighed. 'Wouldn't it be better,' she looked from one girl to the other, appraising each, 'if Jennifer was to see him? No? Well, I suppose you're right, but I don't know what I'm going to say to him, and I didn't go to church on Sunday.'

'No, you were too busy, you let us go instead,' Dahlia instructed her, and Louisa said simply, 'But I hadn't a thing to do and I didn't know you were going till you'd started.'

Here was a Philistine in whom there was no guile. She did not know why Dahlia laughed and put an arm round her broad shoulders in an awkward hug: she would not have understood what Jenny meant when she accused Dahlia of trying to ruin their mother's innocence. It was strange that both girls, knowing what they did about her, should be able to see her as a child whose simplicity could be spoilt: it was a sign of wisdom in them and of an essential honesty in her.

'Don't try to make her pretend things,' Jenny begged. She was smoothing her hair in front of the mirror, for it was nearly supper-time. 'It's horrid! Besides, she wouldn't do it a bit well.'

'Which is your real reason?' Dahlia asked.

Jenny did not answer. She was peering at her reflection.

'The light in this room is very bad. I can't see myself properly.'

'You needn't. You always look the same.'

'Do I? Is that very dull?' Jenny asked humbly.

'It was what made mother think that you were the one who ought to see the vicar.'

Jenny was not gratified. She did not want to please the rotund little clergyman: she wanted to be the cause of Mr. Cummings' generosity, and she felt a stab of disappointment—a little quiver of vexation—when, as usual, he thanked her for his supper without raising his head. If he had wished to keep her there he could not have contrived it better, and though this was her first disturbing realisation of the difference between men and women in their emotional values and possibilities, and she knew that what had been making her look forward to this moment had been forgotten, or never felt, by him, she was determined to bring it to his mind.

'You were very kind to me last night,' she said.

'I beg your pardon?' he said politely.

'You were kind about the bureau last night. You could so easily have taken it from me.'

'You learn not to be in a hurry in our trade,' he said. 'Kitty's just sold an oak chest that my father'd been trying to buy from a farmer for twenty years. Got it at last. We're used to waiting. It's part of the game. I think it's a bit like fishing. It wouldn't be any sport if the fish took the bait just to oblige you.' He lifted a hand and cast an imaginary line. 'I used to do a lot of fishing when I was a boy.'

'And I thought it was all your kindness!' Jenny said, trembling a little in mortification.

'Well, it was, in a way. If you hadn't shown it to me I'd never have seen it. I couldn't take advantage of you, could I? And I won't try to buy it from anyone else.'

'You'll never buy it from me,' Jenny said ungraciously.

'Oh, I don't know,' Mr. Cummings said mildly. 'I generally get what I want when I've set my heart on it.'

Such words had power over Jenny: they made her fearful for her bureau, but otherwise hopeful for her future. 'Do you think anybody can?' she half whispered.

'If you want hard enough and not too much.'

'No, I don't want too much,' she murmured.

'It would be no good setting your heart on Buckingham Palace,' he explained. 'You've got to be careful about what you want.'

'I think that's rather mean. It's just so that you shan't be beaten.'

'It's common sense. What's the good of trying to reach the moon? It's better to aim at a little shop on The Slope.'

'Is that where you want it?'

'It would be the best place in Radstowe.'

'Yes,' said Jenny, clasping her hands, and so she stood for a few moments. 'Yes, and when you walked there in the morning in springtime you'd see the trees in front of the cathedral, like green lace, and in the autumn there'd be the mists and the tower peeping up like a rock out of the sea. Yes, it would be a nice place for a shop. I hope you'll get it.'

Mr. Cummings, in whom a love of beauty had to be controlled by common sense, the site of whose shop would be chosen for the advantage of business and not for the owner's pleasure as he walked there, was anxious to make this plain: he did not willingly leave people in error, and yet he did not speak. Jenny's eyes were shining, she was smiling in selfless pleasure, and this enthusiasm about his affairs suddenly enabled him to see how softly slim she was, how neatly her head was set on her young neck and how darkly the lashes framed eyes of that rare pure grey which has neither green nor blue in it. All unknowingly, Jenny had achieved her instinctive purpose and, as men will, he preserved his new conception of her by encouraging the interest which had created it.

'I might live over the shop and then I shouldn't see the trees.'

'But you'd know they were there and you could lean out of the window.'

'After a bit I'd want the rooms for stock. And I know where I really want to live. At least, I haven't quite made up my mind about it.'

Jenny knew what that meant and perhaps he misinterpreted her smile.

'How would it be,' he asked, 'if you came for a walk with me on Saturday and I'd show you the house?'

She thought it would be a great condescension on her part, but she made allowance for his ignorance in these matters. 'Where is the house?' she asked.

'Over the bridge. In Combe Friars.'

'You can't show me anything there that I haven't seen before. Which one is it?'

'It's name isn't printed in gilt letters on the fanlight. It isn't called Bella Vista or Sunnyside,' Mr. Cummings said, with elaborate sarcasm. 'It's a Georgian house. Red brick.'

'With iron gates.'

'Very fine iron gates.'

'That must be Merriman House.'

'I'd like to show it to you.'

'I've seen it dozens of times,' Jenny said impatiently, 'and with a person who knew just as much about good houses as you do. With my father. You don't seem to realise that I used to live over there.'

'Then, could you get inside the house? The front's all right, but you never know what people will do. They may have thrown out modern bay windows at the back.

63

I'd like to make sure about that,' he said, as though the title deeds were waiting to be transferred and the money was in his pocket.

'No, I couldn't. We were not friendly with the Merrimans,' Jenny said, and her tone put in their proper place these upstarts who had owned the house for no more than two generations.

'No, I suppose you wouldn't have been,' he agreed obtusely. 'But I'd like to have seen inside and I'd like to have the furnishing of it.' He smiled slyly. 'That bureau would look very well in one of the rooms.'

'You must buy the house first, but if you were a millionaire they wouldn't sell it. They're trying to found a family, and there's a son who'll want the house. And you'd only make it look like a museum. I expect they've got lots of ugly things, but it's better to have your grandfather's ugly things than someone else's pretty ones.'

'There,' said Edwin Cummings, 'I disagree with you.'

'And I don't mind a bit,' said Jenny, flashing a rather spiteful smile at him. 'And perhaps you're not interested in grandfathers.' Though this was politely uttered, it was meant as disparagement, for the young man irritated her, and she did not know that the house was taking shape in his mind as an excuse for crossing the bridge with her.

Luckily, he had a sturdiness of character and sureness of himself that prevented any uneasy readiness to suspect insults, and he said, 'I had a very good grandfather myself. He started the business. It's been established for two generations, and I'd be the third if I didn't want my own shop.'

'Then,' said Jenny, 'you're just like the Merrimans, but young Mr. Merriman won't want another house.'

'That's the difference between keeping money and making it. Keeping a lot and making a little. Now my grandfather was a craftsman, but he didn't make a fortune. Couldn't and didn't want to, anyway. I'd like to know how that Merriman made a start.'

'I think it was some kind of food.'

'It would be! Buying and selling. Nothing else! Not even seeing what he was buying and selling, and making nothing except money. But he gets a grand house and starts a family, and they forget about the food and so does everybody else. Landed gentry, I suppose! My father still wears an apron, like his own did, and his hands aren't clean because he's doing a man's job, and a fine job and an honest one.'

Jenny thought of her own father's hands, thin and supple as hers were, and she looked at those of Mr. Cummings—square, blunt-fingered, but extraordinarily tender in their movements. 'You can make things without getting your hands dirty,' she said, 'and why don't you make something yourself?'

'Because when I started work I had no sense. I wanted to wear a stiff collar and a black coat, and now I've got to go on wearing them. But I like my work and I don't particularly want to make a lot of money.'

'You'll have to before you can buy that house.'

'It's a bit too big for me, really,' he said. 'But come and have a look at it on Saturday,' he added, and now he seemed to ask a favour.

'I'll think about it,' Jenny said, knowing that her decision was already made.

CHAPTER VIII

Before Saturday came round again the vicar had called at No. 15 Beulah Mount. He had come and gone like a child's india-rubber ball, lightly bouncing up the steps, into the hall and Mr. Cummings' sitting-room. There he rested precariously, as a ball does, threatening to move at a breath, hovering between stability and motion, and in his repetitive, staccato speech he confirmed his likeness to a ball.

'Yes, yes, no, no, I see, I see,' said Mr. Doubleday, and each phrase was a gentle double bounce in which he seemed to be preparing for the larger, freer leaps of his departure. This he was about to take when Jenny entered the room, not knowing he was there with Dahlia and her mother in attendance, and the rhythm of his remarks had to be changed from a double to a treble beat. He liked to please everybody, and in the comfortable conviction that he had done so he went trippingly down the steps and was carried off swiftly by the slope of Beulah Mount.

'H'm, he's not going to be much good to us,' Louisa said.

'Funny little Doubleday,' Dahlia said indulgently.

'Doubleday? Double chin!' said Louisa.

'Double everything,' Dahlia said, 'until you came in, Jen, and that upset him.'

'And why should Jennifer upset him, I should like to know?' Louisa asked indignantly. 'If he's got a daughter as good, he may be thankful.'

'Am I good?' Jenny asked, thinking of the bureau and

of Mr. Cummings and her desire to keep them both, though she had no real use for either.

'We'll see when you get the chance to be the other thing,' was Louisa's reply.

'And when will that be, said the bells of Hacknee,' Dahlia sang as her mother left the room. 'I can see us both growing into Miss Jewels. Mr. Doubleday has forgotten us already, but we're in the parish and it's Mr. Sproat's duty to see that we don't starve. I wish I knew more about the money. I wish I knew how much father left. It's a pity he didn't give some of it to us and then we could have learnt to earn our livings.'

'But we shouldn't have.'

'No, I suppose we shouldn't have,' Dahlia agreed. 'But I want to know how much we owe. D'you think I could ask her?'

'Don't ask her,' Jenny said quickly, for she did not want to know. A small sum would weigh on her conscience, a large one would cover her like a cloud.

'I expect she's in a muddle herself. And there's the White Farm. That belonged to us, you know. What has she done with that? We've been a pair of babies, Jen, just doing as we were told and asking no questions.'

'We were brought up to be like that,' Jenny said.

Dahlia nervously played an imaginary tune on the window-pane. 'I've a good mind to ask Thomas Grimshaw himself.'

'No, don't,' Jenny said again, and Dahlia turned on her with good-natured scorn.

'Do you think miracles are going to happen?'

Unexpectedly Jenny slowly nodded her head. 'They must.' She paused before she said faintly, 'And there's Aunt Isabel.'

'And there's Aunt Sarah, and one would be about as much good to us as the other.'

67

'Aunt Isabel said if I ever wanted help—'

'Yes, but by this time she's hoping you won't, and getting to feel quite safe and happy about it.'

'She was lovely to me!' Jenny cried.

'Yes, and rather excited. I thought she was silly. She hadn't taken any notice of him for twenty years and cried because she couldn't see him when he was dead. I don't suppose she's ever thought of us again, except to hope she needn't.'

'She said I was like him,' Jenny said stubbornly.

'That's why you'd refuse her charity if she offered it.'

'But it needn't be charity. It might be—kindness.'

'I should hate her to be kind to me,' Dahlia said, 'but she won't be. She didn't like me. She thought I was common.'

'You're not, but you know you have to be careful about your looks.'

'Yes, I've come to the conclusion that it's a misfortune to have wavy hair, especially when it's a queer red like mine. It makes me look so frivolous. And I'm not. I meant to be, but I'm not. I want to be, but I can't. I thought the house would be full of lodgers by now, and all we've got is poor Mr. Cummings, who doesn't know yet whether we're old hags or girls. If only we were full of lodgers, we could pay the debts and have some fun, and I believe we'd get them if we were all older and uglier, and then what good would they be? Oh, I know we'd pay the debts, but I'm remembering that I'm only twenty. I've felt middle-aged since Saturday night.'

'But there are other things,' Jenny said slowly, 'as well as that kind of fun.'

'Yes, there's the museum with stuffed birds and cases full of coins and the backbone of an animal nobody's ever heard of! And the dear old churches! I know. But if

68

you say they're all you want you're not telling the truth, or you're not human.'

'I didn't say so, but you talk about lodgers in such—such a vulgar way as though you wanted to marry one. It's horrid to think about marrying just anybody, to think about it at all until you've got to.'

'Well, I think about it a lot. At least I did until I was middle-aged. Of course, it sounds dreadful to marry a lodger, and I don't particularly want to, so long as I marry somebody, but if you called him a paying guest it would sound charming. Mr. Sproat's one or the other for Miss Jewel!' Dahlia gave her throaty chuckle. 'I'm glad he isn't ours, and I shouldn't like to marry him! But still, they needn't all be like him or Mr. Cummings.'

Jenny felt a little embarrassed. She and Dahlia were changing parts again. It was she who was supposed to be a snob, and now Dahlia was despising Mr. Cummings: it was she who had been serious-minded, and yet she could not emulate Dahlia's earnestness.

'Mr. Cummings,' she said, feeling bound to defend him when she remembered the admiration in his eyes, 'isn't just an ordinary young man in a shop.'

'Well, he's a very ordinary young man in a house!' Dahlia retorted. And after a moment she said rather wearily, and Jenny heard the unusual note in her voice and felt respect for it, 'Doctors and dentists must feel like this when they're waiting for patients and nobody comes except people with bills. We ought to have a notice in the fanlight, but I don't want to vex you, and we can't go out and ask people to come in. I think I'll flatten my hair as much as possible and go and call on Mr. Sproat.'

'Miss Jewel will say he's out.'

'I shall wait until I know he's in.'

'And I don't think he will be pleased.'

'I don't want to please him. I want him to please us.

69

It would be fatal if he liked the look of me. It would make him cross,' Dahlia said, and she laughed with a gaiety in marked contrast to her late weary tone. 'That's why I'm going to plaster down my hair.'

Jenny's eyes filled with tears and she went quickly from the room. She went where no one would find her, to the other attic, used as a storing-place for odds and ends of household goods. Here were her father's iron bedstead and his tin bath, poor gaunt reminders of his life at the White Farm, and Jenny looked at them through tears which were not for him, though it was pitiful to see his bed, the black enamel chipped in places, the two ends, once separated by his long body, leaning together against the wall, and standing in his bath a pair of old boots, mournful, with dejected, crumpled faces. Why had they been kept? Jenny wondered. They were probably found in some corner, during the removal, and thrown into the van. That was better, perhaps, than leaving them to rot in the orchard or to grow mouldy in the deserted house, and Jenny pictured them coming out of their corner or cupboard at night and wandering about the house, with invisible feet inside them. But they were here, close to the room where she and Dahlia slept, and probably, Jenny thought, for she readily endowed inanimate things with human attributes, the poor old things were comforted, but she was in no mood to fancy that her father's protective spirit hovered in the attic. His daughters had no one to protect them, except each other, and Jenny wept because, just for a moment, while Dahlia laughed about Mr. Sproat with the merriment of a girl, she had appeared as she ought to be, free of care and gay and innocent, and it seemed cruel to Jenny, and degrading, that she should have to flatten her unruly hair in order to make a good impression on a gloomy curate.

Jenny looked at the bed and the boots and the bath

with a sort of anger, and she thought they represented in their shabbiness and neglect the lot to which her father had left his children. Dahlia and she would grow shabby: they would age until their faces were crumpled like the boots: they would grow wily in catching lodgers and keeping them: they would be like Miss Jewel, peeping behind her curtains and looking as if she hated everybody. But they would not look like that for thirty or forty years, and Jenny, whose tears had ceased to flow, was able to realise that she exaggerated. Neither Dahlia nor she had the characteristics of the harpy and, she thought complacently, ignorant of what time and disappointment could do to pretty faces, there was no reason why they should be ugly when they were old. And then, finding a seat on an empty packing-case and looking into the future, she saw that there were other dangers than a drear old age. She felt that she was sitting on the edge of a steep slope and she was already sliding down it. Dahlia was sliding, too, and what would be the end of her Jenny did not know. She believed that she herself would not be broken to pieces when she reached the bottom, but she would be maimed, she would limp, she would not hold her head up, she would, in fact, be hardly recognisable as Jenny Rendall. She had such a horror of infirmity that she did not know how anyone unable to run or leap could have a happy hour, and she thought she was to be spiritually lamed, that the standards she had meant to uphold would droop from an injured hand. All physical expressions of strength and beauty, she felt, though she was as yet too young to put her thoughts in order, should have their counterparts within. She had meant to go through life without a flaw, without a halting step, and already she was flecked and hesitant. And what would her father think if he could see her walking across the bridge with Mr. Cummings? Aunt Isabel, noticing him, would never look for her niece by his side. Why, to use his own phrase, had she set her heart on going? She knew and she felt wicked, for he could be nothing to her, with his blunt fingers and his cheap clothes and the thick sturdiness of his figure: nothing but a test for her own powers, a little excitement in the dullness of Beulah Mount and a makeshift of a companion. And thinking thus she tried for the first time to give features and a shape to the perfect companion, the lover who was wasting his time and hers, with other people, in other places. She could not see him. She shook her head and told herself she never would. She would go on slipping down the slope, by Dahlia's side, and Dahlia would have her hair fluffed out as far as possible, and that lovely smile of hers would lose its frankness and her laughter would grow louder as they went down, faster and faster, with the only friends they were allowed to make. Yet as she watched the descent in which she shared she noticed that Mr. Cummings was still on the level ground above, steadily striding towards what he wanted, and she was puzzled. Why should he be up there when she, partly because of him, had already started downwards? She knew there was a moral somewhere, but she could not find it. She was not very anxious to find it. She looked, instead, at the old boots, and wished with all her heart that it had been her mother who had died. She loved her, in a way, more than she had loved her father, but she could have spared a mother more dearly loved than Louisa for the sake of the security and peace and harmony her nature craved.

CHAPTER IX

W<small>HEN</small> Dahlia rang Miss Jewel's bell she was prepared to see a sour face in the narrow opening of the door and eyes that were blank yet sharp. Miss Jewel was pretending not to recognise the bright figure on her doorstep. Not once had she acknowledged the existence of the Rendalls, and no one could have guessed how much they had enriched her life. Louisa had cast one look at her and taken no further interest in a little stick of a woman who would not return her neighbourly smile. The girls knew she watched them from behind her curtains, and Jenny was half afraid of her and pitiful because she was ugly and must be dull, but Miss Jewel was not dull: the Rendalls had saved her from the threatened monotony of her existence.

For years she had feared that the Dakin girls would lure her gentlemen lodgers into marriage, a state of which she had a morbid horror, and leave her to the disgrace of vacant rooms, but Mr. Sproat and the professor never glanced at the windows of No. 16 and Miss Jewel rejoiced, for they were good lodgers, with a bedroom and a sitting-room each, regular in their ways and not exacting, yet while she rejoiced she regretted her security: she was deprived of the necessity to watch them as they came and went. And the Dakins, absolved from evil designs on her gentlemen, gave her no satisfaction. They were innocent of any conduct capable of enlivening her imagination. Even Milly, though she wore a dirty cap, could not be suspected of the kind of wrongdoing Miss Jewel looked for, and now, just when she needed excitement, Fate had been kind to her. There had arrived next door a woman with bright hair which was no doubt dyed, a woman who stood at the area door in a gay overall, showing her bare neck and arms, who loudly scolded the tradesmen and parted from them with laughter. This was bad enough, but not one of Thomas Grimshaw's visits had passed unnoticed by Miss Jewel who, with no more than the help of a middle-aged charwoman, did all the work of the house and still had time to watch her neighbours. The energies which were not given to cooking and cleaning and mending for her gentlemen were used in the hope of catastrophes which would not affect her own existence, and her senses had adapted themselves to her needs. There were few knocks on the Rendalls' door she did not hear, nor was it shut behind anyone without her knowing who that person was. She was aware of Mr. Cummings' arrival and foresaw that he was doomed, yet, day by day, he went punctually to his work, a disconcerting proof that his breakfast was served in time, and punctually he returned, with a regularity which Miss Jewel appreciated in lodgers of her own, though she could find improper reasons for it in a lodger of the Rendalls. That woman, strangely metamorphosed from a handsome hussy in her overall to a respectable woman when she wore her coat and hat, was a scandal, with her weekly visitor, to what Miss Jewel called The Mount, and the two girls were potential scandals. They must be the cause of the young man's willingness to return, but now that the evenings were lighter and he sometimes took a walk after supper alone, she was a little worried. The young scandals remained potential and she began to be impatient, and sometimes she would put her black woollen shawl round her shoulders and step across the road when darkness had fallen to look up at the Rendalls' lighted windows. It was a lucky evening when she caught

74

a glimpse of a head, but she never saw two heads close together and, listening in vain for sounds of revelry, she would tell herself that the quietness of the house was a bad sign. It was always very quiet on Saturday afternoons when that man paid his call and the girls had generally left the house before he came: that, too, was a bad sign, and all the emotions Miss Jewel had missed in her youth were now vicariously experienced. She thought she was indignant and shocked: she was, in fact, bitterly jealous of beauty and admiration and abnormally curious about the relations of the sexes, and to have these things presented to her next door, in the house of a woman who pretended to let lodgings, was a delightful torture. For its assuagement and increase she tried to make friends with Milly, whom she despised as an inefficient slattern. Milly, however, belonged to the league of youth, and though her acquaintance with Dahlia had not prospered, she saw no reason for obliging the suddenly friendly Miss Jewel, who finding this soil fruitless decided to drop a seed into it.

'Take my advice and have nothing to do with them,' she said.

And now the vicar had called and she had hardly recovered from the shock of seeing that undeserved benison bestowed, when Dahlia was on her doorstep asking for Mr. Sproat.

'I was very grand with her,' Dahlia told Jenny. 'I was like Miss Headley when we collided with the boys' school going into church. Do you remember the face she put on? Very calm and sweet and thinking of holy things, but really terrified we were going to giggle. And of course,' Dahlia said thoughtfully, 'I always did. I smiled at Miss Jewel, too, because I'm polite, but I was queenly and hardly knew she was there. And I didn't answer her questions and I got into Mr. Sproat's sitting-room.'

75

'She'll hate you,' Jenny said. 'She'll say nasty things about us to Mr. Sproat. Did he look cross?'

'He wasn't exactly pleased, but he brightened up when I told him we were in trouble. I don't know why he lives in a peaceful place like Upper Radstowe. He ought to live where they have plagues and earthquakes, and then he'd be happy all the time.'

'I expect that's why he doesn't,' Jenny said. She was sitting up in bed, hugging her knees and resting her chin on them, and as she gazed straight in front of her she saw Mr. Sproat joyously tending the plague-stricken and leaping the crevasses left by earthquakes.

Dahlia, undressing, was arrested in the process by a thought. 'I don't believe I'm nearly so stupid as they made out at school. Throw me my nightgown.' She slipped it over her head. 'Lessons didn't interest me, and people do,' she said when she emerged.

'Not all people,' said Jenny.

'No, not all of them. Not Mr. Doubleday or Mr. Cummings. Only the ones who can be useful, and I'm thoroughly interested in Mr. Sproat. He's going to help us.'

'He can't manufacture lodgers for us.'

'He's going to help us,' Dahlia repeated, 'and all because I'm clever. And truthful.'

'Not too truthful?'

'I didn't tell him the family history, but I didn't tell any lies. I meant to, when I went in, but I never can when it comes to the point, and when he began asking questions and wanted to know where we went to school and when we were confirmed and silly things like that, I just told him father wouldn't let us be.'

'Oh, what a nuisance! Now he'll badger us till we are.'

'Let him badger! We needn't do it, but he won't forget us. That's the great thing, and he can't expect us to be confirmed to please him if he doesn't do something to please us. And I told him Mr. Doubleday had called, and I said, in a sort of patient way, Jen, that I was afraid he was too busy to remember us. He liked that! I think little Doubleday's lazy and Mr. Sproat has to do all his work for him. And, as I said before, I think I'm rather clever.'

'You may be,' Jenny said, 'but it's all disgusting. It's not right. It's horrid. We oughtn't to have to do things like that.'

'Yes, I know. We ought to live a perfectly lovely life, with nothing to do and no worries, and be charming, innocent young girls, but we're alive, Jen, and we haven't any money and we've never been particularly innocent. And what harm have I done?' she demanded.

'It doesn't seem honest.'

'What about being in debt?'

'That's different,' Jenny said, with a qualm that sent her under the bedclothes. 'I like to feel honest in my mind.'

'And do you?'

Jenny made no reply. She felt that there was a difference between the material fault of keeping the bureau which would have helped to pay the debt, and the spiritual fault which Dahlia had been committing, and her judgment was in favour of her own offence.

'It's so messy,' she murmured.

'But rather fun getting through the mess, and we can have a bath afterwards.'

'We shan't get really clean, ever,' Jenny said, knowing there were secrets she must always keep from the people she most respected, resenting that heavy burden and realising that it was not her mother's unfaithfulness that troubled her, but her humble birth and the social standing of her lover, with his broken finger-nails and the physique of a large, healthy animal. If her father had loved such a woman as Aunt Isabel, Jenny might have seen sin in the episode, though sin was undefined in her mind, but she could have persuaded herself of its beauty. For her it would be easier to confess to a sinful parent than to one whose speech and manners were embarrassing, and in her own mother she had to confess to all. But she realised, too, that her suffering would seem unnecessary and might appear romantic, a hundred years hence, to a descendant of her own, and that if it had happened to an ancestor of hers a hundred years ago she would feel no shame for it now. Time hallowed and enriched things and hid their faults, and Jenny wished she could remain herself and yet be for herself what she would be for others, were she remembered at all in days to come, with her sordid cares acting like a dark frame to throw up the picture of any happiness or adventures or nobility of sorrow she might have.

Dahlia put out the light, and as she stood with her hand still on the switch, straight and tall in her pale night-gown, and Jenny lay motionless and relaxed, they seemed to be proclaiming their attitudes towards the future.

'Yes, you're just like him,' Dahlia said, and there was not reproach, there was simply acceptance in her voice. 'Keep your dignity and do nothing.'

'And who are you like?' Jenny asked.

Dahlia took a light leap into her bed. 'I don't know. Aunt Sarah, I should think. She's made her way in the world. She started in the scullery and now she's in the housekeeper's room.'

'Be quiet!' Jenny cried. 'And you needn't laugh. It's not because I'm ashamed of her—at least, not only that, but if we talk about her she'll come. You can make people come by talking about them.'

'Nice people?' Dahlia asked hopefully.

'No, only nasty ones,' was Jenny's mournful reply.

CHAPTER X

AT night, three flights of stairs separated the girls in the attic from Louisa in the basement, and then she felt deserted, half timid and quite forgotten in her bedroom. She wished she could persuade one of the girls to share her bed, in the comfortable country way, but they would not even share one with each other. They had been shocked, as at an impropriety, and they had been obdurate, when she suggested that there would be an economy in sheets if they would use the big bed on which she and Sidney Rendall had once slept. She lay in it now alone, as she had lain since her husband set up his iron bed-stead in the little room at the other end of the passage. Solitude had not troubled her there, for she was companioned by all the country noises which town dwellers, expecting peace, find so disturbing, but here she was very lonely, and she would have liked a warm young body near her, she would have been glad to put an arm round it, and she felt she had been defrauded, first in her marriage and then in her children.

Lying there, close to the feet of strangers on the pavement, she was harassed by the lack of lodgers, her debt to Thomas Grimshaw and the expectation of his arrival on Saturday afternoon. She was worried by his patience in pursuit. He gave the impression, when he sat with her in the dark kitchen, of having her at bay, where he would keep her until she gave herself or the money she owed him. His presence was physically oppressive, he had the advantage of her and she knew it, and she wished she could speak about him freely to her daughters. She wanted to explain that episode for which they judged her and make them see it as she did herself, as an impulse so completely and spontaneously physical that, but for its aspect to other people, it would have left no more mark on her than a youthful disease from which she had long ago recovered.

Often her thoughts turned to Sarah. Ten years older than herself, always disliked and distrusted by the franker nature, she was still someone who spoke the same language and had the same early background, and, at a safe distance, Louisa was easily persuaded that, after all, she might like being with Sarah, for she was lonelier here, even in the daytime, than she had been at the White Farm, where the country lay outside her door and she could hear the fowls clucking in the orchard and watch the fields changing from the bare brown of ploughing time to bright young green, from the golden reaping to the stubble, and then to brown again. She missed these things from which she had been glad to go: the sound of the feet on the pavement and the hooting of the steamers seemed unfriendly, and lying awake, as she was not used to doing, she was glad to recover the best memories of her youth, before she had seen Sidney Rendall or Thomas Grimshaw, when she was doing the dairy work on her father's farm and the young squire saw and loved her. She was proud of that young love, prouder still because she had escaped from it for his sake, and taking refuge with an aunt who kept a little paper and tobacco shop in the slums of Radstowe she had dazzled another man with her beauty. This was Sidney Rendall, who strolled into the old theatre one night and saw her leaning against a slim gilt pillar and watching the melodrama enacted on the stage. She was supposed to be selling programmes, and there was not much demand for them in that audience, but Sidney Rendall bought one. He prolonged his stay in Radstowe and endured the melodrama for several successive nights. Like the young squire he was virtuous and wished to marry her, and from him Louisa had no desire to run away. She did not love him enough to foresee disaster for him in such a union, and urged by the enormous aunt who could hardly squeeze herself behind the counter in her low-browed shop, indifferent because she was unhappy, a little flattered by the attentions of another gentleman, Louisa married him, and he was no quicker than she was in seeing the mistake. Because she did not love him her pride was hurt when he gently tried to instruct her in the ways befitting a Rendall. His gentleness betrayed his anxiety not to emphasise the differences between them, and she was determining not to be taught just when he was telling himself she was unteachable, but he was wrong, for she would have responded to frankness. He could not give her that, for it was not in his nature. His pleasure in restraint, in the word not spoken and the caress not given, was incomprehensible and wounding, and forced a reserve on her which seemed like sullenness. Later she interpreted his silence about Thomas Grimshaw as an insult. Indignation, physical roughness, she would have understood: his way of showing her he knew of her unfaithfulness, though he would not speak of it, made her despise him and yet believe he saw her as a thing too poor to be reproached. She could not guess that he had a bitter sympathy for her because they were fellow-sufferers and the fault was chiefly his, but his sympathy was not strong enough to overcome his fastidiousness. He could not forget her affair with Thomas Grimshaw any more than he could bring himself to put a legal end to his marriage. And that was what Louisa feared: she did not want to be parted from the children, and now, when she lay in the dark, she tried not to think resentfully of her husband, because she had a great and consolatory pride in them.

She had written to Sarah because she was angry with them, but perhaps she would not have written if these girls had been what Sarah would expect. She wanted to show them to her relatives who, of course, were thinking they were ordinary girls, and it soon appeared that Sarah was all impatience to see them.

Nevertheless, when Louisa read her sister's letter she rather regretted having sent her own. It might have been just as well to keep Sarah unacquainted with her circumstances. Here she was, giving advice in writing, for Sarah had a fluent though rather incoherent pen, and when she paid the visit she was promising she would have still more to give in speech. Sarah could no more help interfering than she could help breathing, she had an eye trained for the detection of household negligence, and Louisa was not sure that she was wanted in Beulah Mount.

'It's from your Aunt Sarah,' she said, frowning over the letter.

Jenny gave a sharp exclamation. 'Because you wrote to her!' she cried. 'She didn't know we were here, but you've told her and now she'll come!'

'Yes, she's coming, one of these days,' Louisa said, hardly heeding Jenny's cry, and then, looking up and seeing that her face was mutinous and half fearful, she said angrily, 'Of course she's coming, and I'll write to-day and bid her hurry, and stay as long as she likes, too. Not but what she'd suit herself about that,' she added, with her disarming frankness.

'And that might be for ever,' Jenny said.

'And why not?' Louisa demanded. 'Whose house is this, I'd like to know?'

82

'So should we,' Dahlia said seriously.

Louisa faced her two daughters, one in a sort of panic, the other judicially grave, and but for her feeling that they were joined in criticism against her she would have owned to some of Jenny's fear of Sarah and made confession of her difficulties. It was a moment she might have used to her advantage and to theirs, which they might have used if they had known how to suggest comradeship and sympathy, but Jenny was listening to the tramp of Aunt Sarah's feet, Dahlia thought she ought to force an issue, and Louisa saw two feminine replicas of Sidney Rendall judging and condemning her and hers.

All the unspoken resentments of twenty years demanded utterance, and while she hesitated, her thoughts jostling each other so that she could not make a choice of them, her breath was carried away in two hard sobs. For a moment she hid her face in her hands before she rushed into the scullery and banged the door.

Now Jenny's face was white and there were tears in her eyes, 'It's her own sister,' she said remorsefully.

Dahlia left the breakfast table and went to the window. 'It's not our money,' she said.

They were tender-hearted. In this, at least, they were like their mother, who soon returned to the kitchen, openly wiping her eyes, more than willing to accept their bashful amiability.

'You see,' she said, 'Sarah'll come, anyway, whether or no. And I'll tell you what I've been thinking. We ought to have a stone put on your father's grave. Sarah's a rare one for graves and all that. She'll want to see it. We'll never hear the last of it if there's no stone there.'

The sight of her mother still dabbing her eyes with her handkerchief could not entirely subdue Jenny's indignation. This attention to her father's memory was unbearable because it was inspired by the imminence of

Aunt Sarah. 'She shan't see it!' she said, shaking. 'You couldn't let her!'

'I couldn't stop her! And you needn't take me up so sharp, Jennifer,' Louisa said patiently. 'It's not that I care so much for Sarah, but I always made out I was as happy as a queen, and I wouldn't like for her to think different now. So just you go over the bridge and see about it. The sexton has a little place of his own near by, and I reckon you're the one to choose it. And goodness me, we needn't make such a fuss about Sarah. She won't be getting her holiday till the autumn, and nobody knows what'll happen between then and now. We'll have the house full. Let's have the house full and Sarah can say what she likes.'

'I'll go over the bridge to-morrow,' Jenny said. She would have been willing to swim the river for a mother who had pretended she was happy, and in the furtherance of that deception she had no more scruples in pandering to Aunt Sarah about the gravestone. And to-morrow was Saturday, when she was to go for a walk with Mr. Cummings, and the difficulty of starting with him was now solved. She would go on her filial errand and Dahlia dare not laugh if Edwin Cummings were by her side. It seemed irreverent to be mixing the two expeditions and making one serve the other: it seemed callous to take the young man to the grave of a father who would have been indignant at such an escort for his daughter, but it was impossible to please everybody, and Jenny decided that in future she would try to please herself. She would be glad of Mr. Cummings' advice about the stone: he would deal with the sexton more competently than she could, and she had a hope that at last he might listen to what she wanted to say about her father. Not once had he encouraged her past efforts, and she was sure he would not have been anxious for her company if she had not

84

proved herself a better audience than he had been for her, but, when his advice was asked and probably taken, she thought he might feel an interest in the man for whom the headstone was intended. Sidney Rendall in death would become remotely connected with Edwin Cummings, and for Edwin Cummings his existence would begin.

CHAPTER XI

M<small>R</small>. C<small>UMMINGS</small> bought the tickets for the bridge. 'We'll go and see the house first,' he said, characteristically making his plans without consulting Jenny, 'and then I'll show you some other places I like.'

She had been holding her own money when he fore-stalled her at the turnstile, and now she offered it to him. She could not take twopence from a young man who was so intent on saving, nor could she argue with him freely if she were virtually his guest. 'Please,' she said, with that puckering of her eyelids which was her defence against embarrassing moments. 'Because of the shop, you know.'

He walked on, shaking his head, but she stood still, and when he turned and saw her smiling and still holding out her hand he took the pennies meekly, a little triumph that made her want to laugh and run instead of walking sedately. The sun was shining, the world was sparkling, and the smoke of the city, on her left hand, only brightened the sky's blue before the breeze carried it away. It was a magical city, she thought, and she and Edwin Cummings paused to look at it from their airy station. The river ran into the heart of it, but on its way it was caught into locks and spread into basins and spanned by bridges, and to-day the water was the colour of the sky. The cliffs sloped gently to the city in a gracious gesture, as though they slowly opened their hands, made by God, to display the works of man and, from this distance, all the works of man were good. On the Upper Radstowe side houses and gardens clung to the gradually lessening slope until it reached the road where tramcars ran up and down alongside the water, like clockwork toys set going for the amusement of Jenny and Mr. Cummings. The tide was out and no ships passed under the bridge, but there was a constant movement of small craft in the docks: ships, moored to the wharves, mingled their masts and funnels with cranes and chimney-pots and, as far as the eye could see, there were the flattened, coloured roofs of buildings, pierced here and there by a factory chimney or a church spire.

Simultaneously they turned their backs on this and looked seawards. The sea was a long way out of sight and the cliffs, converging loftily, hid the bend in the river where the steamers hooted at high tide with such plaintive warning.

'Let's cross to the other side,' said Mr. Cummings, for the view was obstructed by the upper works of the bridge, those swooping curves of steel which looked like ribbons lightly holding the roadway.

They crossed within a few feet of Thomas Grimshaw's horse and Jenny, who had foreseen the possibility of meeting him and determined not to see him, heard a shouted greeting she could not ignore, but she would not answer his roguish smile with another. She gave him a stiff little bow and saw him look back in amusement at the sight of Jenny Rendall and the lodger.

'That's the man who brings the butter, isn't it?' said Edwin. 'And very good butter it is. Nearly as good as what we get at home.'

'I don't know why you ever left your home,' Jenny said crossly. She could not feel friendly towards Mr. Cummings when she remembered Grimshaw's grin.

'I thought I'd explained that,' he said. 'You see—'

'I know. I remember. But you always say everything

87

is better there. To-day when you had that nice meat pie for your dinner you told me Fanny's pastry was much lighter. I thought it was rather rude.'

'I was only telling the truth.'

'But you only tell it when it's unpleasant.'

'I know I'm getting more than I had any right to expect—far more, but still, there's the fact. Fanny's pastry's the best I've ever tasted.'

'You're only making it worse,' Jenny warned him coldly.

'Well, if I apologise, will you forgive me?'

'Yes,' Jenny said.

'And there's no view like this at home,' he said generously, giving her the credit for it.

'And it was such a good idea to have one side of the gorge wooded and the other bare,' she said. The Downs, topping the bare cliff and trickling over it, looked as though a sculptor had hastily flung a green cloth over an unfinished piece of statuary. 'And don't,' she said emphatically, 'tell me why they are like that, because I know, but I like to think it was just arranged to please us.'

'So it was, I daresay, but no good workman would be satisfied if he hadn't prepared his ground, if he hadn't got a reason for what he did. It doesn't spoil it to think of it that way. It makes it better.'

'I don't care about reasons a bit.'

'Yes, you do, though you mayn't know it. Everybody with taste likes reasons.'

'And have I taste?'

'I'll know for certain when I see how you like my house.'

Jenny raised her brows despairingly. It was no good telling him again that she had liked the house long before he saw it, no good being angry with him for calling it his own, but she told him that she had business to do and it must be done first: she had business in the church-yard.

88

'I never could get really interested in churches,' he said. 'I suppose it's being in the furniture line makes me so keen on houses.'

'My father—' Jenny began, and then she stopped. This was not the right approach to the subject of her father, and she told Mr. Cummings about the headstone.

'Difficult things,' he said, and he clasped his hands behind his back and walked slowly, pondering.

'A black marble slab,' Jenny said, 'but perhaps I'd better tell you about him, shall I? And then you'll see why I'd like a black marble slab, with a figure on it, what they call a recumbent figure, and he ought to be in armour and to seem very far away. The armour and the black marble would give him that sort of look, wouldn't it?'

'It would need an artist to do it,' he said solemnly.

'Yes, it would need an artist,' Jenny sighed, and then was silent. Her own words, her conception of a fitting monument for him, which had come to her almost without thought, on an inspiration, had made her father clearer to her than he had been in life. He had been a man in an armour of inaccessibility, he had always seemed far away, and she saw him recumbent, with hands folded, awaiting buffets from fortune, and she could not speak of him again, nor was that necessary, for Mr. Cummings was receptive and in his serious face, his measured tread, he showed respect towards the dead for whom he was asked a service. She felt no incongruity in making her appeal: her father himself could not have been more mannerly, and she doubted whether he would have understood so well.

'It would be very expensive,' Edwin said. 'It would have to be perfect.'

'I know I can't have it. It was just to tell you what it ought to be.'

'Austere,' said Mr. Cummings.

It was the right word and Jenny nodded in approbation and satisfaction. She felt happy again. She had communicated an idea and this young man was working on it and they were united by it. She felt that he and she were friends, and this was the first friend she had known with whom she need not be secretive: firstly, because he was not curious, and secondly, because he accepted human beings as he found them and kept his critical faculties for other matters. No doubt some of her ease was due to her knowledge that in those ways which meant so much to her she was superior to him, and some of her happiness lay in the remembrance that when she held out the pennies and smiled, he had obeyed her. His clumsy shoes, his ready-made Norfolk jacket, a little too tight across the shoulders, his trousers a little too short, his general appearance of belonging to people who had never had much more than they needed, who had not been owners for generations and developed the careless, unconscious lordliness that accompanies inherited possessions, somewhat diminished her sense of triumph. His dogged manner of walking betrayed the man who had to make his place in the world: it was not the gait of the man who walked on his own land. Clothed by the best tailor in the world, Mr. Cummings would not look as her father had done in his well-worn tweeds, but his bare head was well shaped and his hair grew as it should, and the sun was shining, and she had made him take her twopence.

They had left the road leading from the bridge and followed another at the edge of the wooded cliff, and looking down through the sparse, brilliant green they could see a thread of water: looking across through the screen of the topmost trees they saw the Downs again and tiny figures moving on them. On the other side of the road there were a few houses in big gardens, but they were of no definite period and Mr. Cummings did not look at them: he was still thinking of the headstone, and to Jenny his concentration seemed excessive.

'When we turn into the road to the village,' she said, 'we'll see the road leading to our house.'

'You could have a grey stone slab, you know, with just a simple moulding.'

'Yes, I'd like a slab. Some people think they're cruel looking, but I think they look safe. Oh, it's a lovely day. We might find some violets. Look, Mr. Cummings. Up that road, two miles or more, is where our house is.'

'I've been up the road many a time, and a very dusty one it is. A simple moulding with the name and the dates. We'll see what the sexton man can do.' He took an envelope and a stub of pencil from his pocket. 'Kitty's last letter,' he said. 'I'll use the back of it.' A low wall offered him a table and, first licking the pencil, he drew a rough sketch of Sidney Rendall's gravestone.

'I can't remember the dates, and they don't matter,' Jenny said.

'Any text?'

'No, just the name and R.I.P. I specially want R.I.P.'

'I'll have to do the lettering myself, when we get back. It doesn't do to trust these fellows, but if I give him a tracing he can't go wrong.'

'You're very kind,' Jenny said gratefully. 'I don't know what I should have done without you.'

She sat beside the mound marking her father's grave, while Mr. Cummings talked to the sexton in the small, stonemason's shop near by, and she could not feel sentimental or regretful: she felt drowsy and at peace in this quiet place among the grey headstones, their lettering almost obliterated, the shining angels, the white crosses, the draped urns and broken columns. She was clear of the shadow cast by the church, and the sun was warm, and she was sorry when the voices of the two men disturbed her. The sexton was anxious to show Mr. Cummings examples of his handiwork and to point out the more important graves, that of the late vicar, under a granite cross, and the family vault of the Merrimans, a stone erection like a small house, surrounded by iron railings, and while he kept them in front of this, giving them time to appreciate its grandeur, he turned to Jenny and asked after her mother. His voice was low, suitable for the bereaved, but she did not like his smile. He had lived in the village all his life and it was of Sidney Rendall's young wife he was thinking, not of his widow.

'Let's go,' she said to Edwin. 'It's cold here, in the shadow.'

'Yes, we'll get into the sun and have a look at the house. Pity they didn't make the family grave to match it. It would be the grandfather in the food business who had it built. He must have had his packing-cases on the brain.'

'I wish,' Jenny said, 'I rather wish we hadn't told the sexton he could do it.'

'It'll be all right if I keep an eye on him,' Edwin said reassuringly, and then, seeing her face white and distressed, his own face clouded.

'I feel rather sick,' Jenny said.

'Oh dear!' said Mr. Cummings, instinctively looking round for shelter.

'But I'm not going to be.'

'I've walked you too far,' he said, choosing to take the blame rather than to have no part in this misfortune. 'We'll go to the inn and have some tea, with boiled eggs. Tea in the country's nothing without boiled eggs. Or would that make you sicker?'

'It's not that kind. It's a kind of my own. No, let's look at the house and then we'll try to find some lambs.'

He frowned a little. He was worried about her and that

pleased her. 'I suppose you woudn't care to have hold of my arm?' he asked.

'No!' Jenny cried and she laughed, for the thought of walking through Combe Friars arm-in-arm with Mr. Cummings was a funny one. 'I'm not tottery: I'm not going to faint,' she said, and with the slowness worthy of a really interesting piece of information she added solemnly, 'It's not physical. It's mental.'

Mr. Cummings did not respond in the right way. He said, briskly and kindly, 'You mustn't have fancies, you mustn't have fancies,' and Jenny felt rebuffed, hurt as a child whose confidence has not been respected, ashamed that out of vanity and a desire to be impressive she had trusted him with so small a one as this.

Lagging a few feet behind him, guilty of making a little face at his broad back, she followed him to the gates of Merriman House. They found these open and Mr. Cummings planted himself in the entrance to the short drive, shamelessly gazing at the long, mellow front of the old house. He beckoned her to approach and receive instruction, but she would not move, she would not stare like an admiring, envious tripper. She looked steadily across the narrow road at a high wall sheltering another mansion until the sound of a horse's hoofs drew her eyes to the right and, characteristically, when she saw the radiant figure, with the sun on his fair head and the gleaming coat of his mount, it was herself she saw with greater clearness, and Mr. Cummings, shabby, with dusty shoes, a young man and a girl pausing, on their Saturday afternoon walk, to look with awe at the rider's home.

He did not appear to see them, but he touched his horse with his heel and went smartly through the gateway, causing Mr. Cummings to skip back hastily, for, absorbed in his contemplation, he had heard no sound.

'So that's the third generation of the packing-cases,' he

said. He was a little crestfallen and took his mild revenge. 'I think he might have given me a warning.'

'Do you expect him to have a motor-horn on his saddle?' Jenny asked disdainfully. 'And you shouldn't have been standing there. But I don't believe he saw you. He didn't see either of us. We didn't exist!'

The picture of the young man sitting easily on his horse, debonair and unconsciously arrogant, while Mr. Cummings jumped backwards in his clumsy dusty shoes was etched with acid on Jenny's mind. The wearer of the dusty shoes was her escort, but everything represented by the other young man was her rightful heritage. She suffered Mr. Cummings' indignity in herself and she could not forgive him. Like a French aristocrat before the revolution, young Mr. Merriman had ridden by, spurning the peasant in his path, and it was really she who had sustained the insult which Mr. Cummings had provoked. Probably Mr. Merriman had been innocent of any intention: he had merely reacted, with that touch of the heel, to the presence of such spectators, but her father, standing in the same position, would have had a different effect. There would have been a courteous slowing of the horse, perhaps a pleasant greeting: in that, as in this, Jenny would have been involved, and she felt that Mr. Cummings ought to understand the irritation she could not conceal, instead of being puzzled and placatory with more offers of tea.

'It's so rude to stand and stare at people's houses!' she cried, and her lips trembled.

'Then why didn't you say so before and we wouldn't have come?' he asked reasonably. 'But it's not rude to look at lambs, is it? You said you wanted to see them.'

'I did, but I don't.'

'Or the violets?' he said, gently humouring her. 'Then I suppose there's nothing for it but to go home.'

'I'll go. You needn't,' Jenny said, with decision, and hesitating for a moment, they turned their backs on each other and separated, but Jenny had not gone more than a few yards before she remembered his kindness and her manners, and heedless of the Merrimans' windows she was willing to run after him and ask his pardon, if he would turn his head.

This Mr. Cummings did not do. His back looked stubborn and uncompromising, and his trousers looked shorter than ever when seen from behind, so Jenny continued on her way and she walked slowly, sorry she had been unkind and realising that, under the influence of the gallant figure on the horse, she had treated poor Mr. Cummings as she had treated Thomas Grimshaw when the Dakins were listening on the doorstep. But who, in this case, could have helped it? her heart cried, and her heart ached until she eased it with a story of a new King Cophetua who loved a beggar maid and found she was as noble as himself.

There is no tale so enthralling as the one told by youth about itself, and Jenny was carried through the village on the feet of fancy. She saw no one and heard nothing, though swift cars rushed past and country carts jogged by, until she came to a break in the path set high above the road and saw that she had reached the turning to the White Farm.

A hundred yards away on her left was the curving road above the wooded slope, and still half dazed, though careful to avoid the traffic as she crossed, she found that here, where there was less noise, she could not return into her spell. The sounds were more personal and could not be forgotten: birds were singing in the trees, there were strolling couples in her path, and at the gates of the houses across the road there were waiting cars and boys and girls who talked and laughed together, young men in flannels, more akin to Mr. Merriman than to Mr. Cummings, girls in light frocks and gay woollen coats. They had been playing tennis on the hard courts in Upper Radstowe and they lingered in the gardens before they went in to tea. They would have tea in their nice drawing-rooms, full of flowers and pretty cretonnes, like Miss Headley's sitting-room, and then they would go upstairs and bathe their healthily-tired bodies, brush their sleek heads and slip into evening dresses and descend to dining-rooms sparkling with glass and silver, where kind fathers and mothers smiled benignly at their happy, pretty daughters.

Jenny wiped her shoes in the long grass edging the path. She knew she was invisible to these young people, as she had been to Mr. Merriman, but, she thought bitterly, they would have seen her if she had been beautifully dressed. In the meantime she wiped her shoes for her own satisfaction, wondering if any of those girls had feet as slim. The beggar maid must have had a startling beauty in her rags or the king would not have looked twice her way. Dahlia, with her bright colouring and her face like an impudent, wide-opened flower, might attract the royal attention, but Jenny's charms needed a close inspection. Kings did not go riding about the world deliberately peering into the faces of beggars: they rode, when they were young, for the joy of riding, and probably the one she had in mind had looked at nobody that afternoon, neither at those who were shabby like Jenny nor gay like the girls on the other side of the road. Young men, as she was learning from her acquaintance with Mr. Cummings, had sources of pleasure in themselves: they were free of the feminine desire to be of special importance to a special person, and Mr. Merriman on his horse and Mr. Cummings in his stout shoes could enjoy a lovely afternoon at the end of April and be alone. But was Mr. Cummings enjoying it? she wondered, and she thought, with annoyance, that in all likelihood he was, and she had a vengeful pleasure in the shortness of his trousers until she remembered them as they leapt from the neighbourhood of the horse.

Jenny was not sure that she would recognise the rider if she met him elsewhere or on foot. What filled her mind was the picture he and the horse had made, the contrast he had pointed, the reminder he had given that thus her father must once have looked, and her own brothers should have looked if she had had any. She knew that he was fair, for the sun had burnished his hair and the horse's chestnut coat and made the pair radiantly splendid. Not formally dressed for riding, bare-headed and wearing flannel trousers, he looked as though he had jumped on to his horse to do an errand, as a less fortunate person would jump on a bicycle. It was sad to think that, more closely viewed, he might be quite a plain young man. His eyes might squint or his teeth project but, after all, that did not matter, for she had her vision and she could look at it when she would, though looking at it would not make her happy. Her picture of Kitty and the lavender bushes and Fanny bustling about the house and making pastry much better than Louisa Rendall's was all pleasure. It was peaceful and friendly and could not make her envious, and she thought complacently that those girls might see her as a superior being, as she saw Mr. Merriman, and then she reminded herself sharply that he was not superior and she was not a genuine beggar maid: she was a princess in disguise who must some day be discovered for what she was.

When she reached the bridge the man at the toll-house treated her with the respect due to the princess and the familiarity incident to the loss of her throne. Many a time he had taken money from Sidney Rendall who, in the toll-man's opinion was a real gentleman, and passed him and his daughters on to the bridge. Many a time he had chatted with Louisa Rendall, who was usually alone, and now the poor gentleman was buried, his handsome, inappropriate wife had set up a lodging-house in Upper Radstowe, and the deference once paid to the daughters for the father's sake was moderated by his removal.

Jenny noticed the change as she noticed and exaggerated all such slights, and crossing the bridge slowly she told herself she was not really a definite person, like Dahlia or Mr. Cummings. The toll-man, the girls at the gate, the man on the horse, affected her as though they were contorting mirrors and she was constrained to see herself therein. This, as she knew, was vanity and weakness: there was no need to look, and to do so was inconsistent with the very qualities she wanted to proclaim, and she made another of her good resolutions and walked home briskly, in time to see Mary Dakin, in a new spring hat, descending from a cab outside her door.

Jenny was fated to be troubled, for though Mary smiled at her, it was with a difference, and she passed into the house without a friendly word. Only a few days ago they had been whispering over the garden wall: then Mary had set off humbly carrying her suit-case, to return in a cab and show herself unwilling to acknowledge Jenny's presence.

'Perhaps she knows the hat doesn't suit her,' Jenny thought. 'It's all wrong with her coat and skirt. I suppose it was easier to wear it than to pack it, and perhaps it was given to her by the aunt.' And Jenny, who was much concerned with aunts, imagined that this one of Mary's was a little like Aunt Isabel, but with false pearls instead of real ones, and a little like Aunt Sarah, or she would

99

not have chosen such a hat. She was never to know that it had been bought by Mary in the determination to be as feminine as herself, though later she was to guess that the arrival in the cab had been in the nature of a triumph and that the triumph was of a kind to make friendship with Jenny Rendall unnecessary and inadvisable. Proof of her own power to charm made Mary ashamed of having seen a romantic heroine in the little girl next door.

That half-smile sent Jenny into her own house with a new feeling that this was home, where she had a sister whom she loved and who loved her, with a new recognition that, though her mother lacked all the tenderer, subtler attributes of motherhood, she had a solicitude of her own, expressed materially by a kettle singing on the fire and a meal spread on the kitchen table.

This afternoon there was no sign of tea. The table was covered with a yellow fabric, and Dahlia, who had apparently revised her decision about new clothes, stood over it with a large pair of scissors in her hand, while Louisa sat reading a newspaper at the window.

'Now don't tell me the colour won't suit me!' Dahlia cried. 'I've been to Barley Street this afternoon and bought it very cheap, and I've got another piece just like it, only grey, for you.'

'It's pretty,' Jenny said, 'but it will be prettier when I've had some tea.'

'Tea?' said Louisa. 'We've had ours, and I made sure you'd be having it with Cummings.'

Jenny lifted her head and her voice was a faint echo of her father's. 'Why should I have had tea with Mr. Cummings?'

'Well, dear me, if you go for a walk with a lad, it isn't likely he'd bring you home without it. They wouldn't have done that when I was young.'

'He hasn't brought me home.' All Jenny's magnificence deserted her. She knew she had left the house unobserved by her mother, and she could hear Thomas Grimshaw's thick, soft voice telling Louisa he had seen her daughter with the lodger, making a joke of the matter, because that was how he would be bound to see it, and perhaps knowing that, by doing so, he would take the best revenge for her cold nod and for the old insult he surely had not forgotten. And she was enraged at her mother's commerce with the man: she remembered the sexton's leer, and she saw Grimshaw as the abominable source of every sorrow, but she was incapable of expressing this instantaneous, tumultuous emotion. She could only babble, careless of truth, 'I didn't go for a walk with him! You know, oh, you know why I went to Combe Friars this afternoon. And that horrible man goes and poisons everything!'

'And what man's that?' Louisa asked menacingly, but Jenny did not stay to answer or to see her mother's face change from anger to bewilderment, to hear her say sadly, 'It's not safe to speak to that girl. You never know when she'll fly into a temper. All the same, when Grimshaw told me, I wasn't going to laugh about it. Nobody's going to poke fun at Jennifer, nor at you, when I'm by to hear it.'

It is easy to quarrel, difficult to meet with dignity afterwards, and Jenny was minded to stay upstairs and refuse to minister to Mr. Cummings, but that would only have postponed the awkward moment, which proved not to be awkward at all, for Louisa acted on the adages of her youth—'Let bygones be bygones,' 'Hard words break no bones,' 'Least said, soonest mended'—and she was her usual self as she heaped Mr. Cummings' plate. But Jenny had yet to face Mr. Cummings. They had hardly parted friends, and she knew the fault was hers, but, judging him by her mother's standard of forbearance, she was prepared for geniality, which she would graciously receive.

She saw, as soon as she entered the room, that she would not have the opportunity. Mr. Cummings was not genial, though he spoke to her at once.

'I'll have the lettering finished by to-morrow,' he said, glancing up from a large sheet of paper, 'and you'll have it to take to the sexton any day you like.'

'Thank you,' Jenny said. It was clear that he removed himself from further active interest, and she suffered a little pang, less of shame than of desertion. 'May I look at it?' she asked. 'You're doing it beautifully.' She waited for comments on the size and spacing of the letter, but none came. 'Thank you,' she said again.

He was fulfilling his promise, he was a man of his word, but the zest had gone from the work. She clasped her hands in front of her and said, 'I know I was cross this afternoon. I'm sorry.'

He looked at her, giving her the full gaze of his hazel eyes. They were bigger and darker and less bright than she had yet seen them. 'You needn't be,' he said. 'I've been thinking it out. I know what it was. You were a bit ashamed of me.'

Making no protest, for it would have been useless, she lowered her lids with the long black lashes, and so missed the slight and momentary convulsion of Mr. Cummings' sensible, steadfast face.

CHAPTER XIII

Because Jenny Rendall had touched the almond blossom, Mary Dakin had returned from Wellsborough with her wardrobe replenished in a manner that somewhat shocked her sisters, while it delighted her pretty little mother, whose only grief in life was the manliness of her daughters. Because Louisa Rendall was handsome and jovial with the tradesmen, who took longer than was necessary in delivering her goods and had been known to stand and chat for a full ten minutes, while the landlady next door waited for her milk or vegetables, Miss Jewel broke the habits of her professional lifetime, and, as Mary emerged from her tweeds and severely becoming hats, so Miss Jewel issued from her decent reticence into venomous suggestions about the Rendalls for Mr. Sproat's unaccustomed ears. Her value was in her efficiency and her silence. Remarks about Mr. Sproat's meals, his shirts, which were becoming frayed, or his socks, which defied further mending, messages left for him, occasional comments on the weather, were all that had hitherto passed her pallid lips. Mary's new clothes did not suit her, nor had Miss Jewel's spite the desired effect. She was playing into Dahlia's hands and making it impossible for Mr. Sproat to forget the family. He listened, because he was as much startled as he would have been if a piece of Miss Jewel's furniture had begun uttering human sentiments, but this development in his landlady produced a feeling of determined incredulity which was stronger than his natural aptitude to fear the worst. Nevertheless, Dahlia's visit, of which he had not approved, her irreligious father, her difficulties, her pretty face and voice, took a firmer place in his memory, and he could no longer pass the house without a glance at the windows, or, at least, some thought of those who lived within, and Jenny, leaning from Mr. Cummings' window to flap her duster, would sometimes receive a grave salute.

She dusted that room now with extraordinary care: it was all she could do for one whom she had hurt so grievously that he would not respond to her friendly overtures. There were no more details about Kitty and Fanny, and he was not to be lured into forgetfulness by cunning questions about antiques: she had not the effrontery to mention the gravestone, though his drawing was in the stonemason's hands and the time was approaching when she must go and inspect the work.

The lettering had been finished on that Sunday night, and there was no reason why Jenny should not have delivered it on the Monday, but she waited until Saturday, as though what had happened once on that day of the week could happen on no other, and, quickly dispatching her business and leaving the unpleasant company of the sexton, she wandered about the roads and lanes, expectant of a horseman and disappointed of the one she wanted, yet she was almost glad to have her efforts fruitless. Deeply, she knew that wisdom lay in acceptance, not in seeking the self-torture to which she was so prone. The boy on the horse was a symbol, beautiful in itself, but painful, and Mr. Cummings was a human being who had to be won back to cheerfulness, to the bestowal of another look of admiration, which she would value now, having lost it for a time. Mr. Cummings had risen altogether in her estimation. He had had the wit to think things out, the humility to arrive at the right conclusion, the courage to speak of it, and the pride to withdraw his friendliness, and now that he was in the attitude she thought he ought to take—one of respect and acknowledgment of her quality—she missed her little talks with him, she missed the secret, growing feline satisfaction of lightly playing with him. He was a nice mouse and she would not have used her claws, but she had seen him as belonging to a different genus from her own, and it had not seemed necessary to consider whether he would appreciate her idea of fun; it was now apparent that he would only play on equal terms.

Little of this was definite in Jenny's mind. It was the natural effect of an adolescence which would have been normal if her interests had been less restricted, and, among these, Mr. Cummings, reserved though not sulky, was the chief. A friendship with a girl would have fitted Jenny's mood just as well. She wanted to charm, whether man or woman, more than to be charmed. She was in the state of a creative artist whose impulse had not yet taken shape, and her only medium was herself. Mary Dakin's cool smile had dashed her hope of that particular friendship and killed desire for it. There was something wrong with a girl whose friendliness from the back window could be followed so quickly by coldness: the Mary Dakin who had developed a taste for fussy clothes was not the one Jenny wanted, and with this disappointment, too, there was some sense of release. She could watch the Dakins with detachment: she need not care what they thought of her.

She feared that Dahlia's hopes of Mr. Sproat were also vain, for though he said 'Good morning' as he passed, he did no more, until the day when a duster fell in front of him on the pavement. From Mr. Cummings' window Jenny saw the object flutter from the room above, clear the area railings and land with precision at his feet. It was a noticeably clean duster, and Mr. Sproat did not hesitate to pick it up and, looking at Jenny's window with a smile, he hung it on the railings.

'It's not mine,' said Jenny, showing her own. And, from above, Dahlia's voice called clearly, 'It's mine! I am so sorry. I'm glad it didn't hit you on the head.'

Miss Jewel heard the voice, but, peer as she might from her basement window, she could only see Mr. Sproat's shoulders and his clerical hat. She did not see him remove the duster from the railings and fold it slowly, so that Dahlia, rushing downstairs and out of the front door, received it from his hands, but Jenny saw, and wondered why hanging the duster on the railings was good enough for her and not for Dahlia. She did not grudge this courtesy to her sister and she did not wonder at it when, blushing a little, but frank of eye and smile, Dahlia took the duster from him.

'She's very pretty,' Jenny thought. 'Perhaps he'll fall in love with her.' And with this possibility, sad for Mr. Sproat but exciting for her and Dahlia, in her mind, she turned at the opening of the door to hear Dahlia saying blithely, 'That was a good shot!'

'On purpose?'

'Of course.'

'But why?'

'I don't know. I just felt like it. I'd been waiting for him for ages. I really meant the duster to fall on his head.'

'But you said—'

'Of course I said! It's a new duster. It wouldn't have hurt his old hat. You can't expect a lively young person like me not to do silly things sometimes.'

'But I do hope he didn't suspect you,' Jenny said, rather worried. 'It's a pity, isn't it, that his hair always looks as if it wants cutting?'

'I don't think it matters in a parson. And he has nice

eyes. Rather muddy, but nice when he smiles, like mud with sun on it.' She threw up the duster and caught it. 'Yes, it was silly and it wasn't ladylike! Poor Miss Headley! But you know, Jen, we hardly ever laugh, you and I, though I was laughing upstairs, all by myself, just now, so that I could hardly throw the thing, but we ought to be laughing nearly all the time. I shall have to get that situation and work off my energy, or I shall do something worse. But I do try to be good,' she said, making a small grimace to excuse the sentiment.

'Oh dear!' Jenny said.

'I thought that would please you.'

'Yes. But if you're trying, it means—it means that you mightn't be good, any minute.'

'That's exactly how I feel,' Dahlia said. 'I can't remember the debts all the time.'

'I don't remember them at all. I'm not going to. They're not mine.'

Dahlia heard this in silence. She was not given to reproach or criticism, and after a moment she said slowly, 'It's supposed to be wonderful to be young, and so it is, when you feel like hitting Mr. Sproat, but sometimes I wish I were old. When you're old,' she said, in her ignorance, 'you must have learnt what you ought to do and what you oughtn't. I want to ask mother about the money, but I can't make her cry again, can I? I wish, I do wish, we had one good friend in the world, somebody sensible and kind.'

'Like Mr. Cummings,' Jenny said, spontaneously uttering her considered opinion.

'Is he sensible and kind?'

'He can't help being sensible, and he'd be kind if you let him.'

'Then I think he ought to be encouraged,' Dahlia said, and Jenny drew one of her silent sighs.

'He's not much older than we are, and perhaps Mr. Sproat is going to be our friend.'

'No. When he folded the duster, I thought it was like shutting up a book.'

'But he smiled.'

'There are all sorts of smiles,' said Dahlia.

'Well, you'll see,' Jenny said, determined to have her romance and, two days later, Mr. Sproat rang the bell and asked for Mrs. Rendall.

It was Jenny who opened the door and she took him into Mr. Cummings' sitting-room, to let him see her father's books and to prevent his seeing the bureau, and so much had she and Dahlia assumed responsibility for the household that she waited for what he had to say and tried to make conversation until he asked again to see her mother.

'And me not dressed!' said Louisa. 'Drat the man! What can he be wanting?'

Perhaps Mr. Sproat himself could not have told her. There are obscurities in most men's motives, and, in a member of a profession devoted to helping others, it was easy to suppose himself single-minded, especially easy for Mr. Sproat, who was earnest and unselfish. There may have been curiosity to see the woman who had loosened Miss Jewel's tongue and to discover under what influence these young girls lived: he may have remembered that they were not confirmed, he probably tried not to remember the duster, and he certainly did not realise that, if his motive was not what he thought, he was in a singularly fortunate position to pursue it. No other young man, unless seeking lodgings, would have had an excuse for making Louisa's acquaintance, though indeed, with her, none would have been necessary. And Mr. Sproat had not only had an excuse, he had a practical reason for his call. He had a possible lodger for the Rendalls, if they would not object to a lady, and Louisa's frankness in saying she preferred gentlemen, did much to remove the suspicions Miss Jewel had hopefully offered him, for he was simple enough to think that frankness implied innocence. But when he suggested that it was more suitable for her daughters to attend on their own sex, Louisa's further frankness made him a little uneasy. She thought exactly the other way, she said, but she could not afford to refuse anyone at the moment, and if the lady would call she would be pleased to let her see the rooms.

Mr. Sproat left the house feeling unusually young and doubtful of his wisdom. He did not know what to make of this Mrs. Rendall whom he was suddenly enabled to see with the eyes of the youngish spinster who wanted lodgings. He saw himself, too, as she might see him, when she had called to view the rooms, and without coxcombry, with the experienced caution of the unmarried clergyman, he realised that though Miss Morrison might think he was a fool, she might find a pleasant explanation of his folly in this attempt to install her in a house next door to his own. So close a neighbourhood to one of the ardent female workers in the parish was, in fact, one of the last things he wished for, and, caught all unexpectedly by a disconcerting thought, he stood still with his hand to his lip, the picture of a clergyman in delightful doubt.

At the foot of Beulah Mount Mr. Sproat examined all his motives, and some of them were such as befitted his ideal curate, who was a man somewhat ascetic but not harsh in judgment of those who were not: a hard worker to the glory of God: a consoler and an aid to those in trouble: and some of them befitted an inexperienced, headstrong youth, seeking his own advantage. Yet, as he walked on slowly, Mr. Sproat was not unhappy, though he was puzzled and a little shaken. In that moment when he stood to ponder, he remembered the plans he had made for his life and saw them all in ruins and could not feel a pang, but he also saw the absurdity, the incongruity, the unlikelihood of this emotion that had seized him before he was aware. He saw Louisa Rendall, with her full-blown beauty and the simplicity that might be cunning, seated against a background of many books: he heard the burr of her country speech and her lapses in grammar, and he saw the face of her elder daughter, pretty and gay, yet capable of gravity, and heard her voice, which was low and charming but had a rising note of laughter in it.

'An excellent thing in a woman,' he thought inevitably, and he was astonished at the power of a face and a voice and at his unreasoned conviction that they were what he wanted.

'It's most unsuitable. It's all wrong,' he thought. 'And hopeless,' he added with humility. 'But I wish I could be sure that she meant to hit me with the duster.'

So Jenny's wish for a female lodger was fulfilled. Miss Morrison enthusiastically accepted Mr. Sproat's suggestion, which was begun in a tone of doubt and gradually changed to one of encouragment, as he, like Jenny, saw the value of a Miss Morrison in the household, and, with disregarded shame, realised that what chiefly influenced him was the possible convenience of her presence for himself. For the first time since his childhood, he acted with conscious selfishness, indifferent to Miss Morrison's willingness to take a suggestion as a command, rejoicing in the sudden folly that had overtaken him, determined not to resist its sweetness, feeling that, almost careless of scruples, he was alive at last, but betraying none of these feelings in face or gesture, except to Dahlia and Jenny, who discovered in his serious aspect that, on the whole, his world was behaving well.

'He must be in love with her,' Dahlia said, as she watched him walk sadly down the street and remembered that it was he who had introduced Miss Morrison. 'Curates always fall in love with people no one else would like—those useful-looking women who don't mind about their clothes.'

'Miss Morrison minds a lot.'

'But she looks as if she doesn't, so it comes to the same thing. Is it because no one else wants the curates or because the curates are afraid?'

'What of?' Jenny asked.

'Of loving prettiness, of course. Perhaps they think it's worldly, or wicked—or expensive.'

'But their wives may have been pretty once, and then been too busy, or too poor, to bother.'

'Miss Morrison isn't pretty and never was, but I suppose she's good,' Dahlia said thoughtfully.

Miss Morrison's bright, childish blue eyes, behind her precariously-balanced eyeglasses, had paid little attention to the rooms offered her and she had agreed to the price demanded. She had presented the appearance of a person to whom everything was delightful, and she sustained her sunny, girlish cheerfulness. Hers was a manner to which Louisa Rendall, suspecting patronage, responded with a glumness tactfully ignored by Miss Morrison and shared by Jenny, in whom it was concealed by a reserved politeness. Here was the desired respectable spinster, without the fussiness Dahlia feared: here, also, was money punctually paid, but Miss Morrison's anxiety to be at home in Beulah Mount, to be sisterly with her young hostesses, sympathetic with their mother and comradely with Mr. Cummings, to assert, by practice, her belief that all was right with the world, had the nature of a lesson disguised as play. The sound of her voice, as she chatted to Dahlia, who waited on her with an amused friendliness, her little, self-conscious snatches of song as she ran up and down the stairs, were an annoyance to Jenny, who missed the emptiness and silence of the house and the certainty that, with her mother in the kitchen, there was no one, except Dahlia, to be encountered during Mr. Cummings' working hours. Her favourite post at his sitting-room window was now, by her own act, denied to her. She was not willing to trust the bureau to Miss Morrison and her visitors: she preferred to tantalise Mr. Cummings with the sight of it, and Mr. Cummings meekly crossed the passage and took his meals in the other room.

'It's not,' Jenny said, some days later, indulging a

feminine weakness for unnecessary explanation, 'as if you really belonged to the other one. It always looked perfectly empty when you weren't in it, so I don't think this makes any difference to you. You didn't care about the books and perhaps Miss Morrison will. You haven't noticed the change, have you?' she said coaxingly, as she saw a frown which was only the expression of masculine impatience at unprovoked protesting.

'Have I said anything?' he demanded. 'You know I haven't the right. I'm getting far more than I pay for.'

His eyes rested on the bureau and then on Jenny, and she knew he understood her motive in moving him as clearly as he had understood her shame of him in the neighbourhood of young Merriman.

'Yes, because I can trust you,' she said, dropping her head, using her gift for the fitting attitude without premeditation, with no more than a dawning knowledge of its power, and she heard a long, deep sigh, so startling a sound from Mr. Cummings, that she looked up and saw, with certainty, that his covetousness was not all for the bureau. For an instant, as she remembered his boasted capacity for getting what he wanted, her pleasure was streaked with an absurd fear, but it was the pleasure that prevailed and she turned away to hide her consciousness of an emotion which had survived the wounding of his pride, to hide the gaiety, the sense of life, it roused in her.

Next door Mr. Sproat meditated on the disturbing feelings which had no origin in reason, and knew that their seriousness was not thereby impaired, but Jenny, the disinherited princess, saw reason enough in Mr. Cummings' state and rejoiced in it. She did not consider its gravity for him: she had not her generation's conventional conception of fair play between the sexes and honesty of response or refusal: she welcomed admiration though she

113

could not return it: she felt as though the sun had shone suddenly into a dark room and nothing would have induced her to draw the curtains. In her case, as in that of most young girls who recognise love for the first time and do not feel it, her excitement was chiefly mental. As his brush to the painter and his pen to the writer, was her body, her little head, her thin feet and hands, to Jenny Rendall. These attributes were physical in their nature, but not, as far as she knew, in the use she made of them, for they were the means by which she could express her immature interpretation of life, and her good or evil fortune lay in the fact that they had their beauty for other people and readily and graciously obeyed her instincts.

These warned her not to evoke another sigh from Mr. Cummings, and, if she had tried to do so, she would have failed, for he had recovered his sturdy independence of spirit, he remembered her offences and, referring to her avowal of trust in him, he said that while it sounded like a compliment, it was nothing but a nuisance.

'Then,' said Jenny, 'I absolve you. But you know, inside me,' lightly, she touched herself, 'I can't help knowing the bureau's quite safe, and it wouldn't be with Miss Morrison. She wouldn't know it was good, but she'd praise it, and that would be dangerous, except that she praises everything, to make us feel comfortable, because we keep lodgings. She'd never dream,' Jenny said slowly, 'of telling us her mother made better pastry than ours.'

Opening and shutting the little drawers of the bureau for pleasure in their perfect running, Mr. Cummings pretended not to notice this allusion, and Jenny added maliciously, 'She thinks you have a fine, strong face, and when you have your little shop on The Slope, your customers will be quite certain that you're telling them the truth.'

'And I'll trouble you,' said Edwin Cummings, red with

embarrassment and anger, 'not to discuss my business with Miss Morrison.'

'I didn't know it was a secret.'

'It wasn't.'

'But it is now?'

'Yes,' he said, going to the window. 'The next worse thing to not getting what you want is having people know you can't. If my father doesn't get better, and he's been ailing a long while, it looks as if I'll have to go and take over the shop down there. You see, the girls depend on it.'

He spoke with a dull quietness, but Jenny heard a bitter disappointment in his tone, and, quickly clasping her hands, she said, 'Kitty's clever. Couldn't she manage? But, if she can't, you'll have your little shop down there, instead of here. It will be just the same, in a different place.'

'Ah, you think so?' he said, and his back looked stubborn. 'With four mouths to feed!'

'Not at first,' Jenny said wisely, 'but in time.'

'Yes, when I've bought and sold so much rubbish that I've lost my eye and don't care any longer.'

She could respect this grief and she did not know how to console him. She had forgotten herself and missed the possibility that some of his regret might be for leaving Beulah Mount. The room felt chilly with his sadness and the drizzling rain that blurred the view at which he stared, and, hopeless of giving him other than physical comfort, she knelt down to light the fire.

At the striking of the match Mr. Cummings turned. 'Certainly not!' he cried. 'I can't afford it.'

'Never mind. Neither can I, but I'm going to have it. I always feel cold when I'm miserable.'

If she had not been watching her fire she would have seen a lively look of interest on his face and, as he stood, with a hand on the narrow mantelshelf and his eyes on the kneeling figure, he asked her to tell him why she was unhappy.

'Because you are,' she said, with disappointing frankness. 'I can't bear anybody to be miserable. I ought to be used to it, but I never shall be. You'll feel better if you sit beside the fire, and so shall I. And sometimes what seems to be a misfortune turns out to be just the opposite. It will be much more distinguished to have a wonderful furniture shop in a village than in Upper Radstowe.'

'Well, to start with, it's not a village: it's a small town, and it won't be a wonderful furniture shop: it'll be a mess.'

'Yes, if you don't set your heart on it. But you will, and you'll be famous. And people will come from London and America, to see what you've got. They'll like buying things from a shop with lavender bushes and cobbled paths behind it, and, as Fanny is such a good cook,' Jenny went on with the faintest suggestion of acidity, but sweetening under her own inspiration, 'you could sell home-made cakes and serve teas in the back parlour or the garden, and the tea people will see the furniture and the furniture people will have tea.'

'Then you'd better come and help us,' Mr. Cummings said.

'I wish I could.'

'Why shouldn't you?'

'I have to stay here for the same reason that you may have to go. To help the family.'

He would not have been a man if he had thought their cases parallel. He had plenty of arguments to urge, and they were those sound masculine ones which women answer with feeble logic and the obstinacy of their feelings. Knowing that loyalty and affection bade her stay, Jenny hardly listened to him. Across the passage she could hear Miss Morrison's bright voice talking to Dahlia, and while

Dahlia laughed and Jenny enjoyed a returning consciousness of this young man's liking for her, their mother
was alone in the kitchen. What was she thinking of, Jenny
wondered, while Mr. Cummings talked and believed he
was making an impression? It was easy to forget that
Louisa was capable of thought or any feelings but those
of her healthy body, for her trained patience, imposed on
her peasant power of endurance, produced an effect of in-
sensibility. It was difficult to remember that she was only
forty and had a human need for companionship, difficult
to feel constant tenderness for the woman who had had
her way at the cost of debt to Thomas Grimshaw, but
just such a little rush of kindness as Jenny had felt for
Edwin Cummings, she now felt for her mother, who was
perhaps in greater need of it.

'I mustn't stay any longer,' she said.

'But answer my arguments before you go.'

'Must I? But I can't remember what they were,' Jenny
said pleasantly.

'Haven't you been listening?'

'Not much,' she confessed, and smiled disarmingly.
'But you won't be sad any longer, will you? And, if you
have to go, I'll tell you what I'll do. I'll give you the
bureau. For a present. To put in the window. To sell,
if you like, or to keep in memory of me, and when I'm
rich—and married,' she said thoughtfully, 'I'll drive down
to see you and find out what you've done with it.'

'And I shan't be at home!' said Mr. Cummings angrily.

Jenny laughed and went away, but she was back in a
minute, to find him with his head drooping dejectedly.

'Of course,' she whispered from the doorway, 'I didn't
really tell Miss Morrison about your shop. As if I would!'

Mr. Cummings would have been wise to maintain his
despondent attitude, but he was foolish enough to look
as though a load had been lifted from his mind and to

smile in gratification, and immediately Jenny said, with elaborate reassurance, 'But I didn't invent the remark about your face. Fine and strong was exactly what she said.'

She ran downstairs before her conscience could reproach her for her behaviour, for this desire to tease Mr. Cummings as soon as he looked cheerful, this dallying with a young man whose existence her father and Aunt Isabel would not have recognised, and, at the back of her mind, ready to be produced at need, was the excuse that a little forethought on her father's part and a little kindness on Aunt Isabel's would have deprived her of the opportunity they must have disdained for her. Yet it was a little disconcerting to find that her mother's prophecy of amusement from the lodgers had come true for her daughters, if not for herself. Louisa, sitting in the old wicker chair, with a neglected novelette on her knee, had not the appearance of one whose plans had ripened to success, and Jenny fancied that her colour was less clear, her eyes less bright, than they had been at the White Farm.

'And what,' Louisa asked, 'have you been doing all this while?'

'Talking to Mr. Cummings.'

'And what's Dahlia doing?'

'Talking to Miss Morrison. At least, Miss Morrison's talking to her.'

'And what d'you suppose I've been doing?'

'Thinking,' said Jenny, at a venture, 'that we neglect you.'

'No, no: I've been young myself,' Louisa said. 'And I could be young yet, if I had the chance, but I'm like nothing more than an old potato in a cellar. Still, I'd rather stay and be one than have to hark to that woman upstairs. I wonder at Dahlia, how she stands it. When I don't want to slap the woman, I want to cry over her.'

'Cry over her?'

'Yes.' Over the arms folded high on her broad chest, Louisa nodded. 'She must be feeling pretty bad if she has to make out there's nothing doesn't please her. And she's trying to think she's as young as Dahlia. Well, I feel like that, too, many's the time, only I've the sense to keep quiet about it. But she's a lady and I'm not, and that's where we're different. Now, among folks like mine, an old maid at her age wouldn't be jigging about and wanting to pass for a girl. It seems queer to me that a bit of money and a bit of education makes them want to seem silly longer than they need. Now look at our Sarah,' she went on, and Jenny involuntarily shut her eyes. 'Oh, all right, we won't until we've got to,' Louisa said good-humouredly. 'I'm not very keen on doing it myself. But mind you,' she said, remembering her authority, 'she's my flesh and blood, and partly yours, and I won't have you turning your nose up. But anyway, what I was going to tell you was that I've had a call to-night, and at the area door if you please! Now what did she want to come there for? One of those Dakins. Wants a room for a gentleman over the week-end, so Cummings'll have to come out of that sitting-room.'

'Which Dakin?' Jenny asked.

'Goodness me, I don't know one from the other. Whichever it is, she's old enough to take care of herself, I suppose. You'd better go and talk to Cummings. If we're getting more lodgers we'll have to have one dining-room for all and make the other room a parlour. It would pay us better and save trouble and we'd buy one of these gramophones and have a little life in the place.'

CHAPTER XV

THE thin thread uniting her to Mary Dakin, broken by a
cool smile and a new hat, was spun afresh in Jenny's mind,
though with a difference, by this stealthy arrival at the
area door. Indeed, it seemed to her that the small knot
of personalities in No. 15 Beulah Mount was attached by
slender filaments to the households on either side. Beyond
these a longer, much looser one stretched for her to the
haunts of young Mr. Merriman, whom she never pictured
in separation from his horse, and another, a good deal
tauter, ended in the garden of Mr. Cummings' home,
but none came from outside to make connection with the
Rendalls, except the coarse one from Thomas Grimshaw's
farm and the black one from Aunt Sarah, like a handrail
to guide her whither she was not wanted. Her dread of
Aunt Sarah made her certain that the hand not clutching
the umbrella was tightly holding that communication cord
and would follow it to its end in Upper Radstowe, and,
as once she had looked towards Aunt Isabel for refuge,
she now began to look towards Kitty and Fanny and the
tea-shop. She had a fancy that the sun always shone on
the lavender bushes, that Fanny always sang as she cooked,
that slackness of trade had no correspondence in the step
of Kitty, who, as her brother said, was quick on her feet.
As surely as she saw an enemy in Aunt Sarah, she saw
friends in Edwin Cummings' sisters and envied them for
what she knew she lacked, the anchorage of necessary,
congenial occupation, a knowledge of things outside
themselves, and a resulting sense of security in their own

world. Jenny realised the weakness of her position and did not know how to mend it. She was wobbling on her little pedestal of superiority, precariously condescending to Mr. Cummings and peering this way and that, into the lives of other people, when she should have been establishing her future: but while she was feeble in action she was strong in her belief that no generation had the right to make demands of another and that it would be well for her mother, for Dahlia and herself, if they all went their separate ways before they drifted into habits they could not break.

'Ten years hence,' she said solemnly to Dahlia, 'we'll see how silly we've been.'

'Sooner than that,' Dahlia said cheerfully.

'We ought to be—ruthless.'

'Have a try, then,' Dahlia said encouragingly as she looked at Jenny's mouth and noted the faint tremor of her little chin.

'Perhaps I shall. But oh, I know I shan't! I feel as if there's a hedge round me and it's quite flimsy, but I can't get through it, and I never shall, unless somebody else makes a hole in it.'

'And then what would you do?'

'It would depend on who made the hole,' Jenny said. ' If it was somebody nice, everything would be settled: if it was a nasty person, I think I'd go into a tea-shop, not a hot, smelly restaurant, with young men leaving tips under the plate, the kind you thought of, but home-made cakes and jam and an old garden and nice people coming in cars who would feel awkward about giving me money.'

'Nowadays the nice people don't have cars. All the better, because the common ones wouldn't dare to leave less than a shilling, if they thought you were a lady. I'll come with you, Jen, but I'm afraid I'll never get more than sixpence.'

'You haven't been asked.'

'D'you mean that you have, really?'

'I've been asked to help to start one.'

'By one of the Dakins?'

Knowing that Dahlia would show scorn for anything connected with Edwin Cummings, Jenny hesitated before she made her explanation, and mentally she enlarged the Cummings' house and garden and antique furniture business, so that her words might be the more impressive. 'It was my own idea. People will be thirsty after buying furniture and much more likely to buy it when they've had some tea, and I'd be useful, because Fanny would be busy with cooking and the house and the father, and Kitty knows about the furniture.'

'And what,' Dahlia asked, 'would Mr. Cummings be doing? It was your idea, but who suggested you should help?'

'He did,' Jenny said meekly.

'While he stays here?'

'It all began because he may have to go home and look after the shop. Antiques,' Jenny said.

'Oh, I see! It would be very nice for Mr. Cummings,' Dahlia remarked dryly. 'But we'd lose a lodger. And what should I do without you?'

'What do you do with me now? You're far more friendly with Miss Morrison.'

'That's business. She's so respectable. She's like one of those advertisements signed by eminent physicians, saying that somebody's patent food is pure and wholesome, and the more I go about with her the purer and wholesomer I seem. It's her turn to do the flowers for the church on Sunday, and I'm going to help her, and she's got a jolly class for young women on Saturday afternoons, to stop them from going out with their young men, and I'm going to help with that, too. She's very keen on the jollity. Physical exercises and dancing.'

'Dancing?'

'Oh, not the ballroom variety, worse luck! It's the kind when you stamp your feet and clap your hands and make a noise. It's more for health than pleasure! But I'm longing to see her jumping!'

'Her eyeglasses will fall off.'

'No: she'll fasten them to the little hook that seems to grow out of her bosom.'

'That,' said Jenny, with her quick frown, 'is a word I hate.'

'So would she, except about the Church and Abraham. Anyhow, she hasn't got a proper one, and that's respectable too. She thinks,' Dahlia said, after a pause, 'that Thomas Grimshaw is our uncle.'

'We can't allow that!' Jenny cried.

'I think it's a very good explanation. I haven't said he is, but I haven't said he isn't, and perhaps, now the summer's coming on, he won't be here so often, and by the time the harvest's over I shall have made a real impression on Mr. Doubleday.'

'You couldn't. It wouldn't last with him for more than a minute, unless you kept your finger on the place.'

'There's Mr. Sproat. He's helped us once. Why shouldn't he do it twice?'

'Because there can't be two Miss Morrisons. He's done his duty, and I've noticed that he doesn't look up to say good morning as often as he did.'

'Well,' said Dahlia, 'would you, if you knew you'd see those eyeglasses?'

'No. I never want to look at anybody who isn't pretty, but he ought not to feel like that.'

'Why shouldn't he be as human as Mr. Cummings?'

'Mr. Cummings?' Jenny echoed disingenuously.

'Yes. You'd better be careful, Jen.'

'I'm not pretty,' said Jenny in defence, 'and I'm not

good, and I won't be careful. I've promised to go for a walk with him on Saturday. I don't want to—well, not very much, but we're turning him out of his room for Mary Dakin's visitor, so I had to do something to make up.'

'That's a silly habit to start. If you have to give him a treat when he gives up his room for a week-end, how will you make up when we get another permanent lodger? You'd much better come to the Girls' Class and watch Miss Morrison jumping. You and I don't laugh nearly enough, Jen, and you'll laugh more there than with Mr. Cummings.'

'I'm not expecting to laugh,' Jenny said primly. 'We're going to see the gravestone and I want to have him with me, because I hate that sexton.' She raised her shoulders in a little shiver. 'He knows. Everybody knows, over there, and it's only a few miles away, and, any minute someone might cross the bridge and tell.'

'And we'd say it wasn't true. We don't know for certain that it is.'

'We look as if it is,' Jenny said, chivalrously using the plural pronoun. 'Miss Jewel would be sure about it, Miss Morrison wouldn't stay, Mr. Sproat wouldn't help us, the Dakins wouldn't trust us with their friend. D'you think there's any other family in the world that knows fewer people than we do and knows them such a little, and is afraid of knowing them any better?'

Dahlia listened gravely to this sad question and did not answer it. She stood in the bow window of the bedroom they were preparing for the new arrival and looked at the massed green on the cliff, with the topmost trees seeming to hold on their points a pale blue canopy of sky. She looked leftwards, where the cliff ended and the fields beyond the city lifted themselves with a placidity undisturbed by the noise and movement below, and she might have been comparing the width of a world, full of adventure and excitement for other people, with the tiny circle in which she lived, but she did not look discontented. There was something of her mother's essential patience, some confidence of the future in her face. It was Jenny who looked forlorn, as she sat on the end of the bed and rested her chin on the rail.

'You've forgotten Mr. Cummings,' Dahlia said at last.

'Even with him,' Jenny said bitingly, 'we're not exactly rich.'

'No, but he wouldn't leave a comfortable home for a little thing like that. And I do believe it was a little thing, for her. I'm sure God thinks so—if there is one—but it seems as if little things for mothers can be big ones for their children, so I've decided,' Dahlia said flippantly, 'to be a good girl if I can, and then my blue-eyed babies won't reproach me.'

'And we don't reproach anybody.'

'Oh, Jen, you're doing it now!'

'Only to you and only because it's all so inconvenient. We ought to have gone right away where nobody had ever heard of us.'

'And where would the money have come from? He wouldn't have lent it to us for that,' Dahlia said. And, more than ever, it seemed necessary to use the plural.

In spite of that precaution Jenny's face flushed. She was not sure, she dared not ask, whether Dahlia understood the full implication of her words, but, for Jenny, they changed the forgivable past into the unforgivable present and suddenly, with shame and terror she saw Grimshaw as a villain with three helpless women in his power, taking from one of them a willing, or reluctant, interest on his loan.

This was a moment that demanded action for its relief, and she, who naturally procrastinated, slipped from the room before tolerance and doubt and weakness could persuade her that she exaggerated, and while Dahlia still gazed at the wide, sunny, coloured world, Jenny ran swiftly down the stairs. She was in a cold fury that made her cruel and indifferent to consequences, ready to take this opportunity of returning every pang she had suffered since her birth: but when she reached the kitchen she found it empty.

It was unusually clean and tidy, a fact that had its influence on Jenny's mood. A little fire was burning in the grate and the flames made a soft, lapping sound: the floor shone after its recent polishing: the table was covered with the old checked tablecloth from the White Farm, and half her rage changed to tenderness, for this chance spotlessness and comfort of the kitchen was like the good deed of a naughty child who expects and hopes to avoid upbraiding. And then, through the open doorways leading into the garden, she had a glimpse of her mother's bare arm and gay overall and heard her singing as she hung out the teacloths to dry.

'Oh, with what divers pains they met, And with what joy they went away,' sang Louisa, with such a shaking of the notes, such throaty enjoyment and genteel pronunciation of the syllables as Jenny had heard from the village girls when they sang the hymns in church.

She ought, in that resemblance, to have found fuel for her anger, but she only thought, and was thankful, that her mother was happy, happy enough to sing. Her voice was younger than her body: there was a sort of innocence in the sound, and, softened as quickly as she was hardened, Jenny's taut body relaxed. Not to-day would she discover the sum of money owed to Grimshaw and announce her determination either to be free of obligations towards him or to leave the house: and when her mother ceased her singing and came in from the garden, looking contented and then smiling when she saw her daughter, Jenny saw herself as she would have been if she had fulfilled her intention—a little spitfire, crudely attacking she-knew-not-what stored experience, and perhaps hitting places which were still sore. Like her father before her, Jenny felt, though she would not have admitted, that manners were more important than morals, that outward seemliness and dignity were worth preserving, and, like him, she found a welcome postponement of action in restraint, but she had a genuine fondness for her mother and, swinging to the other extreme of feeling, she was now all tenderness and pity.

'You're looking wan,' Louisa said, 'but I'm feeling livelier. I do believe, Jenny,' and Jenny heard the abbreviation as a sign of her mother's willingness to reject the name Sidney Rendall hated, 'I do believe we've really started. I know this one that's coming's only temp'ry, but where one comes, why shouldn't another? The Dakin girl popped in again, a short while back, and said he'd be here some time Saturday afternoon.'

'I was going out,' Jenny said slowly, 'and so was Dahlia.'

'Well, it doesn't need the three of us to open the door, does it? I'll get dressed directly after dinner and be ready for him.'

The brown eyes and the grey ones met, flickered and looked away, and both women knew that the other was thinking of Thomas Grimshaw. 'It'll be all right,' Louisa said with emphasis. 'A can of hot water in his bedroom and tea waiting in the sitting-room. And Cummings, if he likes, can sit in the kitchen.'

Jenny nodded. She did not think it necessary to say that Mr. Cummings would be more pleasantly engaged. She believed her mother chose this way of telling her that she saw the wisdom of dismissing Grimshaw on this occasion and she had a suspicion that Louisa was glad of the excuse.

CHAPTER XVI

The arrival of a telegram for Mr. Cummings caused some excitement in the household on Friday night. Not one of the Rendalls had received such a message in her life. Even in war-time, when other women had taken those orange envelopes with terror and sometimes opened them to a promise of joy, Louisa had not known this experience, for Sidney Rendall, safe at his clerkly work, had thought it unnecessary thus to announce the inglorious occasion of his return. Dahlia opened the door to the double knock, Miss Morrison tripped to the window and saw the boy on the step, Louisa stood at the head of the kitchen stairs and, before Dahlia had handed the envelope to Jenny and told her to take it to Mr. Cummings, Jenny had time to tell herself that Aunt Isabel was making sudden and generous amends for her neglect. There was no one else of her acquaintance likely to indulge in this reckless mode of communication, and what could it contain but an invitation to her home?

'I thought it might be from Sarah,' Louisa said.

Jenny had not considered that possibility: henceforth she would watch telegraph boys and hear double knocks with dread.

'Only she's not very free with her shillings,' Louisa added.

Mr. Cummings was not very free with his. 'There's no answer,' he said, looking grave.

'Is it bad news?' Jenny asked timidly.

'Yes, my father's ill. I'll have to go home to-morrow.'

'Then,' said Jenny, trying to be helpful and realising that, in his sister's place, she would be glad to know of his reassuring advent, 'wouldn't you like to tell them you're coming?'

'They'll know. There's no answer.'

'There's no answer,' Jenny called softly to Dahlia, who waited in the hall.

'There's no answer,' Dahlia told the boy, but she did not shut the door on him. It was a fine, warm night and very still. The sky had not yet darkened, but the trees seemed to be composing themselves for sleep; some of their colour had withdrawn, their full-leaved branches lay motionless, like cloaks gathered a little tighter against the oncoming chill, and here and there, a single light, beforehand with the darkness, shone through the leaves. No one was visible in the street. Doubtless, Miss Jewel had heard the knock and still lurked behind her curtains, but no one passed. Beulah Mount was a little island of silence, and against it, the noise of traffic, near and far, broke sharply, light-heartedly, or with the dull thud of distant, powerful waves.

Dahlia could not see the river from where she stood: she could see the bridge and hear the footsteps of its passengers hurrying, she thought, to happy trysts or loitering to prolong the happiness enjoyed already. Beyond the bridge was the country, with lanes and woods and secret places for lovers; out of sight, spread the downs, dotted with snowy mounds of hawthorn blossom, edged by thick, sheltering trees, roofed with a great stretch of sky presently to be pricked by stars. Behind this rim of Upper Radstowe, where she stood, beyond and below the slope on her left hand, were hundreds of thousands of human beings unknown to her, and she would not have changed places with the happiest and most fortunate, not because she was content, but because she was at an age when her greatest treasure was herself, exactly as it existed at that moment, when her own experiences, consequent on that self, were the ones she wanted; but she was not contented. The night, the stillness, the sweet scents, her youth and all her senses were telling her to leave the security of the doorstep and find love and laughter under the trees, warning her that if she lost this moment she would not find another, but, while her thoughts and her desires were free and eager, she was the child of her father, the pupil of Miss Headley, the result of early training and habit and of the discipline she had lately imposed on herself, and she did not move, except to sit where she had been standing and clasp her knees. It did not occur to her that though the doorstep was for her a place of safety, it might be dangerous, when she occupied it, for other people, dangerous, for instance, to Mr. Sproat, who went by, carrying a letter to the pillar-box, and returned with swiftness, fearful that the figure, half-seen as he passed, would have disappeared.

Many a time Miss Jewel must have regretted that the houses of her neighbours lay cheek by jowl with hers, and not across the road. She did her best with her opportunities, but there was much she could not see, and Dahlia was now beyond her view, though Mr. Sproat, whose correspondence seemed to be increasing, if the number of journeys he made to the pillar-box was any guide, was just discernible, and what Miss Jewel wished to know was whether Miss Morrison or one of the Rendalls was detaining him. This nightly posting of letters, the frequency with which one was dispatched, to be followed, half an hour afterwards, by another, had coincided with Miss Morrison's arrival in Beulah Mount. Miss Jewel knew all about her. Already bereaved of a father, she had lately lost an invalid mother. She had always been as active for the Church as her filial duties had permitted, and now, apparently, she had severed all hampering domestic ties and was free to devote herself to people who might need her. But how had she come to lodge with such people as the Rendalls? It could only have been through the agency of Mr. Sproat. And what was the cause of these night prowlings and tiny changes in ways and looks which would have been invisible to duller eyes? Miss Jewel was obliged to tell herself that the neighbourhood of Miss Morrison had disturbed him.

Miss Jewel had a natural enmity for other women, as women, and an active one for such as threatened to rob her of her lodgers, but, comparatively, she had a tolerance for Miss Morrison, who was not pretty: who, if she engaged a man's attention, must do it by means of virtues which Miss Jewel, too, possessed, and not by any physical charms, of which, lacking them herself, she had a passionate jealousy. Unfortunately for her, the windows of No. 14 had not the bows which were proving convenient to Miss Morrison at this moment. The room that provided the best view of the Rendalls' step was occupied by the professor, and Miss Jewel was obliged to keep inadequate watch from the basement, whence, after some minutes, she saw an uprising of Mr. Sproat's long body and rightly judged that he had mounted the steps and entered the house. She remembered the telegraph boy, and her certainty about Miss Morrison was shaken. She knew Mr. Sproat's weakness for those in trouble, and she thought he had entered a web in which there were three active, though perhaps temporarily sorrowing, spiders, and, vexed by a curiosity she did not know how to satisfy and a holy horror of her neighbours, she sat listening for his returning footsteps and forgot to turn down his bed-clothes and lay out his pyjamas for the night.

Mr. Sproat, slowly undressing, was vaguely aware of this neglect. His hand missed the garments in their

131

accustomed place and, guided by some effort of memory, fumbled for them under the pillows. Mentally, he was still on the Rendalls' doorstep and his subsequent interview with Miss Morrison was a jangle of words and a blur of eyeglasses and smiles, but he was not in the blissfully unreasoning state of an enchanted lover: he was not at present concerned with his possible effect on Dahlia. Seeing her, as she sat there, he was tutoring himself to believe that a pretty pose, a merry mouth which could take on determined lines, a skin of cream and rose and somewhat unruly hair of a warm, dark red, were as grass and the flowers of the field, and when he had succeeded in this attempt and found it made no whit of difference to his feelings, he condemned the indecorum of sitting on doorsteps and throwing dusters out of windows: he asked himself whether he was likely to hear words of value uttered in that charming voice: he contrasted her lightly-spoken comments on the weather and the night with Miss Morrison's earnest rush into parish matters and, before he had time to control his muscles, Mr. Sproat made a spontaneous grimace. Dahlia might have the limitations of girlhood, but Miss Morrison had girlishness in excess, ruffling her serious speeches and giving a gay ripple to her gravity, setting her hands and her head and her eyeglasses in motion. Only Dahlia's lips had moved in a smile when he stood before her, and he was too much occupied in appreciating a stillness unusual at his approach in the young women of his acquaintance, to find cause for it in her indifference to a man at least ten years her senior and looking more: a man of severe appearance, proclaiming in his garb the service to which he was dedicated, and altogether different from the one with whom she had been picturing herself under the sheltering trees.

Mr. Sproat, indeed, greeting her in a deep voice that

seemed to hold a note of reproach, had been like a cold awakening sponge on the head of a dreamer, yet something of her dream remained in her voice and immobility, and she in her dream, and he in his surprise that at last his journeys to the pillar-box had been rewarded, were both forgetful of Miss Jewel in the basement and Miss Morrison's flanking window, until Dahlia, lacking another topic, told him that the doorstep made a nice seat from which to look at the night, when both the sitting-rooms were occupied by lodgers.

'Won't you come in and see Miss Morrison?' she asked, knowing that Miss Morrison would be pleasantly fluttered and anxious to show him that his friend was comfortably housed.

Mr. Sproat made a step forward and Dahlia took that for assent and led him within doors. A man of his experience in retreat should have had a ready reason for avoiding a lady of whom he saw more than enough to satisfy him in each week of work, but he had not reckoned on Dahlia's desertion, and when she shut the sitting-room on him and Miss Morrison, he felt more than disappointment. Dahlia, he divined with dismay, had put him in the place she considered suitable, while she remained on the other side of the wall with Jenny and Mr. Cummings.

He had had a smile from Jenny as she ran past him, carrying a shabby leather bag. He had heard her say, 'But you can't take your things in a paper parcel!' And her tone was both motherly and amused, and he envied young Cummings, whose hostesses were so different from Miss Jewel, and wished that he too could be managed by someone who was young and pretty.

Miss Morrison did not interpret his slight frown correctly, and, encouraging what she fancied was his mood, to show her tact, she told him of Mr. Cummings' trouble: she indicated that Mr. Sproat's presence might be a consolation, but Mr. Sproat shook his head. He knew better than that. He could hear the voices across the passage and decided that Mr. Cummings was probably supplied with all he needed.

He was not a lively nor a sympathetic companion for Miss Morrison that evening, though he was a lingering one, and his time was not altogether wasted: he learnt that she was interesting Dahlia in church decoration and social service, and she spoke delicately of the contrast between the girls and their mother: she pointed at the shelves of books and raised her eyebrows.

'I'm afraid,' she said, 'he must have married beneath him.' And Mr. Sproat relieved himself of some of his discomfort with a stern rebuke.

'Yes,' he said, glaring at her, 'in a worldly sense, perhaps.'

Now he was ashamed of that remark, born of general irritation and particular annoyance at hearing the expression of a worrying thought. He was quite aware of the inconvenience attached to Dahlia Rendall. Her likeness to her mother was a reminder of it and a disturbance, for he had pride in his cloth and in the family of modest gentlepeople from whom he came, and he was neither young nor old enough to believe that love rode smoothly over obstacles. He wanted to marry Dahlia as much as Sidney Rendall had wished to marry Louisa and, with far less reason, he was much more doubtful of the success of such a venture, but the very coolness of his calculations persuaded him of the sanity of his state and, he told himself, if he went open-eyed into marriage he would avoid its dangers, but he could not repress a wish that Dahlia had been completely orphaned, or on the maternal instead of the paternal side. He was properly modest: he feared he was not attractive, but he was complacent about the advantages he could give her from the point of view for which he had reproved Miss Morrison. Those advantages, however, he decided, as he got into bed, could not be enjoyed in Upper Radstowe, and he saw himself, with a Dahlia who had been confirmed, far away in a country vicarage, and he had covered it with creepers and installed a satisfactory arrangement for hot water before he fell asleep.

Meanwhile, almost within reach of his long arm, Dahlia was making other plans for him.

'I thought it would please Miss Morrison if I asked him in,' she told Jenny, 'and he must have been pleased, too, or he wouldn't have stayed so long. She'll be humming all day to-morrow.'

'But he could come in whenever he liked, if he really wanted to, and, as I said before, he never looks up when he goes by, and you said yourself it was because of the eyeglasses.'

'He'll have to get used to them,' said Dahlia. 'She'd be a perfect wife for a parson.'

'But we'd lose a lodger and I'm afraid we shall lose Mr. Cummings. We simply can't afford to let her marry Mr. Sproat, and I can only hope,' Jenny said solemnly, 'that he'll see her at the dancing class.'

'No, no: he mustn't! She tells me she wears a tunic—to her knees, Jen! But I don't think he has much sense of humour, and of course he wouldn't look at her legs.'

'They're not quite straight,' Jenny said indignantly, as though this fault in Miss Morrison were a personal affront.

'She must have been allowed to walk too soon when she was a baby. Well, we've got something to be thankful for. I wonder if it was care or luck. And I suppose things are divided up pretty evenly, after all. She had a very niminy-piminy mother, distantly related to an earl, or somebody.'

'It's always an earl,' Jenny said. 'But I wish I was, all the same.'

'If you had to have crooked legs as well?'

'No!' Jenny cried, stretching them under the bedclothes. 'No! I couldn't be happy for a minute.'

'That's what I mean,' Dahlia said. 'We ought to be thankful. And the least we can do is to let her marry Mr. Sproat.'

Jenny said no more. She remembered how Mr. Sproat had folded the duster for Dahlia and smiled at her, and she had a feeling that beauty and gaiety might have greater power over that gaunt man than any serviceable virtues.

CHAPTER XVII

MR. CUMMINGS set off early with the borrowed bag on which Sidney Rendall's initials were faintly discernible. Borrowing anything was a violation of his principles, but yielding to Jenny's ideas of propriety was a pleasure he would not deny himself when he was faced with a future empty of such opportunities.

Irritated by her smiling reassurances, he went gloomily, like a patient resenting the serene looks of his friends and nurses who are in no danger or pain themselves and betray the seriousness of his case by their calculated cheerfulness. She could afford to be kind, he thought, when she was getting rid of him, and he turned on the step and told her crossly that, whatever happened, he would return for his box.

Jenny nodded. 'Just for the box,' she said, more in statement than in question. 'We could send it after you, you know.' Then she remembered that he was going on a sad excursion, and thinking it was pleasant to tell the truth and make him happy at the same time, she said simply, opening her eyes wide, 'But I'd rather you came for it yourself.'

Mr. Cummings only looked a little crosser, took off his hat, and marched down the street. Jenny was not distressed. She was learning to recognise the signs of his appreciation and knew he liked her best when she played those little tricks which are age-old and discovered afresh by every girl who wants to tease a lover, and in Jenny they had the fascination of unexpectedness, almost of incongruity: their effect on her proud, often impassive, little face was something to watch for, a puckering of her eyelids, a curving of her straight mouth, and Mr. Cummings, who was doing his best to see her as a priceless museum piece on which it was useless to set his heart, then had the added torture of knowing she was a woman who acknowledged his manhood only as amusement for herself or occasional practical use, and it was no wonder she waited in vain for a backward glance, before she went into the house.

'I'm sorry about his father,' Louisa said, 'but it's a bit of luck for us, just when we'd have had him in the kitchen. He's quiet enough. Fact is, he's too quiet. He's a bit like you, Jenny. When he's not talking, you know he's thinking.'

'Why shouldn't he? Why shouldn't I?'

'Well, it makes me so that I can't forget myself. It's not natural.'

'Thinking?' Jenny asked pertly and, with her head on one side, she smiled in a way which was meant to show her mother that she was being funny, not trying to be clever.

Louisa did not answer. She looked at her daughter and said slowly, 'I've seen many a bird sitting on a rail and twisting its head just how you're doing now, or hopping up for crumbs and keeping a look-out—you know the way they do. Oh dear! It's funny the things you see and never notice till they're not there any longer.'

'We've got the gulls,' Jenny said.

'Oh, gulls! I don't reckon they're proper birds. They're more like foreigners. They're not homely,' Louisa said.

She was inland bred, but Jenny's schooldays had been spent on the shores of the Channel and the crying of gulls and the sound of the wind in the coarse grass had been a harsh and invigorating accompaniment to the grace and sweetness offered by Miss Headley. In Jenny's memory, the winters of those days were composed of dun-coloured water, like rough, unburnished metal which could not take the reflection of gulls in flight, the whistling wind and fine-blown sand. Spring was a flash of wings and a blaze of gorse, with little creeping flames of blue and purple flowers, so small and faint compared with the burning bushes that they must be sought for, and, if her memory could be trusted, there were no wet days in summer. Then the coarse grass hardly rustled above the bleached sand, the sun shone and drew aromatic odours from the earth, and the gulls rocked on water that was almost blue, and, rocking so, they might have been comically conceived toys, rudely cut in wood. Here, in Upper Radstowe, strutting on the mud banks of the river, they were greedy, quarrelsome and cumbrous but, on the wing, their flight contained by the high cliffs, their shadows sometimes splashing the bare rock, they were speed and sharpness and blinding whiteness.

She stood on the bridge to watch them and understood why they seemed alien to her mother, with no cosy nesting in trees and hedges, no song or friendliness for man, and, in Louisa's comment on the gulls, Jenny thought there was a hint of her own foreignness to her surroundings and a nostalgia for the country she had left. It was here, close at hand, and Jenny would be within its borders as soon as she crossed the bridge, but Louisa's need of it was not a conscious emotion, to be assuaged by a temporary return: she was not aware of seeing beauty in trees and meadows and sky: they were a part of her life while she was among them and, when she left them, their separate existence gave her no satisfaction. She would have scoffed at the idea of tramping a few miles to see the place she had willingly deserted. There were plenty of trees in Upper Radstowe if she wished to look at them, with pink and white and yellow blossoms: there were flowers in the gardens and the shop windows, finer to her than primroses and cowslips growing wild. The things over which more sophisticated people grew ecstatic were commonplaces to her and had the importance of the commonplaces to which she had been accustomed all her life.

From both her parents, Jenny had the country in her blood and, inheriting discernment from one of them, she might have seen shapes and colours without his instructive aid. Half-way between his conscious appreciation and her mother's unconscious craving, she felt a lightness of spirit when she reached her native side of the water, though she was going towards the sexton without the support of Mr. Cummings, and there was a permanent mental cloud over the landscape. But this cloud varied in density and she hardly noticed it as she followed the path at the edge of the wooded cliff and thought about Mr. Cummings, at the end of his slow, cross-country journey by this time, facing the problem of the future, and perhaps talking to Kitty and Fanny about the tea-shop. She saw the elder Cummings lying in bed, with his hands folded across his workman's apron: she could not picture him without it, for it was thus garbed that he had first been presented to her imagination, and he would remain aproned, as Kitty would remain looking sadly at the lavender bushes and Fanny would cook and make muslin bags, until she had seen these people in the flesh and had her mental images corrected.

She could not think of Mr. Cummings for long without some reference to herself, and, through this most absorbing occupation the sound of a trotting horse came to her ears. For a moment it was no more than that. She heard, too, the faint crunch of wheels on the soft road but, in the next instant, her body reacted to the thought she had hardly formed and dropped below the level of the path to the sloping ground under the trees. A bend in the road had given her just the time she needed to escape and, from her hiding-place, well screened by branches, she peered upwards and saw Thomas Grimshaw go by, his hard felt hat worn jauntily for Saturday, a little bunch of flowers in his buttonhole.

She was still trembling against the bank when he was out of sight. She detested him for the indignity to which he now reduced her, and then for the greater indignity which she had forgotten too easily, when she heard her mother singing in the garden. But she detested him still more for looking what he was, for the vulgar tilt of his hat, his coarse, ungloved hands and the cut of his stiff new coat, and she sat down among the pine needles and last year's leaves and broken twigs and wished viciously that his horse would fall on the slippery slope to the bridge and throw him out of his cart and kill him. She had youth's hope in a Providence who was altogether on her side and would settle her problems with a sudden, final stroke. Nothing could be easier to Omnipotence than the removal of Thomas Grimshaw, and all she asked was that he should die quickly and painlessly. She forgot to remind herself, as she reminded Mr. Cummings, of the good fortune often inherent in what looks ill, but she had the honesty to admit that, in a world peopled entirely by her family and Grimshaw, she would not have suffered this shame: she might even have been glad of his company and have grown to like him. She saw him now with the eyes of other people, those she knew, or might know in the future, and those who would never hear her name, and the moral aspect of the affair was theirs rather than her own. When she looked forward to the delights which must—because she was Jenny Rendall—be in store for her, they were blocked by the figure of that man, and it seemed to her that she could

141

not reach them without cunning and circumlocution. It was natural to expect the kindly help of Providence: it was not noble, but it was natural to her age and to a pride not yet sufficient for itself, to suffer bitterly at a real or fancied social stigma and, while she sat there, her young face haggard, her widely-opened eyes staring at a glint of river shining through the trees, she made herself a solemn promise that, unless God helped her, she would seek her own pleasure with as little care for other people as her mother had shown in taking hers.

She stood up and shook the dust and leaves from her dress as though they were the prejudices, the virtues and the loyalties she was determined to disdain: then, pushing a way through the trees and bushes, she clambered back to the road at a point some distance from where she had left it, for even in this stern and defiant mood she was self-conscious, and no chance witness of her disappearance must see her emerge from her retreat.

The sternness and the defiance, however, enabled her to deal haughtily with the sexton. The stone was finished, ready to be put in its place, and she sent her gratitude across the country to Mr. Cummings, whose design would, she thought, have satisfied her fastidious father. When the sexton was not looking, she traced with her forefinger the letters which bade Sidney Rendall rest in peace, and she was glad that the villagers and the vicar, perhaps the Merrimans, with their family vault like a packing-case, should see this fitting record of his name, and surely any gossip gathered round it would be shamed into silence by this austere memorial.

She was quieted by the sight of it and if she hesitated when she left the churchyard, it was only for a moment. Her father's daughter did not linger in the lanes for a chance sight of young gentlemen on horses and she turned her face towards home but, virtue seldom being rewarded, she saw Thomas Grimshaw's trap approaching as she walked on the path which was raised above the road. Thus, when he pulled up his horse and called to her, and she stopped because she was at bay, their eyes met levelly. She remembered now her mother's tacit assurance of his dismissal and, though he smiled at her in the way he knew she found offensive, she fancied she could see signs of anger in his mouth and eyes, and anger always frightened her. He must have driven straight back from Beulah Mount, she thought, and in fact he had returned in disgust and met the very victim he most needed. Jenny had always shrunk from him: it was plain that she despised and disliked him: she had once cruelly snubbed him, and he, fresh from a Louisa whose friendliness diminished week by week, and altogether disappeared to-day in a refusal to entertain him, was in a mood to taunt the daughter.

An assumption of familiarity was the best weapon for his purpose and he asked gaily after her young man and why she walked alone, commiserated with her, silently appraised her body from head to foot, and wished her better luck another day, but when she remained speechless, staring with eyes that looked right through him, her mouth drooping piteously, half-open for the words she could not find, he lost his pleasure in a game which suddenly seemed cowardly when it was played with this pale slip of a girl.

'Ah, come on, Jennifer,' he said persuasively. 'Can't you take a joke?'

'Not from you,' she managed to say at last in a strangled voice.

Then he leaned towards her and his face had a purplish flush. 'Not from me,' he repeated slowly. 'Well, you've taken a good deal else, but I'll make you pay for it. Yes, I will! You or her, or the whole lot of you. You'll see!'

He drove on with a flourish of his whip, and Jenny went

forward vaguely until she saw a gate at her right hand, opened it and ran into a field, yellow and white with buttercups and daisies. It was a big field, too big a witness of the tears already streaming down her cheeks, and she sought the shelter of a hedge that made a dark green line across the flowers.

CHAPTER XVIII

'I wish he was going to be a regular one,' Louisa was saying when Jenny went into the kitchen. 'He's a bit grand in his talk, but we'd get used to that, and he's quite different to Cummings. Well dressed, and his suit-case is real leather. He made a very good tea and said he'd be out to dinner. He's out already. And after all the trouble I took with the sweet!'

Dahlia had just returned from Miss Morrison's class, Jenny stood in the doorway with a wilted posy in her hand, and they both looked at their mother, whose face was brighter than it had been for weeks. She was wearing the tight black frock, above it her vivid colouring was coarsened, and Jenny, returning in a dream from the field where she had picked her flowers, wished her mother had been wearing her loose, becoming, working clothes and sitting rather moodily in the old wicker chair. The sight of Louisa, pleased and bustling, her lovely, ample shape constrained by the ill-fitting dress, woke Jenny harshly from her happy trance: her face sharpened and she stepped towards the fire, always burning in that underground apartment, and made to throw her nosegay into the flames. Then she drew back her hand and heard her mother say, 'Don't burn them! It's unlucky.'

'I wasn't going to,' Jenny said.

'Put them in the dustbin,' said Louisa.

'No.' Jenny smiled. 'I'll put them in water.'

'Buttercups and daisies! Why, you can pick those out in our back patch.'

'Not quite the same as these,' Jenny said precisely, and went to fetch water from the scullery tap.

Louisa jerked her head in that direction. 'She's in one of her moods,' she told Dahlia. 'She never goes for a walk without she comes back upset.'

'She hasn't said anything,' Dahlia protested.

'No, but she's looked a lot.'

Louisa had a right to feel aggrieved. She had kept her promise to Jenny: she had received the visitor properly, with hot water in the bedroom and tea ready in the sitting-room and no Thomas Grimshaw in the basement. He had not crossed the threshold. She had told him she was busy, with a gentleman coming any minute, and it was doing the house no good to have him calling every week, and she had the girls to think of. This was what she had been wanting to tell him, for she was weary of a presence that made the kitchen feel small and stuffy. She had outgrown her liking for him and dully resented the unspoken claims he based on their past experiences. She was weary of hearing him tell her that the White Farm, taken off her hands as part of the loan he had made her, was empty still and likely to remain so. It was he who had offered the money, even while he scoffed at her enterprise, and it was not fair—dimly she felt it was not chivalrous—to press her for it indirectly. Now that her affairs looked like improving, she was in a stronger position to resist him, and she knew what it was he wanted. The debt and the failure of her undertaking were to leave her with no resource but to pay or marry him, and there was little chance of her paying. She was not so simple that she could not see all that. For weeks she had been puzzling to find a different solution of her problem and thinking of enlisting Sarah's aid, but to-day she was as sanguine as she had been when she had bought the house. And Jenny must

146

choose this moment to assume her damping little air of superiority!

'She looks,' Louisa said, 'as if she hadn't expected to find us here and didn't like us when she saw us.'

This was an accurate description of Jenny's feelings. From the moment when she had stopped sobbing under the hedge until her return to Beulah Mount, she had forgotten everybody but herself and the young man on the horse. Lying in a crumpled heap, crying with luxurious abandonment, she heard a jingle of steel, felt a light tremor of the ground, and looked up to see again that partnership of man and mount fixed weeks ago in her memory. Again the sun shone on the gleaming coat of the horse and the youth's fair hair, and they approached her across the brilliance of grass and flowers, and did not suffer from their setting. Strength and youth and grace and beauty were coming towards her on a path strewn for them, the horse stepping with the dainty fussiness of a creature who longs to feel his own speed, yielding to the will of his rider, but catching at his bit and shaking his head in remonstrance: the youth sitting easily, conscious of this impatience and his power to control it, and they were both more beautiful than she had thought. Though there was now no Mr. Cummings to discomfort her, there was her own woebegone, stained face, and she shrank closer to the hedge and hoped he would pass her by, but the horse saw the movement, planted his forefeet, looked at her askance and jumped sideways, plainly indicating that, though not fearful for himself, it was his duty to call attention to this strange, stirring bundle. And as young Mr. Merriman saw her half-sitting, half-kneeling there, in an attitude of arrested flight, with her hands at her throat, he called out a word of reassurance. Smiling, she shook her head and looked down, to hide a

147

face not fit to show him, with the last of her tears slipping over her eyelids.

He had seen it, however. He was the young lord of the manor, and if this was not a trespasser she was a tenant. She seemed to be in trouble, and he jumped off his horse and stood near her, holding the bridle, and asking what was the matter. She kept her head down. She had seen what she thought was the perfection of his face, his clear blue eyes, the golden-brown colour of his skin making his hair look pale, a hopeful nose and a kind mouth—the face she had given him in her thoughts. And she saw herself in a crumpled dress with her hat lying by her side and cheeks smeared with weeping, a girl disgraced by crying in the open, like a country girl who must seek the isolation of the fields for her distresses and her loves. And young Mr. Merriman, experienced in village troubles, but still embarrassed by them, thought for a moment that here was another of them. But he did not remember this dark hair, hardly ruffled by the removal of her hat, and he noticed that her hands were gloved, not in the stretched cotton of a village maiden dressed for an afternoon's outing, but loosely, in pale chamois leather stained by its pressure on the grass.

She heard immediately the subtle change in his tone. It had been persuasively cheerful and confident, the voice of the young squire addressing the farmer's daughter: it had become a little nervous, his words were hesitating, and, with a lift of her heart at the kind of recognition she desired and a swift certainty that he had not seen her with Mr. Cummings, she let out a small trickle of laughter.

'I wasn't a bit frightened of your horse,' she explained.

'Of course not.' People of their quality, his tone implied, were not afraid of horses, and she stood up and stroked the soft nose of this one.

She could not remember very clearly all that passed between them, for she had been in a state of happiness that excluded thought. She was content to be with him, to look at him, to find, in this reality, the fulfilment of her dreams. She had emerged from darkness into light and she had forgotten the darkness. She did not know how long they were together, walking up and down, parallel to the hedge and followed by the horse, or standing still for a few minutes and looking at each other across the saddle, talking of she knew not what or talking not at all, but he had certainly told her that he often rode about the fields on Saturdays and she had told him that she often walked there. And after the first encounter she had hardly been conscious of herself: she was absorbed in him. Even when they were parting, near the gate, and he asked her to tell him her name, when he had given her his own, she had answered truthfully, before she had time to fear the associations that name might have for him, but she answered very low, suddenly shy at speaking of herself, and stooping towards her to hear better, he exclaimed, 'What? Jenny Wren?' and then, with a catch of her breath at this escape, she nodded gravely. The name seemed to please him. It pleased her because he had given it to her, and, smiling, without thought of the future, she watched him spring into the saddle, canter across the grass, leap a low hedge and disappear. That was the right way for him to go, swiftly and gloriously, like a centaur emblazoned on a field of green and white and gold. And in a moment the field was empty, but she had gathered her flowers from the place where they stood at parting.

In the first shock of her return to the kitchen, when she saw her mother in the black dress and realised that whether the Merrimans knew anything of her or not, they would refuse to know more, she went towards the fire to burn those flowers, perhaps half enjoying the dramatic gesture, but deeply sensible of the episodic nature of the day's joy. And then every instinct of youth had bidden her keep them, if it was only as an assurance that she had actually picked them in a field where he and she had really stood.

When her mother was not looking, she carried them to the attic; when she and Dahlia were in bed, she suddenly jumped out and turned on the light.

'I thought you were asleep,' Dahlia said. 'I wanted to talk but I daren't wake you. What on earth are you doing?'

'Pressing these flowers before they lose their colour,' she had taken a book from the shelf, 'or drop their petals.'

'Are they so special?'

'Yes.'

'Oh, Jen, tell me!'

'It's not what you think.' She turned and faced Dahlia but she looked at the wall behind the beds and slowly the pattern and colour of the paper faded and gave place to a bright tapestry on which she saw a knight on horse-back, not clad in armour nor in riding dress, but in the flannel trousers, the slack coat and soft shirt in which he, who could do as he chose, defied convention, and Dahlia, eagerly watching her face, saw it brighten, then grow wan again, for, search as she would, her own figure was not woven into the scene. Jenny Rendall was standing in the attic and Jenny Wren had vanished altogether.

'What's the matter?' Dahlia whispered, and the tapestry grew dim and disappeared and Jenny turned out the light.

'What's the matter?' Dahlia asked again. 'Tell me, Jen. You looked so miserable.'

'Did I?' Searching for a satisfactory explanation, she remembered Thomas Grimshaw, almost forgotten until this moment, though it was he who had driven her into the enchanted meadow, and remembering this she also remembered that it was he who had the chief share in exiling her from it: he had given her something of which he had already robbed her, and, on a stifled sob, she said: 'Coming back, this afternoon, I met that man.'

'Which?' Dahlia asked innocently.

'That man,' Jenny repeated with emphasis.

'Oh, that one!'

'And he was horrid, horrid, horrid!' Jenny said, shutting her eyes and pressing her face into her pillow.

'About the money?'

'Yes, but it was the way he looked at me.'

'Did you vex him?'

'I can't help doing it. I make him want to hurt me. But I only said three words the whole time.'

'You'd better tell me what they were,' said Dahlia. And, when the tale was finished, she said: 'Oh, well, we can't help it. It's no good worrying. What a pity Mr. Cummings wasn't with you.'

'Oh, I'm glad he wasn't,' Jenny said fervently.

'But Thomas Grimshaw wouldn't have been rude. Men always behave better in front of other men.'

'How do you know that?'

'I just do know it. He would have been ashamed.'

'Everything,' said Jenny, 'would have been different.' Her sorrow was not so deep that she would have had things changed. She was, in fact, half playing with a sorrow she had not fully accepted. Wonderful things could happen. There were noble people in the world, with candid eyes and kind mouths, who could see beyond material circumstances and deal tenderly and splendidly with the reality hidden from superficial glances. In a hopeless moment she had nearly burnt her flowers: in a tenacious one she had put them between the pages of a book: already she saw herself picking fresh ones, and she resigned her fate to fortune.

'But why,' Dahlia asked, 'are those flowers so special?'

'Because,' Jenny said, 'because—well, afterwards, I had a sort of vision and it comforted me, so I picked the buttercups and daisies and some blades of grass, so that I could remember.'

'Oh!' Dahlia said and was silent. Jenny was queer and poetical and might, in truth, see visions, but Dahlia was not satisfied. She could feel little currents of emotion coming to her across the narrow space between the beds, and when Jenny had stood, straight and pale in her night-gown, staring at the wall, her face was not that of a person who was comforted. 'And that's all?' she asked.

'That's all.'

'Oh!' Dahlia said again, and after she had allowed Jenny time to realise the significance of that monosyllable, she said, 'I'm much more curious about you than you are about me. My flowers were tulips.'

'Your flowers?'

'Only the ones for the church. Miss Morrison wanted to buy lilies, but I wouldn't let her. I said they wouldn't show, and she said that didn't matter because they were an offering, not a decoration, and I said it was silly to offer lilies to the person who had made them, and it was much more important to cheer up the ugly church, and anyhow, tulips were cheaper. She was rather cross, and she thinks it's a beautiful church! But that's only because it's Mr. Sproat's. And he came in when we were arranging the flowers, and she knocked a vase over and he mopped up the water with his handkerchief. And then she actually asked him if he objected to the colour of the tulips, lovely orange ones, and blamed me for it, but she shouldn't have been in such a hurry, because he said he liked it, and then she pretended that she did, too. I hate that kind of thing. I'm not sure that I'll let her marry him, after all.'

'You needn't bother. Wait till he sees her dancing!'

'He's seen her.'

'This afternoon?'

'Yes, he came in for a few minutes. And if I'd had the sense to stay at home I should have seen Mr. Allsop. He sounds rather exciting. Do you suppose he's engaged to Mary Dakin?'

'Not if he's exciting,' Jenny said, and Dahlia laughed.

'You're rather funny sometimes. Well, we'll see him to-morrow. Let's go to sleep.'

'In a minute. Just tell me something. If you didn't know me what would you think of me?'

'I'd think—no, I wouldn't. I don't suppose I'd notice you at all.'

'But if you had noticed me,' Jenny persisted.

'Go to sleep,' Dahlia said, and Jenny was breathing peacefully long before Dahlia shut her eyes. She was a practical person. She was wondering who could have made Jenny ask such an unlikely question and why she was sentimental about the flowers.

CHAPTER XIX

MR. ALLSOP was not at all exciting. He was tall, dark and solemn and a little bald, and Mary Dakin's stealthiness in engaging rooms for him might have been an effort to bring into the affair that element of romance which was denied by his manner and appearance. Dahlia took one look at him and felt a little less reluctance to go to church with Miss Morrison who was waiting in the hall, wearing the grey dress she kept for Sundays, a feather boa to match and a wide black hat with a touch of mauve in it, and holding, on the third finger of one hand, the strap of the little leather case which contained her prayer and hymn books.

Dahlia had not quite forgiven the treachery about the tulips, and her smile, a little too wide and frank, made Miss Morrison feel uncomfortable. She seemed to be smiling in this way to prevent herself from frowning.

'I'm thinking,' Dahlia said, 'that it's perfectly idiotic to go to church on a day like this. But what else is there to do? It's a sort of refuge for the unemployed.'

'Oh, Dahlia!'

'It is! You don't suppose that all those old men and women and all those good, dull girls really like it, do you? They go because it's worse to stay at home. If nobody was allowed to play games on Sunday, or to go for walks, or to use their motor cars, the churches would be full. And, because they're not, it shows,' said Dahlia, taking a deep breath, 'that most people manage to enjoy themselves.'

She was trying to be good, and church was a safe place for the idle who were young and restless and had to be respectable. It was also, for her, the only starting-place whence she might reach a prosperity which would give her the freedom to taste her youth, but she wanted to annoy Miss Morrison and to express her anger that her eager, active limbs should have to keep pace with the ones Jenny despised, that she should be expected to listen meekly to the droning of Mr. Doubleday and the sonority of Mr. Sproat.

'We don't live to enjoy ourselves, dear,' said Miss Morrison, forgetting to be contemporaneous with Dahlia.

'Because we haven't the chance,' Dahlia said, and she stood still under the trees on The Green.

It was too early for the push-carts and playing children of the poorer streets. The mothers had not yet had time to dress their families and themselves in their best, though a few managing women had put the babies in their perambulators and told their husbands to take them out, and those fortunate in peaceful or sleeping infants were sitting on seats and reading newspapers: but the road encircling The Green was already lively with motor cars, shabby ones filled with family parties—fat, cheerful women and red-faced men and a scattering of children, some with gay, fresh young people in them—setting off for picnics, Dahlia thought, and some small, shining ones containing only a man and a girl, and through the noise of the engines and the hooting of horns the single bell tolled warningly from the church.

In a mild protest against Dahlia's mood, Miss Morrison had walked on, and she walked in the dainty tripping way that might have been her mother's when she was a girl. Miss Morrison had been born into a generation that had learnt to walk and to think freely, but she did not belong to it. By character and upbringing her period was

155

that of women who were old and ashamed to be unmarried before they had reached her forty years, and sometimes the burden of sustaining her youthfulness was very heavy. Her attempts were comparable to those of a clergyman who is determined to show himself a man among other men, and it was as free of deceptive purpose. Fostered by a pious wish to persuade an ailing parent that life was joyful, it had been primarily designed as a means of communication with the girls she wished to influence: they were to understand that she understood them and that wisdom could walk companionably with harmless folly: but to-day she could not get into touch with Dahlia. Her girls were often sullen, sometimes rebellious, and then she tried to humour or to soothe them, but Dahlia was not of their class or education, and Miss Morrison knew she had no mental authority over her and she was afraid of the urgent life in the girl's voice, in her gait and her hair and her choice of clothes. Dahlia's dress was home made and of cheap material, the sewing was careless and Miss Morrison feared that the wrong side of it would not bear inspection, but, with a pull here and a pin there she had produced an effect which Miss Morrison's meticulous, old-fashioned dressmaker could not have achieved, nor would Miss Morrison have wished her to do so. Dahlia's frock was yellow, patterned with flowers of russet and apricot, colours allied to those of her hair and eyes and her faintly sunburnt skin, and Jenny, who had chosen them for her, had refused to let her have cowslips in her hat and had bound it with a soft brown velvet ribbon.

Miss Morrison looked back and saw her like a patch of sunlight under the trees, and Dahlia, with long, easy strides, ran towards the maddeningly neat grey figure, to say with a malicious chuckle, 'And the good, dull girls wouldn't go, if the clergymen were women!'

Miss Morrison flushed. 'That's vulgar.'

'It's pathetic.'

'What you said,' Miss Morrison explained.

'What they do!' Dahlia retorted.

'I think,' said Miss Morrison with dignity, though she trembled a little, 'I would rather you did not come in with me.'

'Then I won't. I'll go for a walk. But say a little prayer for me,' Dahlia cried gaily.

Miss Morrison said one for herself. Catching the footstool between her feet, she drew it towards her, raised her skirt, for it was of a delicate shade, and, kneeling, shut her eyes against the faint glow of Dahlia's tulips on the altar. She tried to shut her mind against the memory of her own clumsiness in the vestry and Dahlia's ease: tried to forget that Mr. Sproat had seemed to be deaf and blind on the side of him where she stood and very acute of sight and hearing on the other, and she prayed to be relieved of envy and covetousness and gladness that the girl was not sitting there, like a bright reflection of her tulips. But it was difficult to pray whole-heartedly and she did not pay much attention to the sermon, though it was Mr. Sproat who preached. She could remember his first appearance in that pulpit and her sudden enthusiasm for church and its activities, and Dahlia, with her words about the clergymen, had so surely hit the mark that Miss Morrison blushed again, and she felt a retrospective sorrow for the child and girl she had been. She had not gone to school, and governesses of mature years had taught the prim, spectacled child with the pale, thin hair, and taken her for solemn walks. Carefully shielded, then and later, from all acquaintances who did not satisfy her mother's standards, she had not been popular with her few permitted contemporaries, for she had the pathetic eagerness to be liked, which is repulsive to the happy, careless young, an eagerness which endures rebuff after rebuff before it learns its lesson, and learns it, as it were, by rote, and never rightly understands it. She had at last found safety among the young servants and shop-girls of the district and if they laughed at her behind her back, she did not know it, for she had her mother's faith in the impregnability of a superior worldly position. She had found a modest excitement in chance or calculated encounters with the curate, but slowly this had died of inanition. A few weeks ago Dahlia's words would not have touched her. The admiration she had always felt for Mr. Sproat had become almost impersonal: she was pleased if he showed interest in her or in what she did, but she had given up putting double meanings into his remarks and persuading herself that there was more than courtesy in his eyes. She had almost forgotten those old feelings when she received his astonishing suggestion that she should live in Beulah Mount. Then all the submerged hopes, which had never taken definite shape, floated lightly to the surface of her mind, and, though she would not look at them, their presence made her bright girlishness quite natural. Her friendliness, her sympathy, came from a fount of happiness so full that she need not, could not, be chary with her offerings. It was pleasant, so she told herself, to have someone thinking of her comfort and anxious to have her as a neighbour: she did not grudge the service she thought he asked of her: she was glad to be a guide to these young girls, but not until this moment had she believed that he required no more of her, and because, like Jenny and Dahlia, she had faith in her future, she did not quite believe it now.

Mr. Sproat had not dealt fairly by Miss Morrison, but she did not allow herself to blame him, for that would have implied too much, and, as she forced herself to think of Dahlia in her lovely youth, she also saw a lady clad in grey, with soft feathers at her neck: she saw Dahlia roaming the streets and looking about her with bright, attractive glances, while the grey lady, not young, but gracious, sat modestly in church: she thought of Dahlia's mother in the basement and remembered that her own had been connected with an earl. She shared many of Mr. Sproat's own thoughts, and missed the joy of conscious union. She was spared the knowledge of his decision to ignore his worldly doubts.

He preached, but she did not listen to his counsel, with which, after all, she was familiar. And meanwhile Dahlia was roaming through the streets, her ill-temper gone with its expression, sorry she had vexed Miss Morrison, but innocent of any intention to insult her or realisation that she had done so, for Miss Morrison, to Dahlia's mind, was no longer a dull, good girl: she was a dull, good, middle-aged woman, just a little too dull and not quite good enough to be allowed to marry the curate. The affairs of such people were only interesting when there was nothing else to think of, and she was taking part in the pageant of a fine summer morning in early summer, before the trees had shed their blossom, when the velvet wallflowers in the gardens sent sweet, warm scents across her path, the roses were still a promise, and the late flowering tulips stood straight and motionless in pride of their red and pink and yellow heads.

Miss Morrison and Mr. Sproat were forgotten, but, now and then, among the strange faces Dahlia saw, there came a vision of Jenny's, as it had been last night when she stood staring at the wall. It was a little worrying, but useless to worry, Dahlia told herself. Jenny was secret and would not be questioned. She was capable of making tragedy out of a tiny incident which Dahlia would have laughed down the wind, and the very strength of the affection uniting them made it impossible to force a confidence.

159

Jenny had looked rather serious when she was giving Mr. Allsop his breakfast, and Dahlia would have been relieved to know that this solemnity was not for herself. Jenny was very sorry for Mary Dakin and a little sorry for Mr. Allsop. What poetry, what beauty, she wondered, as she cleared the table, could these two discover in each other. Mr. Allsop looked as if he had been born and bred in a well-appointed city office: a card index and a type-writer and a telephone might have been his earliest toys, a swivel chair his rocking-horse, and a handsome roll-top desk the ambition of his boyhood. He could probably drive a car, but Jenny was sure he could not ride a horse. Where were the swiftness, the colour and the glitter that rushed and glowed and sparkled in Jenny's mind? From the window she had seen him meet Mary on the pavement and when he took off his hat, the little bald patch looked very white against his dark hair. She had heard Mary telling him, in her deep voice, that it was a jolly day, and he had hailed a passing boy and bought a Sunday paper and he and Mary had read the cricket news together. Then, when the rest of the family passed out of the front door and the other girls all said it was a jolly day and marched off with their golf clubs, and Mr. and Mrs. Dakin went slowly down the hill, the lovers were left together—he in his dark blue suit, she in the fluffy dress that did not suit her—and still Jenny could hear them talking about cricket. Were they too shy to talk of other things? Were they afraid to look at each other fairly and exchange securities of endless contentment and a happiness the gay world was painting for them, lest their joy should be indecorous in Beulah Mount? Or did they know they had no such promises to offer, or were they too old to want them?

Jenny saw them pass out of sight and returned to her own work. Already, after a few hours, Mr. Allsop had

160

left his mark on a room untouched by Mr. Cummings' weeks of habitation. There were several of yesterday's newspapers on a chair and she thought of Edwin's carefully hoarded pennies: a neat leather writing-case was on the bureau and she frowned at this familiarity with her treasure: there was a cigar-case on the mantelpiece and the stump of a cigar and grey curls of ash were in the grate.

'I must buy some ash-trays to-morrow,' she thought, flapping out her duster.

Limply her hand fell and rested on the window-sill: then she knelt and looked across the water. Beyond the bridge—that could easily be held by one man with a weapon—beyond the wall of cliff like a barrier, was the Land of Promise which she had forbidden herself to enter any more, but her thoughts might go there, invisibly passing the sentinel, scaling the rampart, finding her golden field, kneeling in the village church, where all good squires and their families attended morning service, sitting on a smooth lawn under the shade of old trees and waiting for the luncheon gong or strolling into the stable-yard where a soft chestnut nose would be poked over the half-door of a loose-box.

Jenny shut her eyes. She was not going. She had half promised to be there on Saturday, but she would not go. He had called her Jenny Wren. What would he say if he knew she was Jenny Rendall? Perhaps he had forgotten her already. His life must be full of pretty faces and good friends and occupations. It would be silly to go. He might have to make an effort to remember her: he might have decided not to see her—poor little Jenny Wren in a crumpled dress, with tears on her cheeks, cowering against a hedge.

'But I did half promise,' she muttered.

CHAPTER XX

Mr. Cummings returned late that Sunday night with the bag in one hand and a large bunch of flowers under his other arm. He let himself in with his latchkey, left his encumbrances in the hall and knocked at the door of the kitchen.

'I didn't know where else to go,' he explained.

He looked tired and hot and rather forlorn, and Louisa kindly bade him enter and sit down. 'The girls are in what they call the garden,' she said, glancing at the open doors, 'and they'll see the stars, if they're lucky, but nothing else. Now, how did you find your father?'

'He was a good deal better this morning,' Edwin said in a very loud voice.

'I'm not deaf, boy,' Louisa said good-humouredly.

'I'm sorry,' he said meekly, but he had made himself heard in the garden, and it was to three attentive women he told his story. His father had had a slight stroke and the doctor thought he would recover and the girls had agreed that it would be best for their brother to return to Upper Radstowe. Business was not brisk, unfortunately, and Kitty would manage with the help of the cabinet-maker, a good workman who could be trusted. It had been hard work to get back on a Sunday, and Edwin had walked three miles to catch a train at the junction.

'You'll be hungry,' Louisa said.

No: Fanny had made him a nice packet of food. He was not hungry, but he was thirsty.

162

'Then I'll make you a cup of tea,' said Louisa. She felt sorry for the lad: she had the quick sympathy of her kind for those involved in illness, and it was unexpectedly homely and pleasant to have him in the kitchen.

Mr. Cummings said he must go and wash. 'And I'd like to return that bag,' he said to Jenny. This second simple ruse was successful, too, and he was able to give her the great bunch of drooping flowers. 'They've had a long journey,' he said. 'They're not what they were.'

'They'll recover. We haven't any flowers in the house and I'll give some to Miss Morrison.'

'Kitty picked them for you.'

'Did she?' There was a warmer note in Jenny's voice. 'Then I won't give any to Miss Morrison,' she said, but she did not bring a deeper shadow to Edwin's already serious face. 'Did she think of it herself?'

'She asked if we had a garden here and I said not what you could really call one and I suppose she felt sorry for you. Kitty thinks a lot of a garden.'

Jenny was not sure that she wanted Kitty Cummings to feel sorry for her. 'But I have other things, you know. All sorts of pictures,' she said, on a sigh.

'Pictures?'

'In my mind. I've got your garden in my mind.'

'Did you go and have a look at the stone?'

'Did you tell her about the tea-shop?'

'She thought it was a good idea, but it's too late for this year. Next year, perhaps.' Mr. Cummings sighed, too. 'I was thinking of you yesterday, going to see the stone. We'll both of us go on Saturday.'

'Will we?' Jenny said, and she walked backwards for a few steps and looked at him over the barricade of flowers. Yes, she had pictures in her mind, those of things she had seen and those of what she might see. There was the old one of Mr. Cummings, skipping awkwardly from Mr.

163

Merriman's horse, and now she had a new one of Mr. Merriman coming face to face with her and Mr. Cummings. It was comforting to remember that there were more bridges than one over the river and other ways than the road of reaching the field, if she decided that the half-promise must be kept.

'Well, I'll go,' he said. 'I'd like to see it. Is it what you wanted?'

'It's beautiful, beautiful,' she said, backing still farther, and the little strain in her voice, naturally taken for thanks and tribute, was the expression of her discovery that no deed could stand alone, that each one depended on the past and affected the future, that even her wish to do well by her father's memory was making life more difficult. There were other bridges, there were the ferries and gates and stiles and footpaths, but there would always be the thought of Thomas Grimshaw, who was not forbidden to leave the roads, and there would always be Mr. Cummings with his love of country walks and passion for old houses.

'No, I won't go,' she said aloud and, without a word, he went slowly up the stairs to remove the stains of travel. He was in trouble and she had hurt him, but she watched him callously. She was enraged at the shifts to which she must be forced in order to have what she skilfully chose to call a simple pleasure, and she was enraged at the insufficiency of her pride. She was of as good birth and education as Cyril Merriman, and she was allowing herself to be cowed by circumstances, yet an inner wisdom warned her that now was the time to teach herself that yesterday's adventure was indeed only a dream and that men were not like women, who could build a permanent and lovely house on the baseless fabric of a vision.

At this moment Miss Morrison opened her sitting-room door.

She had heard the voices and she felt herself so much a part of the household that she ought to give Mr. Cummings a welcome and make inquiries, but she found only Jenny, with both arms round an enormous bunch of flowers, and she retired, shutting the door very quietly. She had seen a girl clasping the gift of a lover and standing so motionless that even her eyes had not moved when the door was opened, and Miss Morrison could not break into the thoughts that held her, she could not bear to witness that frozen ecstasy. She had passed the time for it: she had never known it, and, for a few seconds, under the bright electric light and behind the discreetly drawn curtains, she stared at the carpet through blurred eye-glasses. It seemed to her that filial devotion, a persistent cheerfulness and an earnest desire to leave the world better for her existence, all these were like straws in an east wind, worthless and disregarded, the waste of life that went by unheeded, and she would have exchanged the memory of her duty done and her hope of reward hereafter for such a moment as she believed Jenny was experiencing now.

Then she took up her sewing, for she prided herself on being modern and she did not hesitate to use her needle on a Sunday, and she had a great deal of work to do for the church bazaar. She fixed her thoughts on that and the committee meeting to-morrow, when the decoration scheme for the parish hall and the costumes of the stall-holders would be discussed, and when Mrs. Doubleday, who was in favour of a Dutch scheme, with the ladies in muslin caps and sabots, would be opposed by Miss Morrison's supporters, who had adopted her suggestion of calling the fair Arcadia and set their hearts on being shepherdesses.

Jenny had heard and seen Miss Morrison, but she was in no mood for hearing her say the flowers were lovely, though they were sadly wilted, or enduring her careful avoidance of attributing them to Mr. Cummings' devotion, for, in dealing with the young, she rather laboriously assumed that they were all jolly, natural boys and girls together, and these two, the girl and the woman, remained divided by the door, their ages and their natures, and neither suspected that their troubles had a certain kinship. Jenny was trying to decide on renunciation, and Miss Morrison, making her neat stitches with a hand that was not quite steady, was facing the fact that she had no choice. The boy and girl idea might have applied to Dahlia but not to Mr. Sproat, and it was not natural for him to linger after service in the neighbourhood of The Green, in such a position that he had a view of the hill and the bridge and could intercept anyone who was making for Beulah Mount. Miss Morrison, returning rather later than usual after a chat with Mrs. Doubleday, had pretended not to notice him, but, from her convenient bow window, she had seen a golden-tawny figure coming down the hill, and she had turned away, and it seemed a long time before she heard the expected voices and Dahlia's pretty laughter. In all Miss Morrison's knowledge of him, Mr. Sproat had never made a joke. It was Mr. Doubleday who was the official humorist. And she wondered whether it was she who had been stupid or Mr. Sproat who was now inspired, and it did not occur to her, who naturally waited for masculine leadership, that Dahlia might be finding amusement for herself. She was astonished to see the girl calm and casual when she brought in the midday meal, to hear her say she had met Mr. Sproat and walked down the road with him, and really, he was much more human than she had thought.

'Human?' Miss Morrison repeated. It was a dangerous word.

'Yes, about going to church. He told me he often
166

didn't want to go himself. I hadn't thought of that,' Dahlia said simply.

Miss Morrison smiled in rather a superior way. She knew the trick of confessing to lay weaknesses: it was one she used herself. And, as she sewed that night, it was not Mr. Sproat's occasional lack of clerical ardour that drove her needle in and out so quickly: it was not the certainty that he would never linger on The Green for her: it was the sense of having missed something which was wonderful while it lasted, something that had Jenny and the temporary lodger in its power and was active in the Dakins' house on one side of her and in Miss Jewel's on the other. It had passed her by and, more distressing than that realisation, was the knowledge that it had done well for itself, if not for her. She knew that passion would not have flourished in her thin soil: she did not want it: it would have shocked her. She had always been too old for rapture and too self-conscious to accept love freely, and though she had wished to be loved she had not wished to be desired. She would gladly have kept house for Mr. Sproat, cared for his comforts, trotted untiringly after him to every service and every meeting and believed he was God's deputy, but her imagination shrank from other intimacies.

She settled her eyeglasses with her thumb and finger and a deft, practised turn of her wrist, and believed she had settled something else. She was lonely, but she was at peace, as she had felt when her mother died and the long strain of patient cheerfulness was over. This was another loss, but it was a new gain, for she had found herself. Not jealousy of Dahlia, but the sight of Jenny with her flowers had robbed and then rewarded her, and she laid down her sewing and sank back in her chair with a blissful feeling of relief. It was as though she, who had always been waked early by an alarm clock, was now looking forward to a morning when she need not stir until she chose. Every morning was to be like that, she thought thankfully, and all her early rising had been foolishness. She heard the ringing of the front-door bell and was glad it could rouse neither hope nor disappointment. Through the open window she heard the murmuring of voices and a little catch of laughter. This, she supposed, was Mr. Allsop, escorted by his young lady, and she was not envious, but she was mildly critical of a man who could allow his betrothed to see herself home, though it was only a few steps distant.

Mr. Allsop, however, was not guilty of this ungallantry. They had called for the loan of a latchkey and, when Jenny opened the door, she saw the hasty parting of their hands. They were going for a walk, Mary explained, smiling with her old friendliness, and they might be late, and would it be convenient to let them have the rooms again next week?

'This week,' Mr. Allsop said, more correctly.

'Yes, this week,' Mary said, with a little gasp of excitement.

'On Friday,' said Mr. Allsop.

'Yes, on Friday,' Mary echoed deeply.

Jenny did not smile, but she gave them the key and the promise, and watched them go slowly up Beulah Mount, swinging their joined hands. It was strange, but they seemed to be happy together. She wondered if they were still talking about cricket. She could not imagine what they would find to say about each other.

CHAPTER XXI

M<small>R</small>. A<small>LLSOP</small> left half a crown on his dressing-table, and
Dahlia said she would make a hole in it and wear it round
her neck.

'Don't you do anything so silly,' Louisa said. 'You can
find a better use for it than that. Or you can put it in the
basin.'

This was a cracked bowl, kept, in accordance with her
family's traditions, on the kitchen mantelshelf and used as
a receptacle for the petty cash of the household. Into it
odd shillings and coppers were dropped, and Louisa and
Dahlia had only to reach up an arm—though Jenny must
stand on tiptoe—to increase or lessen its contents.

'I don't know why she thinks it's hers,' said Jenny. 'It
was I who looked after Mr. Allsop.'

'But I found it! All right, you can have it: but I'll look
after him next time and you can have Miss Morrison.
It'll do you good. And as he's coming for an extra day,
perhaps he'll add another sixpence!'

'Well, dear me,' said Louisa, 'what does it matter? We
all share alike, and I never ask where the money goes, do I?'

'Because you don't know how much there ought to be,'
said Dahlia.

'And that's how it should be with we three,' Louisa said,
and she saw a look pass between the girls. It expressed a
faint amusement that she should think them capable of
wrangling about money, but it also asked a question.
Is this the moment? they were asking each other, and
Dahlia seemed to think it was.

'Yes, that's how it should be,' she said. 'That's how it is—about the shillings. But Jenny and I—we don't know where we arc.'

'You're in my house,' said Louisa. 'That's where you are—you and Jenny!' She looked formidable, with her hands on her hips. Again she saw these two leagued together, inhabitants of a different world, who only occasionally seemed reconciled to hers.

'I mean,' said Dahlia stubbornly, 'about the money.'

'What money?' Louisa asked. It was an awkward question, and perhaps, at the bottom of her heart, she hoped for frankness. She could deal with that, but not with the delicacy that made her restive and defiant.

Dahlia hesitated. She was frank, too, but she saw Jenny's face, white and peaked, as it always became when she was frightened, and she compromised. 'If we knew how much we had and how much we ought to earn, it would be easier. It would be more interesting.'

'Well, I don't know myself, and if I did I mightn't tell you. And we want all we can get. And what,' she asked, on a changed note, 'have we got to grumble at? Three lodgers! Well, two and a half, counting Cummings. Seems to me we're doing very well.'

It was useless to tell her that Mr. Allsop was a happy accident. He had booked the rooms for a second and longer week-end, he paid well, and she was more than satisfied.

'And if hadn't been for me, you'd still be at the White Farm!' she said.

'Yes, deadly dull,' Dahlia conceded brightly.

It would not have been dull, Jenny thought: it would have been dangerous. But no. Everything would have been different. Thomas Grimshaw would not have made her cry, and though she must, some time or other, have seen young Mr. Merriman on his horse, he would not

170

have spoken to her. Yes, she confessed, it would have been dull, and she was many years from Miss Morrison's grateful acquiescence.

'So you can be thankful,' Lousia said, ending the discussion. 'And don't forget it's the day for cleaning Miss Morrison's sitting-room,' she added, as she went away.

'I couldn't do it,' Dahlia said guiltily.

'I don't care,' said Jenny, 'and I'm going to keep the half-crown, though I suppose you think it ought to go into the basin.'

'I don't see what difference it makes,' Dahlia replied. But Jenny saw one. The money was her own: she had earned it. It would pay for more than a dozen crossings of the bridge, which she did not mean to cross, or for the little collar and cuffs she meant to make and no one who really mattered would ever see, and she sat, thoughtfully scraping her nail on the milled edge of the coin.

'Let's go and do the sitting-room and throw another duster at Mr. Sproat,' Dahlia said. 'And we must give it an extra good cleaning, because I was rather nasty to her yesterday, and she's forgiven me.'

'She would!' Jenny said.

'Yes, but she didn't. Not in a Christian spirit. Nicely. What awful relations she seems to have,' Dahlia said, taking the framed photographs from the mantelpiece and laying them on a chair when they were dusted. 'We're lucky not to have Aunt Sarah and Uncle Albert in the kitchen. That's another advantage, Jen. We come of people who don't waste their money on photographers.'

'We come of people,' Jenny said grandly, 'who have their portraits painted by Gainsborough, in high-waisted dresses and scarves round their heads.'

'Well, we have handkerchiefs round ours now—to keep the dust off! Look at this one with the side-whiskers! But I won't make fun of her friends. She's going to give us a treat. A real treat, not just being useful and pretending you enjoy it better than anything else. She's going to take us to a pastoral play in the Gardens.'

'When?' Jenny said quickly.

'I don't know. Next month, I think.'

'It's sure to rain,' Jenny said. 'But it's very kind of her.'

'She's going to get the tickets this morning. She was quite excited when she told me about it at breakfast. She's not sure whether we should go in the afternoon or the evening, but she'll decide on the afternoon. Better for young girls! And whether it should be *Twelfth Night* or *As You Like It*. She told me who wrote them and then blushed. Just a slip! So, holding the teapot, I did that sloppy bit about love for her, with heaps of expression. It's funny how I remember it.'

'Who could forget it? "If music be the food of love—" ' Jenny began.

' "Give me excess of it!" ' Dahlia cried, with an emphatic hiss, throwing Miss Morrison's work-bag on the top of the photographs.

'We haven't had any food of that kind since he died,' Jenny said sadly.

'And a good thing, too, because we haven't anyone to love. You never will look on the bright side of things. And I didn't like the concerts any better than the old churches. I used to get fidgets in my feet.'

'And those were the times when he was perfectly happy,' Jenny said, and she thought of her father, sitting between his daughters, his eyes shut, his head turned a little sideways, his motionlessness giving a strange effect of flight. 'Forgetting—and remembering,' Jenny said.

'And that's what you're doing,' said Dahlia, and she looked with amused impatience at her sister, who was like a rebellious young nun in her grey overall, her head bound with a sad-coloured handkerchief. 'You're so busy remembering that you're forgetting to help. If you want to be sentimental you can dust the books. You must earn your ticket for the play. It's her nice, genteel way of giving us half-crowns.'

This was not Miss Morrison's view of her generosity, nor did she wish to educate these girls. Dahlia's somewhat embarrassingly expressive recitation had reminded her of the unenlivened teaching of her own governesses, and checked any tendency to think herself intellectually superior. Her impulse was to give pleasure and to celebrate her painful but salutary catharsis. She was rid of thoughts and feelings which were of no use to her and she had literally waked to rejoice in the silence of her mental alarm clock. She could still do good, she thought simply, but she would do it in her own way: she would no longer be driven to it in a desire for human approbation: she would not feel that time was lost unless it was dedicated to someone's or something's improvement, and she dressed slowly and sauntered through the streets and felt that life was different and she was a changed woman: but she was not greatly changed, and, involuntarily, through habit, her steps quickened. There was the bazaar committee in the afternoon, and Mrs. Doubleday to be frustrated: there was a call to be made on one of her ailing girls, and a tactful interview to be managed with the employer of another: there was her anxiety for Mr. Sproat's welfare to be reconciled with her affection for Dahlia. She was determined to love Dahlia, a task which should not be difficult, and to bring as much happiness as possible into her life and Jenny's, but it was impossible to approve of such a wife for a clergyman as Dahlia would be, or, if she was going too far in her surmises, impossible not to suffer at Mr. Sproat's light conduct. Other men might waylay a pretty girl and talk to her without arousing criticism, though Miss Morrison was herself of those who are quick to discern serious intentions, but poor Mr. Sproat was expected to clothe himself in absolute and permanent discretion when he donned his black coat, and she did not know whether to hope he was frivolous or serious, for his character was endangered in one case and his future in the other.

She pondered these things as she tripped along, but the prayer uttered half-heartedly in church and undeservedly answered last night, was confirmed under the summer sunshine. She was delivered from envy and covetousness, but she was still convinced that she would have fitted Mr. Sproat as a purely spiritual mate.

He was not in need of one, and his black coat did not reproach him, for he was serious and he thought Dahlia must realise his eagerness to know her, even with such slight proof as he had given. He did not reckon with her ignorance of his austere habits and her indifference to everything concerning him except his possible practical use. To his astonished self his conduct almost amounted to a declaration, and this was Miss Jewel's judgment of his behaviour.

After she had seen him walking down Beulah Mount with Dahlia, and lingering in front of the house, she had hard work to fulfil her ordinary duties. Watching her neighbours had long ago become automatic: distrusting and hating the Rendalls had been a pleasure: scheming against them, as was now necessary, constructing scenes of their past and foretelling their miserable future, was a preoccupation which made her careless of the difference between salt and sugar in her cooking, and almost callous to the dishonesty of tradesmen. Miss Morrison had become an ill-used angel for whose sake Miss Jewel would willingly have parted with her lodger: she was living, poor thing, in what was no better than a bad house, and, at the proper time, she and Mr. Sproat should be enlightened. The voices of the girls, coming clearly through the windows, had no charm for Miss Jewel's ears. These two were the offspring of the barefaced, bare-armed, handsome hussy who had unsuspectingly changed Miss Jewel's life into an exciting drama: and who their father was, she told herself, she would rather not inquire, but she was willing to outrage her inclinations in this matter and in others related to it.

With his name painted on his cart, Thomas Grimshaw saved himself a little money in taxes and Miss Jewel a good deal of trouble, which, to be sure, she would not have grudged, and, all unknown to one another, there were three people from Beulah Mount who crossed the river on the next Saturday afternoon: Mr. Cummings and Miss Jewel by the suspension bridge, and Jenny by a longer and more devious route.

She went down a zigzagging path cut in the slope below Beulah Mount, until she reached the road that went parallel to the river, and here she stood for a while and watched the traffic on land and water. She would go back soon, she told herself, but her will was in her feet and they led her over the dock bridges until she was in the other county and she could look back and see Upper Radstowe rising in coloured tiers. It was a sultry, sunless day, threatening a warm, enervating rain: the sky was grey and there was no sparkle on the water, but the roofs and trees and gaudy tramcars, the paint and red rust of ships and their drooping flags, gave to the scene a brightness it never entirely lacked.

'I'll go back now,' Jenny said, pretending she had seen what she came out to see, but again her feet were wilful and they drew her slowly up the long hill bordered by trees, through which she could see the windows of her home. She was level with them now and they seemed to look at her rather anxiously across the wide space

175

between the shores, and she wished the house had an arm long enough to reach her and strong enough to draw her back, but all it could do was to watch her with this anxiety and with entreaty, and soon she was beyond the range of its eyes.

She did not see him at first when she stood in a field where the buttercups looked a little tarnished and the daisies' starched collars had lost their freshness, but, as she advanced, she saw him at the gate where they had parted. He was leaning over it, watching the road which was travelled on this day by Thomas Grimshaw, and Miss Jewel and Mr. Cummings, and it was his dog who gave him warning of Jenny's approach.

CHAPTER XXII

EVERYTHING was different in the dimmed field. He did not come towards her with a jingle and a faint creaking of leather over the soft turf. He came like an ordinary mortal, with a spaniel at his heels, and before they were within speaking distance she had readjusted her conceptions of him. He was a human boy, not a young god, and he had waited for her with as much doubt as she had felt in seeking him and knew a relief, like hers, from disappointment and humiliation.

'I was afraid you wouldn't come,' he said.

'I was afraid you wouldn't,' she said guilelessly.

He was as shy, at first, as she was, but the dog was useful, making a text for talk about other dogs and horses. These were Cyril Merriman's subjects and Jenny was content to listen, because she liked his voice and the movement of his lips and because she had no subjects of her own. When she searched her mind, she saw danger in almost everything she might want to say; she had to be a little ignorant about this district she knew so well: she had to be vague about all her doings, and it was reassuringly easy, though disappointing. He showed none of her curiosity, none of her skill in getting information about his daily life, and, gradually gaining courage, she passed on some of her father's boyhood experiences among the things that Cyril Merriman understood. He learnt what she told him and no more: he did not know how much he was telling her. No one, with eyes to see her grey ones fixed on his face, could have doubted her interest in his dogs and his horses, his travels in the colonies during the last two years, his present occupation of overseeing his father's estate, but her imagination and her quickened perceptions filled in and coloured the outlines he gave her. He loved the country, particularly the part of it his family possessed: he was a practical and enthusiastic farmer: he had a friendship with his father and admiration, but not much liking, for his mother. Music and books and pictures did not exist for him, though she was sure he enjoyed a good tune on a gramophone and read the sporting papers and appreciated a lifelike representation of animals and country scenes: and, with shameful disloyalty to her old beliefs, she decided that this was how a man should be. It was better to be able to guide a plough than to know what the poets said about nature: better to recognise the note of a bird than to distinguish the motifs in a symphony: and skill and fearlessness with animals were more endearing qualities than a fine taste in architecture and pictures and a sensitive reaction to every form of beauty. Jenny was a sudden traitor to the causes she had upheld without much fervour. A world like Cyril Merriman's was the one in which she could be at happy peace. He had the old house, the lawns and trees of her desire. He had work, but he had ease and leisure, beauty surrounded him as naturally as air and was as little consciously regarded. This simplicity of acceptance would have been hers if her lot had been that of the women of her father's house. She did not breathe easily on the heights or value the toil of reaching them. Softly undulating country, sunshine and flowers, were what her nature craved and, turning her thoughts into pictures, she saw gaily-cushioned chairs under the summer trees, and toys scattered on the lawn: she heard the stamping of horses in the stable yard and the barking welcome of dogs, and felt an arm round her shoulders and a light kiss on her hair. She wanted, more than anything, she told herself, to feel safe: safe in love and free from surprises and the need for the cunning she was using while she listened and he talked. And she could get safety if she resigned the other things—her hope of such a life as she had been picturing and her friendship with this boy. She would be safe in the tea-shop with Kitty and Fanny.

Those bulging eyes in Beulah Mount had been rightly anxious when they watched her. It was folly to sit here on a grassy bank with Cyril Merriman. Friendship implied frankness and when it became necessary to be frank, when she had summoned up her courage, the friendship would be gone in the same instant.

'I mustn't stay,' she said, standing up and, when he asked if he might go with her she shook her head, and felt a little impatient, a little scornful of his acquiescence.

'But you'll come again.'

'I don't know,' Jenny said slowly.

'Ah, but you must,' he said. 'If you don't, I'll have to search all Radstowe for you.'

'I'll come again,' she said quickly. She had determined to be wise, but she could not have him looking for her: and it was sweet to hear him. She felt the tell-tale tremor of her chin, and, as though that sign of weakness had emboldened him, he said: 'I want to know where you live—Jenny Wren.' There was a change in the voice he had kept so friendly. 'I want to know where you've built your nest. I'm rather good at finding nests, and I'll find yours.'

'No, I'll show it to you—some day,' she said.

This was not friendship, she thought, with awe. There was a change in his face, too. There was a queer whiteness round his eyes, and the eyes themselves had lost some of their colour, and she knew he wanted to kiss her. This must be love, her heart whispered, and love could be trusted with all secrets and all shames.

'Don't look!' she begged. 'I'll show you.'

'To-day, then.'

'Not to-day.'

'Why not?' he asked, coming a little nearer. After all, he was not acquiescent, and she thought the more of him. 'Why not?' he repeated, but he was hardly thinking of what he said. He was deciding that he must not kiss her.

'Because,' she said, looking about her, 'I want to-day to be just what it has been. I want it to end here.'

'Only if you promise to come soon. Come to-morrow!'

Jenny laughed. He had hold of her hand, playing with her fingers, moving them in turn, backwards and forwards, like a child who insists on attention. 'I'm not going to wait till Saturday,' he said.

'Not on Saturday. But I don't know when I can come.'

'Then you can write to me. If you don't promise to write to me I won't let you go without me.'

'But—' Jenny said again. 'But—' She became aware of the greyness of the sky and she heard the sound of traffic beyond the field and its fringe of trees. The sun was not shining on this meeting, the wheels rumbled ominously, the flowers looked daunted, the leaves of the trees were flaccid under the damp heat, the heifers in a corner of the field—the heifers and the field belonging to his father—were all lying down and chewing sulkily. 'I don't think it's a good day for a promise,' she said. 'It's not a kind sort of day.'

'It's the kindest day,' he said, 'if you don't spoil it.'

'On Thursday then,' she said wearily and, seeing the slight hardening of her face before she dropped her head, he cried, 'You're not angry, are you? I don't want to badger you, but I do want to see you!'

The words sounded childish in her ears. 'On Thursday,' she said again.

'You're not happy,' he said accusingly. 'Have I made you unhappy?'

She looked up. 'You? No!' she said, and she turned and ran from him, but she stopped once to look back and wave a hand.

She wanted to run and run for ever, wearing out a heart that was filled with rage. Slowly, as she answered his questions, that anger had risen in her, like dark water welling up and threatening to overflow the bounds of her control. Her rage was against her circumstances and the people who had imposed that suffering on her. She wished she had never seen him. She had told herself love could be trusted, but it was Jenny Wren he was beginning to love, not Jenny Rendall, and, in the sudden maturity of this moment she saw that he was infinitely younger than she and realised that she would dare to tell a man what it would be hard to tell a boy. It would not hurt a man. He would know what to do with it. He would put it in its place, even though he might decide that the same place was not for him. Even here, she thought, she was unlucky.

Jenny ran fast. She ran by Miss Jewel and did not see her. She was wishing Cyril were a man as old as Mr. Sproat, but not like Mr. Sproat: like no one but himself. She loved his golden-brown skin and his eyes and the way his lips twitched before he smiled. Her pace slackened as she thought of him, but still she saw nothing on the road. She had far outpaced Miss Jewel: she had missed Thomas Grimshaw, who turned in his seat to look back at her, and did not notice a little woman in a tight black coat, for he was very much interested in Jenny and wanted to know whether she meant to cut him and why she ran so fast. Was she trying to overtake young Cummings, whom he had passed near the bridge? She moved well, that girl, he thought, turning again, with her head up, her shoulders back, and an easy stride from the hips. He had a trained eye for breeding and he saw and resented, while he admired, it in her.

He touched his hat to Cyril Merriman who walked towards the village with a dog at his heels. There was no need to touch his hat. He was not a tenant: he farmed his own land, and he was a thorn in the flesh of these people who were as greedy for land as he was, and hated the sight of his small property in the midst of theirs. They had made an offer for the White Farm, but he would not take it. He could afford to lose a bit of money for the sake of thwarting them. Nevertheless he touched his hat, and young Merriman acknowledged the salute with a lift of his hand.

Thomas allowed his trotting horse to fall into a walk. He had plenty to think about and time to spare. He had stayed in Beulah Mount only long enough to ring the area bell and leave an egg-box outside the door, and, when Louisa opened it she would find it empty. That, he thought, would give her a nasty feeling, and she would be sorry, too, not to have the eggs, for she was a ready taker, if a bad giver. That sinister little joke gave him a good deal of pleasure. He was not an ill-natured man, but he had to hit back when he was hurt. She would learn to come to heel, like that spaniel of Merriman's, and a little humiliation would do young Jenny no harm either, but he could not help feeling an angry humiliation himself when he admitted that his marriage to her mother would be the bitterest medicine she could take. And she should have it: he was determined on that. His love for Louisa was a puzzle to himself. With varying intensity, with lapses of casual unfaithfulness, it had lasted for nearly twenty years; its endurance appeared to him as an irrefutable claim on her and his desire was sufficient reason for its satisfaction.

Slowly he drove home, and slowly Jenny was walking across the bridge. Cyril Merriman's face had come between her and her anger. She had to linger while she thought of him and recovered the touch of his hand on hers, and she recovered it with an exquisite physical delight which she had not felt at the actual, troubled moment, and, standing still and lifting her hand from her side, she seemed to give it to him again, limp to his will. Her lips parted, her eyes half closed, and, taking a light, sobbing breath, she felt a slackening of her whole body and a sinking into semi-consciousness as it was gathered into his. This was the experience of an instant, but it left her shaken. She had not known that she, that anyone, could know such an emotion and she saw that it was terrible, like a great wind lifting her from the earth, or a smooth, towering wave engulfing her without a sound. She had thought of love as security, companionship, ceaseless happiness in the presence of another and in the knowledge that she was perfect in another's eyes. She had seen it as the warmth and brightness of summer and the cosiness of a stormy night spent by a glowing fire, and over all there had shone a romantic light, such as had illumined Cyril when he rode towards her a week ago.

She was wiser now, and though she was afraid, she was also emboldened with the calm courage of helplessness. She could not keep her feet in a mighty wind or pit her tiny strength against a swooping wave. She was relieved of responsibility, and in her young mind there was a vague idea that if it had been possible to offer resistance, it would have been wicked to renounce a free and lovely gift.

CHAPTER XXIII

SHE rehearsed what she would say to him. It seemed easy now, with four clear days in front of her and a belief in the overwhelming power of love. She would tell him about her father and the lodgings. And it was not necessary to say more: it was not even right, for though Thomas Grimshaw's friendship with her mother was an unpleasant fact, the rest was guesswork, and, she decided proudly, it was not Cyril Merriman's concern. He should know Jenny's name, he should know where she lived, for she owed him this by virtue of the allegiance her mind and heart had given him. And how simple it would be to say, 'I'm Jenny Rendall. My father was a writer, but he's dead and we haven't very much money, so we keep lodgings in Beulah Mount.' There was no shame in that: there was, indeed, a little suggestion of Cinderella in the story, and her prince would not be outdone by the one who had made no trouble about the ugly sisters. And her mother was beautiful. · She was ignorant, but she was free from any strivings after a false gentility, and he would see and accept her as she was. And perhaps, after all, she and Dahlia were wrong about the past. Perhaps those old hints and bits of gossip were merely maliciousness and jealousy on the part of people who saw a woman, much handsomer than themselves, married to a man of superior station. She wondered she had not thought of that before, and she walked more quickly and saw the windows of her home twinkling in the sunlight. They did not look anxious now—they looked amused. Were they laughing at her, or smiling benevolently and applauding a saner mental attitude? It was the one she had adopted ardently before she descried the sturdy figure of Edwin Cummings ahead of her. He was returning early. He would have to sit in the kitchen. She had no doubt that this was why he had curtailed his walk and, for a daunted moment, she saw the family group with Cyril's eyes. But they were kind eyes; they might sadden for her, but they would never be scornful. And she called gaily to Edwin, who turned and waited.

'I went for a walk, after all,' she said.

'So I see.'

'But I didn't know I was going till I started.'

'Till after I'd started, you mean.'

'No, I don't. I started first.'

'Then I don't know how I missed you.'

'You must have been very careless,' she said gravely.

'Well, I saw everybody else. I met the chap who brings the butter.'

'Driving?' Jenny asked quickly and, with her mind's eye, she measured the heights of the dog-cart and the wall round the field and the thickness of the trees.

'I've never seen him walking. And I met that little body from next door. I think the stone's all right,' he added.

'You mean Miss Jewel?' Jenny asked in a low voice. 'How horrid! What was she doing in my part of the country?'

'Coming out of the post office, when I passed her. He's worked that stone better than I thought he would.'

'Yes, it's lovely,' Jenny said absently. 'I didn't see her. I didn't see you, or Mr. Grimshaw.'

'You haven't lost much,' he said.

'No,' she said coolly. She was hoping Thomas Grimshaw and Miss Jewel had been as blind as she was, but she entered the house with an uneasy feeling in her breast and stood stock still in the hall. From below there came a murmur of voices: in the umbrella-stand there was a strange umbrella with a black crook handle.

'She's come!' Jenny said, and she looked at Edwin with all her woe in her face. 'I knew it would be a black one,' she said, and her lips quivered and then drooped. 'A black one with a crook.'

Not so very long ago Edwin Cummings would have wanted to understand Jenny's trouble before he decided whether he could sympathise, but now, with his decision not to set his heart on her, but to regard her as an exquisite museum piece, far beyond his means, he could treat her with more detachment and try to understand why her designer had made her as she was, and he went nearer and said quietly, as though she were a baby: 'It's an ugly umbrella, but it can't hurt you, can it?'

And she forgot that he was a young man in a bookshop who must keep his distance, and she said simply, 'I don't know. Stay with me. I'm frightened.'

He had the wisdom not to answer. He knew she was not speaking to Edwin Cummings, but to something he represented. He could not deceive himself about that, for her manner was perfectly impersonal. Then she looked round the hall and said, 'And there's nowhere in the house where you and I can sit.'

Mr. Cummings was prompt. 'On the stairs,' he said.

'Yes, just for a minute.' She took off her hat and rested her head against the wall. 'I suppose you never have these feelings.'

'No,' he said. He did not know what they were, but he was sure he never had them.

'Warning feelings. I knew she'd come. But why has she chosen to come to-day?'

He shook his head. He was being very careful, like someone who listens to another talking in his sleep and knows he may surprise a secret to which he has no right—and Jenny's voice had the monotonous tone of a dreamer. But Edwin was not in search of secrets: he was enjoying the privilege of receiving confidences.

'There wasn't a breath of air,' Jenny said in her dull voice, 'and the buttercups were such a funny colour. And then Miss Jewel, and now this.'

'The umbrella?' he ventured to ask.

'Well, yes, it's part of her. I always saw her with an umbrella. She's in the kitchen. I'll have to see her. I'd better go now, I suppose,' she said, hoping to be contradicted.

'Well, if I were you, I wouldn't. Not just yet. I'd go and lie down for a bit. You're tired, aren't you? You might go to sleep.'

'I'd love to go to sleep. Do you think that would be a sensible thing to do, or do you really think I ought to go downstairs?' A little animation returned to her voice. 'Because I always want to put things off and I'd made up my mind I wouldn't. I'm not very brave,' she explained.

Edwin's principles struggled with his desire to please her, to pander to this soft mood in which she asked his advice and would probably be obedient to it. 'Better go down,' he muttered, risking her favour in the cause of courage.

She rose reluctantly, but stood still when she heard steps on the kitchen stairs. Mr. Cummings discreetly disappeared and Jenny waited, recovering her wits and wearing a definitely Rendall expression, only to find it wasted, for it was her mother who appeared and beckoned her into Mr. Allsop's sitting-room.

'I thought I heard you come in,' she said. 'Your aunt's here.'

'Which aunt?' Jenny said perversely. If she had to be brave she need not be agreeable.

'Oh, for goodness' sake don't start like that! You know very well it's Sarah. No sooner were you and Dahlia out of the house than she came—in a cab, if you please.'

'With a bag?'

'It's a small one,' Louisa said propitiatingly.

'There's no room for her.'

'She'll share my bed, and it won't be the first time, so you needn't pull a face. She's not asking to sleep with you. But you've got to come down, Jenny. I've had about three hours of it and my head's turning. Sarah never speaks but what you wonder what she's after, and,' Louisa said rather pathetically, 'I don't like it. She's told me there's dried metal polish on the knocker, and she's had a look at all the rooms and sort of smiled at them.'

'Well, let's go and sort of smile at her,' Jenny said.

'Yes, but you're not to be rude, mind.'

'I'm never rude!'

'Come on, then. She'll get a surprise,' Louisa said proudly, and at these words Jenny renewed her wish to put her head on that broad shoulder and be comforted with a love that was enduring, though it was inarticulate, and would listen, though it would not understand.

But Louisa was not altogether without understanding. 'I don't want her no more than you do, Jenny,' she said.

'Then I don't mind so much.'

'But we've got to put up with her.'

'I wonder why.'

'Well, because—' said Louisa. 'And she'll be going to see Albert. Him and her were always pretty thick together, and she doesn't like me. Never did, from a child.'

'I expect it's because you're beautiful.'

'Oh, go along with you!'

'And she's ugly.'

'You've never set eyes on her.'

'But I know exactly what's she's like. I make people

up,' Jenny said, and she took a deep breath which fell with her next words, 'and they come true.'

'Well, if Sarah hadn't been born long enough before you started that silly trick, I'd say you might have found a better use for your time.'

Jenny laughed: she made a movement towards her mother who did not know how to meet it, but they were together in spirit when they went into the kitchen, and Louisa, standing aside, to give her daughter a better entrance and to watch its effect on Sarah, was disappointed to see nothing more than an amiable smile on her sister's face. She had forgotten that where she had seen one person, Sarah had seen a hundred. Sarah had lost the capacity for surprise, after many years of living in other people's houses and though she could produce the effect of it, at the discovery of an under-servant's misdemeanour or the condescension of her superiors, it was no longer a natural impulse.

'So this is little Jennifer,' she said, with a trace of her native accent, and she arranged her mouth for a kiss, but Jenny had her hand out and her arm was like an iron bar. She would not be kissed except by force.

At this rebuff Aunt Sarah's expression changed a little, and Jenny, the tender-hearted, said hastily, 'We don't kiss much in this family.'

'Then you're not what your mother was at your age,' Aunt Sarah said pleasantly. 'But let me see. You'd be younger than Jennifer is now, wouldn't you, Louisa?'

'I was once,' Louisa said, and her face wore the closed look with which Jenny was familiar.

'Ah, you know when I mean! Never mind! It was a pity at the time and an upset for us all, but it's long ago. We mustn't tell the girls tales about their mother! And this one doesn't look very well. She hasn't got your colour, Louisa. She's been running about all the afternoon,

189

enjoying herself, I fancy, and it doesn't do on a heavy day like this. No, she doesn't favour you. She must take after her father, and that'll be a comfort for you, dearie.'

'Yes,' said Louisa, 'it is.' She looked at Jenny and there was a faint smile on her lips. 'I expect Mr. Cummings will be wanting his tea. You'd better go and tell him to come down.'

'I'd like to see the gentleman,' Sarah said.

'You'll have to, whether or no,' said Louisa.

'And that's because you've made a mistake with your rooms, Louisa. Bedrooms they can't be expected to share—'

'No,' said Louisa dryly, 'I don't fancy Mr. Cummings and Miss Morrison taking to the notion.'

Sarah lowered her lids in disapproval of jesting when business was under discussion. The effect was to make her face strangely blank, for her eyes, brown like Louisa's, but neither bright nor soft and much too near her nose, contrived to give liveliness to a melancholy face in which the long chin occupied an unfair amount of space.

'And I don't know,' Louisa went on, 'which of them would mind it most.'

'Don't be silly, Louisa. We know they can't share bedrooms, but sitting-rooms they can and should. If you'll take my advice—'

Louisa did not stay to hear it. She was following Jenny up the stairs and she called her name with urgency in her voice.

'Jenny!' she said. 'About that kissing.'

'I couldn't kiss her.'

'No, no. I always think she's like a sheep that's been dressed up. You couldn't be expected to kiss her. But of course I kissed him and he kissed me. She'll bring it up again—you see if she doesn't—so I thought I'd tell you. She'll always bring up anything she knows against you.'

'Then we must be careful not to let her know things. If there are any,' Jenny added hastily.

Louisa made no reply to that: perhaps she did not hear it. She did not hear a knocking at the area door until Jenny turned to answer it, and then she said, 'Let Sarah go. It's the groceries and she'll like looking at them. Yes, you'll hear about that again and she'll make the worst of it. It's easy to do that, and I wouldn't like for you to be thinking harm about it. So I thought I'd tell you. He was the young squire, and they found out, and there was trouble. They were afraid he'd marry me and I ran away from home, to Radstowe, to an aunt I had. There was no sense in staying. Nothing but misery for the both of us, for he was fond of me, Jenny, and I was fond of him. I wouldn't have cared if he'd married me or not, but he was good: there was no other way for him. And it wouldn't have done.' She paused and added, 'It doesn't do.'

She had been passionately loved by two men of different breeding from her own, and it was her good fortune to have married the one for whom she did not care and kept the romance of her first love unspoilt by subsequent disaster.

'It doesn't do,' she repeated. 'I know full well your father used to see my aunt each time he looked at me. He couldn't forgive me for her. And it'd have been the same with me and the young squire. But I've never forgotten him. He was good, Jenny, so I had to be. And he's what I like best to remember, except that I ran away from him.'

If her mother had been a different woman, Jenny might have believed that some maternal prescience had inspired her to tell that story. Though the cases were not parallel, they had likeness enough to demand a warning. In each there was an aunt to make a dark background for a young figure, but Aunt Sarah need not become apparent to people who would be unable to forget her, and Jenny was thinking more about her mother, the softness in her manner and her eagerness to preserve from Sarah's soiling tongue what had been beautiful in the episode. She saw a slimly rounded Louisa sitting with the young squire on the sheltered bank of a stream, the sun shining on the water and her bright hair; a Louisa who had not married Sidney Rendall or known Thomas Grimshaw; who was young and innocent, listening to her lover's words and determining to leave, because she loved, him. And then she had married Jenny's father. Why had she done that? Why had she not run away from him, too? Was it because she was beyond caring what became of her?

'I couldn't do a thing like that,' Jenny said, shaking her head at her pale reflection. 'I could never marry anybody else,' and, as she smoothed her hair before she went downstairs, she was glad she was not beautiful. She would have to be loved for qualities more difficult to forget, or to resign.

It was a strange gathering in the kitchen that evening, and she watched and listened, with the acuteness and the detachment of a feverish patient. She missed nothing, but she had a sensation of being somewhere else, and all these people were busy with her future, and she, being absent, was helpless to prevent them. She saw her mother, who had given her that good memory, but who wore her old sullen look while Sarah talked. There was Mr. Cummings, leaning forward in his chair, enduring the monologue with patience: and there was Dahlia, easy and amused, standing against the wall, half-sceptical of Aunt Sarah's familiarity with the great and rich, who, by her own account, found her advice of value, but willing to hear of the loves and marriages, the extravagance or parsimony of people whose names appeared in the society columns of the newspapers, to learn how often the young ladies changed their underclothes and of what materials the garments were composed, and she gave Jenny a look in gay apology for her vulgar curiosity.

Aunt Sarah's talk was like the smell of a perfumer's shop and Jenny imagined the women of her own house in their cool bedrooms, scented with the flowers in the garden below: dainty women, whose personal niceness and adornment were the result of a mental attitude informing all their actions and making fitness and beauty inevitable in their surroundings. She was composed enough to know that Aunt Sarah's anxiety was to impress her own importance on her audience: she resented the supposition that she and the others would be awed, and there was a nightmare quality in the entertainment until she chanced to meet her mother's glance and saw the slow lowering of an eyelid.

Then Jenny laughed aloud, somewhat disconcerting Aunt Sarah, and Edwin Cummings said abruptly, 'Let's go for a walk.'

'Well now, how stupid of me!' Sarah said, recovering herself at once. 'Here I've been chatting and didn't know you young people wanted to be off together. You run away and don't mind me. I'll do what I can to help your mother. She'll be tired, I expect, both you girls being out all the afternoon. I put away the groceries, Louisa, and I found an empty egg-box on the step.'

'Egg-box?' said Louisa.

'Yes. Empty. Name of Grimshaw on it. I've put it in the larder, or did you want it left to be picked up?'

'I don't know anything about it,' Louisa muttered, going towards the larder, and Jenny said quickly, 'Are you coming, Dahlia?'

'No, I'd better stay. Mr. Allsop or Miss Morrison might want something before they go to bed.'

'That's a good girl,' said Aunt Sarah, 'and, after all, two's company, isn't it?'

Jenny stood still on the pavement for a minute, with her fists clenched at her sides. 'Let's talk,' she said fiercely, 'about things. Not people. Things. Let's talk about your shop.'

Mr. Cummings was ready to oblige her, though he was not in her need of an antidote. He shared her feelings about Aunt Sarah, but people were beginning to have importance for him, and he did not feel Jenny's sickness for something hard and definite and exact, like the shapes of the severest types of furniture.

Aunt Sarah had to be discussed with Dahlia, however, when Jenny went up to the attic and found her sister sitting on her bed with a large box of chocolates beside her.

'Mr. Allsop gave them to me. I do hope it isn't instead of a tip. I hope he doesn't take me for a lady. Chocolates are what I call an extra, not a substitute.'

'Has that woman seen them?'

'No. Have one.'

'Then don't let her. Don't tell her anything. She makes things nasty. The more I see of other people the more I like our mother. She's—sort of innocent.'

Carefully choosing another chocolate, Dahlia said, 'I wonder why he left an empty egg-box.'

'Don't. I'm not going to think of that any more, and I don't believe it. How long do you think she'll stay?'

'Don't know,' Dahlia said, with her mouth full. 'I think she's funny.'

'Funny! She's a bad woman! If Mr. Cummings hadn't been so nice I couldn't have borne it when we went out to-night. Pretending we wanted to be together!'

'Well, Jen, he really does want to be with you.'

'I thought so once, but he's been different lately. I think, when people like you, they're inclined to get rather cross, but he wasn't to-night. He was just friendly. It's very comfortable. It's very comfortable not to mind what anybody says or does when he's there. It's such a rest.'

'What from?'

'From what it would be,' Jenny said after a pause, 'if he was—critical.'

'You mean if he was somebody else, don't you?'

Dahlia did not look at Jenny and Jenny did not answer, but when the light was out she returned to the subject of Aunt Sarah.

'The important thing is not to tell her anything.'

'How can I tell her,' Dahlia asked, 'what I don't know myself?'

'Impossible,' Jenny agreed, amiably but finally.

Aunt Sarah did not want to be told things: her pleasure was in learning them for herself. She had always been curious about Louisa's life and the husband and children she had not been allowed to see. She had been jealous, too, and some of her talk, that first evening, had been directed against the superiority of Sidney Rendall's daughters. They must know that she was the trusted friend of people as good as he was, but the satisfaction of curiosity was not the only object of her visit. She wanted the amenities of a home, and here was one where she should be welcome. She imagined herself inspiring affection in her nieces, and Jenny's sudden laughter had been wounding, but the Sarah Lorimer, who, weeping bitterly, had gone to her first situation in the squire's house, at the age of fourteen, who had been bullied by cooks and snubbed by upper servants until her obvious ability had enabled her to bully and snub in her turn, was not likely to show signs of a pain which subsided with her decision that she could never have cared for Jenny. Moreover, Jenny seemed to have settled matters with the young lodger, and, where no interference was possible, there was no interest for Sarah. Dahlia, who listened and asked questions and looked manageable, was to be her care, but natural affection would always have a secondary place in Sarah's life. Her business instincts were stronger and, as soon as she saw the house, she recognised Louisa's waste of its limited capacity for boarders. There was work here for a capable woman who had left one situation and was hesitating about taking another, and Sarah meant to do it. The house was attractive, the situation was good. It was not the place for young men like Mr. Cummings, but for a collection of maiden ladies like Miss Morrison, who would not be liable to removal, who would share sitting-rooms and pay well and have poor appetites.

'How much do you charge the lady, dear?' she inquired delicately. 'And the young gentleman? Dear me!' Sarah made a gentle clicking noise with tongue and teeth. She knew how to undermine self-confidence, and that, a reconnoitring of the neighbourhood and a discovery of the state of Louisa's finances would be occupation enough for a time. She was a visitor: no limit had been set to her stay, and Albert, she assured Louisa, would expect her when he saw her. But she would not be a burden: she insisted on doing the shopping, and she made a respectable figure when she walked down Beulah Mount in a neat tweed coat and skirt and a monumental hat.

Mr. Sproat saw her, approved of her appearance, and rejoiced in another female lodger for the Rendalls. For Mary Dakin she had the interest of one who had slept under the same roof as Mr. Allsop. Miss Jewel saw and heard her and knew that lodgers did not carry marketing baskets or call their landladies by their Christian names, and she recognised the heavy black hat as the badge of authoritative service. This was a woman who, like herself, would buy economically, manage competently, distrust everybody, and make a success of a house which had been doomed to failure, and the exultation stored in Miss Jewel's lean breast, throbbed less vigorously. This woman would be a formidable enemy, if she were not a valuable ally.

Sarah had heard of Mr. Sproat as the benefactor who had introduced Miss Morrison, and she considered him with an appraising eye, for Miss Morrison was to be the nucleus of the group of spinsters and it would not do to lose her. A glance at the Dakins' windows, which wanted cleaning, a glimpse of Milly's soiled cap, argued little comfort for Mr. Allsop when he married the daughter of that house, and he had the appearance of a man used to comfort and good food. Sarah knew the signs. The nod he had given her, as he stood in the hall and said a few words to Dahlia, before he went away on Monday morning, was the sort of nod she respected: it was accompanied by an indifferent glance, the look of a man who employed people and kept them in their places. That was the proper behaviour for gentlemen towards those who served them, unless you had been in the family for years, and then a little teasing and the use of a nickname were delightful. Sarah had had more of the first kind of treatment than of the second, but in her imagination, and in spite of frequent changes in her ascent to the housekeeper's room of a rich but far from noble family, she was one of those old servants in whom young people of the house confide more readily than in their mother. That was what she wanted Dahlia to do. She was a pretty girl in need of guidance, which Louisa was too ignorant and careless to give her. She would be easily flattered by a gentleman's attention, and though Mr. Allsop had nodded to Aunt Sarah in the correct manner, he had been talking to Dahlia in a different one. Her mother had married a gentleman, but this was a piece of luck not likely to recur, and it would be better for Jenny to look after him next time he came. No one would want to talk to her.

Already she was in control of the household and treating her nieces as members of the staff. She had reached this position when her attention was claimed by the shops, but while her keen eyes were examining the goods and her air of knowing what she wanted was producing it with dispatch, her brain was working on the bigger problem, like a machine conscientiously revolving, though its minder was looking another way. After all, she found herself thinking, as she walked up Beulah Mount with her laden basket, it might be just as well to have both girls out of the way. There were not enough bedrooms in the house but, with the attics occupied by lodgers, at a slightly reduced charge, there would be five spinsters in residence, and perhaps more, if sisters or friends would share a room. That would pay very nicely, and two active, middle-aged women could easily do the work of a house which could not be expected to support a family. Louisa was nothing but a child. She had chosen a handsome-looking house with a good view, but that was all that could be said for her. She was not what Sarah called a good cook, and she was wasteful, and she would have to learn not to throw away the bacon fat each morning, or cut away half the potatoes with the peel. 'I'll have to do the cooking myself,' Sarah thought, 'and Louisa must wait on the ladies.' She would do the cooking and the catering and she would see that there was no more extravagant buying of groceries by the single pound: and here Sarah frowned, for this method might indicate a lack of ready money. She had a little store of her own, not to be touched, not to be mentioned to the improvident, and perhaps, after all, the plan was foolish. She was only fifty and there were at least ten years in front of her when she could be employed and paid by other people, but then, at the end of those years she would not feel like embarking on another venture. No, this was the time, she decided, putting her basket on the step before she opened the door. It was a good door, a good knocker, too, though badly cleaned, and she could not resist removing a glove and scraping at the dried metal polish with a finger-nail, but she was interrupted in this occupation by a greeting. Miss Jewel, standing at the bottom of her area steps, had bidden Sarah good morning and worked her unaccustomed lips into a smile.

CHAPTER XXV

From Monday evening until Friday, Mr. Cummings returned to the possession of his sitting-room, and Jenny had no scruples about lingering there when her light services for him were done. While he read the works connected with his business, or seemed to read them, she sat at the window and watched the progress of the evening. When the blue of the sky faded, the woods grew darker, as though they took the colour into their care and would keep it for the morning: then the sky whitened, like a face blanched by disaster, and slowly drew a black veil across it, but the stars blinked through with their eternal humour. There was nothing to grieve about, they seemed to say: this was a nightly occurrence: sometimes the thickness of the veil obscured them, but they were there, finding amusement in what they saw below, though there were wars and pestilences, troubled hearts and Aunt Sarahs in the kitchen.

'There's a very bright one,' Jenny said in a low voice, 'just beyond the woods. A specially bright one.'

Edwin made no remark. He could see her little head and profile against the window, for it was not yet dark outside, and a few eager stars were early at their stations. It was dark within the room and he had put down his book. Jenny, occupied with her own thoughts, did not recommend him to turn on the light, nor was he anxious to draw attention to himself. He was quite aware that this room was a refuge for her and that, for some reason, she preferred his presence to his absence, though she hardly noticed him, and he doubted whether she had noticed the infrequency of his evening walks or the change in her own behaviour towards him. She had been different since the Sunday of his return from home and still more different since this last Saturday when he had watched her coming across the bridge and seen her stand still and put out a hand. He fancied she was ill and sought support, and he took a few steps towards her, and then he turned and hurried forward. He had seen something he was not meant to see: he was trying now not to go where her thoughts were taking her, but it was impossible not to be conscious of herself. Her capacity for sitting still was remarkable, and, in anyone else her idleness would have been reprehensible. Kitty and Fanny, who worked much harder than she did, always had something to read or something to sew in the evenings. Jenny looked as if she had dropped into Upper Radstowe from some secret habitation of her own and had arrived without her luggage, with none of the odds and ends with which women like to surround themselves, and she did not seem to miss them or to need them. She was not concerned to justify her existence. She existed, and, for Edwin Cummings, this was enough.

'I wonder if there's a bright one shining over us, too,' she said.

'I daresay you could think so, if you wanted to.'

'And that's just what I don't want,' Jenny said. 'Not yet, anyhow. Not till Aunt Sarah goes away.' There would be less harm, then, if a guiding star shone near her home, but, whether Sarah went or stayed, whether the star shone or not, Thursday was drawing near and she wanted it to come and longed to push it back.

'And when will that be?' he asked.

'I don't know. She came with a little bag, but she's sent for her box. A tin one, I expect.'

201

'The tin ones stand a lot of knocking about,' he said tolerantly. 'And, I must say, she's a very good cook.'

'As good as Fanny?'

'Better.'

Jenny turned her head towards him. 'It's a very queer thing,' she said slowly, 'that the only nice remark you've made about us should be about her.'

'I must tell the truth,' he said.

'And it seems to come so easily to you,' Jenny said with polite envy.

'I think she's a nasty woman, if you'll excuse me saying so, but a good cook.'

'Yes, she's nasty. She must be, or she wouldn't have made friends with Miss Jewel. She's been in the house and seen all the rooms and she told us they were spotless. I hate that word. And then she smiled at Dahlia and me in a roguish sort of way.'

'I shouldn't mind her,' Edwin said comfortingly.

'Of course you wouldn't. Why should you? So long as she cooks well. But, Mr. Cummings, do you always tell the truth?'

'I've never had the need not to,' he replied.

'You've never pretended a reproduction was an antique?'

This roused him. 'I should hope not!'

She had not chosen the perfect simile and she tried another. 'But would you own up if the parts that didn't show were different from the rest, different from what the customer would expect?' This was wrong, too. A piece of furniture might keep its defects concealed as it stood motionless against a wall, but no human being could stay in a field for ever. She was not a separate thing. She could not be judged, though she ought to be, entirely for herself.

'You know very well I should, and so would you.'

'Yes,' she said solemnly. And, in a different tone, she

said, 'Put on the light and we'll talk about things again. I'll draw the curtains and shut out the star. The star,' she repeated, looking at him as though she would permit a question, 'and Miss Jewel, too. Oh yes, she goes across the road and pretends to look at the river and the lights, but I think she's watching us. Perhaps she's lonely,' Jenny suggested hopefully, and again she seemed to invite a comment, but Mr. Cummings made none. He opened the illustrated paper he had been reading and prepared to instruct her in the peculiar qualities of the walnut period. He almost forgot his heartache when he was teaching her.

'The period Kitty likes best,' Jenny said. Try as she would to be interested in things, she had to connect them with people, and she looked at the bureau and then at him. She did not know that she was different, but she knew there was a change in him. He was much less ready to talk about himself and his affairs. He was worried about his father and disappointed about his shop, and, as she had told Dahlia, he showed no tendency to be cross, a suggestion of indifference which was a challenge even to a girl whose spirit was across the water, under the brilliant star, and, looking at him almost tenderly, she said, 'If you've set your heart on it, I'll let you have it.'

'I've given up setting my heart on anything,' he said grimly.

'Then I should think you're the only young person in the world who has,' was her reply. And cheerfully, a little mockingly, she added, 'Perhaps you'll start again some day.'

'And what,' he asked, breaking through his reserve, 'have you set yours on?'

'Just being happy,' she said.

It seemed a reasonable desire. It was known to every member of the household, and Edwin Cummings' resignation was simply a short cut to it. Miss Morrison, taught by a wrong deduction from the expression of Jenny's face, believed she had discovered her mistaken choice of paths, and now, equipped with a spiritual outfit for first aid, she was following that of others. Louisa's immediate view of happiness was the departure of her sister, whose company was increasingly oppressive, but her ideas of hospitality were those of her childhood: when relatives came to stay at her father's farm they settled down for weeks, and it was natural that Sarah should send for her box. Dahlia's readiness to enjoy herself and make the best of things was a wise foundation for whatever future might be built on it, the instinctive precaution of a nature far less optimistic than any other in the house. These people were all, consciously or unconsciously, in pursuit of happiness. It was Sarah Lorimer who found happiness in the pursuit, and the difficulties in the way were her pleasure. She was half-sorry to have been helped by Miss Jewel, but Miss Jewel had given no aid but what suited her own purposes. She had an eye as keen as Sarah's. They recognised and distrusted each other's breed, and if Sarah despised Miss Jewel as a little provincial person who had seldom been beyond Radstowe, Miss Jewel detected and disliked the general toleration which was the result of Sarah's experiences. Sarah had not Miss Jewel's abhorrence of sin, and, had she possessed it, she would not have seen that Mr. Sproat was sinning against himself and his landlady when he cast his eyes on Dahlia Rendall. Miss Jewel was wisely silent about him, except to praise him, but she skilfully introduced the subject of Thomas Grimshaw, and she was encouraged to sustain it, and when Sarah ended the interview with the majesty proper to the housekeeper's room, tempered by neighbourliness, she had decided that one middle-aged woman could easily manage her sister's house and Louisa would be happier across the river. There was no occasion for rivalry between the houses. Miss Jewel could keep her precious gentlemen and Sarah would specialise in spinsters.

She stepped back to look up at the house and she felt that access of admiration which comes with the promise of possession. She would pay Louisa a fair rent for it, but she must have it to herself. There was no hurry, she needed a holiday, but she could not be idle. She was doing the cooking of which Edwin Cummings so much approved, and she was always at the door before Louisa had a chance of answering it, thus depriving Miss Jewel of one of her strange pleasures. Louisa appeared less often in the area, affronting Miss Jewel with her bare arms and neck and her air of being in no hurry, of having all the time in the world to waste, and the right to look decent women in the face.

Louisa submitted to Sarah's aggressions, as she had submitted to her life with Sidney Rendall, but she had a feeling that life was repeating itself. Here was another person robbing her of her children. They would not stay in the kitchen, and she did not blame them. Dahlia, who had begun by easing the situation, had quickly tired of it, and, by the Tuesday evening after Sarah's arrival, she had developed an enthusiasm for helping Miss Morrison to make things for the church bazaar. She would have been very well satisfied to listen to more of Aunt Sarah's stories, if she had confined herself to them, but Jenny was right about her. It would not do to tell her anything, and Dahlia was afraid of her own tongue, for Aunt Sarah could make suggestions and ask questions which the unwary might repulse too eagerly or hesitate to answer. So Dahlia escaped when she could and, though Miss Morrison was dull, there was a grateful innocence in the atmosphere of her sitting-room. She did not realise that her mother would feel deserted and, oddly enough, it was Jenny whom

Louisa chiefly missed, and she, her mother thought, was probably sitting in her bedroom and wasting the electric light. But here Sarah was better informed. She had an extra sense for knowing the whereabouts of everybody in the house, and, when it failed her, she made normal use of her eyes and ears. She had a very quiet footfall, and, if she did not see a streak of light under Mr. Cummings' door, when twilight had fallen, she knew he was not alone, for young men did not sit by themselves in the dark, though girls occasionally might.

This was very well, but Sarah liked things definite. 'I think they must have had a tiff,' she said to Louisa on the Thursday night.

'Tiff?' said Louisa, glancing up from her novelette. The stories she read were very much like Sarah's, but she was not impatient of them in print. She did not expect what she called sense in literature, and a semblance to her ideas of truth was the last thing she asked of it. 'I've never known them quarrel,' she said.

'Well, I think they've started. She looked very pale to-night—not that she's a healthy-looking girl at the best of times—and he's gone off for a walk by himself.'

'I don't know what you're talking about,' Louisa said. 'I thought you meant the girls.'

'I meant one of them.'

'Well, I haven't got one that isn't healthy-looking. Dahlia's a picture, and Jenny—'

'Ah, she's like her father, dear. I don't wonder you think a lot of her, and you can't blame young Cummings, can you? And why should you? Dahlia will marry better than that—like you, dear, because she has the looks, but he'll do very nicely for Jenny.'

In Sarah's imagination one of the occupants of the attic had gone already, and, by the time it was needed for a lodger, Dahlia would have gone too, or she would be sharing the basement bedroom with her Aunt Sarah. She was not sure that she would not prefer to have the girl about her, but there was no doubt the others needed settling for their own good, as well as Sarah's own, and she smiled into Louisa's astonished and angry countenance with sincere conviction that her schemes would minister to the well-being of the family. They would not have been perfect to her mind if she had seen them otherwise, yet, though she did not know it, there was very little for her to do. She was to assist in the development of a little drama and to influence it here and there, but the stage was set and the parts were assigned to the actors before her plans were laid.

CHAPTER XXVI

Mɪss Mᴏʀʀɪsᴏɴ hoped Miss Lorimer did not feel hurt by Dahlia's absence. She would be delighted to ask her into the sitting-room, if she would care to come, but no doubt she had plenty to say to her sister.

'Heaps,' Dahlia agreed.

'She seems to be an admirable woman. So business-like!' Miss Morrison said, as she searched among her bright pieces of silk and cloth and tried to remember which one she wanted. 'And so fond of you all!'

Dahlia was dressing two small dolls. She sat close to the table and kept her work on her knee. Miss Morrison was short-sighted: she was busy with her needle-books and her pen-wipers and her pin-cushions. The table was strewn with materials which were to be converted into objects as different as possible from the uses to which they would be put and she could be trusted to attend to her own affairs.

'I can't find that merrythought,' she said. 'I washed it thoroughly this afternoon and I made sure I'd brought it downstairs.'

'Perhaps the cat's had it,' Dahlia said.

'I don't think so, dear. There was no meat on it. I was going to dress it up like a little old woman, for a pen-wiper. These comical little things sell very well and cause amusement.'

Dahlia glanced round. 'It's sitting on the top of that photograph, the one of the gentleman with side-whiskers.'

'So it is!' Miss Morrison's laughter tinkled out. 'I

remember now, I put it there for safety. That's my great-uncle Frederic. I never saw him, but he was always in the drawing-room at home and I think he has a fine face.'

'Was he related to the earl?' Dahlia asked innocently.

'Oh no, dear. Now, where's that cloth? He wasn't even a Morrison, but he married one. These relationships are a little confusing. I'm sorry to say that I started by calling your aunt Miss Grimshaw. Seeing the name on the cart I thought it must have been your mother's.'

'Very confusing,' Dahlia agreed. 'What did Aunt Sarah say to that?'

'I found I'd made a *faux pas*—a false step. She just changed the subject.'

'Silly old fool!' Dahlia cried. She could not endure a duplicity in which Sarah shared. 'Why couldn't she say he was no relation at all!'

Miss Morrison was too much puzzled to object to this abuse. 'But I thought he was an uncle. I thought he must have married another sister, and, when your aunt changed the subject, that there might be a little unpleasantness in the family.'

'There's plenty,' Dahlia said, 'but he's not an uncle.'

'But you didn't— And I made sure—' Miss Morrison began, but she, too, changed the subject. 'Can you see the red and black cloth, dear?'

'Here's the red. I'm using the black, but I shall have finished in a minute. We've known him all our lives. To tell you the truth,' Dahlia said, and she looked rather fiercely at Miss Morrison, 'I let you think he was an uncle because people are so stupid.'

'Thank you, Dahlia,' Miss Morrison said politely.

'They imagine things, but I was stupider to care.'

Miss Morrison's cheeks were pink. It was more difficult than she had supposed to be consistently fond of Dahlia, and she said with dignity, 'No nice-minded person would have thought any harm of visits from an old friend.'

'In our position, we have to be careful,' Dahlia said. She knew she had made another mistake. Her own knowledge had infected her with suspicion of everybody else, and her cheerfulness failed her. She felt something like Jenny's rage against circumstances, and, in this moment of anger with herself and with Miss Morrison, whose lips were pursed and whose eyeglasses waggled, she popped her little dolls on to the edge of the table.

'I think these are comic and they ought to cause amusement,' she said.

Miss Morrison, gazing with distress at the unmistakable representations of Mr. Doubleday and Mr. Sproat, the one rubicund and paunchy, the other sallow and cadaverous, could find nothing to say before there was a knock at the door and Jenny entered. Aunt Sarah was in the kitchen, Mr. Cummings' room was empty, she was tired of weeping in the attic and she came here to be with Dahlia, though she must be with Miss Morrison, too, for she felt lost and cold and shipwrecked: but a sparkle of amusement came into her tragic, red-rimmed eyes when she saw the little figures, and she said admiringly, 'How clever! Who thought of it?'

'Me!' Dahlia said triumphantly. 'I painted their faces this afternoon and I've just dressed them.' She was marching them up and down the table and now she handed one to Jenny. 'You be Mr. Sproat and I'll be Mr. Doubleday. I had to paint a permanent smile on him. It's good, isn't it? I like his fat cheeks: and look, I've made Mr. Sproat's hair creep down his neck, the way it does. Their hats were rather difficult. Take them off and we'll walk them into church.'

'But they haven't got their white things on.'

'No. I'll have to make them a set of those.'

Miss Morrison had turned aside. She believed that all
this was aimed at her and her enthusiasms, but she was
not sure: she wanted to protest against Dahlia's irreverence,
she felt hopeless of making any impression on these young
pagans, and, with her anger, there was a secret pleasure.
Dahlia could not care for Mr. Sproat: she was not worthy
of him.

'I'll preach,' Dahlia said.

At that Miss Morrison spoke. 'Not in my room,' she
said.

'No,' Dahlia said at once, 'I won't. You wouldn't like
it. But you do think they're funny, don't you? I'm not
being rude about them. I haven't made them a bit funnier
than they really are.'

'I believe you could get a living by it,' Jenny said.
'You could do famous people, or people in books, and
I'm sure Kitty Cummings would have them in her shop
and sell them for you.'

'I don't think Dahlia would enjoy that,' Miss Morrison
said in a new voice. 'I'm afraid she would not be so clever
if she were not unkind. I know there are some people
who think clergymen must be funny, just because they're
clergymen, but I see no reason why good men should be
mocked.'

'I don't believe Mr. Doubleday's good, just because
he's a clergyman,' Dahlia said, 'but I'm rather sorry about
Mr. Sproat. He makes a lovely doll, but I know he's as
good as gold.'

'Do you?' Jenny asked doubtfully, but with willingness
to discuss the matter.

'Yes,' said Dahlia, looking at the doll, 'and I'll wash
some of the paint off his neck.'

'And what makes you think Mr. Sproat is good?' Miss
Morrison asked coldly.

Dahlia gave her the full gaze of her brown eyes. 'It's just a feeling I have,' she said.

There was another knock at the door and Aunt Sarah appeared, to inquire, in her best manner, whether Miss Morrison would see Mr. Sproat.

'Hide the dolls!' Miss Morrison cried shrilly. Dahlia slipped them under the cushion of a chair, and Mr. Sproat heard two peals of laughter, one high and silvery, like water falling, the other lower and warmer, like the same water finding its way among mossy stones. He met two girls in the doorway who managed to smile at him with moderation, but he could see they found it difficult, and he was sure they would immediately seek some place where they could continue to enjoy their mirth.

It was a long time since he had heard such laughter. The good, dull girls made responsive noises when they were required: there was a sort of defiance in the delighted shrieks of the girls at the mission, and the laughter of Dahlia and Jenny came nearest, in character, to that of the middle-aged women at the Christmas treat who laughed because they were honestly amused: but the sounds were very different.

There was a look of pleased surprise on the face Mr. Sproat turned towards the door and of regret that the two had gone. He was, in fact, defeated in his object by this departure. Like Miss Jewel, he sometimes crossed the road to look at the river and the lights, and, as he crossed back again this evening, he could see into Miss Morrison's lighted room. She had forgotten to draw her curtains, and his first thought was that her tiresome, modest habits had probably deprived him of many other glimpses of Dahlia, as she sat in the beautiful attitude of a woman sewing, but at the same moment he was making for the Rendalls' door. This was the action of the natural man who was becoming stronger than the cautious curate, but he took advantage of his office when he asked for Miss Morrison.

He had asked for her and he had hardly looked at her: he had given her no separate greeting, and when the door was shut he became aware that something was amiss. She was standing by the empty hearth and one hand rested on the mantelpiece. The framed row of relatives behind her stared severely at Mr. Sproat, but she did not look at him and she was impressive in her unwonted stillness.

'I seem to have spoilt a joke,' he said awkwardly.

'You can share it if you like,' she said, and, acting without thought, under the impetus of all her emotions, she went to the chair and took the dolls from their hiding-place, but one of them she held behind her back.

Miss Morrison was never to analyse those emotions, but the look he had given Dahlia, who was flippant, and not given her, who was serious: the mockery of the two girls, painful in its gaiety and disregard for her: still more, Dahlia's faith in the goodness of Mr. Sproat, had stirred the pathetic little fire she had tried to keep warm for him, even when she resigned him, and it flared up in its last sparks, and she hoped they would scorch him.

'Dahlia has been dressing dolls,' she said, and she handed him the representation of the vicar.

Mr. Sproat was delighted with it. He laughed heartily, a little maliciously, and she knew that some of his enjoyment was at the discovery of Dahlia's cleverness and humour.

'And here's another,' she said, 'for the bazaar. Dahlia thought it would cause amusement.'

His face fell, and, with a valiant effort he pulled it up again. His laughter was rather hollow, and gingerly he laid both dolls on the table. 'Very funny,' he said. For a moment he seemed lost in thought, then he looked up and

213

said, 'I don't think it would do to sell the vicar, but you can put any price you like on me.'

She recognised his heroism and she fancied that this was his declaration of devotion to the girl who laughed at him and a gentle turning of her own spitefulness against herself. She had not known she was capable of it. She saw black regret ahead of her, but, in the meantime, she knew she must try to resume her normal manner.

'Certainly not! It was just a joke. And Dahlia has talent, hasn't she?'

'Evidently,' said Mr. Sproat. He was not thinking much about her comic view of him: they would both have to get used to that. He was facing a future with a young wife who would probably never consent to being confirmed, and finding that he did not mind whether she was or not, and he heard a good deal of laughter in the vicarage clad with creepers and properly supplied with hot water. He had known there would be youth and beauty there: he now knew that there would be a point of view which was not necessarily his own and a humorously critical attitude towards the small happenings of life. He had been right in thinking she was what he wanted: her physical charm was not a disguise: it was, he decided, the reflection of her character. This was a strange conclusion for a man whom she had caricatured. It showed that he was deep in love. He accepted the consequences of his plunge and refused to taste a single bitter drop in the water.

He rose and said good night to Miss Morrison without explanation of his call or apology for his departure, and he found Dahlia sitting on the doorstep.

'Did she show it to you?' she asked at once in a serious tone.

'Which?' asked Mr. Sproat.

'Both,' she said.

He put his hand to the back of his neck. 'Yes, I saw them both.'

'I want to tell you I'm sorry about it because you've been so kind.'

'Kind!' he exclaimed.

'Getting Miss Morrison for us. And I'm afraid,' she continued honestly, 'if you're cross you won't get us anybody else.'

'But I've noticed a strange lady—'

'Very strange!' Dahlia said with a chuckle. 'A visitor. An aunt.'

'And I'm not cross,' said Mr. Sproat. It occurred to him that as far as Dahlia was concerned, it was not worth while to bother about lodgers, but he told her he had hoped the family was now out of its difficulties.

'Do people ever get out, if once they start them?' she inquired earnestly.

'Certainly.'

'I mean by some other way than prayer,' she warned him, and she added quietly, as a simple statement of opinion, 'I don't suppose you've ever had any.'

He was a little ruffled. No man likes to think his path an easy one, but no lover in search of opportunities allows his pride to forfeit them, and he said resourcefully: 'Suppose you tell me about yours. It's a fine night. Let us walk round the hill.'

'The nights,' Dahlia said, on a sigh, 'have been terribly fine lately.' Here was a man seeking her company, here was the summer night, and again the trees were dark and motionless and inviting, but where was the secret, joyful excitement she had imagined? Smiling a little, she stood up and shut the door behind her and walked solemnly with him up the street.

Miss Morrison's curtains were still undrawn and her head rested on her bright silks, in close neighbourhood to Dahlia's dolls. She was not grieving after Mr. Sproat. Even her admiration for his spiritual qualities had been

215

based on misconceptions. He was no more spiritual than other men. She grieved because an interest, an excitement, so small that it might have been allowed her, had been taken from her life, and because she had lost her dignity. It seemed impossible to stay here any longer. Any other place would do as well as this one: any other place would be better, for she felt that every one was as conscious of her folly and her sin as she was herself. She did not know how she could meet Dahlia or endure the remembrance of this night. To hurt him and damage Dahlia in his eyes had been her objects and she had failed in both: she had failed in love and she had not acted like a lady. She felt old and lonely and perfectly indifferent to the success of the bazaar. What did it matter whether she was a Dutch peasant or a shepherdess? Her heart was empty: she neither gave love nor received it and there was no one in the world who cared about her.

She did not know that Miss Jewel, on the other side of the road, was working herself into a passion of pity at the sight of the bowed head.

CHAPTER XXVII

Miss Morrison need not have been anxious about depriving Aunt Sarah of her niece's company. Sarah liked Dahlia and, as a visitor, might have taken a little trouble to secure her affection, but, in her own mind, she was not a visitor and she had plenty of occupation. From the reserve of both girls in replying to questions and their careful disregard of suggestions, she had corroboration of Miss Jewel's hints about Thomas Grimshaw. Sarah cared nothing in the world for Louisa's past, except as it might influence the future, and in that future she was interested. An adept at innuendo, she practised it for pleasure when it was not needed for business, and innocent under-servants had fancied themselves and their families guilty of unsuspected crimes when Sarah went about her peculiar way of satisfying her curiosity. If not meaning to be unkind can constitute humaneness, Sarah was humane. Her imagination was better controlled than Miss Jewel's and it was more limited. It was bound by her own experiences and, as she was in-sensitive, she did not realise that she might be inflicting torture.

This was not what Louisa suffered, but she was made uneasy by sympathetic remarks about her marriage and her loss, and questions about Sidney Rendall's illness and his funeral. She answered with a brevity which might have been attributed to grief, but she had neither the skill nor the desire to make her abruptness emotional. In the past she had tried to make Sarah believe she was as happy as a queen, and she began to wonder whether Sarah had ever been deceived.

'You don't want to talk about it,' Sarah would say sympathetically, and then ask another question which was difficult to answer. Sarah, thought the simpler Louisa, might have been living at the White Farm with them all the time, so deftly did she touch the weak places of the alliance. She discovered that Louisa had never seen the children's school or met or parted from them at the station, that it was Sidney Rendall who chose the very boxes in which their clothes were packed, and saw to it that the clothes were exactly to the school pattern. And here a real sympathy was roused in Sarah: this was insult as well as trespass on woman's province.

'Well, dearie, all I can say is that if it had been me—'

'But it wouldn't have been,' said Louisa.

Sarah let that pass. She was not to be diverted. 'If it had been me, I wouldn't have been too particular about keeping my side of the bargain.'

Louisa felt mentally hemmed in by Sarah, just as she felt physically at bay when Thomas Grimshaw sat in the kitchen and, when he called on Saturday, and was ushered in by Sarah, who had been on the watch for him, the combined pressure was too much for her and she went upstairs and wandered aimlessly about the house where there was no room she could call her own.

She tapped at the door of Mr. Allsop's sitting-room, to make sure he was not within, and, getting no answer, went and stood at the window. There were people passing up and down the road, there was the usual throng of Saturday afternoon traffic over the bridge, but Louisa, who, immured in the White Farm, had thought she would never tire of seeing so much life, hardly looked at it to-day. Her eyes were fixed on the cliff across the water, where

218

the trees were thick with their summer leaves, and she was thinking that everything was different since Sarah's arrival. The girls were anywhere but in the kitchen, and as though, like their father, they could not see their mother clearly through the shadow cast by their aunt, they paid her less than their former attention. She was linked with Sarah in their minds: yet, now and then, there was a puzzling sweetness in Jenny. What puzzled Louisa most was a sense of change in herself. Her body was tireless, but she felt tired and, if she could have filled the house with the friendly, jovial lodgers of her first hopes, the pleasure would have been in the thought of their money, not in their company. There were to have been husbands for the girls among them: now, such marriages would not have pleased her. Young Cummings was a nice lad, but he was not good enough for Jenny. Her feeling, which she could not have expressed, was that both girls must be destined for some specially romantic and lovely future, and she hoped it was a long way off. She wanted to keep them with her. She was giving mental birth to these children, now that they were her own, and the energy she had thought to spend on herself was transmuted into a preoccupation with them, the more intense because she did not understand them. Their unexplained comings and goings she took as a matter of course. Her own mother had never questioned her until troubles arose, and then, indeed, there had been questions enough. Dahlia and Jenny had the same liberty. On Saturday afternoons they were always out: they escaped as Louisa was escaping now, and she sometimes thought Jenny must be doing what she had often done with her father, looking at things simply because they were old or ugly. Though she did not understand the taste, she accepted it as a sign of a different upbringing from her own, and she could well believe that old churches and museums

were tiring enough to change the quality of Jenny's
pallor, but she wondered why they reddened her eyelids. In the evenings she often sat with Mr. Cummings,
and Sarah would come downstairs and knowingly nod
her head, but lately Dahlia had been there too, deserting Miss Morrison and the work for the bazaar, and
she would not have intruded on a pair of lovers.
It was all Sarah's fault, Louisa decided, and even
Miss Morrison was not quite herself, and while this
was a relief to Louisa, who preferred her in an abnormal
state, it was a symptom of the vague discomfort in the
house.

'Well, I dunno,' she muttered. 'I'll have to get rid of
her.'

The girls would come back, wanting their tea, and they
would swallow it quickly and leave the kitchen if Sarah
was in it, and, as she thought this, a little flicker of family
loyalty darted through her breast. Sarah was not as bad
as all that: she might almost be taken for a lady, but
Louisa knew that the girls' objection to her presence
was her own.

'She makes you afraid to think,' was her explanation.
She was now probably learning from Thomas Grimshaw
all she wished to know, and then she might be satisfied
and go and worry Albert.

She was surprised to hear the opening of the area door
and to see Thomas mount the steps and walk down the
street towards the stables where he left his horse and trap.
He had not waited long for her return, she thought, and
she felt a little vexed and uneasy. He was a weariness to
her, but while she had power over him she need not
greatly trouble about the money, and she realised in her
dim way that there was seldom a moment in life when
a favourable circumstance was not accompanied by a
disadvantage.

She waited at the window until she saw him drive by, without a glance at the house, and again she was a little vexed. She wanted to be done with him, but it would be queer to learn that he had done with her, and she looked after his broad back with a sort of jealousy and some satisfaction that, wanting her, he was not seeking consolation in a Saturday night in town. She watched him on to the bridge and out of sight, and she felt a reluctance to go downstairs and hear the comments of Sarah. Praise from her had a way of sounding disparaging and she generally praised people, so Louisa lingered, in a state of uncertain loyalty to Grimshaw, and saw Miss Morrison hurrying home. She looked tired and hot, and Louisa opened the door to her.

'And where's Dahlia got to?' she asked.

'She has not been to the class with me,' Miss Morrison said breathlessly.

'And quite right. You really didn't ought to go jumping about in the heat,' Louisa said, and she looked at Miss Morrison, who was no older than herself, and thought she was a poor, weak thing, with her narrow shoulders and long back. 'You'd better have some tea,' she said.

'Wait a minute, Mrs. Rendall, please. I want to speak to you.'

Louisa followed her into the sitting-room, moving slowly behind the other's agitation, then standing in her unconscious grace, while Miss Morrison first straightened her eyeglasses and then pulled off her gloves.

'And better for the girls, too,' Louisa said, 'to be outdoors, weather like this.'

Miss Morrison's lips trembled. 'They can do what they like in future. I'm going away, Mrs. Rendall.'

'A holiday'll do you good.'

'Altogether,' said Miss Morrison. Louisa's first thought

was that it would be unpleasant to make this report to Sarah. 'You mean we're losing you?'

Miss Morrison bowed her head. Her mind had been made up while she conducted a class of three listless young women who had no more attractive occupation for the afternoon. A larger muster might have given her courage to continue her life in Beulah Mount, but this lack of enthusiasm settled her wavering mind, and she took the first opportunity of making her announcement, lest a second should find her more timid and uncertain. The last week had been very painful. Dahlia's courteous attention had been almost unbearable. Somehow, Miss Morrison divined, she knew that Mr. Sproat had seen the dolls and Dahlia did not look abashed. With her cheerfully distant manner she seemed rather to be sparing Miss Morrison all possible embarrassment, and even pitying her a little. It was a case in which apology would deepen the offence and explanation would be more revealing to herself than Miss Morrison could bear. And there would still be Mr. Sproat, in Beulah Mount, unless he and Dahlia left the neighbourhood together, and she was determined to be the first to go.

'Well, I'm sorry,' Louisa said. 'I hoped we'd got you settled. If you're going somewhere else in Upper Radstowe it'll look bad for us.'

'No. I'm going to travel. I ought to have gone away before, when my dear mother died. I'm not very well. I ought to have a change.'

'There's nothing like a change,' Louisa agreed, and, as she spoke, she wondered if Miss Morrison, too, would be disappointed. 'Oh well—' she said.

'I shall be going at the end of next week, and, of course, I shall pay you what you consider right, instead of notice.' She sank back in her chair. The ordeal was over and there remained nothing more to fear except the awkwardness of her farewells, the question of gratuities, and Mrs. Doubleday's reproaches for leaving the bazaar, after getting her own way about the shepherdesses. 'But I'm not well. I'm afraid I shall have a breakdown,' she said to herself in rehearsal.

As Louisa went down the kitchen stairs she also rehearsed a little speech, but she did not make it. She merely said bluntly that Miss Morrison was going the next week.

'She'll have to pay for the month,' Sarah said sharply, and then, shaking her head and smiling indulgently, she said, 'Oh, Louisa, Louisa, you're not the one for the job. What's she complain about?'

'Needs a change, she says.'

'And I've been doing the cooking myself!' Since her talk with Thomas Grimshaw she was not so set on keeping Miss Morrison as the core of her group of lodgers, but she remarked that it might be just as well to have a few words with her.

'You'll leave her alone!' Louisa retorted. 'She's the right to go if she wants to, hasn't she? The house isn't a prison, is it?'

'Don't use the word!' Sarah exclaimed. 'It makes me feel uncomfortable. I'm worried for you, Louisa. That's the truth of it, and, when I think of the money you owe, and a lodger going, I don't like to hear you talk of prisons.'

She saw an amused and somewhat scornful expression on her sister's face, and understood that suggestions made to a shrinking little servant, under suspicion of theft, were too primitive for Louisa.

'That's only my joking way of putting it, dear, but you're my sister and your trouble's mine. I'll have to get you out of it and I think I can. He didn't strike me as a very patient kind of man, Louisa. He's fond of you, dear, I could see that, and it seems a pity— But there, if you won't, you won't, and we'll just have to buckle to and scrape here and pinch there, until we've paid him. The girls will have to do without their little pleasures, and I'll spare no pains to work the business up for you. I'll stay with you, Louisa, instead of seeking another situation.'

She paused for the gratitude she did not expect to get, and Louisa made no answer. She was thinking of Thomas Grimshaw. He had been quick in speaking of the money, but it was hardly fair to blame him. He must have fallen into Sarah's smiling trap before he knew it had opened, and maybe his hurried departure had been made in anger at himself. She did not want Sarah to stay, but she was a little frightened now about the debts and she had faith in her sister's ability. They would make money more quickly with her help. Moreover, Louisa always gave way before a superior force: it was part of her patience and incapacity, and she knew she was no match for Sarah. It would be impossible to turn her out, if she did not wish to go.

'I'll stay,' Sarah repeated, looking noble. 'And, now Miss Morrison's going,' here she made a clicking sound of distress, 'we'll do what I said about the sitting-rooms. Young Cummings will be glad enough to use the kitchen till he can set up a little home of his own, and the sooner the better, it strikes me, for Jenny.'

'What d'you mean by that?' Louisa asked quickly.

'Nothing particular,' Sarah said, 'but there's nothing like marriage for keeping a girl out of mischief. You know that very well yourself, dear, don't you?'

Louisa let that pass, but her face reddened and she put her hands firmly on her hips. 'If I hear a word against Jenny, or Dahlia, or him—for he's a good, steady lad—I won't have you in the house, Sarah, so now you know. You wouldn't stay if you didn't want, and you'll go, mind, if I hear any more of it. It's my house—'

Here Sarah gave a polite little cough and Louisa left the kitchen, to find, again, that there was nowhere in the house where she could rest.

'Unless it's the girls' attic,' she said to herself, almost tearfully, 'and p'raps they won't mind for once.'

CHAPTER XXVIII

She sat down on the edge of a hard chair, feeling like an intruder, and looked at the neatly-made beds, each with its nightdress-case on the pillows—Dahlia's, a gay one made of cheap lace and silk and Jenny's of coloured linen, worked with her initials—and she knew that each contained a garment of corresponding character. Dahlia, she thought, was more what she had been when she was a girl, though she had never had a nightdress-case, or any apparel but the plainest: Dahlia was pretty and good-humoured and naturally lively and ready for a bit of fun, yet it was Jenny for whom Sarah had expressed anxiety. That, as Louisa knew, might mean nothing more than a wish to create discomfort and a sense of her own omniscience, and it had certainly produced uneasiness, for Jenny was almost as much a closed book to her mother as the ones on the shelves behind her head. Everything in the room—the books, the photographs of school groups, Dahlia's caricatures, a water-colour painting of sea and sand dunes—emphasised her small share in the lives of her children, and they would politely hide their astonishment and, perhaps, their displeasure, when they came home and found her in their room. But she did not move. She wanted to be with them, for they were hers and she had a passionate desire to protect them and a fear that, in her ignorance of all their thoughts and feelings, she could not do it. Moreover, she believed that they had sat in judgment on her and, with their father's courtesy, tried to conceal their sentence of disapproval.

226

It would have been a comfort, at this moment, to have been able wholeheartedly to blame herself, but emotion did not make her dishonest. She thought her offence was small and the world's condemnation out of all proportion to it, yet she would have hated, though she would have understood, such a slip of virtue in her daughters, and, for the first time, she saw a sort of indecency in expecting them to be tolerant of Thomas Grimshaw. She saw that Sarah was the unpleasant solution of an awkward problem. She must make money for them all and free them, and the girls would be patient when they were given a reason.

She was glad it was Dahlia who first returned and asked gaily, with admirable presence of mind at this invasion: 'And what are you doing in our room?'

Louisa appreciated this manner. It was the right one, and she answered in the same spirit. 'Running away from Sarah!' she said, and then she went on quickly. 'Miss Morrison's given notice. We're going to feel the loss, and, before Jenny comes in, I'd better tell you. Sarah's staying, she'll help us, we've got to let her stay. I owe a lot of money to Thomas Grimshaw and she'll help us pay him. The sooner the better. Then we'll go off somewhere else and you and Jenny can have your chance. There wouldn't be any need,' she said persuasively, 'for me to come with you if you didn't want it.'

'And leave you with Sarah!'

'I wouldn't like it,' Louisa admitted, 'but I was never one for standing in a girl's way. Suppose you and Jenny married, it would be the same thing.'

'Yes, suppose!' Dahlia said.

'Well, your aunt's talking about young Cummings for her and she'll have found someone for you before long, I dare say. And anyhow, what's the matter with Jenny? She's not herself.'

'Isn't she?' Dahlia was sitting on the other chair and

trimming her nails, with a towel spread over her dress to protect it, and Louisa watched the operation and felt half proud of her daughter's daintiness and half annoyed.

'And you've not said a word about the money.' It would be better to be scolded than to be in doubt of Dahlia's thoughts.

'What's the good? Besides, we've known for ages. Mr. Grimshaw told Jenny weeks ago. But not how much.'

Louisa had long guessed their suspicions, but that Thomas should have been the source of their knowledge was a blow that benumbed her for a time. She was conscious of a contraction of her whole body, a strange sensation of desiccation, while her mind registered the fact of his treachery, and when feeling rushed back with the colour in her cheeks, it was with so much bitterness of disappointment in him that a more introspective woman might have been persuaded that she had always loved him: she knew, at least, that she had trusted him and his love for her, and there was desolation in knowing that she could do so no longer.

'You might have told me,' she muttered.

'I did try to,' Dahlia said, and Louisa nodded, her lips drooping like an unhappy child's. 'Oh, never mind, never mind!' Dahlia begged and, throwing aside her implements, she knelt down beside her mother. 'It will be better now,' she said, 'when we three are all friends, and we'll work together.'

'I'm no good to you,' Louisa mourned. 'Worse than no good to the both of you. And it's all come together. Sarah and Miss Morrison and him. But I've done with him,' she said, suddenly pushing Dahlia from her and openly wiping her eyes. 'He can come and see Sarah all he wants, but not me. Well, there's Miss Morrison's supper to see to, whether she goes or stays. And, I must say, Sarah looks the kind of woman that would take a

lodger's fancy. Different to me,' she said simply. 'But if
it was only me, surely she'd stay now Sarah's come.'

This humility was painful to the guilty party, who could
not tell what she believed to be the truth. 'Mr. Sproat
will find someone else for us,' she said.

'I did think he might be marrying her, so we'd have
lost her anyway, and now there'll be Mr. Allsop marrying
that Dakin girl and he'll be off, too. We'll just have to
make the best of Sarah. And Jenny'll not have to make a
fuss about it. Where's she got to, this afternoon?'

'I don't know,' Dahlia answered truthfully.

'And where've you been?'

'Into the city to look at a church with a leaning tower.'

Louisa threw up her chin. 'Well, on a day like this! If
it had been Jenny, now, I wouldn't have been surprised.'

'Neither should I. It's some people's idea of amusement.
And I saw other things, you know. I'm always pleased
when I see the ships among the streets. They look like
tall weeds in a pavement. But on Saturday afternoons all
the best shops are shut.'

It seemed her fate to be taken on instructive expeditions,
but she sympathised with the difficulties of Mr. Sproat.
He wanted to be with her and he did not know how to
manage it, and the leaning tower had beckoned him and
offered an educational excuse. Her confidences had been
scanty when she walked round the hill with him and
gave him no pretext for continued counsel, and though
this invitation was one which a more occupied young
woman would have refused, she liked Mr. Sproat, and he
had had his hair cut, and, still better, she liked watching
his shy approaches and wishing she could tell him what
he ought to do and say. She was surprised to find herself
much more interested in the tower than she had been
when she saw it with her father, and her erratic memory,
producing things she had never meant to remember,

229

enabled her to make several intelligent and appreciative remarks. She saw a complacent expression on his face, the one lovers wear when their faith is unexpectedly justified, and at once she confessed to her quotations. He was no less pleased. A father who had taste and education was a valuable possession, even though she had lost him, to a girl with a mother who was an awkward one, and Mr. Sproat commended her for treasuring his words.

'I don't know why I do,' Dahlia said. 'I wasn't listening. I never did. It all bored me so much, and really,' she went on, smiling with the frankness that seemed half mutinous, 'I meant to pretend I'd made it up myself!'

'It bored you,' Mr. Sproat repeated, thoughtfully. 'Then why did you come to-day?'

'Because you asked me, of course.'

'And do you always do what people ask you?'

'If it's a good thing,' she said, with too much gravity to deceive him, and he laughed and said he wished he knew what she considered good.

'Tea,' Dahlia said, and Mr. Sproat found a tea-shop and a quiet corner—which was not what she wanted—and put her into a tramcar when he had to fulfil another engagement. She wondered whether he really had one, but she was not anxious to walk with him up Beulah Mount.

'I'll tell Mr. Sproat to-morrow, if I see him after church,' she said to her mother. 'I'm sure he'll help us.'

'Then he'll have to do it quickly, but I've got some hopes of Sarah. It's not as if she won't be working for herself. She's not said anything about it yet, but she'll soon start bargaining about her share. She won't let the house be empty,' Louisa said, having no suspicion that an empty house was just what she and Thomas Grimshaw wanted. Nothing else, they had agreed, would bring Louisa to her senses.

Remembering her mother's tears, Dahlia could have cried, too, when she had gone, but she did not dwell on the details of that pathetic interview. She was beginning to be impatient for Jenny's return. She could hear Mr. Cummings splashing in the bath, after his dusty walk; his second bath that day, she thought with approval; and Jenny lingered still. She had not, then, been out with him and as safe as Dahlia had been with Mr. Sproat. In the mind of Dahlia there were but two kinds of men: the safe ones, like these two, and the dangerous ones who, so far, only existed in her imagination, but came to life when she looked at the summer night. They had no faces and no definite personalities: they were waiting under the trees, or on the hill where she had walked securely with Mr. Sproat, and one of them was the man she was going to love, and she thought she would love him with rapture, without judgment, with indifference to the faults of character that made him dangerous and wonderful. His eyes would not have the guarded look she had seen that afternoon, nor would he almost shut them, now and then, as though he gave himself a moment's freedom from her charm. This was amusing, in Mr. Sproat, and gave Dahlia a sense of power which she was anxious to exercise on someone else, but not on the real lover. It would be impossible, there would not be time. She saw love as the instantaneous coincidence of two natures, a sort of miracle which it would take another miracle to undo, and productive of a happiness inconsistent with a pale face like Jenny's and quivering sighs.

Dahlia had heard those sighs when she was supposed to be asleep, and they were so separate from her idea of love that she could hardly believe it was the cause of them. But what else, she asked herself simply, could take her sister on mysterious errands, and, in alternation with her looks of woe, give her the appearance of someone secretly enchanted? And it was with just such an air of moving in a magic world that Jenny at last entered the bedroom and gave Dahlia a smile of vague recognition.

'I've been waiting for you for ages,' Dahlia said.

Jenny took off her hat and gloves: even in moments of abstraction her movements were precise. 'Waiting for me,' she repeated, and she seemed to be weaving a little web of sound about her, to keep out irrelevant matters.

'I didn't know where you were and I was worried. Where have you been? Oh, Jen, why don't you tell me? I didn't know, and things have been happening.'

'Happening?' Jenny's voice was different, with an edge of fear on it.

'I wanted to tell you myself. I didn't want you to hear it in the kitchen.'

'What?' Jenny said, with her hand at her throat.

'Miss Morrison's going.'

'Oh! Do you mind? I suppose it's because of the dolls. We were rather rude, and I'm sorry, but I don't like her much.'

'I like her money. And mother told me about the debts. And cried. A little. She was sitting here when I came in. There was nowhere else for her to go. It's very awkward to lose Miss Morrison's money.' She paused. She saw that Jenny was hardly listening, that her mother and Miss Morrison and the money were not present to her mind, but she knew that her next words would reach her. She did not understand this shrinking horror of Aunt Sarah: she accepted it with the rest of Jenny's strangeness.

'So,' she said gently, 'Aunt Sarah's going to stay and help us.'

'Stay? But no, she can't,' Jenny said quickly. 'She can't stay! I mean—then I can't live!'

She dropped on to a chair and, for the second time,

232

Dahlia knelt and put her arms round a sufferer. She knew she could not comfort: she could only hold Jenny tight and put her own cheek against Jenny's wan one. 'Oh, Jen, Jen, Jen,' she said coaxingly, 'what's the matter? You're such a silly. You do exaggerate, you know.'

Jenny's answer mystified her, but it was made with reassuring calmness. 'I don't mind telling lies if they're true,' she said, 'but mine aren't and they're all wasted. And I'm wasted,' she added through trembling lips.

CHAPTER XXIX

Since the Thursday when Jenny set out to tell Cyril
Merriman her name and habitation she had seen him
nearly every day, though sometimes only for a few snatched
moments. She had wept that evening before she found
amusement in Dahlia's dolls, because she had failed in
candour. As soon as she saw him, she knew she could not
let him see Aunt Sarah. Her mother had a right to be
acknowledged and she tried to believe he would accept
her as a simple and beautiful country woman. She was
ignorant, but she was not common. She could be trusted
to meet a friend of Jenny's without the arch glance and
jaunty speeches Sarah would produce, and Sarah's manner
would inevitably affect his judgment of her mother and
herself. Therefore, she thought swiftly, when he took her
hand, she must be wary until Sarah went, and the Jenny
she showed him on this and other days was one she did
not know herself and one who fascinated and puzzled him.

She could have forgiven herself for all the little wiles
with which she kept him off: the offence that lay like a
material burden in her breast was the use to which she
had put Aunt Sarah. There was ignominy in that, but
she had started on it almost before she was aware. He
could not come home with her, she said: she could not
stop for more than a few minutes, because there was an
aunt staying with them at home. She had to hurry back
for attendance on the aunt: she did not want her to see
him—and here she made a little face of genuine dislike—but
quickly, as though he had the power to see, through her

234

mind, Aunt Sarah as she really was, she began to describe some of Aunt Isabel's attributes, and, worse still, some of her possessions, and allowed him to assume that this was the one who was their guest. She drifted from one aunt to the other, and so, proudly, to her father, saved herself from a positive lie and learnt that deceit grows easily in the mind to which it is once admitted. She was ashamed, but she could not retract until years of trust in each other would make the revelation tolerable and something to be laughed at together. And occasionally she thought of Edwin Cummings and his integrity.

It was no wonder she had a pale face and tired eyes. They were both too young and innocent to need any stimulating elusiveness in their love. Almost in the same moment they had recognised each other, and all their instincts were for frank avowal and perfect confidence and Jenny, longing to give him everything, had to ward him off, to keep him at a little distance, but not too far, to play at an uncertainty she did not feel and so postpone his further knowledge of her. She was cleverer than he was, and while she loved him for the ease with which he could be beguiled, by a word or a look or a movement, she felt a maternal pity for his slower wits and a fear of his greater honesty. But it was not hard for him to be honest: his life was set in pleasant, open places, and he knew nothing of dark corners. She dared not let him see hers yet: she could not risk the loss of him until there was less danger.

All this was a mental strain and a kind of torture, forgotten now and then in the happiness of his company and the courteous young respect with which he submitted to her retreats. Sometimes he held her hand, but he had never kissed her before this Saturday when she heard that Aunt Sarah was to stay. Her lies were wasted and she was perjured: her mind was in a confusion she could not clear. She had told herself that when Aunt Sarah

235

went away the lies would be almost true, for Aunt Isabel actually existed and neither of them would be in Beulah Mount. And now Aunt Sarah was a permanency and she would never see him again of her own will, and her memories were ruined by her own cowardice, all except her memory of this one day.

They met in the wood on the side of the gorge, where Jenny had once hidden from Thomas Grimshaw: and when she had gone a few yards down a tiny track, slippery with pine needles, she saw him below her, standing in a small level clearing. The sunlight was on him as he looked up at her and she gave a little stifled cry and stood still. The leaves of the birch trees were like myriads of golden coins held in clusters on silver wands: they moved on a light breeze that gathered and then scattered the scents of summer, and the sunshine brought out the smells of warm earth and resin. The sound of a tug hurrying down the river, the distant clanging of tramcar bells on the road near the docks, seemed to make walls round the wood: the sun was shining, it was high summer, they were in a world of their own and no one else existed. She looked down at him from her high place, like a lady watching her lover from a tower. His head was bare, he had thrown off his coat and looked taller and slimmer without it, and the wind stirred his shining hair and the soft fabric of his shirt. He was as radiant as he had been when he found her weeping. And he looked up and saw her small oval face, very pale against the dark background of trees and slope: her body was bent towards him over the foot pointed for the descent, her arms were slightly raised for balance. She looked as though, with another lift of them, she would leave the ground and flutter down to him, and he opened his own arms. At that signal, careless of where she set her feet, she ran towards him with a speed she would not, if she could, have lessened.

Their hands met and with what to her was miraculous, yet natural, ease, he took the shock of her descent, before his arms went round her. There was no timidity or hesitation in this embrace: their bodies might always have known each other. Her face burrowed into a neck that smelt of clean, sunburnt skin and, with the ecstasy of contact, there was also a deep sense of peace. She was safe: nothing could hurt her: she was wrapped in the exquisite tenderness his youth felt for hers. She could hear tiny woodland sounds through the murmuring of his voice, calling her foolish little names, and with the wish that they might stay like this for ever, they both drew apart and she shut her eyes for his kiss.

The spaniel came back from an expedition of his own among the bushes, trundling contentedly towards his master, to find his sacred person involved with another. He sniffed at Jenny, knew her as the one who had lately interfered with all his walks, gave a sigh and settled himself at a little distance. He was a young dog, but he was too old to be surprised and not too old to feel aggrieved. He knew he would have to wait indefinitely, and he lay with his nose on his paws, twitching his ears at the new tones in Cyril's voice and unobtrusively taking up another station when they went, hand in hand, to find a resting-place under a tree. He had been useful once, when these two found nothing to say to each other, and now, though they hardly spoke at all, they had forgotten him.

They were making the best of this good hour. Cyril asked no questions and made no plans to have this relationship properly acknowledged by their families. He was practical and conventional, but to-day he was a poet, and he did not introduce his prose into the lyric they made together. Whether Jenny would have told him everything is doubtful, but when she thought back to her perfect faith in him, to the ease of a mind which had forgotten its troubles, she believed she would have done it. She was never fortunate. The skill with which she had eluded him at other meetings failed her when, in the first wonder of their love, he might have heard all she had to tell him and belittled its importance. And what, after all, would there have been to tell? Her father had married beneath him, her mother was supposed to have been unfaithful and her Aunt Sarah was common and hateful and thought she was genteel. Yes, it would have been easy with the people far away, with no chance of seeing Aunt Sarah, obsequious and playful towards Cyril; if her mother's supposed lover were not called Thomas Grimshaw, a man who would touch his hat to Cyril. Theoretically, the story was not difficult to repeat: practically, to a young girl on whom it had weighed all her life it must always have been bitter: to tell it to Cyril Merriman, who was the young squire of the country-side, whose family probably, whose servants certainly, knew about the Rendalls, it would have been an heroic effort. He spared her that and so permitted her to think she would have made it at a word from him.

This time, it was he who said she must go home and, at once, she obeyed him. They were both wise to-day, not consciously fearful of spoiling their emotions by prolonging them, but acting spontaneously under the inspiration that had controlled them since the first sight of each other in the wood. Walking on the sides of his feet, so that he could look down on her as they ascended, he pulled her up the slope, and she, whose small body was compact of muscle and who could have run upwards almost as far as she had run down, hung rather heavily on his hand to please him.

The dog went first, quietly delighted to have this tedious experience ended, and when he reached the top of the bank he turned and watched them, and wagged his tail encouragingly. His eager eyes, his bushy tail, begged them to persevere and promised them his own success, and still they paid no heed to him.

'Poor little love,' Cyril was saying. 'You look so tired, but we are nearly there.' His head was almost on a level with the road and the dog gave a series of joyous, congratulatory barks.

Jenny was not tired, but there was a heavenly languor in her mind and she shut her eyes, glad to know she could follow him blindly. From her position she could hardly have seen Thomas Grimshaw if her eyes had been open: the sound of wheels and hoofs on the sandy road had no troubling associations for her, but he, driving by in great content after his interview with Sarah, heard and recognised the dog and then the top of Cyril's head. He raised himself from his seat, to catch the expected glimpse of Jenny, dropped back at once, whipped up his horse and was round the corner before she had reached the path. Cyril saw his back and felt a momentary annoyance lest the fellow had noticed Jenny, but she did not see or hear or think of him and she parted from her lover in the perfect happiness of her drugged mind.

'The same place on Monday,' he said, and she nodded, her great eyes shining.

He had told her to go home and she was going, but she went very slowly, as though she carried a vessel brimful of some precious liquid and must not spill a drop, and not a drop did she lose as she wandered up and down the roads, sat in a muse on a seat near the bridge, crossed the water, at last, and went up to the attic. And there the vessel was overturned. The beauty she had stored and cupped so carefully was gone. She could persuade herself that her falseness was the only real barrier between her and Cyril, and it was fatal. Even to his simplicity, perhaps because of it, it might seem that she had trapped

239

him into what she knew he saw as a betrothal, and made her confession afterwards. Could he think that? she wondered piteously. She had told him lies and why should he not suspect her of others, when he saw her mother and Aunt Sarah? She did not believe he would understand. He was too young and too candid to be capable of thinking with her mind. His life had been too smooth, his position too assured, for him to realise the difficulties of hers. And though he might still love her, he would have to learn to love a different person. She could not bear teaching him that hard lesson and watching him hide his struggles. She must leave him with what he had: it was the best she could do for him now, she thought, in a misery too deep, at present, for pain, and she did not know that all her instincts were bidding her protect her own memories too. She was afraid to test him. She had to keep her certainty of his perfection.

CHAPTER XXX

I⊤ is comparatively easy to be brave in the first shock of a catastrophe, and Jenny saw with indifference the anxious, almost apologetic look of her mother and the curious glances Aunt Sarah cast at her through her newly-assumed air of authority.

Sarah was busy at the gas-stove in the scullery and she had the girls standing behind her with their trays for a considerable time before the soup was ready to be served. Jenny did not care. The stirring of the soup and the hissing of the gas were part of the nightmare in which she was held helpless. It was Dahlia who protested.

'I call this a waste of energy,' she said. 'There's nothing more tiring than standing still and holding out a tray.'

'If you'd put the cruets on the table, as you ought, instead of on the tray, there'd be no need to hold it out till wanted. You'll know better another time. Everything on the table beforehand is my rule.'

Dahlia made a face at her aunt's back. If they had to put up with her they must get amusement out of her, and it was important that Jenny should laugh to-night because she was unhappy and, in the future, because only as a joke would Sarah be endurable. She was not a guest and she was not the head of the household, and until she justified her manner with money for the business or a stream of lodgers, Dahlia would not submit to being at her orders. She looked at Jenny, but she was occupied in staring, with the intentness of dislike, at her aunt's long profile.

'Cutlets and peas for the next course,' Sarah announced, 'but no peas for Miss Morrison.'

'Who said so?' Dahlia asked.

'Common sense,' said Sarah.

'Doesn't she like them?' Jenny asked quietly.

'I couldn't say, dearie, but she doesn't like us and we can't waste peas on her.'

'Mother,' Dahlia stepped towards the kitchen, 'Miss Morrison can have peas, can't she?'

'Why not?' Louisa said. She had nothing to do. Sarah was at the stove and the girls were ready to wait on the lodgers. She might as well have been in the garden with Edwin Cummings who had carried a kitchen chair there, to be out of the way until he was called in for the family supper.

'Miss Morrison will take peas,' Dahlia said genteelly, 'and if you haven't bought enough for two, Mr. Allsop needn't have any. I wish he could have all his meals with the Dakins.'

'I couldn't fancy anything that girl with the dirty cap had laid hands on myself,' said Sarah, 'and, by what I see the tradesmen bringing, they don't keep a very good table.'

'Does that matter,' Dahlia asked, 'when it's covered with a cloth?'

She had won a half-hearted smile from Jenny and Sarah said sourly, 'You're very saucy to-night, aren't you? The soup's ready. Now don't stay talking to Mr. Allsop.'

In the hall, before they separated, the girls stood and looked at each other across the plates of soup, and Dahlia smiled in the expansive way that meant mischief.

'This is fun, Jen,' she said, with more amusement than she felt. 'It was awful when we had to be polite, but now we can tease her and I shall stay with Mr. Allsop the whole time. If we're parlour-maids, we're parlour-maids, and I ought to stand behind his chair.'

'That,' said Jenny, 'is just what she wants you to do, or she wouldn't have told you not to.'

'Why should she?'

'I don't know, but don't do it.'

'That depends,' Dahlia said. 'I can't sacrifice my own pleasure to spite her.'

'Pleasure!'

'It might be.' Her afternoon with Mr. Sproat had been instructive in more than architecture, and it had roused a desire for further knowledge. Was it possible, she wondered, to make Mr. Allsop's eyes assume the guarded look she had seen in Mr. Sproat's?

'Oh, Jen,' she said, 'you needn't look like a funeral. The world's not as bad as all that. And the soup's getting cold. "The funeral baked meats did coldly furnish forth the marriage tables." Where does that come from?'

'From somebody who knew everything,' Jenny said mournfully as she went towards Miss Morrison's door.

Aunt Sarah was not altogether to blame for Dahlia's flippancy. Mr. Sproat had his share in it and so had Jenny, for when Dahlia was worried her spirits rose, and she gave Mr. Allsop his soup, saying cheerfully that it was rather cold, but she was speaking metaphorically when she said she would stand behind his chair.

She saw him raise his eyebrows. 'But I don't like cold soup.'

'No, it's horrid, isn't it?' she said sympathetically, 'but this isn't quite cold. It's lukewarm.'

He raised his eyebrows again, with a difference. He had an inborn objection to not getting what he paid for, but he was quite willing to be amused by a pretty girl with a voice noticeably charming after the deep chorus of the four Dakins, and he talked to her and allowed her to talk to him while he hastily swallowed the soup and ate the rest of the excellent meal Aunt Sarah had prepared, but he was much more experienced than the curate and he loved his Mary, and when Dahlia took away his last plate she felt an increased liking for the more appreciative Mr. Sproat.

She turned her sense of failure into a semblance of success. 'I've found out quite a lot about him for you,' she said pleasantly to her aunt at supper. 'I thought you'd like to know that he's a partner in a draper's shop in Wellsborough.'

'Oh, a shop!' Sarah did not approve of retail trade. 'Well, it's nothing to me, dear, what he is, but I always thought he had a money look about him.'

'He's not as bad as that!' Dahlia protested.

'Bad?' said Aunt Sarah.

'And it's the best shop in Wellsborough, of course,' Dahlia said dryly, 'so Mary Dakin won't have any bother about her clothes.'

No one responded to this remark and altogether it was rather a silent party, only enlivened by Sarah's distress at Jenny's lack of appetite and the efforts of Louisa and Edwin and Dahlia to protect her from this attention. Each one would begin a sentence and stop half-way in it to let the others proceed, and all three sentences would fall short while Sarah went on steadily with remonstrances and kindly speculations and advice, until Jenny cried desperately, 'Leave me alone! Must I even eat to please you?'

After that no one spoke. Aunt Sarah looked patiently misunderstood and at the end of the meal she generously said that Jenny must be excused from washing up, and so made sure that both her nieces would busy themselves at the sink, while she rested in the kitchen. Edwin Cummings helped them, in his shirt-sleeves, and polished the spoons and forks with the energy of his anger. Louisa stood at the garden door and stared at her walled enclosure, and they all knew that they were in silent league against Sarah.

'All the same,' said Louisa, 'if I was you, Jenny, I'd go and have a bit of a lie down.'

'Oh, I shan't lie down,' Jenny said, 'but I'll go upstairs and read.' Why, she asked herself, should she lie down to-night in particular? She might just as well, and she wished she could, lie down for ever. She turned to Edwin who was washing his hands under the tap. 'What are you going to do?'

'I don't know.'

'Well, when Miss Morrison leaves there'll be somewhere where we can sit.'

'Is she going, too?'

'Too?' said Jenny.

'Well, I mean, I may have to any time.'

'I'd much rather you didn't,' Jenny said, with decision and this expression of her preference sounded like an order.

Dahlia was amused. She had never spoken like that to Mr. Sproat, and he matched Edwin Cummings in her mind. Edwin Cummings was Jenny's Mr. Sproat, better looking but of inferior station, more devoted but, perhaps, less manageable, and Dahlia wished Jenny would tell her whether she had found a very different person in the woods or whether she, too, was waiting for him.

'Yes, we'd all be sorry,' said Louisa, and from a more adroit parent, this might have been an attempt to lessen the emphasis of Jenny's statement.

'And nobody sorrier than me,' he said. ' I know very well I've had much more than I had any right to expect.'

'And that was only because there was nobody else to have it. Now, why don't you wait about at the top of the stairs and listen if Mr. Allsop goes out and then you can

245

slip into his room till he comes back and he'll never be the wiser.'

Edwin Cummings, who had not known the need to tell a lie, now condescended to act a mild one. When Mr. Allsop went out, leaving the smell of an excellent cigar behind him, Edwin walked boldly into the sitting-room, stayed there for a few minutes and then left it with a loud shutting of the door, and stole across the hall and up the stairs. Among his good habits was that of wearing slippers in the house and he hardly made a sound until he knocked at Jenny's door.

'It depends who it is,' came her voice in answer, and he opened the door for a modest crack and said, 'It's me.'

'I don't mind you,' Jenny said.

He shut the door quietly and looked at her as she sat on the edge of her bed. She was not reading, her hands were clasped on her knee, her smooth dark head was bowed and, speaking rather breathlessly, he said, 'I don't think I can bear it!'

'None of us can,' Jenny said grimly, 'and there's no reason why you should. But it's only for the week-ends, and I suppose some day he'll marry Mary Dakin and then he won't come any more. I used to feel so sorry for them both, but I think they're happy. I used to be sorry for me'—she looked up and smiled in puzzled wonder at herself—'and now, when I look back, I think it was all rather nice. Dahlia told me I would. And you'll have your room again on Monday.'

'I'd rather be in the kitchen, even when your aunt's there. I wasn't thinking about your aunt. Jenny—what I can't bear is for you to be unhappy.'

She shook her head. 'I'm afraid you'll have to.' It seemed quite natural that he should grieve for her—it seemed the proper tribute to her sorrow—and she felt a mild astonishment when he began to speak about himself.

'I thought I'd get over it,' he said. 'I thought I could manage just to like you. And I can't. I meant to love you and say nothing. I didn't mean to say anything, even when I was outside the door, and now somehow I can't but tell you. It seems as if there's no help for it.'

'No, there's no help for it.'

'And if I have to love you, what am I going to do?'

'You'll have to do what I'm doing,' she said. She felt that he was telling her about someone else: she could not apply his words to herself. She wanted Cyril and could not have him, and poor Mr. Cummings loved someone who did not want him, but, as there was no one in the world like Cyril, her sufferings were greater than those of anybody else. It was strange to hear Mr. Cummings expressing the same thought.

'Ah, but it's worse for me! It isn't you that you're in love with!'

'No.' Without surprise she accepted his knowledge of her state and she heard his words only to make use of them. 'How much,' she asked, 'could anybody love me? Could he love me if I was wicked?'

'It would be easy.' He covered his face with his hands. They were not so brown as Cyril's and they were square, but they were just as clean: they looked clumsy, yet they were sensitive, but Cyril would never hide his face like that. He would set his lips and scowl if he were troubled, he would never make an emotional gesture, and she felt a faint scorn for Edwin Cummings who had not the same patrician control, but, as she realised when he dropped his hands, he had not been concealing agony: he had been concentrating on the arrangement of his thoughts.

'It doesn't matter to me whether you're good or bad,' he said. 'There's no sense in love. You're proud and selfish and sometimes you're unkind and you're for ever thinking about yourself, and,' he added, with a wry

247

humour, 'I can't wonder at it! I don't love you because you're good or clever. I love you because you move the way you do and sit like you're sitting now, and because you've got such lovely little feet! I'd do anything in the world to make you happy. I'd rather you were happy than I was.'

'Would you?' Jenny said. Was this how Cyril loved her? Was this how she loved him? She was not sure, and suddenly she was assailed by a sense of waste. Here was love being offered to her and she could not take it: here was a man spending himself fruitlessly on her, and she said sadly, 'You ought not to love me.'

'I know.'

'And you mustn't.'

'I've tried not to.'

'At first,' she said, 'I didn't properly understand that you were talking about me. I was rather—rather muddled. I felt as if it was somebody else. I'm sorry. I'm sorry. Oh, we're both unhappy!' She lifted her arms towards him and he came and sat beside her. 'Would you forgive me anything, anything, anything?' she asked, looking straight into his eyes. 'Yes,' she sighed, 'I believe you would.'

'And it's all wrong,' Edwin said, his heart hopelessly at war with his common sense.

'Yes, it's all wrong.' Why should she be so sure of the man she did not love? She knew she could trust him to the world's end, but she did not want to go there with him: she wanted to go with Cyril, though he might leave her by the roadside. She had no right to suppose him capable of desertion, but she had a calm and profound conviction that love for him must be a fitting complement to the only kind of life he knew.

'No, there's no sense in it,' she agreed. 'It's just something we can't help. She bent towards him. He was the only one who understood. 'Don't go away,' she said.

But it seemed that, in spite of his boast, there were limits to what Edwin Cummings would do for her. 'Not if I can help it,' he said.

'But you must help it—so that you can help me.'

'You could come, too,' he said.

'Could I?' Frowning a little but unembarrassed, she asked, 'Should I have to marry you? Because, you know, I don't think I could.'

He rose from his knees. There were also limits to his endurance and he did not answer her question. 'You could help Kitty in the shop.'

'I'd like that and I'd like the garden. Oh, but how could I leave the others with Aunt Sarah? You say I'm selfish and now you're trying to make me worse.'

'I shouldn't like to do that,' he said anxiously, and Jenny laughed. She heard the sound and was amazed at it. She thought she had finished with laughing.

CHAPTER XXXI

Beulah Mount looked stately and serene in the summer moonlight. The houses had lost their individualities, like a row of sleepers, resembling each other in pathetic unconsciousness, and because the houses were old, it seemed that they must be dreaming peacefully of their past, undisturbed by the new lives they sheltered. Anyone crossing the bridge at this quiet hour, hearing his footfalls startlingly loud and hollow on a road contracted by night and loneliness into a thread thrown over an immeasurable abyss, might have seen those houses as reminders of everything beautiful in an older world, the sorrows and vexations and passions merged by time into romance: he might have wondered at the willingness of man's mind to let ugliness slip into oblivion so that beauty may stand clear, and have found in this faculty, according to his own prejudices, a human need to see things better than they are, a proof of the superior power of good, or a faint reflection of a greater mind, incapable of preoccupation with evil.

Of all the houses, the one with the double pair of bow windows seemed most filled with memories, and it was difficult to believe that it could also hold a modern repetition of those old emotions, heartaches and uncertainties and self-seekings. Jenny had once tried to see her situation as a descendant of her own might see it a hundred years hence, as the man on the bridge might see her home, and she knew it would be a story for smiles and pity and even for a sort of envy. The envy would be for the retrospective romance of her ill-assorted parents, the beauty of their daughters, and the bad aunt in the kitchen: the smiles and pity would be for the weakness of Jenny and her old-fashioned fears and uncertainties. Her grand-daughter or great-grand-daughter, living in a changed world, would be puzzled, but, if she had a picture of the small pointed face with the wide eyes that seemed to anticipate grief and yet to be astonished when it came, she would feel a pride in Jenny's history. In her sorrow she was making pleasure for the future, but she could not be expected to find consolation in that and she lay stiff in her bed, afraid to make a movement lest it should release the feelings she must control.

'Jen,' Dahlia said softly. Her bright conversation while undressing had not roused Jenny to any apparent con-sciousness of her surroundings. Slowly she had taken off her clothes and neatly she had put them by, but she might have been doing everything in her sleep, and since then Dahlia had been testing all possibly interesting subjects and rejecting them, until she wisely settled on the one she believed to have a large part in Jenny's gloom.

'Jen!' She made a chuckling noise meant to suggest mirth, but the face Jenny could not see was troubled. 'I'm starting a campaign and you must help me. The only way to deal with Sarah is the way she deals with us. Let's imagine all the nasty things we can about her— they're certain to be true—and then we'll hint about them. It's so easy. You just say "Ah!" and shake your head and the guilty conscience does the rest.'

'I thought we had to be good and put up with her.'

'So did I, but I've been thinking. I can, when I try hard. Now just answer a few questions. Do you remember how Miss Headley used to look as if she was thanking God when we answered properly, or asked an intelligent question? We really ought to have done it oftener, but we didn't realise what a difference it made to her. Well—do you think Sarah is sacrificing herself to the good of the family?'

'No,' Jenny said promptly.

'Quite right. Do you think she has an axe to grind? Remember my first question and your answer.'

'Must have,' said Jenny.

'Where?'

'Here.'

'Clever girl! Then we needn't be good. And there'll be very little to do when Miss Morrison's gone. There'll be plenty of time for fun.'

'It was fun that's driving Miss Morrison away, wasn't it? Is that what you mean?' Jenny asked, with a note of hope in her voice. 'Are you going to drive Sarah away?'

'No, I don't mean that,' Dahlia said gently. 'I mean that if she wants to stay she will, and what we do won't make her go. It wouldn't be right to get rid of her, even if we could, till we've paid the debts. After that—'

'After that,' Jenny repeated, 'we shall be old women! What will anything matter then?'

'We shan't be old women next year, or the year after. Would that be soon enough for you?' Jenny did not answer and Dahlia cried, in exasperation, 'Why don't you tell me what's been happening? If it will help you, I'll poison Sarah to-morrow!'

'It would be in the papers,' Jenny said at once. 'That wouldn't do us any good.'

Dahlia nodded to herself in the darkness. There was someone else in Jenny's case. 'Well, then, if God took her to himself without any fuss, would that make you happy?'

'I thought it would, but it was only an excuse. Nothing can help me.'

252

'You mean there'd still be me, I suppose, and mother, and the lodgers?'

'Don't ask me anything.'

'It would do you a lot of good to tell me.'

'No, no,' Jenny grieved.

Dahlia turned on her side to face the other bed. 'Jenny,' she said, and the name she never used was a sign of her earnestness, 'I think you're in love with a snob!'

'Why do you think I'm in love at all?'

'Don't be silly,' Dahlia said practically. 'You don't go across the bridge to look at the buttercups and daisies or pick them for the sake of pressing them in a book, and not even you would go to the churchyard two or three times a week. You're in love and you're ashamed of your family. And if he makes you feel like that, he isn't worth a button.'

'He doesn't know about my family.'

'I thought not! You'd better tell him at once and get it over.'

'It sounds easy, doesn't it?' Jenny said wearily.

'It would be easy for me. I shouldn't care. If he thought I was ruined by Aunt Sarah, he'd be ruined for me.'

'And what about Thomas Grimshaw?'

'Same thing,' Dahlia said cheerfully.

'And suppose you found he'd been deceiving you— rather meanly?'

'I'd never think of him again. Oh, poor Jen! You mustn't care. He's not worth caring about! Why, you'd never be able to trust him again, all your life! Don't worry, poor little love.'

This was the first endearing term Dahlia had ever used towards her: it was what Cyril had called her, and she began to cry, quietly at first, then with deep sobs following each other so closely that they choked her, and

253

she sat up in bed and rested her head against the rail and wept with an abandonment that had its dignity.

Dahlia sat in the same position to keep her company and felt a great bitterness for the deceiver and a great love for Jenny. 'Poor little thing,' she kept saying to herself, but she did not speak aloud, and as the sobbing gradually ceased she found her thoughts turning to Mr. Sproat. If he was beginning to like her he was doing it with his eyes open and treating her, nevertheless, with respect, and she did not think he would deceive her. That was the wry way of things, she thought. She did not care for him, who could be trusted, and here was poor Jen breaking her heart for someone who, somehow, had betrayed her. Dahlia stole a look at her. She had slipped lower in the bed and her dark head was on the pillow, her slim body hardly raised the bedclothes, and she seemed mysterious and almost sacred to Dahlia in this sad acquaintance with love. It was strange to imagine Jenny yielding so much as a kiss, but, if she did that, it would mean that she would give everything for the asking, and Dahlia was deeply troubled. It seemed to her that such a passion must be caused by something more than a wounded mind. 'She'll never tell me. She'd rather jump over the bridge,' she thought, and she felt inexperienced and friendless, but determined in protection and loyalty. Then, as she settled down to sleep, she remembered Jenny's words about her wasted lies and, taking another look at the proudly-cut little features, wondering what kind of man, what strength of emotion, could make Jenny deny the character they expressed, she felt a little less anxious about the bridge.

These were some of the difficulties hidden in the house that looked so serene in the moonlight. Mr. Allsop was probably the most contented person under its roof. His comfortable love for Mary jogged on its friendly course:

254

his talk with the little girl who waited on him—with this diminutive, in spite of her height, he expressed his sense of her social inferiority—had been a pleasant accompaniment to his dinner. She was very pretty. Her skin had the colour and softness of a peach, and he wondered idly how she kept it so, for his Mary's was distinctly weatherbeaten, and he was so well pleased with having treated her like a lady that he had half a mind to flatter her with a little harmless dalliance which, he was sure, would not come amiss.

Mr. Cummings had gone sadly and sensibly to sleep. He had done what he could. Jenny knew now that he loved her, and staying awake and thinking would be useless: he did not even speculate about this lover of hers and marvel that he could make her unhappy or resist her loveliness: when he did not understand a thing and had no chance of enlightenment, he shut it out of a mind needed for other matters.

Miss Morrison, thinking nervously about her travels, which so far had not taken her beyond the south coast of England, felt like a desperate adventurer setting out for a strange land. To-morrow would be her last Sunday in Upper Radstowe. She wished there were someone who would miss her but, with the self-protective imagination which her life had created, like a covering shell which made her invulnerable unless she thrust her head beyond it, she saw herself as an interesting figure, standing on Beachy Head and gazing seawards—not young, not beautiful, but mysterious in her gentle reserve and in the memories she seemed to see on the horizon.

The other pair of sisters in the basement, both large women, made bulky mounds in their bed. Neither of them had any active distaste for the physical proximity of the other, and if Louisa was conscious of Sarah's mind working in the darkness, Sarah remembered Louisa only as one of the strings to her bow. She had so many that she did not know which one to use first. Chance must decide, but she fancied that one of those connected with Jenny would be chosen. She did not like Jenny, and she had discovered a similar feeling in Thomas Grimshaw. In Sarah's eyes and his, she was a haughty, two-faced minx, too fine for amiability towards either of them, but not beneath carrying on a secret intrigue with young Merriman. Several times, as he had told Sarah, he had seen them together: an accidental glimpse of them had led him to watch for others, and to-day, though she was still in ignorance of this, he had seen them emerging, hand-in-hand, from the wood. And, at the same time, thought Sarah, masking her satisfaction with indignation, she was playing a double game with Edwin Cummings.

Sarah was decently careful in the management of her meditations. She did not put things crudely, even to herself, but she registered facts and knew where to find them when they were wanted. There ought, one way or the other, to be no difficulty about Jenny. There would not, she hoped, be so very much difficulty with Louisa when money ceased coming into the house and ought to be going out of it, but whether girls who had to be supported would be more favourable to Sarah than Louisa's loneliness in their absence, she could not be sure. It would be a fine thing if Mr. Allsop took a fancy to Dahlia. Dahlia and a wealthy draper, Jenny and the young squire, would be partnerships worthy to be mentioned casually to future lodgers, but it was Louisa's marriage to Thomas Grimshaw on which Sarah was really determined. She would get the house on easy terms as a reward: moreover, it was the respectable and proper ending to Louisa's amatory career, and, even failing the draper and the young squire, it would be easy to get rid of the girls.

These plans passed smoothly through Sarah's mind.

They would settle themselves with an imperceptible shake from a master hand, which, in other respects, meant to be idle until it could work for the sole benefit of its owner. She had a great sense of power as she lay there at the bottom of the house, as though she supported the whole superstructure, and Louisa and her daughters were the props which had become useless, had become obstructions, and must be moved as soon as possible. She was in that state of the schemer which is more blissful than accomplishment, but her fellow-conspirator next door was less content. This was the difference between the constructive and the destructive mind, between seeking material advantages for self and the feverish desire for disaster to others. The advent of the respectable Miss Lorimer was not the advantage Miss Jewel had expected. Miss Lorimer apparently treated Thomas Grimshaw as a friend and her presence at these weekly interviews took all the spice from Miss Jewel's vicarious enjoyment of them. However, for Mr. Sproat she still had the knowledge she had gathered in her excursion across the river, and she hoped for an opportunity of hurting him through the daughter as well as through the mother. Like Sarah, but not patiently, she could bide her time, and, like Sarah, she was to have very little influence on the sequence of events. She was the bogey who could not really frighten the children, and Sarah was not much more than another one made by Jenny for herself.

CHAPTER XXXII

Miss Morrison bought parting presents for everybody, including Edwin Cummings. To him, who did not smoke, she gave a pipe in a neat case, for she was one of those people whose preconceptions are not corrected by observation. She proffered handbags of suitable size and strength to the two women, but, in choosing her gifts for Dahlia and Jenny she paid a tribute to their youth and forgave the pain it had cost her. She felt proud and a little tremulous when she unpacked the parcel from London, for it contained more than two wide scarves in lovely colours: it contained magnanimity, thwarted affection, and proof of her thoughtfulness and taste, and from those gauzy folds there might be wafted regrets for her departure. Indeed, so charming was the behaviour of the girls under this well-chosen generosity, that it was Miss Morrison who felt regret and, with a little encouragement, she might have been persuaded to stay: but persuasion was not in Louisa's character, it did not suit Sarah's purposes, and it would have come with indelicate suddenness from the happy recipients of her gifts. But they did feel the kind of sorrow youth spares for those who seem rather pathetic and unimportant, and they wished they had taken more pains to make her happy. She had taken some for them. Her letter to the shop must have been explicit, and the person who carried out the order must have been intelligent, but only Miss Morrison knew how well her wishes had been fulfilled. The girls saw the fitness of the presents to their individualities, but they missed the symbolism at which she had aimed.

'I've never had anything so beautiful in my life,' Dahlia said solemnly, wrapping herself in the scarf of apricot and faint pink and misty brown, the colours she had worn on that Sunday when Miss Morrison's sterile romance had ended. 'But there ought to be a looking-glass in every room. I must go upstairs, but I'll come back in a minute.'

'You can go into my room and look in the long glass,' Miss Morrison said. Generosity is its own increase, and pleased with her discrimination and her willingness to make this girl more beautiful, Miss Morrison was almost capable of inviting Mr. Sproat to see her thus adorned.

'It was so clever of you to choose those colours,' Jenny said. She smoothed and patted her own scarf, but she did not put it on. Her eyes shone because the thing was lovely and saddened because she would have no joy in wearing it. Her spirit was across the water and her heart ached with her pain and his: her ears were alert for his footstep and she was afraid to leave the house lest she should meet him, afraid to stay within and be discovered, and she half hoped he would accept the few words of un-explained farewell which would reach him before the time of their appointed meeting. She could not bear to think of him waiting in the wood, looking at his watch, pretending it was fast, making excuses for her delay, mounting the slope to look for her on the road, descending again to call for her among the trees. She had told him that Jenny Wren had gone away for ever, but the ideal lover would not submit to such a disappearance. He would look for her and, perhaps, when he found her—perhaps, she thought, as she wandered from room to room and window to window, in the joy of success after despair—all would be well. She played, as was inevitable,

259

with the thought of going to him and making her confession, after all, but Dahlia's words stuck in her memory. He would never trust her again. Was it possible to love without trusting, she wondered. Her own longing for the sight of him, the physical need she had of his presence, the touch of his hands and the strength of his arm, persuaded her that there was nothing he could do to alienate her. The joy she had in his little tricks of speech and manner seemed guarantee enough of an enduring satisfaction: her senses roused, only to suffer starvation, trusted to his to break down the barrier she had raised, but, obedient to the instincts which had quickened under this experience, she constrained herself to wait until he came into her life again, not as a boy on horseback, gently pacing the summer grass, but as a man, fiercely riding down obstacles and doubts in the pursuit of his desire.

'I hope you are pleased with yours, too,' Miss Morrison said, fearing it might be disappointment that kept the girl so quiet.

Jenny's scarf was also commemorative of the Sunday when Miss Morrison had learnt that love was not for her: its pale blue and pink and green and grey were the colours of the great bunch of flowers over which Jenny had gazed with the blind eyes of an enchanted dreamer. Touching the almond blossom one day in spring she had unknowingly stirred Mary Dakin to a discontent which became a power to attract Mr. Allsop and, on a night in summer, she had, as unconsciously, robbed Miss Morrison of her belief in her own womanhood.

'Is this,' Jenny asked, laying her hands gently on her present, 'as much like me as the other is like Dahlia?'

'Yes,' said Miss Morrison, steadying her eyeglasses, 'I think it's like someone who is young and happy, so happy that she can't believe it's true. But it is true, you know,' she said, beaming bravely on Jenny who gave her an uncertain smile. It was difficult to believe that Miss Morrison could be inspired to prophecy, but easy to accept anything as a sign.

Dahlia returned, weaving her scarf about her. 'I shall try it on to-night when I haven't any clothes on,' she said.

Miss Morrison frowned and flushed. She had never seen more of herself than was unavoidable in the processes of her toilet and this frank paganism removed the regrets that had been gathering round her. She thought of the misguided Mr. Sproat and she was re-established in her belief that she could not love Dahlia for more than a few minutes at a time.

'Then,' said Dahlia, intent on this vision of herself, 'I shall look like the picture in Miss Headley's study. You know, Jen, the one where Venus is standing on a cockle-shell, with hair rather like mine. We'll have a tableau, and you can be the girl in the flowery frock. Or we'll take turns, if you like.' She turned to Miss Morrison. 'It's a lovely picture. If you go to Italy you'll see it.'

'Yes,' said Miss Morrison, thinking of Eastbourne, wishing she knew to what picture Dahlia referred and feeling a little abashed by an intimacy with art in her landlady's daughter.

'I always looked at it,' Dahlia went on, 'when Miss Headley was lecturing me, so the time wasn't wasted, after all. I used to believe she had those pictures on the walls because she knew she ought to like them, but now I believe they were for us, too, and she knew they'd stay in our minds if she didn't talk about them.'

'She used to talk to me,' said Jenny.

'I know. And explain things. But you're different. I don't like to have things explained. If they need that, there must be something wrong with them. There won't,' she cried gaily, 'be any need to explain me when I'm wearing Miss Morrison's scarf!'

'Perhaps,' said Miss Morrison, bringing herself back into the conversation as she delved among the odds and ends in her handbag, 'perhaps you'll wear it when you go to the play, next week, in the Gardens. I bought three tickets, for you and Jenny and me, but as I can't go, I'm sure you would like to take your aunt.'

Dahlia put out her hand for the tickets, but before she took them she said, 'They're not on that condition, are they? Because we'd simply hate to take our aunt.'

'Oh, Dahlia! That's not grateful!'

'To you? We're very grateful to you, aren't we, Jen? And we wish you were coming with us.'

'Thank you, dear, but I was thinking of your aunt. She told me she has given up an excellent situation to stay here and help your mother.'

'Did she? Dear old thing! And we didn't know! But I'm sure she wouldn't be happy, Miss Morrison, if she went to the play and left mother behind. Mother will adore the funny bits and dear old Sarah will have a lovely time, being unselfish'—Dahlia's tender tones ended in laughter—'and looking in our drawers!'

'Oh, Dahlia!'

'But she won't find much! No incriminating documents, are there, Jen?'

Jenny shook her head. She recognised the warning under the pretence of fun, but she possessed nothing interesting to Sarah and she believed she might be almost happy if she had one letter from Cyril to keep safely near her heart.

Miss Morrison, though shocked, was rapidly considering the contents of her own drawers and finding a barren satisfaction in her blameless past. 'I don't think you ought to talk like that,' she said.

'I oughtn't,' Dahlia agreed. 'It's bad policy, and if you hadn't been going I shouldn't have said a word. But we needn't take her, need we? We'll take mother. It's *Twelfth Night*, and she'll like that. And it's in the evening. I did hope you'd choose the evening!'

Jenny looked with envy and admiration at Dahlia; for her, the darkness of evening was an added excitement, not a welcome obscuring of the family party, and she actually looked forward to hearing the loud laughter from which Jenny shrank. She had heard it in the cinema when it was mercifully mingled with other noises of the same kind, but how would it sound from an expensive seat in the Zoological Gardens? Sir Toby Belch might prove less amusing than the comedians who followed each other at an inhuman speed, through windows and over roofs and after motor cars, and suffered falls from which they rose with renewed vigour, to the joyful shrieks they could not hear. And perhaps the lions will roar, she thought, and she also thought that it was Dahlia who should have loved Cyril Merriman. She would have told no lies: she would have presented herself to him as she was, and re-treated with a gay pride if she was not altogether to his liking, and it was she who was the true aristocrat, because her spirit was free.

In the kitchen, whither they carried their presents, they found Aunt Sarah examining her stout bag. She smiled at it indulgently and said nothing. For her, who had received handsome tokens of appreciation—which the Rendalls had not been privileged to see—from employers who were much more like friends, this was a poor and unworthy tribute, and with a sort of tenderness, a masterly gesture, she laid it on one side.

'But you've let the cat out of it,' Dahlia said. 'We'd no idea—had we, Jen? But you mustn't do it. It wouldn't be right.'

'I don't know what you're talking about, dearie.'

'Ah, you're just pretending,' Dahlia said gravely,

shaking her head and watching for those signs of a guilty conscience. 'You didn't want us to know, but we've found out. We know what you've done and we disapprove of it.'

'Oh, do you?' Sarah said tartly, but quickly she recovered her virtuous serenity. 'I haven't done anything, nor won't, that isn't for your good and your mother's.'

'But you ought to think of yourself,' Dahlia said, smiling.

Louisa looked a little puzzled. She opened her lips to speak, then shut them. She had plenty to say about that, but she must not make Sarah angry. She was half jealous and half doubtful of Dahlia's manner and it would be just like the rest of her life if Sarah took the love and confidence of her children, but she was relieved of her anxiety when she met Dahlia's sly glance of amusement and saw it passed on to Jenny and returned. Alone, she was not a match for Sarah, but, through her, the girls and she might come to understand each other, and then what she saw as a necessary evil would be turned to an unexpected good.

CHAPTER XXXIII

THERE was a constant ringing of the front door bell during the last few days of Miss Morrison's sojourn in Beulah Mount, and the state of the doorstep was a grief to Sarah, who was unwilling to clean it herself and powerless to have it done by anybody else. Louisa cleaned it early every morning and it was not her fault that the weather had turned wet.

'It's bad for the house,' said Sarah.

'Not when it's you who open the door,' Dahlia said, with her wide smile. 'Besides, it's nice for Miss Morrison to see the footmarks. They're like flowers scattered in front of her. I can plainly see the shape of Mr. Doubleday's boots. He turns his toes in and Mrs. Doubleday turns hers out. And heaps of the good dull girls have called. It's wonderful how fond people are of you when you're going away.'

Fortunately this thought did not occur to Miss Morrison, and she departed happily in the belief that she had been more successful than she thought, a belief that sustained her in a short farewell interview with Mr. Sproat and sent her towards Eastbourne with a high heart. A little encouragement, a little faith in her own powers, and she saw that watering-place as no more than the shore from which she would presently plunge into the perils of the Continent.

'I shall write to you from abroad,' she told Dahlia, who saw her off.

'Send me a postcard of the Botticelli, won't you?'

'Of course, of course,' Miss Morrison answered. The faint shadow of her comparative ignorance fell on her and almost spoilt her pleasure in a corner seat and safe-looking fellow-passengers.

Dahlia did not pursue the subject. 'I'm sorry you're going,' she said.

Miss Morrison nodded brightly. Among all the other pretty speeches, she took this one for granted. 'I've had so much kindness,' she murmured.

This was one of the happiest days of her life, but Dahlia was sad as the train left the station. Miss Morrison seemed to her like a waif, driven out into a world she did not understand, and she might have been kept safely in Beulah Mount if she had been treated with more kindness. Dahlia had the chivalry of a young woman for an older one and she refused to consider Mr. Sproat's part in Miss Morrison's flight. She stood on the bridge of the dirty, noisy station and thought of her own faults. She had always tried to prick Miss Morrison where she was most vulnerable, yet how could she help it? She was irritating, her eyeglasses waggled, and she had that covering of self-satisfaction with which Providence often protects the fundamentally sensitive and uncertain. It had been stripped from her for a short time, but already it was growing again and perhaps there was no need to worry about her. There were other, nearer matters for Dahlia's consideration. Miss Morrison had gone, but Jenny remained, a little ghost wandering about the house, clasping and unclasping her hands, refusing to be laid by the simple expedient of speech. Ghosts always told their troubles to mortals and, immediately, their restless haunting ceased, but not a word could Dahlia get from this one. Only to her and to Edwin Cummings was the ghost apparent, and he, though he could not lay it, could give it a sort of peace. Jenny would sit still in a room with him, and it was fortunate that, on this day when Mr. Allsop was arriving, Miss Morrison's room was empty.

Dahlia let out a sigh. Like everybody else, she wanted to change the world and its inhabitants to suit herself. A very little change to Edwin Cummings and he might marry Jenny: a very little change to Mr. Sproat and Dahlia's life would be full of glorious excitement, of listening for his footstep and watching from the window: less desirable and less necessary and just as impossible were the changes in herself and Jenny which would solve their problems.

She stood on the bridge at the top of the steps and looked down at the platforms where trains came and went and people got out and in, and she forgot that she might be an attractive and conspicuous object. A great many passers-by must have glanced more than once at the girl who seemed to be awaiting an arrival, and envied the person she was to meet, but only one of these stopped and spoke to her. This was Mr. Allsop, holding his good leather suit-case, wearing his well-cut blue serge clothes and removing his hard felt hat.

'Were you waiting for me?' he asked in a jocular manner.

'Of course,' Dahlia said seriously and as she looked at him without smiling and noticed the small red veins in his middle-aged cheeks and wished he would not wear his office clothes when he went courting, she knew he half believed she spoke the truth. There was a flash of doubt and surprise, instantly extinguished, in his eyes, and a little pleased movement of his lips, and she felt scornful of his absurd readiness to think he could attract her and angry at his estimate of her taste, but she had more control over her features than he had and she preserved her gravity.

They passed together out of the gloomy station into the sunshine of its wide approach, and here Mr. Allsop signalled to a cab and handed Dahlia into it.

'We shall get back very quickly,' she said.

'Not so quickly as you think,' he said. 'We're going to stop and have an ice.'

'Are we? Do you want one?' she asked.

'Well, no, not particularly. I thought you might.'

'No, thank you,' she said. She looked demure: she wore an expression of meek content at being carried home in a cab, and he could not guess that her enjoyment was in his embarrassment. He was going to patronise her with an ice, amuse himself a little and then get rid of her: he had not reckoned on her company to Beulah Mount, but she intended to stay in the cab as long as she chose.

'Some tea, then?' said Mr. Allsop hopefully.

'I don't want anything, thank you.' For a few moments she looked out at the busy streets and then turned towards him. 'You don't generally come in a cab, do you?'

'No, I don't,' he said shortly, and sank back in his corner.

Dahlia sat forward, balancing herself easily to the jolting of the cab and giving him a view of her hat, the tip of her nose and the pretty line of throat and chin, and these charming curves increased his irritation. It was his thrifty habit to proceed to Beulah Mount by tramcar and omnibus, and he saw the inconvenience of being extravagant on this occasion. Mary would be watching from the window: she would not be human if she did not feel surprise at seeing his companion in luxury, and he hardly knew how to explain her presence. There had been times when Mary had met him at the station and had not been indulged with a private conveyance: he had been able to postpone his kiss until they reached the shelter of the house, and if this girl had given herself the trouble of eating an ice, he would have had his hair cut afterwards and arrived in Beulah Mount alone.

Dahlia gave him time to think this out. She could feel his sulkiness like a third person in the cab and she came to a conclusion which she did not recognise as a commonplace. The man was nothing but a baby, good-tempered when he had what he wanted—and how self-confident he looked when he accosted her!—and helplessly cross when things went wrong, and she knew that part of his sulkiness came of the same sense of failure with which he had afflicted her the week before, exaggerated, in his case, by her indifference to his condescension. A little girl like Dahlia ought not to refuse an ice when it was offered by a man like himself, and if she really had other business at the station, why had she walked off so readily with him? He could not reconcile this behaviour with her detachment and he was struck by the painful thought that she considered him too old to be interesting.

They were going slowly up the steep Slope and Dahlia remarked that the summer sales had begun and that Mr. Cummings worked in the shop at the corner.

'Would you like to go in and see him? I can drop you there, you know.'

'No, thank you,' she said again. 'He's not supposed to have callers in business hours, and he's buried away somewhere at the back, among the old books. You mustn't suppose that he's just a young man behind a counter. That annoys him. He's an expert.'

'H'm. I shouldn't think there's much in that.'

'Much what?' Dahlia asked.

Mr. Allsop had a vulgar impulse, which he repressed, to say that he referred to the base metal which enabled him to take her home in a cab. 'Not much future,' he said.

'And when people say that they mean money and

motor cars and large houses. Mr. Cummings doesn't care about such things. He likes beautiful, rare ones.'

'Including yourself?'

It was now Dahlia who had a vulgar impulse, but she would not indulge him by yielding to it and she said carelessly, 'No, I'm not old enough.'

The cab had turned off Nunnery Road and passed the concert hall, built in the supposed style of a Greek temple, and Jenny would have cast a thought at her father, but Dahlia was looking out of the other window. 'When we come to Albert Square, will you stop the cab?' she asked. She had punished him enough for his conceit, she had no wish to punish Mary Dakin as well, and though his manhood insisted on a polite protest, her womanhood was entirely free from the supposed desire to rouse uneasiness in another woman's breast. Moreover, it gave her special pleasure to stand at the cab door, when she had alighted, and to say sympathetically, while she smiled at him radiantly, 'Isn't this a relief!'

It was a great relief, but Mr. Allsop felt foolish, though the tact she had displayed with no more conscious purpose than the avoidance of silly explanations, had an exciting effect on him. It gave to their innocent companionship a slight air of intrigue, restorative to his self-confidence, foreign to his nature, but, he thought, probably inherent in hers, and he knew he would be able to reply with whole-hearted reassurance to Mrs. Dakin's weekly plaint that they had not a room for him in the house. He had never regretted his insistence on making his own arrangements for bed and board. He had better food at the Rendalls' and refreshing lulls from the cheerful monotony of Dakin conversation, and he hoped no particular engagement had been made for him to-night. It would be amusing to continue his intercourse with Dahlia in the key of her last remark.

For a minute she watched the disappearing cab. She was almost innocent of Jenny's desire to mark the difference between her education and her situation: her pride was of another kind: it rested on the independence of her spirit and her faith in herself, and Mr. Allsop's offence was not so much condescension to his landlady's daughter as a fatuous belief that the company of a man, even a middle-aged one and slightly bald, must be welcome to a woman.

'Silly old thing,' she muttered, stepping backwards before she turned, and nearly colliding with Miss Jewel.

Miss Jewel almost smiled at Dahlia. Some small part of the reward due to virtue was hers. She had been torn this afternoon between a desire to rest on her horsehair sofa, close to the open kitchen window, and another to do her shopping in streets cheaper than those near Beulah Mount, for she never allowed her tradespeople to feel secure of her custom, and now, with her basket laden and her weekly accounts lessened by a few pence, she had witnessed this little episode which, for her, had more than a slight air of intrigue. So she almost smiled when Dahlia apologised prettily and offered to carry the basket, and she accepted the offer, in a grudging manner but with epicurean delight. It was a dainty mental feast to Miss Jewel to hear Dahlia prattling amiably, to see her accommodating her long stride to her own short one, and making nothing of the heavy basket that contained food for the lodger who would certainly not be reft from Miss Jewel by this girl. But the possibility of losing Mr. Sproat was not the chief cause for enmity: it came from the twist in her own character and the frustrations in which she believed she gloried.

'Like mother, like daughter,' she thought, taking covert upward glances at the tall, slim figure, and she saw it without being moved to the compassion of maturity for the young and light-hearted. Miss Jewel was not mature:

she had grown old, without ripening, in mind and body, and she had an insane hatred of physical fulfilment or its promise. She saw its promise—and suspected its fulfilment—in Dahlia: she saw, too, the superiority of a new scandal to an old one and the power of the two together.

'So you've lost Miss Morrison,' she said.

'Yes, we've lost her,' said Dahlia. 'You're luckier than we are. You don't lose yours.'

'No, I do not,' said Miss Jewel. 'But I wouldn't call it luck. If there's one thing I do believe it's that some of us get our deserts in this world.'

'I hope so,' Dahlia said.

'Do you?' Miss Jewel asked, with emphasis, and she stood still to look Dahlia up and down.

'It seems a sensible idea, and then we can start afresh in the next world.'

'Not everybody,' Miss Jewel said, tightening her mouth. 'Only the good ones.'

'And here the wicked flourish like the green bay tree,' Dahlia said cheerfully.

'No they don't.' She could not allow this either. The statement was destructive to all her hopes of present happiness. 'They're cut down in this world and burn in the next.'

They had arrived in Beulah Mount. Dahlia handed her the basket and, hiding her horror of the triumph in the little black woman's voice, she said lightly, 'I shall ask Mr. Sproat about that. I'm sure he doesn't believe it.'

CHAPTER XXXIV

It was rather sad to go into Miss Morrison's room and see it bare of all her fussy little possessions. The gay work-bag, the writing-case, the ornamental blotter, the row of framed relatives had gone, and the gentleman with side-whiskers lay, face downwards, at the bottom of her large trunk, but when Dahlia looked in, as people will always look at a room lately vacated, she did not find it empty. Jenny was at the side of the window, standing pressed against the wall and holding the curtain back a few inches, so that she could see out without being seen.

She dropped the curtain and moved towards Dahlia. 'Mr. Allsop came—in a cab. He must have been in a special hurry to see her.' Jenny's tones were flat, but, for a quick ear, there was a note of tired envy in them.

Dahlia pretended not to notice it. 'Lucky Mary!' she said. 'Did she trip out to meet him? She does try to trip sometimes, when she remembers.'

'No. She shouted from the window.'

'Not maidenly,' Dahlia said with disapproval. 'What else did you see? You were spying through the curtain, like Miss Jewel.'

'I wasn't spying!' She had been watching the bridge. She watched it whenever she could steal away by herself and be reasonably sure that Aunt Sarah would not find her at a window. Cyril had told her that he seldom went into the city: he loved his fields and woods and this was a busy time of year for a farmer, but she could not believe he would not come and search for her, and she imagined

273

him studying the directory, making notes of all addresses where someone called Wren might be found, and knocking at each door in quest of her. She wondered if he would tell the police to find a pale girl with dark hair who answered to the name of Jenny.

'I wasn't spying, but I saw you with Miss Jewel.'

'I hope she'll tell Mr. Sproat I carried her basket. His eyes don't brighten, they sort of glower, when he hears of a kind deed! I haven't seen him since Sunday—not to speak to.'

'Why should you?' It was a long time since Jenny had thought of Mr. Sproat's smile as he picked up and folded the duster.

'Oh, I don't know,' Dahlia said, and, like Jenny with Cyril, she imagined what she would do in his place.

Jenny forgot that a blow to pride and trust might temporarily deaden a heart to tender sensations, and Dahlia was fortunately unaware of Mr. Sproat's battle with himself. He knew he was going to lose it and had no wish to win: the country vicarage was slowly being furnished and he, who had never put foot to a spade or plucked a weed from a garden bed, was planting peas and cabbages and spraying Dahlia's roses. Mr. Sproat was greatly changed. The ardour formerly roused in him by sin and trouble had slackened: his eyes were growing sharper to discover virtue, which need not be stern to be commendable, and where he had expected moral principles to stiffen the souls under his care, he was surprising a desire that they should have ordinary human happiness. He was a little worried by his own laxity: he knew the cause, and it was not a reasonable one: it was a charming face, a lithe, well-proportioned body, and a belief, grounded on little more than his wish, that these were the outward signs of inner perfection. But sometimes he thought he might be wrong, and then a drear rain fell

274

on the vicarage garden, and the rose-petals lay discoloured on the sodden earth. This thought came oftenest when he caught a glimpse of Louisa Rendall and remembered Miss Jewel's disquieting words about her, long ago. Louisa was a grave disadvantage, and, though it could not change his purpose, it did postpone definite action. He saw Dahlia oftener than she saw him: nothing she did jarred on his taste, but he had missed the pleasure of seeing her with Miss Jewel's basket, and, as Jenny was quick to point out, it was not likely that she would report this kindness.

'I don't know how you managed it at all,' she said. 'She always pretends not to see me.'

'I know,' Dahlia said slowly, 'but I nearly knocked her down and I suppose she liked it.'

'Did she ask questions?'

'I can't remember any.'

'She must have wanted to find something out. She's dangerous.'

'Oh,' said Dahlia, with the irritation of her regret that Miss Jewel must have seen her leaving the cab and Mr. Allsop, 'you think everybody's dangerous.'

'Yes, I do—nearly everybody.'

'And she's rather a little viper, I know. She believes in Hell—she told me that—but I don't see how she can send us there.'

'I wish Miss Morrison hadn't gone,' Jenny said unexpectedly. 'She was silly, and it's nice to have her window, and we can sit here to-night, but she was a clean person.'

'So is Mr. Cummings.'

'Oh yes, but I feel as if we need as many as we can get.' She began to walk up and down the room. 'And we need something to do. Dusting and sweeping, that's soon done, and four of us doing it!'

'There's the play next week.'

'Yes, yes. But something to keep us quiet—to keep me quiet.' Her voice rose a little. 'I can't keep still,' she cried plaintively, and she looked at Dahlia as though this were her fault and could, at her will, be mended.

'Come for a walk, then.'

'I don't want to go out.'

'You haven't been out for days, have you?'

Jenny hung her head. 'Only down the street.'

'Let's dress some dolls,' Dahlia said, after a moment's rapid thought. 'Pretty ones, this time. And we'll tell Mr. Cummings and perhaps his sister will sell them for us.'

'If we could do that—' Jenny said. 'And quickly, quickly! Let's pretend we've got an order and we must finish it by Monday.'

'All right, I'll go and buy the dolls if I can get the money out of the basin without Sarah's seeing.'

'It's not her money.'

'No, but I hate to let her see me doing anything. I'm getting as bad as you about her. Where's Mr. Allsop's half-crown?'

'Spent, long ago. At least,' Jenny said, 'it seems long ago.'

'And he gives me chocolates! He has no sense. Never mind. I'll go and rob the till.' She went, but she returned to pop her head round the door and say, 'I wonder if Mr. Allsop would like a set of Dakins. I could make them very funny.'

'I don't think you'd better be funny again,' Jenny said, and she went back to the window.

She wished night would come with its dark curtain, though at night, when there were fewer people abroad, each footstep in the street sounded very loud and purposeful and frightening. She held her breath until the steps passed on, and, with this respite, felt a cold exhausting

276

sense of desolation. It would be better to-night when they dressed the dolls, working against time, with fingers so active that the mind must not wander from them, while Edwin Cummings sat in the background quietly turning his pages and silently protecting her.

Dahlia, who had gone out to buy those dolls, as she would have run to fetch medicine for a body in danger; Edwin Cummings, who watched this case of illness in which he could do nothing but wait for a possible crisis, were accepted by Jenny, with the selfishness of an invalid, as ministers to her needs. The atmosphere of love which they cast about her was all she wanted from them: she breathed it as her right and offered only unspoken gratitude in return. She did not know what she would do without them and, as there flashed into her mind a picture of Cyril on the doorstep, demanding admittance, and Cyril entering the room where she and Dahlia and Edwin sat, she saw herself springing up and standing beside his chair. He would take care of her, he would not let Cyril be angry, she thought, and, when she heard the actual turning of the door-handle, she had a moment's panic because she was alone.

'Sarah said she was going out,' Louisa told Jenny, 'and I've seen her go,' she added, in simple humourless comment on the nature of Sarah's statements.

'I didn't notice her.'

'She moves very quiet,' said Louisa. 'Says she's going to see about lodgers. She'll call at the hotel and have a talk to the manager. She says we'll be handy when they have an overflow, which, by what I can see of it, is what they never have. And we'll have to put an advertisement in the paper. We didn't think of that, Jenny. Well, the house feels more my own when she's out of it, so I thought I'd come up here.'

'But why don't you come when she's in the kitchen.'

'Well, if I did,' said Louisa slowly, 'wouldn't she come, too?'

'But you'd have us.'

'Yes, but you'd have her.'

'It's not fair—' Jenny began.

'That's what I think.'

'I mean not fair to you.'

'It's my own fault,' Louisa said. 'Funny thing is, when you think about it, everything's your own fault, only it doesn't stop with yourself.' These statements, this un-accustomed framing of her thoughts, came slowly from Louisa. 'Easy if it did,' she said with a sigh.

'Yes,' Jenny agreed, but she was not thinking of how her actions might affect other people: she was considering how her mother and her father and Aunt Sarah had affected hers.

'And you can't start again,' Louisa said. 'Not fresh, anyway.' She was looking back, through Thomas Grim-shaw to Sidney Rendall, and through him to the young squire. 'But when I did start,' she went on, 'I was doing right. And what's come of it?'

'Doing right?' said Jenny.

'Well, I told you, that day Sarah came. I ran away, didn't I? But how did I know where I was running? It seems as if there ought to be someone to tell us.'

'I wish there was,' Jenny whispered.

They did not look at each other. Louisa stared at the uneven line of the treetops, making a jagged palisade against the sky: Jenny looked at the hands folded on her lap: and between the two women there passed an invisible shuttle, carrying threads of sympathy, of possible con-fidence, but the threads were frail, the shuttle moved uncertainly, and the fabric was not yet firm enough for testing.

'Anyway,' said Louisa at last, and her big mouth

278

turned down derisively, 'there's one person here who thinks she can tell us all we want to know. But she doesn't tell right, Jenny. I don't believe she tells right.'

She rose and, still looking at the trees, she stood with her hands fixed on her hips. She could not bring herself to say more: she could not tell Jenny that Sarah had seldom opened her mouth during these last days, except to refer, directly or indirectly, to Thomas Grimshaw, to mingle, with tenderness for the widow, a suggestion of what was due to the living, to utter hints of the comfort in atoning for past offences and to grieve at the woeful burden of debt and at responsibility for the girls, to sigh and then to promise cheerfully that she would set things right. It was worse than having Grimshaw himself in the kitchen. Louisa was sore against him for his betrayal of her to Jenny, but he was a human being to whose feelings she knew she could appeal, while Sarah was like the darkest part of Louisa's memory, her worst fears of the future, in a woman's shape. What Sarah said mattered very little, for Louisa had her own sturdiness of opinion, but what was said repeatedly had the harassing quality that drives people to act against their inclination and their judgment. On the other hand, she was not so stupid as her sister supposed, and this advice, this kindliness, sometimes gloomy, sometimes jaunty, was overdone.

'She wants to get me out of the house,' Louisa thought. 'I won't go. She wants me to marry Grimshaw. What would happen to the girls? They shan't stay with Sarah. And I don't want to marry him. He hasn't treated me as he should. Funny thing, if I married him to please her!'

Nevertheless she was worried. She had rushed into this scheme in the optimism following her liberation from Sidney Rendall. She had kept a few hundreds of her small capital for immediate needs and the rest had gone towards the purchase of the house. There would not

279

have been enough for that and the furniture without Grimshaw's help. He had bought the White Farm at not a penny more than it was worth and lent the rest of the necessary money. A man with no purpose but the expression of devotion would have paid an absurd price for the farm and allowed her to believe she owed him nothing, but Grimshaw was careful of his money: he laid it out where he thought it would be profitable, and though he expected no return in cash, he had risked it, on an inspiration, for what he valued even more. It was he who had managed the business for her and explained as much as he knew of the mysteries of banking. She had learnt to draw a cheque and she no longer enjoyed this experience, for she was only too well aware that her little fund of money was diminishing, but whether the house was more hers than his and what the law and he could do to her, she did not know. And she wished, as her daughters had often done, for a friend who could be trusted and who was wiser than herself.

'I shouldn't wonder,' she said suddenly, 'if that Cummings hasn't a good business head. He's a nice lad, Jenny. When he came, I didn't care about him. To tell you the truth, I grudged him what he was getting, though goodness knows I never stinted him. He's the one good thing we've got, coming here. It isn't what I thought it would be, and I don't want what I thought I did.'

'What do you want, then?' Jenny asked.

'I want for you to be happy,' Louisa said. 'And I've as good as fetched Sarah here to torment you. Dahlia's got such a spirit she can stand against her, but you're different. Always were, from a child. And anyway, what does Sarah do to harm us?' she inquired of herself aloud. 'It's nothing you can lay your hand on. If it wasn't for the money— But there, it's no good fretting. Come a year or two and we'll go off, the three of us, like I told

Dahlia. Only, I'd like to see you happy, Jenny,' she said softly, awkwardly. 'It's not just Sarah, is it? You've only to tell me and I'll do anything I can to make you happy.'

She looked at her daughter, whose face might have been cut in pale stone with a bright patch of colour on each cheek-bone, and it was Louisa who showed emotion. Jenny could not feel it. Her mind received the words, like an echo from Edwin Cummings, and while it acknowledged their sweetness and their surprise, she was frozen by the mockery of them from her mother's mouth. Her very existence meant unhappiness for Jenny.

'Oh, well—' Louisa said, after a pause. It was too late, she thought, for the confidence she would have welcomed, but she stood there for a few minutes so that she should not show her hurt and trouble Jenny with an abrupt departure.

CHAPTER XXXV

Iᴛ is easy to interpret the actions of other people according to the desire of the observer, and Mr. Allsop, at first a little cross when Jenny brought in his dinner, was soon mollified by the thought that Dahlia was either teasing him with this substitute or cautiously retreating from danger, and he returned to the Dakins' house in the good spirits which, with his arrival in a cab, had revived in Mary the first excitement of his courtship.

This was only Friday: Saturday and Sunday and an hour or two of Monday held, in promise, many opportunities for treating the girl with the indifference she deserved, the dignity he hoped he could assume, or enough suggestion of admiration to make the following Friday interesting. Mr. Allsop was not consciously disloyal to Mary: his temperate affection for her had never wavered. It was Mary he wanted to marry, but he saw Dahlia as the born plaything, and, if he was not much mistaken, she accepted and liked the part assigned to her. He missed the serious-ness which Mr. Sproat discerned, and he was not capable of evoking it. She was like a piquant sauce to the good, honest daily fare of Mary and enabled him to appreciate it better.

Miss Jewel, going out to get a breath of air at the time when she knew Mr. Allsop had his evening meal, suffered a disappointment without mitigation, at the sight of Jenny in the sitting-room: and Mr. Sproat, served later with his own dinner, was distressed by Miss Jewel's attentions. He liked to prop a book against the large cruet-stand and

282

read in a peace which was only interrupted by visits to the window, and to-night Miss Jewel seemed to find difficulty in leaving him. She made a small, dark cloud, threatening to burst in the room, and, when she brought his fruit and custard, she emitted a noise which came to his ears like the distant roll of thunder.

'So poor Miss Morrison's gone,' she said. 'They'll feel her loss in the church, Mr. Sproat.'

'Yes, indeed,' he said. He did not want to think about Miss Morrison. He had not been single-minded towards her or towards the Rendalls when he installed her next door, but Miss Jewel would not allow him to forget her.

'How she come to get landed in that house,' she said daringly, 'is what I could never make out. And a real lady, too. Well, she's gone, but, if I'd been her,' Miss Jewel's voice rose and quickened, 'I'd have shown them up first. The mother's a bad lot and the daughter's going the same way.'

'Which daughter?' Mr. Sproat asked before he could stop himself.

'The one that looks as if she would.'

Mr. Sproat put down the sugar-basin and turned a dark glare of indignation on her. 'I don't listen to gossip, Miss Jewel. Kindly leave the room and be careful not to spread your malicious lies where they may get you into trouble.'

'The trouble isn't for me,' she said, as she slipped through the door. She was shaking violently, but she had seen that his hands were not quite steady. She supposed her lodger was lost to her, but she had gained more than she would lose, and she had not scraped and pinched for years to no avail. She had earned freedom of speech and the luxury of hatred, and though she dreaded entering the room to remove the cloth, she had the courage of her vices and the strength of her certainty that he was troubled.

Mr. Sproat pushed his plate aside. He could not conceal

283

his trouble from himself. He did not trust his landlady's judgment, but he had never taken any pains to understand her character: she had been efficient and generally silent and he saw no reason why she should make a sudden excursion into fiction, yet he remembered that she had done so once before concerning the same characters, and that there could be no smoke without fire. He could not console himself with the knowledge that Miss Jewel was a small and active volcano and might be making all the smoke herself: his own doubts about Louisa Rendall returned to him, and while he refused to harbour any against Dahlia, he had to admit that she was a stranger and a lovely one, subject to all the perils that trip the feet of beauty.

His appetite had gone, but he drew back his plate. He would not give Miss Jewel the satisfaction of seeing the food untouched, and he ate the fruit, carried home by Dahlia, without suspecting that it was given to him in the agreeable form of raspberry fool because it had been bought cheaply, in a crushed condition.

Meanwhile, Dahlia was innocent of any desire to tease Mr. Allsop, disappoint Miss Jewel or worry Mr. Sproat. She wanted to keep Jenny busy in attendance on Mr. Allsop, for Edwin Cummings' refusal to give extra trouble by taking his meals in the sitting-room was a mistaken kindness.

'Quite the son of the house,' said Sarah, with the smile that made her long, melancholy face grotesque.

She rather regretted that pleasantry next day, when she heard what Thomas Grimshaw had to tell her. By his account, this affair with young Merriman was more than a mild flirtation, and indeed, on the faces of Cyril and Jenny he had seen expressions which he called queer. He had no language to describe and no power to understand the grave happiness of passionate young love.

'Holding hands,' he said, 'but they looked queer.'

And Jenny had looked queer on the evening of that day and had gone early to her room. Sarah clicked her teeth and shook her head and Grimshaw had a revulsion of dislike for her and for himself. He was not deceived by Sarah's sorrow. He knew she felt, as he did, that there was a possibly useful weapon in this knowledge, but he wondered if it was a dirty trick to tell tales of Jenny, badly as she had used him.

'I think I'd better tell her mother,' he muttered.

'You'll do no such thing,' Sarah said sharply, and added gently, 'Worrying the poor soul, and maybe there's no need. And she's gone out, Mr. Grimshaw. I don't think you'll see her to-day.'

Grimshaw muttered something else that Sarah did not catch, and though she was busy with thoughts about Jenny, telling herself that the poor child should not be wronged if Sarah Lorimer could help it, she realised that it would never do for this man to grow weary of Louisa's caprices, and she spoke soothingly and encouragingly to him. She had to be vigilant for everybody, and the importance of one scheme must not make her forgetful of another.

'I sent her out myself,' she said. 'And the girls, too. I thought we'd better go into the accounts and we don't want to be interrupted. I'd like to know just where we are.'

He paid no attention to that, but said grimly, 'Yes, the girls take care to be out when I'm coming.'

'What's that matter? Jenny will be across the bridge, I suppose. Dear, dear!' Tolerance for youth's folly was mingled with anxiety in Sarah's sight. 'You must keep a look-out for her when you go back. We want to know all we can. We've got the girl to think about, Mr. Grimshaw.'

He made no reply and took his leave abruptly. She

could do all the thinking she liked, but he would not help her. She was not a comfortable ally. She had the effect of making him dissatisfied with himself, with his tales of Jenny and the pressure he had determined to put on Louisa. 'I'll have nothing to do with it,' he decided. 'And Louisa can keep the money. What's the good of a woman who hates the sight of you?' There were plenty of girls in the country-side who would be pleased to marry him and his farm, girls younger than Louisa and as good-looking, and he would make his choice of one of these and settle down and forget the other, but as he went home, on the roads overhung by trees in heavy leafage, he was wondering what it was that made one woman seem so right that everybody else seemed wrong.

Sarah was astonished and a good deal disconcerted by his departure. 'Funny!' she said to herself, and her long face lengthened, in thought, not in dismay. Something had gone wrong and she did not know what it was. Only kind and sensible remarks had passed her lips and she was left alone to search among them for her offence. She had been left alone last night, too, and she was genuinely puzzled. It was true that Jenny had always avoided her—poor Jenny, she remembered to think tenderly—but the character of Dahlia's amiability had changed, even to Sarah's obtuseness, and last night Louisa had gone out of the kitchen in that lazy, slow way of hers and sat upstairs with the young people. 'Funny!' Sarah said again. It was a strange way to treat a woman who had spent the afternoon tramping here and there, making inquiries, giving information, sowing seeds which were not expected or desired to come up before the autumn. She had tried to imply that the house was full at present, but that there would be room for privileged persons later on. This was her plan and the one of which Grimshaw had approved and now he refused to discuss money matters and he had gone off in a huff, and men were so unreasonable that she could not be sure when he would return. It might have been better to have kept Louisa at home.

'Well, I don't know,' Sarah said, for once admitting ignorance, and she saw the possibility of a future in which she was not mistress of this silent house, in which she returned to another situation, lost it after a few successful years and had to find another. Her career had been a steadily and quickly rising one until she reached the housekeeper's room but, this was another puzzle and she did not attempt to solve it, the same room was never hers for long. There were no complaints of a definite nature, she left with good recommendations, but she went.

'But there's one thing,' she thought. 'I'm spending nothing while I'm here.'

She might have found an explanation of these dismissals in the restlessness she felt this afternoon, because the house was empty. Where power was given to her she had to use it in her own way: in this case she had taken it, but there was no one present on whom it could be practised and Miss Jewel was the only person within her reach. She had received all the information she expected from that quarter, but she would have the gratification, at this weary moment, of talking herself into reassurance.

She and Miss Jewel were spared the sad spectacle of themselves, seated side by side on the horsehair sofa. They could only see and criticise each other. Summer and winter, Miss Jewel wore a closely buttoned black, stuff dress which might have been designed by modesty for the protection of beauty, but there was no grace of any kind in the small body and the sharp, closed face. It was many years since she had first seen her plainness of feature and the mean lines of her figure, seen them through eyes and heard them mocked by lips which were beautiful to her and desirable: she was a girl then, with feelings which differed from those of luckier mortals only in their greater keenness, and, for any satisfaction in her existence, it had immediately become necessary that she should make a virtue of an impotence to charm and feel hatred for those who had the power.

Sarah, large and heavy-featured, her head crowned with the monumental hat—for she was not familiar enough with Miss Jewel to appear bare-headed at her door— ought not to have roused enmity in the other's breast, but she was Dahlia's aunt and Louisa's sister, and Miss Jewel's little outburst the night before had not released much of her stored indignation: it was only the first trickle and it had begun to clear the way for the volume that pressed behind: a few more drops would finally displace the small obstructions of caution and precious secrecy that blocked the passage.

Sarah was insensitive and her object, in this visit, was to talk herself into a confident humour. Glibly she used the names of titled people: with admirable carelessness she mentioned the quantities of eggs, cream and wine that went to the making of soups and sauces in the households with which she had been connected. She took Miss Jewel's stillness and her stare for signs of awed attention and when her voice, like a blunt, but fiercely wielded knife, broke across these details with an irrelevant suggestion, it was a second or two before Sarah could make sense of the words.

'You must find those girls of yours a handful.'

'What's that?' said Sarah.

Miss Jewel repeated her remark and Sarah took time before she answered it. She saw a gleam behind the opaqueness of the little black boot-button eyes. The indignation of a loving aunt, repudiating the suggestion, might increase that gleam, but it might quench it. Sarah,

288

as well as Mr. Sproat, knew that there was no smoke without fire, no fire without a spark to set it going, and she was interested in that spark.

'So you've noticed that?' she said at last.

'Noticed it!' Miss Jewel cried, and with the cry, the last pebble, keeping back the stream, was shifted, and Sarah heard a steady torrent of words in which cabs and wronged betrotheds and assignations jostled against each other. She looked serious and said nothing. The afternoon was turning out well, after all. She was to have her hands fuller than she expected, but they were large and made for use and fortune was offering what she wanted. She had a solemn conviction that the wishes of the worthy were fulfilled, that such a chance thought as she had cast towards Mr. Allsop in connection with Dahlia took root and fructified when the right person cast it.

'There'll be trouble there, if there isn't trouble already,' Miss Jewel said. The pace of the stream had lessened and Sarah was placidly afloat on the calm water. Miss Jewel was not satisfied, for Sarah gave the impression of being able to steer herself and her relatives into safety, and Miss Jewel was glad she had pushed Mr. Sproat into a backwater, instead of involving him in the flood.

'I'm obliged to you for telling me, Miss Jewel,' Sarah said, with dignity. 'You've done what you thought right, but I may as well tell you I don't believe a word of it. Not a word. I've had a lot of experience and I know how mistakes are made. Now there was my Miss Marigold, high-spirited, I'll allow, but as good a girl—'

'Oh stuff!' said Miss Jewel. 'I suppose seeing's believing.'

'Seeing with my own eyes would be believing,' Sarah said.

'Very well, then,' said Miss Jewel, and the interview ended in common satisfaction.

CHAPTER XXXVI

Mr. Sproat was now learning the difference between sorrow for the sin of people who had no other importance to him and the dread of it in someone who had become dear. It was his nature to be pessimistic and his new habit of greater kindliness had not yet reached a sturdy growth, nor was his love, as he discovered, of the kind to defy unpleasant suggestions. It was a pity not to be able to see himself as a knight, prepared for mortal combat with anyone who offered the smallest affront to Dahlia Rendall, but he faced the fact that her beauty, her easy good nature, alarmed while they attracted him. He faced the meaner fact that the mother and the aunt were what really made him doubtful about the correctness of his judgment. If Dahlia had been mothered by the late Mrs. Morrison, who was querulous and of poor constitution in mind and body, but distantly related to an earl, Mr. Sproat's reproof to Miss Jewel would have had a blasting dignity. The truth was that he secretly felt she had the right to criticise these people, who were of her own kind, while he was predisposed to suspect them of bad behaviour, because they were not of his social order, and he postponed further furnishing of the vicarage, which was his usual occupation when he went to bed. But it was dreary work to try to compose a sermon and it was worse when the light was out, to see himself standing in the pulpit, talking of faith and charity to a congregation in which Dahlia had her place. Her mouth would be grave and her eyes bright with a gay mutiny as they saw into a heart capable of being disturbed by the malice of his landlady, and he remembered her honesty and how readily she had confessed to boredom with her father's architectural excursions, but that frankness was the only virtue of which he had proof, and he, too, was honest and he would not pretend his love was firmly fixed. What else did he know about her? What did he know about any girl? Why should Miss Jewel, hitherto almost guiltless of gossip, attack the Rendalls without cause and for the second time? And, at that question, Mr. Sproat's imagination began to work, and he ground his teeth as he pictured Dahlia in the arms of another man, and groaned mentally when it was thus revealed to him that it was not her spirit with which he was most concerned.

Dahlia would have been very much amused, and a little scornful, if she could have seen him twisting in his bed as he tried to conquer the flesh and forgot the Devil, who was assailing him with the suspicion that Dahlia was not worthy of the vicarage and the vicar, and forgot the world, which also had its influence on his state. In spite of the guarded look in Mr. Sproat's eyes she did not suspect him of being as much subject to physical emotion as the unknown man who waited for her among the trees, but she liked Mr. Sproat and she was a little hurt when she met him on Saturday afternoon and received an unsmiling greeting.

She was returning, with her mother, from a walk they had taken on the Downs, while Jenny, defrauding her aunt of a rare opportunity, was keeping very quiet in the attic: it was an entertainment that cost them nothing, and neither Dahlia nor Louisa had been much enlivened by it. There is a subtle, mental necessity to enjoy what has been paid for, this stimulus had been wanting, and Dahlia felt a revival of cheerfulness when she saw her friend striding up Beulah Mount. She slackened her pace, expectant of a little conversation, but Mr. Sproat gravely passed on. This was not in disapproval of any supposed offence of hers: it was penance for himself and, like other people who are troubled about their souls, he did not consider that hers might be injured for the benefit of his own.

She was surprised to feel a small pain that stayed like an obstruction in her throat and to find herself making excuses for him. Somebody was ill and he was rushing to the sick-bed: he had urgent business with the Vicar: she would see him to-morrow and be restored to confidence in his friendship, but when she saw Aunt Sarah looking at her with a new kind of curiosity she immediately connected it with Mr. Sproat's changed manner and wondered, though she would not ask, whether the two had met that day. Jenny, who was not fit to be told, however casually, of Dahlia's little worry, would have been ready with an explanation: she would have harked back to the old story and remembered Miss Jewel's ominous journey across the bridge. But Jenny was the invalid: she had to be spared, to be kept busy with the dolls and, if possible, diverted with a humorous rendering of such little happenings as came Dahlia's way. These efforts and these attentions were not begrudged: they were Jenny's right because she was Jenny, but to-day Dahlia could not be funny about Mr. Sproat and she felt still less inclined to be funny on Sunday.

She walked home from church very slowly, giving him the chance, as usual, to overtake her on The Green, but on this morning, when the sun was shining and the old trees dipped their branches under a warm breeze, he went by hurriedly, with a hearty professional comment on the weather.

'Pig!' Dahlia muttered, flushing all over. 'All right! I shan't go to your dull old church to-night.'

Jenny, seeing her then, might not have been so sure that Dahlia would have dealt high-handedly with Cyril, but her doubts would have been unfair to Dahlia, who kept her griefs to herself and hid her wounds, whose spirits rose in defiance of trouble and whose pride demanded from someone the tribute Mr. Sproat had denied her. Mr. Allsop was the obvious person: he was the only one within her reach. Since she had parted from him in Albert Square, she had pretended not to notice his pleasant overtures, chiefly because he was conceited and must be snubbed, but also because she distrusted her strong desire to obey her instincts. She wanted to be good. She was a victim of the lasting inconvenience of self-indulgence, and though she had not yet seen the man who could tempt her to follow in her mother's steps, she knew that her impulse to attract where she did not love was like walking on the edge of that path and enjoying an excitement for which she was not prepared to pay. Now she felt justified in amusing herself with Mr. Allsop: it was the illogical, but natural, retort to Mr. Sproat's cold manner: it was the reaction of a child who, wrongfully distrusted, determines to give cause for that distrust. Thus, Mr. Sproat, thinking about himself, indirectly played into the hands of Sarah and Miss Jewel, yet, strangely enough, left them empty.

'You can get on with the dolls,' Dahlia said to Jenny, 'and I'll look after Mr. Allsop.'

Jenny was in a state when she did what she was told, so long as the task kept her in the house. She did not like waiting on Mr. Allsop: she much preferred sitting with Edwin Cummings, who had been very helpful about the dolls. It was his idea to dress them in the periods of certain articles of furniture in his father's shop and set them up there, in the hope that clever Kitty, a competent saleswoman, would be able to dispose of them, and on Satur-

293

day morning, he had used some of his employer's time in finding suitably illustrated books which he carried home to Beulah Mount. Dahlia had spent a few shillings on ribbons and laces, for there were no rich remains from handsome dresses, no old finery in the house, but she could make a plain piece of stuff look like a brocade by tracing a pattern on it in gold paint, and Edwin Cummings knew what patterns were correct and would see that no others were reproduced.

Dahlia was receptive of his information because it was interesting to her and it was evident that he looked on her with the approval he had hitherto withheld, but the real bond between them was Jenny. Though Dahlia had her moments of irritation with her, and he may have known them too, they both loved her, and she had those supremely feminine qualities which made her grief seem the greatest there had ever been and her needs the ones that must be served. She was not spoilt, she made no actual demands, but she had power to touch their hearts, perhaps for no better reason than the casting of her body in its particular mould. With these two she allowed herself to be the tragic figure she believed she was: the pride on which she prided herself went down before their assured affection, but she had not altogether deceived her mother, and Sarah's marked kindness might have roused her suspicions if most of her acuteness had not been concentrated in her ears. The pain of loss and the shame of her cowardice were almost forgotten in her stretched attention. She was glad Cyril did not come, she hated him for not coming, and each day seemed to be the one that would bring him and make her happy or miserable for ever. She did not realise the strength of hopes based on the impossibility, the madness, of a world without him and, to pass this time of waiting, she sewed the dolls' clothes as quickly as she could with the neatness necessary to their natures and hers, but the very precision of her stitches, the exactness with which she pushed her needle in and drew it out, added to the tension that was drawn over her like some tight fabric that would burst with a prick.

'Why don't you read to me?' she asked Edwin, on Sunday night, and her tone implied that this was a request often made before and unkindly refused. 'It's so quiet,' she said.

'Is it? Seems to me there's a lot of noise outside—people passing all the time.'

'That's what I mean,' Jenny said.

'And the tide's full. The steamers are hooting up and down the river.'

'I hadn't heard them,' she said. 'I want you to read to me in a loud voice.'

He hesitated, in the embarrassment of one who is not used to the sound of his own voice expressing the thoughts of others, and she reminded him of his promise to do anything in the world for her. Unseen by her, his face reddened. This was the first reference she had made to his avowal, and she made it with an unconscious callousness and a disregard for his feelings which showed him the state of her mind and the small part he had in it.

'What shall I read, then?' he asked, going towards the bookshelves.

'It doesn't matter. I shan't be listening.'

Apparently studying the rows of books, Edwin mastered the excess of his anger, but it might have been heard in his loud, monotonous tones and his unintelligent manner of reading. He had to make a noise and he did it, and the noise was a steady cursing of that fellow across the bridge who had injured Jenny: it was a declaration of his own folly and of the weakness and selfishness in her, which, perversely, made her no less lovable, and gradually the

295

indignity of this situation changed to absurdity, and he read on through a grim smile.

Jenny looked up and saw it. 'Is it funny?' she asked.

'Very, I think.'

'Well, it's after ten o'clock, so we can stop.'

'Thank you,' he said with exaggerated meekness.

'If you don't mind, I mean.'

'I don't mind at all.'

It was after ten o'clock and the perilous, the hopeful, day was over. She need not listen any longer and she seemed to emerge from the taut tent of her suspense and to see the familiar room for what it was and Edwin Cummings as a person.

'I'm afraid,' she said, opening her eyes wide, 'I'm afraid I haven't been very nice. I didn't listen to your reading.'

'Neither did I,' he said.

'I thought you were enjoying it.'

'No, you didn't.'

'But I saw you laughing.'

'Not at the book. At myself.'

'Why?' Jenny asked uneasily.

He looked straight into her eyes and again she saw that his were hazel with bright lights in them. It seemed a long time since he had looked at her like that, when he sat beside her in the attic, and then the lights had glowed, but now they sparkled.

'Because I've no sense,' he said, 'and because I saw what a fool I must look, reading I don't know what out of I don't know what book, to someone who'd told me she wasn't going to listen! It's not a man's job, not mine anyway, and it's not one you ought to have put me to.' Her eyes, staring at him, filled with tears, but his sternness did not waver. 'You've got to help yourself.'

'I can't,' she whispered.

'And I won't do it for you,' he said.

Her arms dropped to her sides, and from one hand a naked doll hung by a limp limb. She was parting with one of her anchors, the stronger of the two, the one on which she thought she might ride out the storm. She could not believe he was deserting her and, as he saw her woebegone and helpless, he may have remembered her as he first knew her, courteously condescending to the young man in a shop, for he said, astringently, 'I thought gentlefolks knew how to hide their feelings.'

He watched for a lift of her head. She dropped it and said, 'I don't belong to them,' but when she did raise it, a moment later, it was with the startled fling of an animal surprised in its thicket.

There was a step in the hall, the opening of a door, and a sudden confusion of voices.

'No, no!' she cried and she rushed to him and clung to his firm arm. She put her mouth close to his ear. 'Don't let him come in,' she said in a slow, difficult whisper.

CHAPTER XXXVII

J ENNY's fears for herself were unnecessary. No stranger to the house had entered it, but why Sarah should have noiselessly opened the sitting-room door at the very moment when Mr. Allsop was kissing Dahlia, and what impetus hurled Mr. Sproat into the room shortly afterwards, Dahlia did not know. Shaking though she was with rage and mortification at her aunt's quietly menacing suggestion that Mr. Allsop had dishonoured her niece and would have to make proper amends, she wanted to laugh when Mr. Sproat burst in, but she smiled amiably and said, 'It was all my fault. I made him. I wanted to see what it was like,' she rubbed her cheek with her handkerchief, 'and it was horrid.'

Mr. Allsop, standing with his shoulders against the mantelshelf and trying to look like a man of the world who knew how to deal with the ridiculous situation and was biding his time to speak, lost some of his nonchalance at Dahlia's words. It was humiliating to hear the girl telling what was, in fact, the truth, for he had not meant to go as far as kissing, and he did not know how to endure her insult without laying rough hands on her. And what was this curate fellow doing? Mr. Sproat was holding to the back of a chair and staring at Dahlia, when he ought to have been thundering reproaches at the wicked man, and somehow this did not fit Mr. Allsop's instant and characteristic suspicion that the whole affair was a trap. He glanced at the windows, where the curtains had not been drawn, raised his eyebrows and picked up the cigar he had laid down.

'And on a Sunday night, too!' Sarah said for Mr. Sproat's benefit, with pious sorrow. She was as much astonished as Dahlia by his appearance, but she was not amused, and she was regretting the part she had played. Yielding to her usual temptation to act over-quickly, she had nipped this bud instead of allowing it to blossom, but, with Miss Jewel's sharp elbow, like a skewer in her side, she had been literally spurred into the house, and she had said things to Mr. Allsop which were altogether unjustified by the occasion. They had been in her mind since yesterday, the proper remarks for the reprobate who must make honourable amends to the victim, and they had slipped out too soon. Just for a moment Aunt Sarah believed she had blundered, but at once adjusting her opinion to her circumstances, she saw that another deserting lodger was of greater advantage to her than a probably barren flirtation.

All this was revealed to her while Dahlia spoke and rubbed her cheek, before Mr. Allsop, carefully ignoring the interfering though silent Mr. Sproat, asked with dignity for his bill, announced his intention of going to the hotel for the night and his belief that this sudden departure would not look at all well for the house. Three magic words, wiping out all past deficiencies, promising an earthly paradise, passed through Sarah's mind. She saw them neatly printed on the cards she would disperse in the neighbourhood. 'Under new management'! She almost uttered the words, but what she actually expressed was her sorrow and shame at her niece's light behaviour.

'What a fuss!' Dahlia said. 'Why should Mr. Allsop go? It will be very awkward for him.'

'Not at all, thank you,' he said coldly, and his eyes looked like stone balls. 'I shan't find it awkward in the least.'

'That's all right, then,' Dahlia said. She had been thinking about Mary and she wondered what tale he would tell her. 'It was all silly and not important, but I'm sorry. And it was horrid,' she added, when he left the room, followed by an obsequious Sarah. 'It was so stupid of me not to draw the curtains first.' She drew them now, and Miss Jewel missed the sight of Mr. Sproat slipping into the chair he had been holding. He bowed his head. This was the sort of remark he found so baffling in Dahlia, and, he had to admit it, so delightful.

'It was vulgar,' he heard her say. 'Jen will be furious with me. Still, we have to learn by experience. Nobody else has ever kissed me and it will be a long time before anyone else does! I think I'll go and wash my face.'

'Wait a minute,' said Mr. Sproat.

'I won't be scolded,' she told him. 'It's quite punishment enough to lose a lodger, and that's the second one I've driven away. Besides,' she said mildly, 'it's not your business, is it?'

'It seems so to me,' he replied.

'But how did you know he was kissing me?'

Mr. Sproat frowned. She ought to have avoided the use of that word: she seemed to have no shame. Yet in this frankness he faced again what he had seen when he burst into the room, a sort of innocence that made him murky to himself and quenched the primitive rage roused by Mr. Allsop's embrace. When he saw her, flushed and vexed, but incurably humorous, he forgot Mr. Allsop in the blissful certainty of his own love. She might kiss everybody in the street and, though he would not like it, he would forgive her. But what right had he to forgive or withhold forgiveness? He had a salutary moment of humility: he realised the spiritual dangers of his office.

'How did anybody know?' Dahlia said.

'I think—' said Mr. Sproat, and then he paused. He

300

must be honest. 'I saw your aunt and Miss Jewel on the other side of the road—'

'Watching, I suppose?'

'I—I suppose so.'

'And what were you doing?'

'I went out, too.'

'You must have been a nice little party,' Dahlia said bitterly.

She sat still, looking down at her clasped hands. It was Jenny's attitude, and if Mr. Sproat had ever been observant of the younger sister, he would have seen, now, one of those family likenesses which have little to do with shape or colour. Dahlia was thinking with great concentration, and when she looked up she said quietly, 'I don't think I can stay in the house with Aunt Sarah and I don't wonder Mr. Allsop won't. She's a wicked old woman. Jen said so from the beginning, but I didn't think people were really as bad as that.' She lifted her hands an inch or two from her lap and slowly dropped them, a gesture infinitely pathetic to Mr. Sproat. 'We haven't a friend in the world,' she said.

'Except me.'

'I thought that once, I don't know why, but I did, and it was a comfortable feeling, but yesterday and to-day you weren't nice to me. Had you seen me in the cab with Mr. Allsop?'

'Cab? No.'

'Miss Jewel did, and I thought she might have told you. She must have told Aunt Sarah and then they watched. What a fool I was? But why were you there?'

'I often walk up and down in the evening,' he muttered. 'You know that. I walk up and down and hope I shall see you. Sometimes you sit on the doorstep, and I've seen you through the window sewing. But no!' He gave the table a loud knock with his clenched fist. 'I was watching—like the others! I—Miss Jewel had said things—'

'Miss Jewel!'

At the sound of that cry, Mr. Sproat had to readjust his views of Dahlia's social inferiority. Her voice, her speech, he had always recognised as belonging to his own world: he was now obliged to absolve her aunt and mother from any influence on her standards. 'I'm not deaf,' he explained. 'I couldn't help hearing what she said. You can't suppose I encouraged her, but—I had to make sure.'

'And you've made sure,' Dahlia said scornfully. 'And if Mr. Allsop had been a nicer man and nicer looking and not bald, I should have let him go on kissing me! Until I remembered Mary Dakin. I wish I'd remembered her. I hope he'll tell her it was all my fault.'

'I think you can rely on that,' Mr. Sproat said dryly, but she would not allow the sneer to pass unchallenged.

'Is that what you would do?' she asked.

He took a little time before he answered, and then he said, 'I might. If I was afraid of losing you.'

'Me?' Dahlia said.

'Yes,' said Mr. Sproat. 'And I know I'm worse looking than Mr. Allsop, but I'm not bald.'

There was a slight softening of Dahlia's lips. Her criticism of his behaviour underwent the inevitable change. 'But what I can't understand,' she said, as though Mr. Sproat's sentiments were quite natural and need not be discussed, 'is why Miss Jewel wanted to interfere.'

'I'm glad she did,' he said. Without Miss Jewel he would not have had this sureness of his feelings, this uplifting pride in victory over his prejudices, for, deep in his heart, almost unknown to himself, there was a sense of his condescension towards Dahlia's family, if not towards her: there was a faint surprise that she seemed unaware of it.

'Are you?' she said. 'But you haven't stood here and

302

heard that—that snake suggesting that you'd been compromised, as they call it, and ought to be married. That's what she was hinting at, when you came in. How would you have liked that? I want to wash my face, but I can't wash my mind.'

'But when your conscience is guiltless—'

'Don't be silly!' Dahlia said. 'And it isn't guiltless. There's not much difference—' She hesitated, choosing her words for his sake, not her own. 'I mean, the feelings are the same. Not that I had any feelings. I just wanted to have them.'

Mr. Sproat flinched visibly. He had seen, and tried not to reproach, weeping penitents: he had warned brazen young women who were running and dragging other people into danger, but this calm acknowledgment of motives, this frank realisation of their nature, lay outside his experience, he did not know the correct response, and slowly it dawned on him that she knew as much as he did and dealt with her knowledge more courageously. He wondered where she had learnt it in her twenty years of life, and whether she would be willing to impart some of it to him. It had been he who was to give, furniture and hot-water system and flowers and a modestly established place in the world, and she was to accept his offerings gladly and repay him with beauty and laughter: with those he would be well rewarded, but he knew now that if she were ever his she would bring him a dowry outlasting beauty and preserving laughter, and for the first time his spirit was humble before her.

An unusual, whimsical smile played about his mouth. Last night he would have seen, in any proof of Dahlia's light-mindedness, an absolute remedy for what he feared was a physical passion, and here he was, conscious of a charm it was not easy to forget, but far more impressed by the wholesomeness of a fearless mind.

'He's left his cigar-case,' she said, 'but he hasn't gone yet, so I'd better give it to him.' She looked at the bulging expensive case as it lay on her palm. 'He's just like that,' she said. 'Oh dear, isn't it all stupid? And now you won't try to find us any more lodgers, will you?'

'No.' He stood up: he was trembling a little. 'I want you to marry me,' he said.

She let the cigar-case slide on to the table, she brushed the infected palm, and Mr. Sproat took courage, but when she said, 'Are you just being kind?' his heart sank. She saw him as a man in a black coat, like the doll she had dressed, with no urgencies of his own, only the bleak desire to do his duty, but she was not smiling and for that he was thankful.

'Because I love you,' he said.

She sighed lightly. Her first kiss had been a sordid business: the first words she heard from a lover had none of the breath-taking rapture she had imagined, but Mr. Sproat was wrong about her vision of him. The man who has declared his love to a woman can never look quite the same to her again. Dahlia would not be tempted to laugh at him until she loved him, and she did not love him yet.

'I like you,' she said. 'I want you for a friend. I like you so much that I might get to love you, but perhaps you wouldn't wait as long as that. I like you very much,' she said slowly, more to herself than to him, 'but marrying's different. I hated Mr. Allsop when he kissed me. But then, I didn't really like him to start with. What I feel,' she said, frowning a little, trying to make things clear to them both, 'is that I shouldn't like to lose you. That's not love, is it?'

'It's what I feel about you.'

'But I shouldn't mind losing you now and then.'

Mr. Sproat turned aside. He was hurt by that comparison of his possible embraces with the kiss of Mr.

304

Allsop. He felt angry and humiliated. He forgot she was his spiritual superior, he remembered her mother and her unspeakable aunt: he was a clergyman of the Church of England, offering all he had to a girl who had just allowed a lodger to kiss her, and she treated him like a piece of merchandise to be taken, perhaps, but more likely to be rejected.

When he looked at her again there were tears in her eyes. He had never pictured her in tears and this womanly weakness pleased him.

'I ought to have said thank you,' she said, 'but I was trying to be truthful.'

'I don't think you can help that,' he replied.

'And I think it's lovely of you not to mind—not to mind all this, but I should have hated you if you had.'

He knew she did not refer to the Allsop incident and, in emulation of her, in honour to her, he said, 'But I did mind a little. Rather a lot.'

He could not see himself as he made that confession, but Dahlia saw him and the eyes she had likened to mud, with the sun shining on it, were very bright and steady.

'You mustn't mind—anything,' she said.

'I won't,' he promised.

They heard Mr. Allsop leave the house, careless of his cigar-case. They heard him go, with loud footfalls, down the street. The sound grew fainter and died away and, as they listened to the silence that seemed to throb a little with the beat of his march, they were not thinking of him. They were testing the feelings they would have if they heard each other's retreating footsteps.

'I'll come and tell you when I know,' Dahlia said quietly. That was like her, too, and Mr. Sproat strode into the night, up Beulah Mount, round the hill, down the Avenue and up on to the downs, and it was very late when Miss Jewel heard him come home.

CHAPTER XXXVIII

Eᴀʀʟɪᴇʀ in the year, when the Rendalls jogged in the wagonette from the White Farm to Beulah Mount and saw their changed lives stretching, like the road, in front of them, they could not see how they were to affect their neighbours, or picture their benign old house as the centre of a tiny storm. Louisa, sitting with her knees spread and her ungloved hands resting on them, picturing a house full of those jolly lodgers she no longer wanted, had no forewarning of the hatred she would rouse in Miss Jewel's lean breast. Dahlia would have laughed joyously at the thought of attracting a sombre, rather sallow curate, and imagined herself treating him with a gay heartlessness, and Jenny, looking at the fields and woods where she was to meet her lover, that ideal lover who was actually to appear in the flesh, had no vision of another young man to whose arm she would cling, asking for protection. She would have been amazed to know that, however indirectly, she was to prepare Mary Dakin for love and Dahlia would have shrunk from the idea of troubling that love for a moment. But these things had happened and, on that Sunday night, the three elder Miss Dakins, their parents and Miss Jewel's professor were the only people in the three houses who were not uneasy. Even Milly, of the stout boots and dirty cap, was a little disturbed: she was loyal to the family romance and, like Mary, she had noticed that on this day Mr. Allsop's meals had occupied more time than usual: he had retired earlier for the night, yet the light from his sitting-room made a golden splash on the road for a long time afterwards. Mr. Allsop, however, marching back manfully, next morning, preferring to present himself as a dashing but repentant blade rather than as the cat's paw of a naughty young woman, was to make himself more lovable to Mary and to love her better. The Rendalls had done no harm to the harmless: possibly, the gifts life brings, whether they seem good or bad, are of a neutral character until they are handled by the receivers, moulded by them into fair or ugly shapes and painted in bright or dreary colours, and Mary Dakin and Mr. Allsop, simple and ordinary human beings, took this little misadventure with sense and spirit and turned it into good fortune. Dahlia's anticipations of wry looks from next door, Miss Jewel's hopes of horrible wranglings and broken hearts were not fulfilled, nor was Miss Jewel in any mood, next morning, to waylay Mary Dakin and pass the news to her: she remained in her lair, dreading the moment when the Dakins and the Rendalls would observe the removal of Mr. Sproat and his possessions, and seeing, with dismaying clarity, the difficulty of explaining his secession without damage to herself.

Dahlia had her apprehensions, but she could not altogether regret her behaviour. While she hoped for the best for Mary, she was more concerned with the good bestowed on herself. It was no longer necessary to wash her cheek clean of Mr. Allsop's kiss. Mr. Sproat had metaphorically done that for her face and for her spirit and, on this night, when she went to bed, it was she who undressed in a sort of dream.

'Why were there such a lot of people in the house?' Jenny asked, and Dahlia, that guardian angel, returned to the duties she had temporarily forgotten.

'Mr. Sproat came in and we all had a talk,' she said. When she looked at Jenny's little pointed face, peering

307

over the bedclothes, it seemed a pity to tell her about Mr. Allsop and she could tell no one about Mr. Sproat.

'Yes, I know. Mr. Cummings went and looked. But why?'

'Why not?' Dahlia said, standing before the glass, in her nightgown, and studying her reflection.

'He needn't have come in with such a rush. He frightened me.'

'Well, you see,' Dahlia said, trying on one of her hats, 'Mr. Allsop had to go off in a hurry. He won't be here for breakfast.' It was a poor explanation, but it was good enough for Jenny. Sarah had found it good enough for Louisa, who did not give another thought to Mr. Allsop's sudden business, and she had other things to think about when next Friday came and did not bring him.

Jenny said, 'Oh! Well, I suppose he'll come back to her,' and Dahlia took off her hat and did not try on another: it seemed too heartless, and if Mr. Sproat had been handy she might have promised to marry him there and then. She was not in love with him: she did not want to be in love as Jenny was, broken-spirited in sorrow and probably slavish in happiness: she wanted to be saved from that, but she rejoiced in being loved and before she went to sleep, in that assurance, she asked a question of Jenny.

'Do you think,' she said slowly, 'I could ever look like Mrs. Doubleday?'

'How could you? You haven't got horse teeth.'

'But from the back, Jen,' Dahlia persisted.

'No, your waist's in the right place and hers isn't.' Jenny had an unerring eye for physical defects. 'And her legs must be fastened in badly, or she couldn't throw her feet out.'

Dahlia repeated the statement she had made long ago. 'We have a lot to be thankful for,' and as Jenny sighed, she said, gently, 'Yes, Jen. You'll get over this. People do, you know. And you told me once that you couldn't be happy for a minute if you had flat feet.'

'If I'd had flat feet—' Jenny began, but she finished her sentence in her mind. Cyril would not have loved her: he would have been kind to her when he found her under the hedge but, after he had seen her walk, he would not have asked her to meet him, and she would have gone home, burdened with hopeless love and the sad feet that would cumber her all her days. Under this thought and her memory of Edwin Cummings' coldness and the rigidity of the arm to which she had clung, she recovered a little of her pride. She could not bear being taunted by him: she would show him that she did come of gentlepeople, though she had denied her kinship with them. She had been wearing her heart on her sleeve and there had been no sign of his, when she held his arm. She had disappointed him: it was strange to suffer because she had disappointed a young man in a shop.

'If only I needn't listen all the time!' she thought.

She could relax when she lay in bed, but with the slackening of her muscles, as though a door had been opened, her mind was filled with intensely vivid memories. She could live over again every moment she had spent with Cyril, from the first meeting in the green and golden field to the day when the field was tarnished under the leaden sky and, through all the others, to the one when she had carried home her brimming cup of treasure and dropped it on the attic floor. But now the attic had disappeared: her body was not in the bed: she was crying again under the hedge. She heard the soft thud of hoofs, the flowers stood up among the grasses, solid and shining: he bent over her, kind and embarrassed, but she spoke and smiled and his face and voice subtly changed, and slowly, forgetting nothing, she went through each hour. The first touch of his hand made her own hand tingle, she smelt warm earth and resin and saw the pale yellow birch leaves held in bunches on silver stems: she heard the hooting of the steamers, the jangle of tramcars, the sound of oars in their rowlocks and she ran down the steep hill-side into his arms. Then the wood, patched with black shadows and strips of sunshine, Cyril himself in his soft, white shirt and her face against his tanned neck, were all blotted out in a darkness that swayed with her own giddiness. She had no identity: she was neither Jenny Wren nor Jenny Rendall: she did not think back through these last days, so few, though they seemed like years, or forward to an endless future without him: she was young love, young desire, wrapped and rocked in the ecstasy of a caress which was more perfect in the liberty of her imagination than it had been in fact. It was almost as though, half conscious, she floated on a smoothly heaving sea and, without a struggle, she sank into it and slept.

This was her nightly solace, but there was no comfort in the morning when Dahlia's bright head, the slow, rhythmic movements of her mother, Aunt Sarah's sharp looks, overlaid by piety, and Edwin Cummings' hurried eating of his morning porridge, were the attributes and actions of people in another world, and they were enviable for the calm ordinariness of their existence, for the freedom with which they could go out and walk about the streets, indifferent to being seen, or sit in the house, careless of knocks or footsteps.

'I shan't go to the play,' she told Dahlia. 'You can take Mr. Cummings.'

'I'm not going to take anybody,' Dahlia said. 'Mr. Sproat—what an awful name it is!—I met Mr. Sproat this morning and he's got a ticket for me, so'—she managed to put a little reluctance into her voice—'I shall have to go with him and you can take Edwin Cummings.'

'Couldn't Sarah go instead of me?'

'I wouldn't let her hear a word of it. She's not fit to hear such lovely language.'

This was startling from Dahlia, and Jenny looked at her with a spark of interest. 'You called it sloppy when you recited it to Miss Morrison.'

'There are lots of funny bits, too.'

'Yes, I know,' said Jenny, thinking of her mother's laughter.

'And it would do you good.'

'It might do Sarah good.'

'No, she's a hopeless case, and, don't you see, Jen, she'd spoil it for everybody else. People would be afraid to laugh, if she were there, because they'd be sure there was a nasty meaning in the joke, and the sloppy bits would curdle, they would taste sour. Though,' she added thoughtfully, 'I don't believe anyone would hear them. The actors wouldn't be able to speak. They'd come slipping through the trees and then, suddenly, they'd be struck dumb—when they felt Sarah. No, she mustn't go.'

'It seems to me,' Jenny said slowly, 'that you're rather excited because you're going with Mr. Sproat.'

'Because I'm going to wear my flowery dress and Miss Morrison's scarf. I haven't been to a party since I left school and what parties those were! The boys huddled in one corner and all of us pretending they didn't interest us any more than the girls, and Miss Headley being so careful not to watch us! Of course, I'm excited. Wouldn't it be terrible if it rained?'

'It wouldn't matter to me,' Jenny said, but secretly she longed to go to the Gardens. She knew there would be release and assuagement in hearing immortal words beautifully spoken, coming across the twilight straight to her heart, and she thought that if she could sit there, with Cyril beside her, it would be like marriage. 'A marriage of true minds,' she said to herself, but she doubted whether it would be like that for him. She could imagine how he would fidget and look round at the audience, like a bored child. He was like a child, in some ways, she thought, loving him the more for it, and he would hardly come all the way from Merriman House to see a play by Shakespeare: he would expect it to be dull.

'All right, we'll take Mr. Cummings,' she said.

'I'm not going to start with Mr. Sproat,' Dahlia explained. 'I've told mother, but nobody must tell Sarah.'

'But he knows about her.'

'Of course he does. I don't mind his seeing her, but I couldn't bear her to see him.'

'And he won't be sitting with us.'

'No.' Dahlia resented this implication. 'Do you suppose he'd mind, if he was?' she asked, lifting her head.

'It's different for a parson,' Jenny replied, making excuses for the offences she had not given Cyril a chance to commit.

It was a fine night and Dahlia wore her flowery dress and scarf. She had the shoulders for a shawl. They were what her mother's must have been when she was a girl, and though these were still magnificent, they were hidden under her black coat.

'You look so nice without a hat,' Jenny said, putting her head on one side and peering at her mother in her old, half-timid, coaxing way. 'I'll lend you my scarf if you'll go without a hat. Then your dress won't show. It's a shame that you haven't got a nicer one.'

'What does it matter about me?' Louisa asked. 'Whoever sees me?'

'We do,' Jenny said.

'But not much,' Louisa answered without bitterness. 'And d'you think I'd take your scarf? I want to see you wearing it. I'll go in my coat and hat. I'd feel undressed, else. But Jenny, if you're thinking I'll look queer, in those good seats with all the grand people, I'll stay at home.'

'No!' Jenny cried, and the vehemence that reassured Louisa was directed against herself. She would not be ashamed. The matter-of-fact way in which her mother recognised her difference was more painful, at that moment, than any raised eyebrows of the Merrimans, and Jenny said stoutly, 'There'll be nobody as beautiful as you.'

This was probably true, but the other beauties would not notice their rival: her colour would be drenched, her shape hidden by the unbecoming black.

'Well, I'd like to go,' Louisa admitted. 'It's a long time since I've seen a play.'

It was more than twenty years since she had sold programmes at the old theatre down in Radstowe, and there Sidney Rendall saw her leaning against one of the slim gold pillars, looking like Ceres, he thought, and enthralled by the melodrama being played on the stage which famous actors and actresses had once trod. The old playbills hung in the corridors, but the names on them meant nothing to Louisa: they meant little to Sidney Rendall when he returned, night after night, to look at the young goddess who held, instead of a sheaf, a bundle of programmes under her arm.

She did not look like a goddess when she stood on the pavement of Beulah Mount, waiting for the rest of the party. She looked—Jenny saw it and shut her cruel eyes for a second—like a servant being taken for a treat by the daughters of the house.

There was no need to blush for Mr. Cummings. His clothes were good, because cheap ones were not economical; his hair, as Jenny had often noticed, had no erratic, betraying growth, and there was nothing to be betrayed, except the fact that his father was a fine workman and

3¹3

wore an apron and soiled his hands. The one thing Mr. Cummings would not have been suspected of was an interest in the beautiful antique. He might have been an engineer or a sailor: he looked as if his hands served his brain. Jenny was satisfied with his appearance and more than satisfied with Dahlia's, for, once out of range of the Dakins' windows, she had the radiance of a girl who knows she looks lovely and expects confirmation of that knowledge in a lover's eyes. Miss Jewel saw it through her curtains and felt a bewildered rage. Where were the dust and ashes that should have been on Dahlia's head?

CHAPTER XXXIX

THERE was a gay scene on the road lying between the Zoological Gardens and the Downs. Upper Radstowe had a taste for culture when it could be combined with a social function, and all Upper Radstowe was driving or walking towards the gate. The plays of Shakespeare, performed in the theatre, never filled the house, but this was a sort of intellectual garden-party, and no one of any importance meant to miss it.

The unimportant people were clustered on the gentle slope edging the Downs. They could sit there and have a good view of the arrivals and, with the amazing generosity of the poor, they enjoyed the sight of ladies in flimsy frocks and men in white shirt-fronts entering the portals denied to themselves. When the entertainment began they might see the illuminations among the trees and catch a waft of music: meanwhile, they were content with the frocks and the opera hats and the shining cars. Young men and girls lay on the bank and occasionally interrupted their love-making for a look at the road, but the middle-aged women looked at it all the time and paid little heed to their children, who were screaming among the hawthorn bushes or rolling down the slope, though now and then a mother would shout a mechanical, disregarded threat, or administer a slap to a passing child.

The reverend gentleman, waiting at the gate, was known to some of these women from the poor streets of Upper Radstowe and so was Mr. Doubleday, but more distantly. He advanced, beaming, turning in his toes, tripping on them lightly, giving his two nods to all his acquaintances, ready to give them to strangers at the least encouragement, and Mrs. Doubleday marched by his side, with her toes turned out, but she did not smile. While Mr. Doubleday glanced at the people on the bank and gathered them, with that look, into the general festivity, her permanent state of mind was one that turned pleasure into duty. She was there as the guardian of her husband, whose geniality was sometimes overdone, and as a guarantee of the Church's recognition of the arts.

'Ah, Sproat, Sproat!' said Mr. Doubleday, lifting a hand in greeting. 'What a gathering! What a gathering! Waiting for friends? That's right. That's right.' He squeezed himself through the turnstile and bounced forward, his head, as quick as a bird's, jerked this way and that: his eager eyes missed nobody, yet nobody made more than a passing impression on his mind. Mrs. Doubleday had more concentration. She kept her attention on Mr. Sproat, to whom also she was a sort of guardian. She expected him to meet a bevy of what, in Church circles, are known as lads, but she saw him detach Dahlia from an oddly-assorted group and disappear with her in the crowd. That was the young woman whom Miss Morrison had brought to church, the daughter of her landlady, unsuitably dressed for her station and most unsuitably companioned, and she spoke her disapproval to Mr. Doubleday.

'Oh! Pity, pity!' he said vaguely, to oblige her, but he did not think it was a pity: he thought it was delightful for a young man to see an irreproachable entertainment with a charming girl by his side.

Mrs. Doubleday was deciding to speak tactfully to Mr. Sproat. 'It would never do,' she informed her husband, and she thought of Miss Morrison suddenly leaving the bazaar in the lurch after getting her way about the shepherdesses, and she wondered whether tact were really what Mr. Sproat needed. 'I'm surprised at him,' she hissed in Mr. Doubleday's ear.

'Yes, yes,' he said soothingly, lifting the tails of his coat and glancing round in a last search for familiar faces, before he took his seat. He could see Mr. Sproat sitting with his arms folded across his chest. He was a good fellow, a little too earnest in well-doing, but a hard worker, a hard worker, and that was what the rotund Mr. Doubleday appreciated in a curate, but Mrs. Doubleday was mentally removing him from Upper Radstowe, little knowing that, in imagination, he had gone already.

The gathering twilight, the grass turning black at his feet, the faint sound of violins being tuned, out of sight among the trees, the murmur of voices from the wide semicircle of spectators and the stir of moving people, the sudden shattering roar of a lion disturbed by this untimely invasion, made a magic envelope for Mr. Sproat in which he and Dahlia were enclosed. He looked impassive and rather stern, as though he had been brought there under protest, but it was a sense of beauty that kept him so still. He did not look at Dahlia, though, as she leaned forward in her chair, he could see the back of her pretty neck by merely lowering his eyes. Looking at her was not necessary: he could feel her presence and the loveliness of the warm night through every pore of his body, and when the musicians quietly took their places at the side of the lawn left empty for the players, and the unearthly sound of strings stilled the rustling of the audience, the magic envelope was thickened and nothing came through it except the music and the stars, until it was broken by the sudden, brilliant lighting of the green stage and the appearance and voices of the actors.

317

What spoilt the happy spell for Mr. Sproat wove a self-forgetting one for Jenny. The seats, chosen with such promptitude by Miss Morrison who, perhaps, from her boarding-house in Eastbourne, was incorrectly picturing the happiness she had given, were in the front row and in the middle of it, a conspicuous position, without a screen of chairs for Louisa's widespread knees, the hands turned inwards on them, her elbows threatening Edwin Cummings on one side and Jenny on the other, and, until the play began, Jenny was very uneasy and looked steadily at the empty stage in the common belief that if she noticed nobody, nobody would notice her, and she hoped, in spite of herself, that her attachment to her mother was not obvious. In a country inhabited by savages whose standards were incomprehensible, Jenny might have forgotten Louisa's little oddities of manner: she would certainly have been glad of her company. No savages would fluster Louisa Rendall and the people composing this audience were much less dangerous, and therefore less important, but for Jenny they were important and might be dangerous, and the physical security she would feel if her mother stood between her and brandished spears, was wasted in the Zoological Gardens of Upper Radstowe, though the lion roared behind his bars. Jenny was safe here from everything except the criticism she dreaded, and the possibility that Cyril was standing in his place and scanning the rows of faces. Why had she come? she asked, in a panic, making herself as small as possible, trying to make her mind a blank, so that her thoughts would not draw Cyril's eyes. Each minute the night was growing darker, but each minute loitered heavily. Why had they arrived so soon? Yet, if they had come later they must have made a little procession across the open space and everybody would have seen them.

'I wish they'd get started,' Louisa said in a loud voice.

'The lady behind wants you to take your hat off,' Jenny said.

Louisa turned to look at the lady and then, slowly, rather resentfully, she removed the obstruction and pushed it behind her feet.

'I can't see Dahlia anywhere,' she told Jenny with reverberating consonants.

'The music's beginning. We mustn't talk,' Jenny whispered.

'Oh, well—' said Louisa, settling into her seat. She accepted the hint without understanding it. She did not know what the music was for, except to cheer things up a little and make an accompaniment to her own comments, but she was obediently silent and as much enchanted as Jenny when the play began. Perhaps the words, strange to her, as to many better educated people in the audience, words which would have been almost incomprehensible if she had read them, carried her back, on the mere pleasure of the sound, to her youth when the young squire loved her and, heedless of the future, she had been happy. Perhaps the emotions underlying her pleasure were no less intense than her daughter's, though she was not able to put them into language, and in hers there was no pain, for they had the beauty given by distance, and the scoldings and the heartaches were forgotten. It was like remembering a dream in which the sun shone with peculiar brilliance on running water and on flowers: the stream gurgled through a familiar meadow, the flowers were the common ones of the field, such flowers as Jenny had gathered and brought home, but the dream revealed them as themselves, and, for a brief space, Louisa saw them as fresh and lovely creations offered to human eyes for the first time. That dream had come to her when, at the foot of the stairs in Beulah Mount, she told Jenny

319

about her lover, and it returned now, in the darkening gardens. It was the best thing in her life: she had done nothing to spoil it and it stood clear, separated from, though it had led to, everything that followed. It was like a shining jewel in a dark case, like an inspired and glowing painting on a dingy wall.

Remembered happiness did not come in the same way to Jenny. First, she felt the safety of the darkness, then, in that security and in the glorious sense of isolation produced by the presence of many strangers, her mind seemed to leap from her body and she saw her story as one that might have been acted on the stage in front of her and she had a sort of pleasure in it. She was Viola who loved the Duke, but she was a sadder figure for whom there was no happy ending, and she was young enough, and, at this moment, enough enchanted, to enjoy the sadness of carrying her romantic love through life as a secret, beautiful burden, and she forgot that, outside these gardens, beyond the reach of these voices, there was the common daylight of many to-morrows.

The polite titterings evoked by Toby Belch and Andrew Aguecheek, who seemed themselves to doubt the humour of their representations, brought her back to the present moment, and she glanced at her mother who was staring stolidly at the comic men. There was no need for a roaring lion to cover Jenny's confusion. Louisa was not moved to the point of loud laughter, and she did not know that this was where she was expected to feign amusement if she did not feel it: she smiled because one man was fat and the other thin, and she looked distrustfully at Malvolio's struttings. This was not her idea of fun. When she wanted what she called a good laugh she knew where to get it, but she was contented here and she was soothed. She forgot Sarah and Thomas Grimshaw and the money, and she was proud of Jenny, with her small head rising above

the filmy scarf, and of Dahlia, somewhere out of sight with
Mr. Sproat, and when her attention wavered and she
discerned the heads and shoulders of other girls, she could
see no one comparable to her daughters.

'It's a bit long, isn't it? Getting tired of it?' she asked
in a loud whisper. Jenny's head drooped now: she was
not looking at the stage, and, without raising her head,
she gave it a tiny, irritable shake, denying the suggestion,
bidding her mother be quiet.

Louisa lifted and dropped her shoulders. She had done
something wrong again: she wished she were different.
In Sidney Rendall's lifetime she had purposely and
defiantly sustained the peasant standards he despised: he
had done his best to keep the children from her, and,
with her own pride, she had helped him. Now that they
were her own she wanted to be like them. Pathetically
she was trying to understand their values and to make
hers fit them, and though she seldom wasted bitterness
on the past, she had a strong feeling of anger against her
husband. He had not given her a chance, she thought:
he had done wrong by them as well as by her and,
if they had not been the girls they were, they would
have gone off and left her before this: they would not
have been seen with her among all these grand people
in the Gardens. She wanted more time to get closer to
them. Already, in these few months, their relationships
had changed. Sarah had done something towards that.
Dahlia and Jenny, with small attentions and little, friendly
looks and unspoken criticism of their aunt, which once
Louisa would have resented, were trying to draw their
mother into their own fellowship. She believed they liked
her: she knew she loved them with all the force of her
liberated affection, but time was passing, and Dahlia
was sitting somewhere with Mr. Sproat, and here was a
lad on her left hand who would be glad enough to take

Jenny from her—and if it was not Edwin Cummings it would be someone else.

'And what'll I do then?' she asked herself and, like many another mother, she wished time would stand still for them and keep them as they were, while she advanced towards understanding them — towards, she thought humbly, being worthy of them.

The play was ending. Jenny was sitting on the edge of her chair as though she wanted to be off already, but Louisa's attention was now on the stage again. It was a pretty play, she decided: she liked the dresses and the lights and the festal feeling of an entertainment in the open air, but these people in the play had made a lot of difficulty about nothing: nobody with eyes in their heads could have mistaken the girl for her brother, but Louisa clapped loudly with her strong hands before she stooped for her hat, put it on carelessly and turned to smile at Jenny, between relief and pleasure.

Jenny was not by her side. She was not in sight: she had slipped away with the first stirring of the audience.

'Gone after Dahlia, I expect,' Louisa said. 'We'd best sit here for a bit, till the crowd's out, and maybe she'll come and fetch us.'

CHAPTER XL

THE stage lights were put out and the trees, which had been a mere background for the players, seemed quietly to take a step forward in the darkness. With dignity they resumed their individuality and asserted their right to the earth where they were rooted. Their branches were motionless, but it was as though they drew a faint sigh of relief, like people who had endured with courtesy the tiresome company of guests at last departing. Then the audience, on the farther side of the semicircle, broke across the open space and blocked the view of Edwin and Louisa.

'Best wait till they've gone,' said Louisa, as she sat back and drew in her feet lest they should be trodden by the people carelessly passing, and she added doubtfully, 'Jenny—she's not like other people. She's dainty. I reckon she ran off so's not to get pushed about. She was never one to be touched much—from a child. Or else,' Louisa continued, 'she wanted to remember it, just as it was. It sorts of spoils it when you hear everybody talking, and you've got to get home, and Sarah'll be in the kitchen. She'll be having a quiet think all to herself up in the attic.'

Edwin made a sound which could be taken for assent, but he had no belief in Louisa's explanations. He was wishing he had been sitting next to Jenny, for he must, he thought, have known when she was seized by the instinct to run, and he could have followed her. It was hopeless to attempt that now, and he fixed himself in his chair, but the imagination which, until he knew her, was limited to plans for his perfect shop and dreams of the choice pieces he would buy and reluctantly yield to purchasers, went roving over the Downs and ran through the streets: it slipped on to the bridge and stood by the railings. They were high railings, designedly high and designedly spiked, but imagination easily surmounted them, hung by a pair of slim hands on the outer side for a second and dropped in a pale bundle from which the ends of a scarf flew out.

Edwin Cummings shut his eyes. His common sense defied this vision: he was reassured by the belief that such things could not happen to anyone he knew, but, for all that, he was held by the vividness of his picture, and he saw a horrible fairness in such an end for Jenny. She was not like other people: she had that strange, elusive quality of specialness, and, just for an instant, the thought of her, dead and marble cold, was agonisingly lovely to him. It immortalised her aloofness and her youth, presenting them to him, to be carried secretly while life lasted.

'We'd best be going,' he heard Louisa say.

He did not move immediately. He was still held by that vision, and then, in a panic, he opened his eyes, knowing that he could not rest until he found her, but before he could spring up and while Louisa still kept her seat, a young man walked across the empty, grassy space and stood in front of them. There was no doubt of his identity in Edwin's mind. This was the man for whom Jenny listened and his footsteps had not made a sound. She had listened, and, at last, when she was not here, he had come silently.

The sky would get no darker to-night: the lamps edging the paths and a few inquisitive, heartless stars were not bright enough to make Cyril Merriman more than a figure

324

with a pale oval for a face above the pale front of his shirt, but Edwin saw the carriage of his bare head and his slim body, and felt, unwillingly, his own urgency in the other man, heard it, too, in the controlled words he uttered.

'There was a lady sitting here,' he said. 'Sitting here— Was she—? I think she was with you. Could you tell me where I can find her?'

'Jenny, is it?' Louisa said, looking up at him.

'She's not here,' Edwin said in a harsh voice.

'So I see,' the other answered, in a cold, level tone: and he did not look at Edwin, who saw the dark blots of Cyril's eyes extinguished by the lowering of his eyelids. His face was plainer now, but perhaps it was not plain enough to show the slight spreading of the nostrils which was apparent to Edwin's fancy.

Jenny had run away: Jenny had clung to his arm and bidden him refuse entry to the owner of the steps she feared, and this fellow with the good manners and the charming voice should not find her if Edwin Cummings could help it, but while he made this resolution, it wavered. He had a feeling that things must happen as they would, that so it might be best for Jenny, since Fortune, seeing her as he did, must wish to please her, and already he heard Louisa saying, 'Is it my Jenny you're wanting?'

There was hesitation in the young man's voice. 'She was sitting here,' he repeated. 'Her name—' He stopped. It seemed as though he could not pronounce her name in the hearing of this woman who sat with her hands on her knees and used the possessive pronoun. She was the sort of woman who usually stood up when he spoke to her, and her next words startled him. They surprised Edwin Cummings, and Louisa herself had her pride in them.

'And anyway,' she said amiably enough, 'I don't know who you are, young man.' The mother of girls like Dahlia and Jenny did not answer the questions of strangers.

'It must be a mistake,' he muttered, and he turned away, but he turned back and his voice was young and troubled: his need forced him to condescension.

'But she was sitting here. She spoke to you. I'm Cyril Merriman of Merriman House, across the river.'

There was a movement from Edwin Cummings, unnoticed by the others. This man, for whom Jenny listened, was the descendant of the foodstuff merchant, the future owner of the house on which Edwin had nearly set his heart, the carelessly arrogant horseman who had almost ridden down the stranger within his gate, and Edwin had a fierce desire to pay him physically for that moment. Cyril Merriman's haughty indifference was negligible, but Edwin had not forgotten Jenny's shame, and there was a grim satisfaction in thinking that this was he who would some day lie under the monument like a packing-case, without ever having understood its ugliness. But, Edwin thought wildly, he would put Jenny under it too, if he could: he would have her to live with him in the fair old house his grandfather had bought but had not planned, and when she died she would be hidden and stifled under that monstrous, expensive expression of the family's importance.

'No!' Edwin said aloud. But Louisa was speaking and his exclamation ran into his words.

'Merriman!' she said. 'Well, then, I've seen you when you were a bit of a lad, riding your pony on the roads. I'm Mrs. Rendall. I lived at the White Farm, near your place, for more than twenty years, but I'm living now in Beulah Mount.'

'Rendall? At the White Farm?' he said. 'But— Rendall,' he repeated, emphasising the first syllable.

'That's my name,' Louisa said with a nod. 'Number fifteen, Beulah Mount. I've started a boarding-house there, since my husband died. Well, not what you could rightly call a boarding-house, but I take lodgers. Mr.

326

Cummings, here, is one of my lodgers. Well, really, at the present, he's the only one I've got.'

'And she lives there?' Cyril asked in a low voice.

'Of course she lives there!' Louisa cried with neighbourly good humour. 'She's my own daughter.'

The upward fling of Cyril Merriman's head, his hastily-muttered, 'I don't understand it,' was meat and drink to Edwin Cummings, and with consolatory self-satisfaction he knew that nobody connected with Jenny, were they murderers or thieves or vagabonds and not Jenny herself, if she were one of these, could turn him from his love for her or discompose him for a moment. She was Jenny, and, in a flash of time, he saw her, disdainful and selfish and sweet: he searched for the secret of her charm for him, and suddenly he sprang up, in his necessity to find her, to be more active than this Merriman who, even in the darkness could not hide his discomfiture and indecision.

Edwin might have been more tolerant if he had understood the confusion created by the difference between Louisa's surname and the one by which Cyril knew Jenny, and not only by the difference, but by the curtailed likeness. Many memories, many doubts, were passing through his mind. He was trying to explain inconsistencies and to connect divergences, and he was interrupted, as Edwin was stayed in his flight, by a voice calling his name, by the faint swish of draperies and the appearance of a tall woman who walked with authority across the grass.

She halted within a few feet of the party, saying, with impatience, 'Why are you so long, Cyril? We are all waiting for you.'

'Yes, I'm coming,' he said. 'Mother, this is Mrs. Rendall, who used to live at the White Farm. I expect you know her.'

There was a pause in which Mrs. Merriman stood very

still. Then she said, 'No, I don't know her,' in a cool, level voice, as though Louisa were not there, and she walked away quickly, saying, 'You must come at once, Cyril.'

This was difficult for the young man, and, muttering something, he hastened after her.

'Oh, well—' said Louisa slowly, getting up from her chair.

With her back to Edwin she pushed her hat farther on her head: she made a pretence of feeling for something in her handbag.

'That was disgusting!' he said.

In this matter, too, he was ignorant of causes. For him Mrs. Merriman's conduct was that of an ill-mannered snob, but Louisa knew better. It was virtue's rebuff to sin, that sin, so slight and so forgivable in her own mind. What she did not know was that legend had been very busy with her name. For Mrs. Merriman the affair with Thomas Grimshaw, who would not sell the White Farm, whose land was an independent smear on the Merriman acres, was enough to make Louisa invisible to decent eyes, but the country-side had been generous in giving her other conquests, and if Cyril had heard of none of them, this was due to his indifference to gossip and his absence from home since he became a man.

Louisa suddenly sat down again. These few seconds of concentrated thought had been exhausting. The young man who wanted Jenny, Jenny who had run away and was unhappy, Mrs. Merriman's rebuff, Jenny who was unhappy and ran away, though the young man was looking for her, over and over again she fitted these pieces into their places: some necessary connections were missing, but it was not long before she saw herself as the centre of the pattern.

'Don't mind her,' Edwin said. 'Come home now.'

They could hear a man's voice warning loiterers that the

gates must be shut. 'All out! All out!' he cried, and there was a mournful finality in the sound.

'We'll have to find Jenny,' Louisa said.

'Yes, we must find her.' He slipped his arm through Louisa's and guided her past the disordered chairs, on to the gravel path and through the gate.

'Wait a minute till I take my hat off,' she said. 'It's hot. My head's hot. Pity but what I didn't keep it off all the time. Jenny said I was better without it, but there, what matters the hat?' She quickened her steps. 'It wouldn't have made a bit of difference.'

Past the fountain, up the avenue, across the foot of the hill and down Beulah Mount, the two went hurriedly. Their thoughts went quickly, too, and Louisa's travelled on a path she had not meant them to take. They crossed the bridge—where those of Edwin Cummings lingered for a minute—and marched steadily on the long road to Grimshaw's farm, and, as they went, they cast back, now and then, to Louisa's own young squire. She had been right to run away from him, but why should Jenny run from hers? Jenny was different, she was a lady: Mrs. Merriman could not turn up her nose at Jenny, and Jenny's mother had a plan which would make all well.

'She'll be in bed by this time,' Louisa said, but when they reached the house they found Sarah in it alone. 'Jenny not back yet?' Louisa asked.

Sarah shook her head in disapproval. 'No, nor Dahlia,' she said, and at once Edwin Cummings went out quietly.

'Dahlia's all right. I know where she is.'

'Ah, it's Jenny you're worrying about.'

'There's plenty of time yet. It's early. I'm not worrying,' Louisa said hastily.

To that Sarah paid no heed. She had endured several hours of solitude and inactivity, and she had to make the worst of what was offered to her now. 'Goodness knows where the girl's got to,' she said. 'But don't say I didn't warn you. If I was the girl's mother, I'd be across the river, come to-morrow, and I'd ask young Merriman what he's after. There's trouble there, Louisa. Jenny's looking ill, and if you won't believe me you can ask Mr. Grimshaw and he'll tell you what he's told me.'

At these words Louisa found herself trembling a little, not for Jenny's immediate peril but for her own fortitude. Grimshaw had told Jenny about the money and he had told Sarah. Sarah, if she spoke the truth, had been his confidante again, and Louisa was more angrily hurt than she had ever been before, but her pride inspired her to say scornfully, 'You and Grimshaw! You're a pair of clever ones! And all the time there's not a thing you can tell me about Jenny that I don't know already.'

'Well, then,' said Sarah, 'I wonder at you. If I was the girl's mother I'd be over the bridge to-morrow.'

'Don't you worry. I'm going.'

Sarah's eyes sharpened. 'You'd better take me with you, Louisa. I'll know how to talk to them.'

'If you stir a finger—' Louisa began threateningly, and Sarah assumed her meekly pious expression.

'Oh well, dearie, you know much more about these sort of goings-on than I do. Like mother, like daughter,' she said with a sigh.

CHAPTER XLI

As Edwin Cummings passed through the hall he picked up a letter and put it in his pocket. It was from Kitty: it might contain bad news, but he would not stay to read it. All the circumstances of his life unconnected with Jenny had fallen back and left him and her in a circle of darkness where she evaded and he pursued.

He went first towards the bridge and stood at its entrance. No one was crossing. The bridge, outlined by lamps, seemed aloof from human interests. It looked as though it had created itself for its own satisfaction and lighted these inextinguishable lamps at the same time. They burned with a steady impassivity, and no little figure, standing under the cold lights and then dropping into the gulf at which they gazed, would have moved them to a single flicker. They were horrible to Edwin as he looked at them: they seemed remorseless, symbols of cruelty, and he turned away. He had an irrational feeling that it would please them if he passed the entrance and made known his fear, and he was afraid of his fear. It was foolish, he did not believe in it, yet it was there, and thinking of it might draw Jenny to this place. He went back to the point where the roads to the bridge and Beulah Mount converged. He would stay there and wait for her and take her home: he would stand between her and his fear, with its power to produce what he dreaded. Why had such a thought come to him, he wondered. It was outside his character. It came, he felt, from her conception of herself, from her belief in the intensity of her own sufferings, but Jenny was not to touch tragedy, though she approached it, and presently, coming in little runs down the hill, not keeping to the path but sheltering among the bushes on the rough ground, he saw her and felt a great reaction of anger. All his muscles, unconsciously tautened, ached violently as they slackened. He wanted to scold her harshly, he was furious with himself: but when he met and took her unresisting hand she seemed to him like a little animal, scared by something it did not understand, blindly finding its way home.

'Oh, Jenny, where have you been?' he asked.

'Over the Downs,' she said, 'and looking at the river, and then I thought it must be time to come back.'

'And you didn't think that we'd be worrying about you. You're not kind, Jenny.'

'No, I'm not kind,' she said. She stood and looked at the quiet streets. 'Nobody!' she said. 'And on the Downs there were only lovers and a few lonely ones like me.'

'It wasn't safe,' he muttered.

'Safe! No one can hurt you if you pretend you're not there.'

'Then,' he said roughly, 'what made you leave the Gardens?'

'I wasn't pretending hard enough,' she whispered. 'I didn't want to.'

He sighed, let go of her hand, and thrust his own into his pocket. 'I've a letter from Kitty,' he said, 'but I haven't read it.'

'Read it now, under this lamp,' she said.

'No, your mother's waiting for you.' He felt tired and far away from her. He had been braced for a sorrow with its own beauty, and though it was not fair to blame her, who had no suspicion of an anxiety out of all proportion to its cause, he was jaded by this calm anti-climax and weary of himself and her. He knew she was reassured by his presence. She was no longer a little frightened animal it was impossible to scold, and, suddenly cruel as he remembered Cyril Merriman, he asked sharply, 'What name is it you've been using? Were you ashamed to use your own?'

She gave him a quick, fearful look. She stopped and raised her arms a little and the ends of her scarf flew out with the movement. It seemed as if she would fly, too, but the door of the house was open: Louisa was standing there, and, for the first time since she was a baby, Jenny went for refuge to her mother.

'Ah, you've come back,' Louisa said, moved, like Jenny, beyond embarrassment. 'Come in here for a bit. I want to talk to you.'

Edwin read his letter in the hall and tried to fix his mind on it while he listened to the murmuring of voices in the sitting-room. He read it twice, then folded it and put it in his pocket. There was bad news, but grief for his stricken father and anxiety for his sisters had to wait. He spared this moment for himself. He would be glad to go, he decided. It seemed a long time since he resigned his hope of the little shop on The Slope. He had given it up without much pain, because Jenny had slipped into its place, but for Jenny he was not much more than an occasionally useful policeman, and it was not in such a capacity that he meant to spend his days. He would return to the second-hand furniture shop, the bundles of old school-books and forgotten novels, the odd bits of china and the rare excitement of a treasure, and some day, when Jenny was married, she would drive down as she had promised, to see what he had done with the bureau, but the bureau would not be there: it would be in Merriman House, or Mr. Sproat would write his sermons on it and there would be no need for Jenny to ask news of it. He did not want her to drive down and see him: he wanted to remember her as part of the past that could not be renewed. He had his business to follow, and he knew, well enough, that gradually he would forget to remember her. It would be the easier because he would not know how to picture her in surroundings different from Beulah Mount, and, as he thought this, he remembered Cyril Merriman's mother sweeping over the grass, and her voice when she said she did not know Louisa Rendall: he remembered the young man, puzzled and hesitant, meekly following his mother, and did not trust his valour. It seemed to him that perhaps, after all, he wished to stay, and, when the door of the sitting-room was opened and Jenny appeared, he said gloomily, 'I'll have to go home before long. My father's worse again.'

'Is he? Was that in Kitty's letter?' Jenny said. 'I'm sorry.'

'I'll have to give notice at the shop.'

She nodded. Her eyes were shining, though her face was grave.

'A month's notice,' he said.

'Yes,' she agreed. 'I'm sorry about your father. I'm sorry you'll have to go. You've been so kind,' she said, smiling a little, like one who has a tenderness for past unhappiness, and she went upstairs without a word of more regret.

And this was she who had once commanded him to stay and told him she could not do without him! She had stood there listening to him because she was naturally courteous: she would have listened like that to the whine of a beggar. He knew she had forgotten him before her foot was on the first stair.

How could she remember anything except her mother's story? Cyril had come and asked where he could find her: he knew where she lived: he had spoken to her mother and he would surely come to-morrow. There was still

Aunt Sarah to be presented, but what did she matter? They would be able to laugh at her together. Aunt Sarah was the name her cowardice had given to all her difficulties, and now the worst of them were over. The singing in Jenny's heart was in a minor key. She knew things would not be easy, but Louisa's tenderness had sweetened the soothing balm she gave: her optimism and her resolution to remove what she believed was the only obstacle between Jenny and young Merriman, had made her rendering of the story much more favourable than Edwin's would have been. There was no sense, Louisa thought, in worrying Jenny about Mrs. Merriman: that little matter was soon to be set right and the child would be happy. She should have, without injuring anyone, what her mother had resigned for her lover's sake, and she would know what to do with it, and, while Sarah punctured the stillness of the night with advice about what should be said to the Merrimans, or left unsaid, and what ultimatum should be delivered, Louisa saw Jenny's shining eyes and heard such confidences as she had never expected to hear from that proud daughter. The sacrifice of Louisa's own pride was nothing. Thomas had not treated her fairly: he had gone behind her back. Yet she could understand that, too. She could forgive him. And Louisa drew a deep breath in the basement room where she lay with Sarah. There was space, out there, in the country. Garden and fields were round about the house: the doors stood open, and through them came all the sounds to which she was accustomed, the clucking of fowls, the tramp of nailed feet on the flags, the clink of pails, and the lowing of cows waiting to be milked.

'Oh, well—' thought Louisa, making her usual comment.

Such was her simplicity and such her faith in Jenny's inheritance from her father. When, according to her notions, her own social offence was wiped out there would

335

be no other difficulty. Jenny's case was not like her own. Jenny was an educated lady, and the Merrimans, for all their wealth, were new people in comparison with the Rendalls. This was the first time Louisa had paid any tribute to her husband's family, and she did not ponder on the strangeness of finding value in what she had most bitterly resented.

Unknown to anyone except Sarah, whose mysteriousness was not noticed by two girls with plenty to preoccupy them, Louisa set off, next morning, on her mission. It did not occur to her to write to Grimshaw. She had no time to waste, yet she did not take the shortest road. She went downhill to the ferry instead of crossing the bridge, and Jenny, once more stationed at the window, but no longer hiding behind the curtains, saw nothing alarming in the direction of her departure. Jenny watched the bridge. As each hour passed she told herself the next would bring him. The morning went by and she saw the absurdity of expecting him before the afternoon. But that passed, too, and the quick beating of her heart slowed down. She could invent a hundred reasons for his delay, but they did not comfort her. He knew where she was and, in his place, she would have been on the doorstep with the dawn, and she began to put her own interpretation on her mother's tale: she saw how scanty its details were, but she would not ask any questions. She clung to her hope, though there was a gathering hardness in her thoughts of him, and this enabled her to meet Louisa's happy face with cheerfulness and to make a pretence of knowing what went on around her.

Louisa had not tried to renew the emotion she had shared with Jenny. She had an instinctive fear of advancing unless the moment propelled her. She had done what she could and she was not surprised at the young man's absence. No doubt he was having a hard time with his

336

mother, who would presently be discomforted. She had another secret pleasure in Sarah's baffled curiosity. Louisa's serene expression was the only hint vouchsafed of what had happened across the river. Sarah could not rest without the full report, and Dahlia, the only member of the household altogether ignorant of what was stirring, was made uneasy by her aunt's behaviour, the noddings and shakings of her head, which were unheeded now by Jenny and Louisa. She had failed in her attempt on Mr. Allsop: she might be planning something as shameful in regard to Mr. Sproat.

'I don't think she knows,' Dahlia said to Jenny, 'but if she finds out she'll spoil it somehow.'

'Knows what?' said Jenny.

Dahlia's surprise was a reproach. She had given freely to Jenny and she expected some sympathy in her own concerns. 'About my being friends with Mr. Sproat.'

'Oh, Mr. Sproat. But I thought he was such a wonderful person that Aunt Sarah couldn't matter.'

There was a touch of spite in this remark, but Dahlia pretended not to hear it. 'No,' she said on consideration, 'she doesn't really matter.' This was true. There was something pathetic about Sarah during these days. She was without her favourite occupation: she seemed to have lost her gift for making people uncomfortable. 'But,' Dahlia said, 'I don't want smudges on things.'

'He's rather smudgy himself.'

'He's not!'

'I only meant because he's black,' Jenny explained. 'Have you seen him since the play?'

'Of course I have. Every day. And several times.'

'Not in Beulah Mount,' Jenny said. If they had met there she must have seen them.

'There are other places,' Dahlia said.

Yes, there are other places, Jenny thought. There were

337

the woods and the fields, but it was impossible to imagine Mr. Sproat in such settings. How would he look in his black coat and clerical hat, standing in the little clearing of the wood, while the leaves of the beech trees made a sound like a fairy clapping of hands? Would he open his arms to a Dahlia who would run into them?

Jenny frowned and said in a puzzled tone, 'Do you like him?'

'Yes, I like him.'

'Do you love him?'

'No,' Dahlia said coolly, 'but I'm going to. I think it's best to be friends first.'

'It isn't romantic.'

'It will be romantic afterwards.'

'After what?'

'When I've married him,' Dahlia said.

'Oh, don't, unless you love him!' Jenny cried.

Dahlia's lips twitched a little in amusement, but she said gravely, 'I don't believe much in this love. Look at our parents. What did that come to? Look at you, Jen. What's that coming to?'

'Ah, that's cruel!'

'It's not. Somebody has to talk sense to you.'

'Very well, then,' Jenny said, and her words came in jerks because she was sobbing without tears. 'I'll tell you.' Three days had passed and she would deceive herself no longer. 'Nothing will come of it—nothing, nothing!'

'Poor Jen,' Dahlia said softly. 'It's a shame to be happy when you're not. And how can I marry him and leave you and mother with Aunt Sarah? And not a single lodger when Edwin Cummings goes!'

'Is he going? Yes, he told me. I'd forgotten. I'd forgotten everything. I thought Cyril would come, but he hasn't come,' she cried. 'He would have come at once, wouldn't he? Unless he's ill. He might be,

338

mightn't he? But he's not, he's not!' A change that frightened Dahlia came over her face: the hands she had been clasping and unclasping fell to her sides. 'I think I'm going to hate him. I shall like that,' she said in a hard voice.

CHAPTER XLII

Tʜɪs seed of thought was quick in sprouting. She did not water it with tears, but she tended it with her recovered pride. He did not care for her enough to see past her mother. He was like her father, who had always seen Louisa shadowed by the colossal aunt, and the humility of her love became a shame to her. She had told lies because she was afraid of losing him and, while she scorned herself, she could feel little stabs of apprehension that shook her breath when she wondered what her mother had said to him and how she had behaved. Edwin Cummings might have told her and, once or twice, she was tempted to ask him, but she was afraid of hearing things which would be painfully added to those she must forget. She did not want to feel more bitterness towards the mother who had been so tender and made confession natural, who now moved about the house as though she had a sure cause for happiness. Jenny's mind was tormented between love and hatred for her and for Cyril. She believed she was on the topmost peak of suffering: she could go no higher. It was physically impossible to stay there much longer, and soon she must be granted the power to begin her slow descent into the valleys, where she would not be scorched by sun or numbed by cold, those temperate valleys from which Dahlia never strayed.

But Jenny was mistaken. She had farther to go yet. She had only reached the false top of the mountain, and it was her mother who smilingly beckoned her upward.

'Jenny—' she began timidly.

A week had passed: she was not blind to the change it had made in Jenny. Her face was thinner and her eyes seemed bigger, and Louisa wished she had not spoken to her about the young man and kept her on this stretch, but it had been necessary to make sure that Jenny loved him, and now she brought news that would make her soft and young again and gay, like Dahlia.

'Jenny,' she said, 'come away with me to the attic. We'll be quiet there. Dahlia's out. Better lock the door. You never know with Sarah, but there's a stair that creaks and I think we'd hear her. Dahlia's out again with that Mr. Sproat, I fancy. D'you think, Jenny, she's going to marry him?'

'I suppose so,' Jenny said.

'Then, if she's to be married, too, I've nothing more to worry me.' She sat down and dropped her head, and, when she raised it to look at Jenny, there were tears in her eyes. 'I was married myself, this morning,' she said. 'I've married Thomas Grimshaw.'

Jenny's clenched hands went to her mouth and stayed there, pressing it hard. Over them her eyes glared at her mother. That gesture and that look might have been born of an ecstasy too great to be believed—the sudden, amazing solution of her troubles—and, interpreting them thus, Louisa said quietly, 'I wasn't going to have the Merrimans saying things against you. When I saw her that night, and she wouldn't speak to me, I knew how it all was, and I thought, well, that's easily settled. I reckon that's why he hasn't been to see you, but it will be all right. His mother would be nasty about it, I know. She'd make it hard for him, and he's only a lad when all's said and done, but she can't be nasty now. I was young, Jenny, and I wasn't happy. I don't see who's the right to blame me, and anyway it's all over and it's put right and you can look the Merrimans in the face.'

Jenny pressed her hands harder. She must not laugh or scream. Through the disastrous folly of this action she was mercifully allowed to see the shining goodness of her mother, but, thinking in pictures, as was her habit, she tried to imagine her established in Grimshaw's farm while she herself was welcomed in the house of the Merrimans. Louisa, out of sight, might by some miracle have been forgiven for her daughter's sake. Settled on the land the Merrimans coveted in the midst of their own territory, married to the rough farmer who was known to have been her lover, it was madness to think they would accept the daughter. The pictures went like lightning flashes across Jenny's eyes and what she saw most clearly, what troubled her most, was the pitiful uselessness and simplicity of this sacrifice, the weakness of confessing a fault which need not have been acknowledged. In self-defence Jenny had tried to deny it, and succeeded so well that she had learnt to ignore it, but now, plainly, it was a greater obstacle than her mother's speech or Aunt Sarah's servitude. She doubted whether her mother's death would have removed it.

Jenny had been mad but she was shocked into sanity, and her chief need was to defy her cowardice and to be purged of her lies and disloyalty, and she determined to see Cyril. Yes, she would see him. But how could she return and tell her mother she was not going to marry him? Where would be the consolation in hearing—what was the truth—that she did not wish to marry this laggard lover? She would speak too late to save her mother. Therefore, thought Jenny, ready to make sacrifice for sacrifice, she would do it, if he asked her: she would endure a martyrdom of slights, she would spoil his life for him and rejoice, knowing that her mother would think herself rewarded.

She knelt in front of Louisa's chair and rested her hands

on the broad lap. 'Did you want to marry Mr. Grim-shaw?' she asked gravely.

'It was the best thing.'

'But will you be happy?'

'What would I do anyway, without you and Dahlia? And there's the money, and he's always wanted me, and I like the country. I've sadly missed the fowls,' she said simply. 'And there'll be a bit of money for you both. There's no debts now, you see, and we'll sell this house, and what was your father's will be yours. I've settled that with Thomas. That'll put Sarah out! But we won't tell her yet. Not till you're settled, Jenny. Oh, I like him well enough. We'll get on. This isn't the place for me, and do you think I'd stay with Sarah? It seems as if it was all arranged for the best.'

'Kiss me,' Jenny said. 'I'll write to him now. I'll see him to-morrow.' She knew he would not refuse to meet her. 'But suppose—suppose—'

'I'll have done my best,' Louisa said, 'and d'you think he could look at you and not want you? He'll be able to laugh at his mother now! It's easy seen I'm not a lady, but what does that matter when you are?'

'I'll go to-morrow,' Jenny repeated.

She was in a fever to see him: she longed to look at him and know his power had gone: she wanted to tell him that her mother's love was greater than his poor substitute, and, in this mood which was less sane than she believed, she hoped he would beg her to marry him and she would consent in the exquisite joy of despising him because he had dared to despise her. 'And yet,' she said to herself, 'I shall always love his face. I know what it will be like when he's middle-aged and when's he's old. It's the face I want.'

She had seen it last above the rows of spectators in the Gardens, with the light from a lamp shining on his bare head, as the sun had shone on it in the wood, and she had not looked again. He was standing behind the chairs, scanning the dim faces, and she knew the moment when he found hers. Now her letter was on its way to him he would find it when he came down to breakfast, and in the afternoon he would meet her in the field, not in the wood, and she wondered whether the place would mock her with its first brightness or wear its second, threatening aspect.

'I ought to burn the flowers I picked,' she thought. 'I mustn't keep anything.' But she could not bring herself to destroy them, and, at that admission of weakness, she began to be afraid. For a little while, in the attic, she had been brave and defiant: she could not sustain this exultation, and she found that though the happiness of love or hatred could be contained within herself, she wanted to make others conscious of her doubts and misery. She felt neglected by Dahlia, who was always here and there on her own business, and she looked with anger at Edwin's impassive face. She was amazed at his callousness for her suffering.

'We ought to be dressing those dolls!' she exclaimed. 'We haven't touched them for a week.'

'Why don't you get them, then?' he asked mildly.

'I don't know where Dahlia is.'

'You know where the dolls are.'

'Yes. But—'

'But you want someone else to fetch them and sit beside you, and I daresay you'd like me to read to you.'

'I don't want anybody to do anything for me.'

'Then you've changed,' he said.

'Yes, I've changed. When people try to help you they do the last thing you want.' And in the realisation that her mother's action had doubly bereft her of refuge, she cried, 'Where am I to go?' Was she to accompany her mother to Thomas Grimshaw's farm? Must she beg a home of

344

Dahlia? She could not picture herself alone and her present mode of life, hateful as it had once been, seemed pleasant and safe when she was faced with losing it. She was not quite nineteen. She could take her father's money and learn to earn her living, as she had desired. She would be rid of these relatives who hampered her. She would go each morning to her work and return at night to some hired room where there would be no one to vex her and no one to give her that indefinite special treatment she had always accepted as her right. Looking back, she realised how often her mother had hesitated before she spoke, lest Jenny should be upset, how quick Dahlia was to soothe and cheer.

'What's going to happen to me?' she asked, with the quietness of her lonely little hired room.

'How do I know?' he said. He did not know and he gave the impression of indifference. Jenny's grave happiness on the night of the play had slowly changed to wide-eyed anxiety. It was evident to him that Louisa Rendall had given her some hope which was unfulfilled, and, under his stolid exterior, he raged against the fellow and her lack of pride. That night and the next day he knew the empty peace of responsibility removed and desires finally out of reach, and here was his responsibility back again and his desires were coming nearer.

'I don't believe you care,' Jenny said.

'I'm tired of caring.'

She turned away. 'I don't seem able to make people like me for very long,' she said.

Edwin shuffled his feet. He found it difficult to be cruel. 'Because you only like them yourself when you're in trouble. I know just how happy or miserable you are by the way you treat me. When you're happy, you don't see me. It started that Sunday when I came back from home and brought you the flowers from Kitty. It's been

345

going on ever since. To-night you want someone to comfort you. To-morrow—'

'To-morrow!' Jenny said, on an upward breath, and she heard the hope in her sigh, and Edwin heard it too.

He stood up and, with his hands in his pockets, he looked down at her. 'What time are you meeting him?' he asked, and, because he was standing over her and looking stern, she replied before she remembered to be offended. Then, shrinking from him, she asked, 'How did you know. And you'd no right to ask me.'

'I hadn't any right. And I know because I love you.'

'Still?' Jenny said. 'Then why,' she asked, turning his statement to her own advantage, ignoring its dignity and pathos, 'why don't you say I can go home with you and help Kitty and Fanny in the shop?'

'And to-morrow you might tell me that, after all, you didn't want to come. I'll wait till you know your own mind and, by that time, I may have changed my own.'

'You're sure to,' Jenny said, from the depths of her certainty that she would never get what she wanted.

CHAPTER XLIII

Next day, when she started in a drizzling rain, she remembered his avowal, and was glad, and still she failed to see what it might mean to him. To-day, more than ever, she could think of people only as they affected her. He loved her, and it was some time since she had thought of him as a young man in a shop. He was solid, in a world that seemed to shift behind the veil of rain: he was certainty to a mind that did not know itself: he was the strong place in which she could find shelter if she returned beaten from her foray into the farther county, and, while she remained in sight of her home, she went forward boldly. She thought her mother might be watching from a window, and she was grateful for being allowed to slip out of the house as though she were going on an errand to the shops. No significant smiles, no jarring words of encouragement had speeded her. There were occasions when Louisa behaved with the tact of fine feeling and Jenny's loyalty revived. She feared her own weakness: she knew she might be too submissive when she was faced with Cyril, but she was determined to hear nothing against her mother.

The rain came down heavily as she turned into the road edging the steep wood, it pattered on the leaves which had once waved in joy for her, and Jenny's footsteps lagged. It was right that it should rain, it had never rained before when she went to meet him, and the skies were crying for her because she could not weep herself. She felt cold and listless. She was protected by her school mackintosh

347

and sou'wester hat, and her feet were stoutly shod, but she was chilled and she thought it would be a happy thing if she could fall ill and die. She would be buried with her father, under his name and the prayer that he might rest in peace; her own name would be traced in Edwin Cummings' lettering. She wondered whether Cyril had seen that austere stone slab and whether its dignity would be a reproach to him or a warning, and she knew it would be neither. She knew the limitations of his imagination. She was going to face them, like a wall in front of her, and, when she crossed the road and opened the gate into the field and saw him standing a few yards away under an umbrella, she gave a little laugh and a smile tilted her lips as she approached him. No one with any imagination would have brought an umbrella to this interview: no one whose view of her had not altogether changed would have refused to take a step towards her. He seemed faintly ridiculous and very young, and the smile remained on her lips, but it was not so easy to keep it there when she looked into his face. Like those who claim to be unmoved by the sight of death because the spirit has left the body which is worthless, yet have to recognise that this is the representation they have known, these the hands they have touched and these the lips which have parted to speak to them, Jenny looked at Cyril and saw what he had been for her and hoped piteously that the spirit would flutter back.

His first words told her it had gone for ever. 'It's no good meeting like this,' he said sulkily.

'I wanted to say good-bye,' Jenny said.

This answer confused him a little. He had expected pleadings and explanations, and indeed she had meant to explain, but it was he who started to do that.

'If you hadn't deceived me—' he began, and she said quickly, 'It wouldn't have made any difference.'

348

'But it would.'

'How?' she said. 'I'll tell you.' She paused, amazed at her own calmness. 'If you'd known what you know now you'd never have met me again. And you see,' she said, puckering her eyelids, 'I wanted to meet you. And I did tell you my real name, but you didn't hear it properly and I was a coward. I liked you so much,' she said simply.

'But Jenny— How can I? I mean—you must see for yourself it's impossible.'

'What?' Jenny said. She heard the rain drumming on his absurd umbrella, and, less noisily, on her hat.

'You're getting wet,' he said, and he came nearer, to bring her under his own shelter, but she stepped back.

'What?' she repeated.

'Going on with it,' he muttered. 'I mean, you've got to think of your family.'

This, no doubt, was the text of his mother's sermons, and it was in the tip of Jenny's tongue to tell him how her father had pitied the Merrimans' lovely old house for having to harbour people who were new to it, but she decided that it was not worth while. She was busy wondering where his love had gone, and why a mere fact displeasing to him should enable him to look at her with such hard eyes. Love seemed to be a very fragile thing. Where was her own for him? She saw it like a gay butterfly, happy in the unconsciousness of its brief span of life and broken by a careless hand or foot, by something alien to itself. But love was said to be as strong as death, and many waters could not quench it nor the floods drown it, and here was the rain, washing away what once she and Cyril had felt for one another.

'It never rained before when we were together,' she said aloud, 'so we couldn't know, but we know now, and it's all over. If you had been older,' she said, 'I should have

349

told you everything at once—at least I think I should—but you were too young to hear it without hurting me. I don't like being hurt.'

'You hurt me, too, and everything might have been all right if you had told me.'

She shook her head. 'You know it wouldn't. You're not strong enough. And,' she said, not meaning to be cruel, stating what she believed to be the truth, 'if I hadn't deceived you, you wouldn't have such a good excuse. It's much easier for you, this way. You've got a grievance. It's queer,' she said, looking past him at the rain streaming down as though it were determined to blot out the scene of their happiness and, failing to hide it altogether, hissed more viciously in its resolve, and again she thought it was not worth while to tell him that what seemed strange to her was the swiftness with which he, who had been her joy, was changed to an ordinary young man, standing in a wet field under an umbrella. 'I shan't always love his face,' she said to herself. 'It isn't the one I knew.'

'So good-bye,' she said. 'I wanted to finish it neatly,' she explained with a little gesture. 'I didn't want to leave it ragged.'

'Jenny—!' he said, and she knew he would have loved her always if she had not been Louisa Rendall's daughter.

'You don't understand anything,' she said, thinking of her mother. 'You never will. But it's not your fault,' she added gently as she went away.

It had been easy. No word had been spoken about her mother, but when she was beyond his sight Jenny wept for her lost love and her failure to feel the proper pain, and her tears were mixed with the rain on her cheeks. She did not know what she could say to her mother who had married that man for her foolish sake, and, on the bridge crossed so many times in happiness or sorrow, in the blindness of her infatuation or with eyes open to her peril, Jenny stood stock still, not, as once before, living again her hour with Cyril, but appalled by a new vision of herself. Who was she, what had she done, that anybody should be sacrificed for her?

'It's awful! It's awful!' she sobbed, running forward, ready to fling herself at her mother's feet and beg forgiveness, but, at the other end of the bridge, she was met by Edwin Cummings.

'I don't think—I'm afraid—I'm afraid I shall never be any better,' she stammered.

'You'll have to get dry first,' he said.

She laughed at that and asked him what he was doing here and at this hour, and perhaps it was a sign of grace that she did not take his presence for granted.

'I thought you'd be back by about now,' he said.

'Oh—' Jenny said, with her little moan, and again she stood still for a moment. She could see the bow windows of her home, and through the rain they looked at her benevolently. They were not worried about her any longer and they were able to take a mild interest in the activities on the pavement.

'What's happening?' Jenny asked.

'It's Mr. Sproat moving,' Edwin said.

'Not going right away?' she exclaimed.

'Your sister says he's got rooms in Albert Square.'

'Oh,' Jenny said again. 'She didn't tell me.'

'You wouldn't have listened.'

'Don't preach at me!' she cried. 'There's no need. Just let me enjoy not being afraid of anything. I was afraid of Miss Jewel and Aunt Sarah, but they can't hurt us now. I feel—I feel— What do you feel?' she demanded suddenly.

He tightened his lips. He had learnt to be cautious with Jenny, and she said in a low voice. 'Let me go home with you. And,' she said, offering him compensation, 'you'll have the bureau, after all.'

351

He shook his head. 'Not without you, Jenny.'

'I'll take it with me. It will be mine, and when you want it you can ask for it.'

Without waiting to see how he received these words she ran into the house and up the stairs into the attic. There she leaned against the door she had shut with a bang and her breath came fast. She saw that she had settled her own future. She had bound it to the old house and the garden with the cobbled paths and lavender bushes, but she had bound it to peace and safety. She smelt the lavender under a hot sun and heard the sounds of sawing from the workshop and of Kitty singing in the house.

'Yes,' she said, nodding her head in approval.